M000119448

Visit Logos online at www.LogosPub.com.

Visit JP Robinson's website: www.JPRobinsonBooks.com

In the Midst of the Flames

Published by: Logos Publications, LLC, PO Box 271, Lampeter, PA 17537

Library of Congress Control Number: 2019954688

Paperback ISBN: 978-0-999-7793-5-4

Hardback ISBN: 978-0-999-7793-6-1

Printed and bound in the United States of America

What Readers Are Saying

[In the Shadow of Your Wings] ". . . Robinson's eclectic array of characters and high-stakes scenarios make for an immersive beginning to a series that will appeal to fans of war dramas."
—PUBLISHER'S WEEKLY

[Bride Tree] "An enchanting romance woven with espionage, and a power struggle that will keep any historical fan charmed and mesmerized."—READERS' FAVORITE

"If there's one thing I've come to expect from Robinson is that he has a non-stop ride packed in his novels."—A.M. HEATH, Author of *Ancient Words* series

[In the Shadow of Your Wings] "Wow. This story had characters from every walk of life-in all aspects of that time period. So beautifully written on how their individual stories intertwine. This is a must read for historical fiction lovers.

The author does a perfect job at setting a clear stage for so many stories, characters and their hardships. Absolutely mind blowing how the plot unfolds. Amazing!"—TARA

[In the Shadow of Your Wings] "Fantastic WWI historical fiction book. Fast paced, you won't want to put this book down. Great story, characters and believable. Looking forward to reading more of the Northshire Heritage series wish they were available now."—CAROLINE

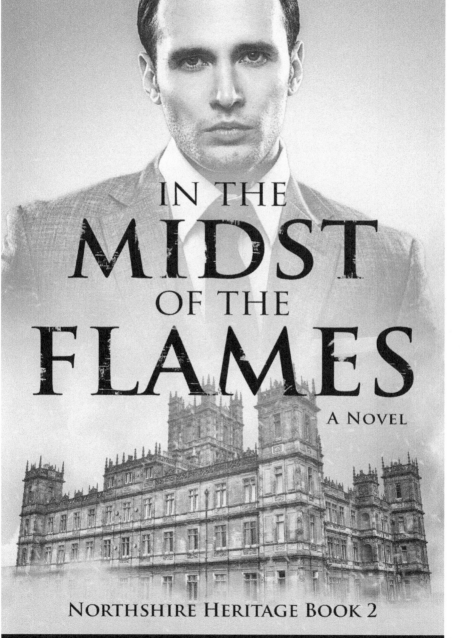

IN THE
MIDST
OF THE
FLAMES

A NOVEL

NORTHSHIRE HERITAGE BOOK 2

JP ROBINSON

JP ROBINSON

Dedication

To my sister, Rachel. There comes a time when all God's prodigals make the choice to return home.

While all events, characters, and the assasination plot in this book are fictional, the story of *In the Midst of the Flames* was inspired in part by its true-life historical counterparts. The heroic sacrifices of soldiers and nurses, the struggle for independence by the Irish insurgents, the attitude toward the war in Germany, and the spy-fever that swept through Great Britain were all pivotal aspects of the Great War that posterity must never forget.

Cast of Characters

THE BRITISH

The Steele Family

Thomas Steele—head of Northshire Estate and the Bank of England

Malcolm Steele—Thomas's son, Commander of the 7th Batallion, Northumberland Fusiliers

Leila Steele—Malcom's wife, former German spy and heir of Northshire Estate

The Thompson Family

Will Thompson—Malcolm's former friend now in a German POW camp

Eleanor Thompson—Will's wife and military nurse working as a volunteer with the Red Cross

Prominent members of Northshire Staff:

Harold Greyson—butler and Thomas's personal assistant

Jenny Edwards—lady's maid to Leila Steele

Prominent politicians in Whitehall, London

David Lloyd George—Prime Minister of England

Robert Hughes—head of the British Secret Intelligence Service

Earl Curzon—President of the British War Council

Alfred Milner, Bonar Law, Arthur Henderson—members of the British War Council

THE GERMANS

The Meier Family

Burkhard Meier—landowner near Munster, Germany

Adele Meier—Burkhard's wife, mother of Katja

Katja Meier—daughter of Burkhard and Adele, sister of Markus (deceased)

The Haber Family

Fritz Haber—scientist, husband of Clara and Charlotte

Clara Haber—deceased wife of Fritz

Hermann Haber—son of Fritz and Clara

MISCELLANEOUS:

Charlotte Nathan—Fritz Haber's mistress

Werner Jaëger—head of German Foreign Intelligence (Department 3B)

Nathaniel Leonard—captain of Northshire's guards

Aengus O'Malley—London-based gang leader and affiliate of *Sinn Féin,* a militant Irish political party

Karl Schmidt—Fritz Haber's colleague and friend

Uther Klein—general and regional commander of the Munster POW camp

Elijah Farrows—Farmer and pastor to Northshire's tenants

Lt-Colonel James Stewart—Malcolm's commanding officer in the British 28th Division

Arthur Hoffman—member of the Swiss Federal Council

General Falkenhayn—the German army's Chief of Staff

JP ROBINSON

Prologue

Amsterdam, Netherlands. October 1914.

"**I**n thirty seconds, you will die." The hammer of the black Luger slid in place with an unfeeling *click*. He pressed the gun hard against her forehead. "Now"—his voice was as unfeeling as the metal that bit into her flesh—"tell me what you know."

Leila Durand squirmed, twisting her bound wrists, as she glared at the small but powerfully built bearded madman, whose black-gloved hands peeked out of the sleeve of an equally dark greatcoat. His clothes were that of a businessman—a starched white shirt, a black suit that was just visible beneath his coat, and a solid black necktie. But the hard glare in his eyes and the pressure of the gun against her forehead left no room for doubt. This man would kill her.

Give. She again wrenched her wrists hard, ignoring the pain. They were bound behind a straight-backed chair, plaited together by knots of coarse rope that cut into her skin. Chains, wrapped around her chest and arms, held her immobile.

I'm trapped.

He grinned at her, the whites of his teeth at odds with the darkness that cascaded from his hooded eyes. She tried to ignore the wild galloping of her heart and focused on the circumstances that had brought her here—wherever *here* was. All she knew was that she was in some hole in the ground in neutral Amsterdam with a maniac who meant to kill her.

Unless, of course, she spilled her guts.

After two years of clandestine field operations for the German government, Leila had been ordered to return to Antwerp for an intense two-week training session. This was to be expected, given the recent outbreak of the Great War.

Her instructor was none other than the formidable Elsbeth Schragmüeller. Two days ago, Elsbeth had sent her to shadow a British agent in Amsterdam who was to meet a contact at a shipping house.

The man had held a brief conversation with a newspaper correspondent—an Allied spy no doubt—and Leila had managed to get close enough to hear most of his conversation while remaining unseen.

Elated by her initial success, Leila had slipped off into the growing gloom and headed toward the train depot where she would catch the last train across the border. But her trip back to the *Kriegsnachrichtenstelle,* or espionage training school in Antwerp, had been cut short as a group of men materialized out of the darkness and blocked her path on the deserted street.

A quick glance in the dim light around confirmed that escape was impossible. The high walls of Amsterdam's dikes rose on both sides. She had whirled around, only to see four men rushing toward her from behind, weapons drawn. Heart sinking, she had raised both hands in surrender. There was no sense dying here.

After jerking a black hood over her head, they had dragged her into some sort of abandoned warehouse then, sometime during the night, she had been roughly thrown into the small confines of this windowless tomb.

Who were those men? Gritting her teeth, Leila strained again at the bonds. She had eluded death in the street only to die in a cellar. Questions hummed in the back of her mind like whining mosquitoes. *Who is he? British? French?*

Leila gave herself a stern mental shake. Right now she had to figure out how to get out of this mess. The questions she could shelve off for another time. *If there is another time.* A single candle blazed on a wooden table, transforming her abductor's face into a contorted mask of demonic frenzy.

"I'll only ask one more time." He drew back his hand and slammed the butt of his semiautomatic pistol against the side of her face. "What did you hear?"

Leila's head whipped to one side as the metal connected with her skin. For a moment, the candle seemed to wink out. She blinked rapidly, knowing that if she lost consciousness now, she would never wake up.

"N-nothing." Her breath came in short, ragged bursts. The pain was blinding. "I don't know what you're talking about."

She looked up at him, ignoring the throbbing in her skull. "I told you. I'm just a student. That's all. A student."

He dropped into a crouch, teeth bared. "Do you take me for a fool?" He raised the gun and pulled the trigger.

Pft!

The bullet sped by her neck and bit into the chair, sending splinters of wood into the air. A silencer had absorbed most of the sound, but she could swear that the pounding of her heart would've drowned out the noise of the shot anyway.

"The next one will be in your eye." He laid a gloved finger on his pursed lips. "The right one, I think."

Leaping forward, her captor grabbed her hair with his left hand. Leila cried out as he jerked her head backward.

"Tell me!" His shout made her ears ring.

Tears leaked out of her eyes.

I won't. He won't break me.

She shook her head as she gasped out the words. "I . . . don't know . . . anything!"

He slammed his fist onto the chair, and, with a growl, tossed the gun onto the table then withdrew a wicked-looking knife.

She stared, wide-eyed and chest heaving as he twirled it around in his hand. "W-what are you doing?"

He threw her a wolfish grin. "I'm going to cut off one of your ears. Do you have a preference?"

"N-no, no!" She writhed in the chair, desperate now. Her mind whirled. *Is information worth such a price?* She wavered but then a spark of rebellion surged in her, rising above the throbbing pain and fear.

"Then tell me what I want to know." He placed the edge of the knife against the fleshy part of her right ear. "Tell me." The knife bit into her skin and she felt a fiery finger of pain then the slow drip of a trickle of blood.

"I can't!" She was gasping now and soaked with sweat. Her bladder felt like it would burst at any moment. "Nothing. I've nothing to tell, I swear it."

"You're lying!" He pressed in deeper, the edge of his knife cutting into her pale skin.

A ragged scream ripped out of her throat. *I won't . . . give . . . in!*

"Nothing!" The cords of her neck bulged as her wails filled the room. "Nothing . . . to say."

He fell silent then eased the pressure off her ear and withdrew.

XIV

Sobbing, Leila trembled in the chair, watching his every move with wide eyes. He straightened, pulled a handkerchief from his breast pocket, and wiped her blood off the edge of the blade.

She knew from the slight sting on the right side of her head that he had cut her, but not deeply. *God . . . oh God.*

With a terse nod, he strode over to the far wall then pulled on a cord. Electric light flooded the room, making her wince.

"Open your eyes, Leila Durand."

Hesitating at first, she obeyed, licking her lips.

He leaned casually against a wooden table with his arms folded across his chest. Her eyes darted to the gun and knife which rested on the table near the flickering candle.

"I am General Werner Jaëger, head of His Imperial Majesty Kaiser Wilhelm II's Foreign Espionage unit called Department 3B."

She gaped at him. "You're . . . "

"I am your commanding officer." A thin smile played about his lips.

"B-but—"

He held up a hand, forestalling the swarm of questions that hummed in her mind. Or was that ringing sound her battered head?

"Elsbeth, cut her bonds."

Footsteps sounded behind her and, after a brief moment, the ropes, then the chains, slackened, and fell. Leila rose and turned, rubbing her chafed wrists.

"Fraülein?"

"Well done, Leila." Her teacher nodded, the corners of her thin lips turning upward. "Well done indeed."

XV

General Jaëger stood upright, clasping his hands behind his back. Keeping a wary eye on him, Leila retreated behind the chair.

"Don't worry, the test is over." Jaëger stood still. "Elsbeth spoke well of you and it appears her judgment was correct."

Leila's fingers probed the wound behind her ear. The flow of blood had stopped. "Test?"

"I wanted to see if you would break under interrogation." He motioned toward the table. "What I saw is . . . encouraging. The British aren't as ruthless with captured female spies as I can be. If you won't break under my interrogation tactics . . . "

Her eyes widened as the implications of his words sank in. Shadowing the supposed Englishman, her abduction, imprisonment, and torture—it had all been an elaborate scheme to see how much torture she could endure.

"But why?"

The papers in the Netherlands were full of advertisements posted by both the Germans and British soliciting informants and espionage agents. It was difficult to believe that all prospective recruits were subjected to such brutality.

General Jaëger rocked back on his heels, his eyes probing her battered face. At length, he reached inside his pocket and pulled out a sealed envelope.

"Your orders are here, written in code. Read them. Memorize them. Burn them."

She took the envelope and slipped it into the pocket of her wrinkled skirt. "I will."

"There is something else." Werner came closer, and this time she held her ground. He nodded his tacit approval, his eyes shifting to Elsbeth's impassive face then back to Leila.

"What I am about to say is *not* written in your orders." He drew a cigar from his pocket, lit it, and inhaled deeply before speaking again. "In the event that the Fatherland loses this war, the kaiser has ordered me to develop a contingency plan. It is called *Herkules*. To execute this operation, I will need to have agents already in place, ready to move at a moment's notice."

She furrowed a brow, trying to think past the pounding in her skull. "That is what this was all about?"

"Precisely." He drew again on his cigar. "If *Herkules* is carried out, it will end European civilization as we know it."

Releasing his breath in a cloud of smoke he said, "When the heads of all our enemies gather together to sign a peace treaty, you and the other agents will follow specific directions. All non-German heads of state will be assassinated in one blow."

A chill ran through her. "All?"

"All." His eyes probed hers. "Germany will take advantage of the ensuing chaos and will seize control of France and England in a final bid for power. Leaderless, the nations will fall at our feet. Now, I am certain you understand the need for my little experiment." He gestured toward her ear.

"I-I do." She had been right. Ordinary agents were not subjected to this level of interrogation. Gingerly, Leila touched her ear again. An odd sense of pride swelled within her. It was an honor to have been chosen. *And I did not give in.*

Jaëger sniffed. "Elsbeth will see to your wounds." He gently touched her cheek. "When they have healed, you will depart for Great Britain and the home of Sir Thomas Steele."

He tossed the still-burning cigar onto the floor and ground it underfoot with the heel of his black boot. "If you do not wish to be a part of *Herkules*, speak now and I will end your life mercifully."

XVII

Werner jerked his head toward the chair. "What you saw is only the beginning of what I will do to you if you betray me."

Leila lifted her chin and stood with shoulders straight and chest thrust forward. "You've seen me prove my loyalty to the Fatherland, General." She fixed her green eyes upon his unblinking stare. "I will not fail you."

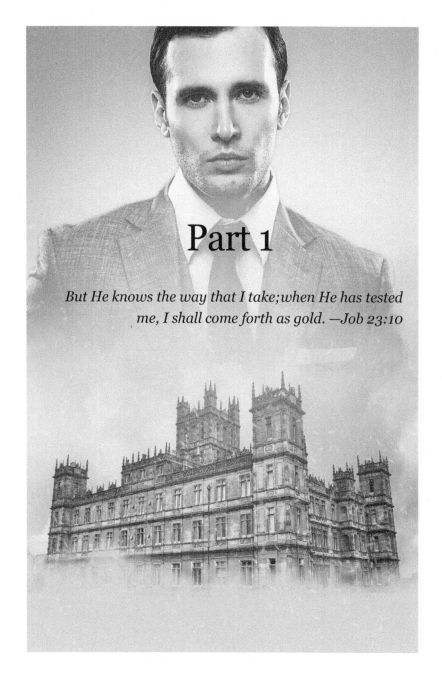

Part 1

But He knows the way that I take; when He has tested me, I shall come forth as gold. —Job 23:10

JP ROBINSON

Chapter 1

March 1917. German Military Headquarters at Castle Pless.

Fritz Haber, renowned scientist and mastermind behind the development of Germany's chemical weapons, skulked down the hall of Castle Pless, the historic site of headquarters for military operations on the Western Front. Shoving his hands in his pockets, he hunched his shoulders, eyes darting around with each step. Haber had one wish, one which all his scientific endeavors had failed to produce—to become invisible.

But achieving invisibility was not his only failure—far from it. Each *click* made by the heels of his black boots on the castle's tiled hallway reverberated in his skull, hammering two words over and over through his mind with a ferocity that made him cringe.

You failed.

Failure. The word summarized his life.

With a shudder, he glanced around again. Once he would have found the notion ludicrous. The very thought that the great Fritz Haber could fail at anything was simply preposterous. *You failed.* But it was true. Failure was all around him, in everything he did.

His eyes failed to grasp the archaic beauty that surrounded him, missing the arched doorways, vibrant tapestries, and mounted heads of various types of wildlife that decorated the castle walls. He failed to notice the obvious awe on the faces of the crowds that lined the hallway, applauding as he stalked passed them.

Only one image burned before his eyes, obscuring all else from view. It was a haunting memory of the fateful night on which his life had plummeted into ignominy. He saw afresh his wife's bloody corpse prostrate on the stained grass. His gun was held between her slack fingers as though he himself had killed her. Perhaps, in a sense, he had.

Haber had pioneered the age of chemical warfare, seeking to add more glory to his already illustrious name. Fearing that Clara's scientific genius would eclipse his own, he had shut his wife out of the project. He had mistaken her for a rival instead of seeing her as a partner. In retaliation, she had tried to thwart his greatest contribution to humanity. Science had been his god and he, Fritz Haber, had sacrificed everything upon the altar of his deity.

But his sacrifice had been in vain.

Clara had committed suicide after finding him in the arms of her rival, the siren named Charlotte Nathan. It was Clara's final act of desperation, her ultimate plea for him to abandon the selfish road he had chosen.

Haber bunched his fists against his temples as a memory of his blood-stained hands flitted through his skull.

Failed. His marriage had been a disaster.

He lurched forward.

His son, Hermann, had been the first to arrive at his mother's side. Clara had died in his arms.

Fritz slammed his eyelids shut. As a father, he was nothing short of a disappointment.

"*Herr* Haber."

He jerked to a halt, his eyelids flickering open. General Paul Hindenburg stood before him, arm raised in a stiff salute.

Fritz swallowed. "Yes?" It was a question, as though he was not sure of his identity. But he wasn't. Not anymore. Could the *real* Fritz Haber have fallen so low?

How art thou fallen, oh Lucifer. Like the archangel, pride in his abilities had engineered his downfall.

The general lowered his arm. "His Imperial Majesty, Kaiser Wilhelm II, desires your presence. He is about to meet with Chief of Staff Falkenhayn."

Haber removed the rounded *pince-nez* from his eyes. Here was the evidence of his greatest failure. "The kaiser."

He had promised Germany's monarch a quick victory with his celebrated poisonous cloud of gas. While his new weapon had eliminated thousands of the enemy, the war dragged on. French scientists had developed gas masks and even gas weapons of their own to counter the devastation he had unleashed.

Just as Clara predicted.

To others he was still a hero, but when he stared into the mirror with glazed eyes, Fritz Haber saw nothing but a shadow of the man he had once been. When he had received the kaiser's summons, ordering him to Castle Pless, he knew that the time had come to pay for his failure.

"Are you ready?" Hindenburg motioned toward the looming doorway.

Wiping his glasses, Haber put them back on his face. "I am ready."

Ready to account for his empty promises. Ready to be disgraced. He could expect nothing else. In the kaiser's Germany there was no mercy, only justice. And he was as guilty as any man could be. Whatever punishment the kaiser planned to inflict, he was ready.

———————————◆◆●◆◆———————————

General Erich Falkenhayn, chief of Military Staff, bolted out of his chair as the door to his office flew open.

"Who dares—" The words died on his lips as Germany's emperor, Kaiser Wilhelm II, swept into the room, flanked by Falkenhayn's rival, Paul Hindenburg, and the chemist, Fritz Haber.

"Your Imperial Majesty." Falkenhayn bowed deeply—a gesture that the emperor did not acknowledge.

Distancing himself from the others, Wilhelm, a tall, gray-haired, boar of a man, stumped around Falkenhayn's desk while keeping one hand on a long, black walking stick and eyeballing his general in silence.

Falkenhayn knew that the kaiser's deformed left arm was virtually useless, but he made a conscious effort to keep his gaze from wandering toward the man's congenital defect, focusing instead on the string of medals that decorated the kaiser's chest.

The sharp upturned corners of the emperor's moustache bristled as he leaned over the desk. "I am not pleased, General Falkenhayn. Not pleased at all." He slammed his walking stick onto the wooden surface before him.

Falkenhayn's face burned as he moved to the front of his desk and sank into a hard, wooden chair. He had the sinking feeling he was about to be disciplined like an unruly student and, as such, he played for time. "Is there something specific you wished to discuss, Your Majesty?"

Wilhelm barked out a dry laugh. "Something specific? No need to play at the fool, General; you already are one." He straightened with an exasperated sigh. "I never wanted this war. You and the other generals forced my hand."

The kaiser mimicked Falkenhayn in a falsetto tone. "'For the glory of the Fatherland,' you said. 'Our destiny is to conquer' you said. Well, where is all this *glory* now?" His blue eyes drilled into the Chief of Staff's skull. "Where is it?"

As if on cue, Paul Hindenburg stepped forward, offering a newspaper to Falkenhayn who glared at him then let his gaze fall to the paper.

BERLIN STARVES!

Falkenhayn's eyes rolled from the headline to the photographs of long breadlines. "T-this is typical, my Kaiser. War produces suffering both for those in the field and for the home defenders." Shrugging, he glanced up at his sovereign. "My strategy of maintaining a strong offense on the Western Front and a passive approach in Russia is sound." He glared at his rival, Hindenburg, again. "Despite whatever fabricated criticisms you may have heard."

"The fact remains, Falkenhayn, that we have been at war for over two years!" The kaiser looked over Falkenhayn's shoulder to scowl at the chemist. "Despite *Herr* Haber's breakthrough with the poisonous cloud of gas, Germany is no closer to victory now than we were *before* we lost the better part of two million men."

Falkenhayn shook his head. "War was the only option, Your Majesty. I-it was the only path to the glory your family name deserves!"

"So you've said before." Wilhelm spoke through clenched teeth. "But I fail to see how liquidating my own army will ensure my kingdom's greatness."

At this, Hindenburg stepped into the conversation. "The Russians have grown weaker, but they are still a powerful enemy.

If the Americans break their neutrality and join the fight, we may not win this war."

"I have just returned from the Western Front." Falkenhayn pushed himself out of the chair, right hand bunched into a fist. "We crushed the British at the Somme last autumn. The morale of the army is high, my Kaiser."

"Morale does not win wars, General. Or haven't you noticed that?" Wilhelm sucked in a deep breath, held it, then released it slowly. "I have convened this meeting to discuss preparations for all possibilities."

Bile rose in the back of Falkenhayn's throat as he stared into the older man's eyes. "You cannot mean . . . ?"

"I mean that I will do whatever it takes to ensure my empire survives this global catastrophe." The kaiser's gaze shifted from one man to the other. "We will prepare to initialize Project *Herkules* unless the course of this war shifts in our favor."

Falkenhayn stiffened. "*Herkules*?"

Hindenburg nodded, face grim. "*Ja*. It may be the only way of snatching victory from the jaws of defeat. If all else fails, *Herkules* will paralyze the governments of Europe while giving us the chance to launch a new, unexpected offensive."

The kaiser's voice filled the silence that followed this analysis. "My son, Prince Wilhelm, is now thirty-five years of age. If we fail in this endeavor, gentlemen, he will have nothing to rule when I die. The people are hungry, the people are angry. We need a quick end to this war to ensure that my kingdom survives."

Turning, he crooked a finger at Fritz Haber. "Come, *Herr* Haber."

The chemist shuffled forward and bowed. "Your Majesty." He spoke with the rasping wheeze of a man approaching the grave.

"You promised a swift victory with the help of your cloud of gas, *Herr* Haber, yet all I see are dead German soldiers and starving civilians." Wilhelm shrugged. "Your efforts in Galicia have been commendable, true, but still . . . no victory."

Haber hung his head. "I will not ask for clemency, Your Imperial Majesty. I do not deserve it. I only ask for a few days to set my house in order before I am executed."

Silence filled the room. At length, Wilhelm cleared his throat. "You have not failed, *Herr* Haber, at least not utterly. You are considered a hero by many."

Retrieving his cane, he limped around the desk. "Besides, to kill the greatest mind in Germany would be to destroy the man who carries the key to *Herkules* success. No. Gas is the ultimate weapon, but its implementation must be precise. It is through *Herkules* that you will redeem yourself."

Haber's bald head glistened as he bobbed it downward once more "I am . . . grateful for your continued trust." He looked up, licking his lips. "My colleague, Karl Schmidt, and I will do everything in our power to produce whatever your Majesty desires."

Wilhelm thumped his walking stick twice against his palm. "What I desire? I want another gas that can be used against our enemies. I want an antidote that will save the lives of any Germans present when this weapon is unleashed. Is this possible?"

Straightening in a slow motion, as though he were in pain, Haber met the kaiser's gaze. "There was a time when I would have said that I could do anything. That time is past." He removed his *pince-nez* and continued. "However, there are certain molecules that, if manipulated, may help us succeed. I will need time. Time in my laboratory with my colleague."

Wilhelm motioned to Hindenburg. "See that he gets it and whatever else he needs."

Falkenhayn narrowed his eyes. The kaiser should have spoken to him instead of his subordinate. "There is a problem. General Jaëger believed there was a traitor on *Herr* Haber's team."

"I understood that was taken care of." Hindenburg cocked his head to one side.

"Yes, well—" Falkenhayn was careful to avoid looking at Haber. The man had no idea that his wife had been executed to save his life and also upon suspicion that she was an agent of Great Britain. He believed it to be suicide and no one present was about to reveal the truth. He chose his words carefully. "Apparently we were mistaken. The possibility exists that the British have turned a member of Haber's team."

The kaiser shrugged. "His team is not working on this project. It is just himself and his colleague, *Herr* . . . ?"

"Schmidt." Haber spoke up. "Karl Schmidt."

"You trust this man?"

"Oh, yes." Haber nodded while stepping forward. "His loyalty to the Fatherland is beyond question."

"Then, General Falkenhayn," the kaiser said turning toward him, "we do *not* have a problem."

Falkenhayn went rigid. Unleashing *Herkules* was a mistake, one they all would regret. "B-but to initialize *Herkules* we must know where the Allies will demand we sign a treaty of surrender."

Cradling his deformed left arm in his right, Wilhelm strode over to the other side of the massive room. A painting, dubbed the *Proclamation of the German Empire,* stood in prominent relief against the surface's cream paint. In the painting, the gilded walls of the Hall of Mirrors of the French palace at Versailles rose around a group of German officials who celebrated a recent victory over France with swords plunging into the air. Defeated French officials looked on with downcast eyes as the German conquerors established their obvious supremacy.

"You know there is something about the French that I admire." Wilhelm cocked his head to one side.

Falkenhayn slid closer. "What is that, Your Majesty?"

Wilhelm kept his eyes on the tabloid. "They neither forget nor forgive. It makes them almost predictable." He gestured toward the painting. "A century before this day, Napoleon Bonaparte crushed our armies. Here, in France's celebrated Hall of Mirrors, we took our revenge." He turned to his Chief of Staff. "Now, if you were French and obsessed by a ridiculous sense of honor, where would you insist a peace treaty be signed?"

"At Versailles?" Falkenhayn blinked. It made sense. It made perfect sense. But *Herkules* was a diabolical plan, one that would stain Germany's honor to time immemorial. It would unhinge the governments of Europe if not the entire world. Only the individuals in this room even knew of its existence. "It will take time to initialize *Herkules,* my Kaiser and"—he dropped his gaze to the floor—"there is a problem."

Wilhelm made a growling noise in the back of his throat. "I do not wish to hear of any more problems, General."

"Forgive me, Your Majesty, but I must speak. You will recall that Department 3B," Falkenhayn said, straightening as he spoke, "the division that oversees European espionage, has come under my control."

"What of it?" Wilhelm tossed his walking stick to Hindenburg, who snatched it out of the air in a smooth motion, then turned back to him.

Falkenhayn followed the interaction with a furrowed brow. *Something is not right.* Clearing his throat, he continued.

"The division's head, General Werner Jaëger, has been in Britain for over a year seeking a rogue agent—a woman named Leila Steele."

"Stop wasting my time, Falkenhayn." Kaiser Wilhelm folded his arms across his chest. "Get to the point."

"Y-yes, my liege. The fact is, this woman is more dangerous than any of us could have predicted. I received a report last August from two of our agents in Britain in which they stated they were treating General Jaëger for a severe gunshot wound. I assume he was hurt in his attempt to silence her."

"Since August? Seven months to recover from a little scratch?" Wilhelm spun on his heel. "Did you not inform him I demanded he return to Berlin?" The question was again directed at Hindenburg.

Falkenhayn recoiled. This blatant disregard for hierarchy could not be tolerated any longer. "Majesty, I—"

Wilhelm cut him off with a glare then turned back to Hindenburg. "If you sent for General Jaëger, then why isn't he here?"

"I *am* here, my Kaiser."

Eight eyes swung in unison toward the back of the room where a series of seven black alabaster statues, that honored German iconic figures, lined the rear wall. The dim light cast by the electric lamps had not permitted Falkenhayn to see that an eighth figure was among them. Or perhaps he had been too flustered by the kaiser's sudden approach to notice. But Werner had been in place *before* the kaiser entered the room. The realization that he had been the unwitting object of Jaëger's scrutiny for at least the past thirty minutes made the hair rise on the back of his neck.

"General Jaëger." Falkenhayn forced a tight smile. "You are—"

"Alive." Jaëger separated himself from the shadows and came forward. A black suit covered a white, slim-fitting shirt that was open at the neck. His hair, black and flecked with silver, was neatly combed and a thin, well-trimmed peppered beard formed a neat square around his mouth.

Jaëger stepped forward with a slight limp then bowed low before the kaiser. "Your Imperial Majesty."

"Tell me this, General. Why is it that, after more than a year of searching, you are unable to destroy a product of your own making?"

Werner's black eyes did not leave the kaiser's face. "I am not a man to make excuses."

"I have not asked for any!" The monarch pounded the floor with his cane.

Werner's voice was as smooth as silk and was barely above a whisper. "Leila Durand killed my son. She is alive because fate has been kinder to her than it has to me. The only reason that I am here instead of on her trail is because I was summoned. As we speak, I am laying a trap for her that cannot fail." His gaze slid to Hindenburg. "I will kill her."

An uneasy silence filled the room then Falkenhayn cleared his throat. This was his chance to distance himself from the political fiasco unfolding around him. Perhaps, if he could convince the monarch that it was Jaëger who was at fault, he could regain the kaiser's trust. "May I point out, my liege, that Leila Durand is one of the few agents who know of *Herkules*."

The kaiser pivoted toward him, lips curled in a feral snarl. "Imbecile! You shared that kind of information with a traitor?"

Falkenhayn recoiled. "S-she had been vetted by the best and given clearance for this task." He dropped to one knee. "How could so intricate a plan be executed without already having agents in the field?" He thrust a shaking finger at Werner. "I acted upon General Jaëger's recommendation."

"Get up. What is done cannot be undone." Wilhelm shifted his withering gaze to Werner. "We cannot risk sending any men into Britain to clean up General Jaëger's mistake."

Werner dipped his head. "The mistake, my liege, would be to enact *Herkules* at all. It is a reckless plan, guaranteed to fail."

"Explain yourself, General." Hindenburg moved forward to stand next to the kaiser.

"Leila Durand is no fool." Werner's face was impassive. "For two years before the start of the war she succeeded at missions where others had failed. Before briefing her on *Herkules*, I had her abducted and taken to a cellar in Amsterdam. After a day with no food or water, I tested her to the limits." A muscle twitched in his jaw. "She never broke."

Falkenhayn pushed himself upright, sensing an opportunity to redeem his place in the kaiser's favor. "Obviously your methods are outdated, General. Her loyalty has been turned. Thanks to you, we now have a rogue agent free on the loose and she is armed with crippling information."

"It was not her courage we lost." Werner pinned him with his obsidian stare. "It was her heart. It was the one possibility that none could have foreseen—that of a spy falling in love with her target."

Wilhelm flung his arms out in an exasperated gesture. "Yes, well, the loss of her heart doesn't do us much good, now does it?"

Haber coughed. "Majesty, we could proceed by simply changing the name of the operation. Even if this . . . Leila came across the term, she would not know what it means."

"A good suggestion." The kaiser tapped his pursed lips with his finger. "Very good. What do you propose?"

A spasm crossed Haber's face and he dropped his gaze to the white tiles below. "I would suggest *Hubris,* your Majesty."

"The fatal pride that precedes defeat." Wilhelm barked out a sharp laugh then brandished a fist. "It is perfect. The arrogance of my British cousins led to this war. The pride of the nations who aligned themselves against us prolonged it. In one blow, they will all fall at our feet."

He turned back to the painting of Versailles on the wall. "We have no time to waste. *Hubris* may be our key to victory."

"My liege." Werner limped forward. "Changing the name does not alter the fact that Leila knows what the plan entails."

"Then you, General Jaëger, must see that she dies." The emperor drew himself to his full height. "Even if the British suspect foul play, when they see our men in the same room with their leaders, their fears will be laid to rest. An attack on this scale is unprecedented and is therefore impossible to my unimaginative cousins. Besides, turncoats are always held in suspicion. The British will have difficulty believing a woman who betrayed her own people. What is to prevent her from lying to them?"

"And of our agents in the field?" Falkenhayn spoke again. "Anyone involved only knows the name *Herkules.* It would be difficult at best to inform them that it is the same mission under a different name."

"Hindenburg will find a way." Wilhelm turned to the pasty-faced cretin. "Can this be accomplished, General?"

Hindenburg bowed low. "Consider it done, Excellency."

"Ah!" A grin slid over the kaiser's mustachioed face. "The perfect answer." The smile faded as quickly as it had appeared as his censuring glare rolled from Haber to Jaëger. "This is an opportunity for you both to redeem yourselves. *Herr* Haber will develop an antidote that immunizes our men from a gas attack while you, General Jaëger, will destroy your own creation. Do not return to the Fatherland until the girl is dead."

"I understand, my Kaiser."

Wilhelm raised a warning finger. "Fail me again, General Jaëger, and not only will you die, but your name will die as well."

"My name?" Werner frowned.

"It is only because of your past record of exceptional service to the nation that you are still alive, General Jaëger. If you fail in this simple task, history will bear no record of your existence. Your name will be stricken from our military records. Your son is dead, you have no family. Nothing to show you ever lived. You have six months to finish this. Do not fail me."

Werner blanched. "I understand," he said again. This time, Falkenhayn thought he detected a slight quaver in his voice.

Wilhelm's eyes probed his face for a long moment, then he turned to Falkenhayn. "Unfortunately, my *former* Chief of Staff, a monarch's clemency can only extend so far."

Falkenhayn's mouth went dry. "Former?"

"General Hindenburg is your replacement." Wilhelm gestured toward the beaming fool. "Give him what he needs, then pack your bags and get out."

"M-my bags, Your Majesty?"

The monarch shoved his way past him but looked back at the door. "You have cost me two million soldiers, Falkenhayn. Two million." His eyes narrowed. "Like the French, I never forgive . . . and I *never* forget."

Chapter 2

March 1917. Berlin, Germany, Dahlem suburbs.

Fritz skulked through the busy streets of his hometown, his shoulders hunched, and black top hat pulled down over his brow. He shoved his hands into the pockets of his dark coat, sinking into its protective embrace. The warmth of spring had yet to reach Germany, and Fritz was grateful for the chilly air that allowed him to cover his identity with both coat and hat, affording him the blessing of anonymity. But he did not wish to escape his neighbors as much as he did his memories.

Berlin was a painful place, full of ghosts that taunted him from the shadows. His eyes rolled over the square through which he shuffled. Here, Clara had rallied the pacifists of Berlin, calling them to protest his use of chlorine gas as a weapon. He hurriedly crossed the square and turned down an empty street. The heels of his shoes clicked against the hard stones below and Fritz slowed his pace as he approached a snow-covered area, lined off by a black chain-link fence. He stared in mute despondency at the ghostlike tombstones then dropped heavily onto a bench.

Here, Clara was buried. At least her ashes were.

Sweat trickled down his neck despite the frigid air. How many times had he wronged this woman? Would she have killed herself had he been more attentive? His brow furrowed. Then again, how many times had she slandered his name, turning their private quarrels into a public feud?

He sucked in a deep breath. This was not the time to look back. A new challenge had presented itself in the form of the kaiser's request. He was to develop a synthetic compound that could act as an antidote to gas poisoning.

Haber absently removed his hat to wipe the sweat from his bald head. *But how can it be done?*

"Fritz? Fritz Haber?"

He froze, recognizing the lilting voice that made his blood run as cold as the snow-littered ground. Oddly enough, there was a time that voice had turned his blood into fire. Slowly, he shifted toward the woman who had been his accomplice in sin.

She took a few steps forward then faltered. "I . . . it's been over a year since I've seen you. How are you, Fritz?"

With a soft sigh, Fritz took in the sight of Charlotte Nathan. A fashionable black hat adorned her dark hair. A bright blue top brought a splash of color to her beautifully pale cheeks and graceful neck and a long black skirt fell to her black boots. Her eyes glowed with a warmth that touched him, even as he shrank within himself at her approach. In her hands she held several wrapped parcels. Germany was suffering the ravaging effects of war, but it seemed that even hunger bowed to the beauty of this woman.

Fritz rose and made a slight bow. "It is good to see you again, Ms. Nathan."

She arched a quizzical eyebrow, gliding over the snow toward him. "Ms. Nathan?" She lowered her voice. "For you, I am Charlotte. *Only* Charlotte. Or have you forgotten?"

Fritz looked away, a lump rising in his throat. "No . . . Charlotte. That is the problem. I have not forgotten." He turned toward the cemetery. "I cannot forget my guilt, m-my stubborn pride. It became my god, you see. And I offered my wife as a sacrifice."

Charlotte laid a warm, gentle hand upon his arm, turning him toward her. "Don't think like that Fritz. You and I, we love each other, *ja?* We always have. What happened with Clara . . . that's not your fault. I don't blame you, no one does. All that matters is that we love each other."

Haber pulled the *pince-nez* from his nose and wiped his tearing eyes. "Love?" He scoffed. "Charlotte, you must understand that I am a scientist. Unless something can be proven, it does not exist. What we call *love* cannot be measured; it cannot be quantified or analyzed. Love is simply the metaphysical combination of random hormones that produce chemical reactions. We interpret this as emotion when it is nothing more than an ordinary, biological process that leads to human reproduction!"

With a grunt, Fritz rammed the *pince-nez* back onto his nose.

"Are you quite finished?" Charlotte tilted her head to one side, mouth upturned in an incomprehensible smile.

He shoved his hat back on his head. "What do you mean?"

Instead of answering, she let the packages fall to the ground, leaned forward, and pulled him into a passionate kiss. She held him close for several long moments and, at the warmth of her embrace, Fritz felt the ice in his heart begin to thaw.

At length, Charlotte pulled away. "I won't quibble about the details of love, Fritz. The fact is that you need me. And I need you. I need you to get out of this slump that you're in and reach for the stars."

Impetuously, she kissed him again, kissed him as though her life depended upon the passion of this moment. This time it was Haber who broke away first, breathless and confused.

"Glory is waiting for you, Fritz. Waiting for us."

Glory. Something stirred within him, an old hunger that had lain dormant for many long months. He closed his eyes, afraid to surrender to its siren call. "No, Charlotte. I am a changed man. Clara's death has—"

"Clara's death has made a way for us to be together." Charlotte held him at arm's length and he opened his eyes.

"What are you saying?"

"Can't you see?" She gestured toward the graveyard. "All that held you back is now gone. You're free to be the man you've always dreamed of becoming."

Her voice softened, and she laid her forehead against his own. "I'm also free, Fritz. Free to . . . become your wife."

"My what?" Fritz jerked back as though he had been scalded by a hot iron.

Smoothly, Charlotte pulled him back toward her, intertwining her fingers with his own. "Think, my love. Your son, Hermann, needs a mother, and you, well," she said with a wink, "*you* need a woman."

Haber stood as still as a stone, his mind reeling under the barrage of emotions that Charlotte had so easily unleashed. To his shame, he had fallen for her charms before. She knew how to manipulate his weaknesses. But he had to admit that her words, though unexpected, made sense. He put no faith in love, but logic dictated that he bring a female into his home to help him raise his teenage son.

He gnawed at the inside of his lower lip. As she insinuated, nature itself mandated that he find a wife. If not Charlotte . . . then who? *Still* . . .

"Normally it is the man who proposes to the woman." He shifted uncomfortably.

"When has our relationship ever been normal, Fritz?"

There he had to agree. "All the same, I will need time to think it over." He dipped his head, stood abruptly, and held out his hand. "In the meanwhile, walk with me."

He helped her gather her parcels then turned toward his home.

"Where are we going?" Charlotte slipped her hand in his.

"I do not know. Perhaps nowhere." Haber shrugged then slanted her a glance. "Or, perhaps, we are going toward the future. Time alone will tell."

———————— ◆•●•◆ ————————

Later that evening, Charlotte padded down the hallway toward Fritz's study, her black coat draped over her arm. After taking lunch, they had spent the afternoon discussing the events of the past year. Fritz had gone abroad, seeking consolation by burying himself in morbid plans of gas attacks. He had also attended several symposiums where, to his horror, he had been shunned by various members of the scientific international community who considered his creation of the poisonous cloud an act of murder. Guilt over Clara's death coupled with the loss of his reputation had nearly broken the wretched man's mind.

As soon as his son, Hermann, had returned from school, Fritz had escaped to the sanctuary of his lab. Charlotte had chosen to hide her irritation at his absence and had devoted the rest of her day to getting reacquainted with Hermann. Now that evening had come, it was time for her to go home, but she would not leave without putting herself once more at the forefront of the scientist's enigmatic mind.

Charlotte did not need to ask directions to his office from the servants who scurried out of her way like rats before a feline predator. A smile tugged at her lips. She rather liked the comparison. Like a cat, she toyed with her prey—Fritz. He was the man into which she longed to sink her claws. Not for his looks of course, but for the prestige that he offered. No matter what delusions the international community held, when Germany won the war, the world would bow at the feet of the man whose intellect had sent tens of thousands to their graves. And she would be right at his side.

Charlotte scoffed as she passed a photograph of Clara that still hung on the wall. "When I move in, you'll be the first thing to go."

Clara. The petulant fool had not known how to handle her husband. Fritz's ego demanded praise and Clara had failed to give him that adulation. Despite his earlier grief-induced confession, Charlotte knew that science was not Fritz's god. That place was reserved only for himself. She was prepared to be his most ardent worshipper for as long as it suited her purpose.

In return, her husband would lay wealth, power, and honor at her feet. Her social circles would pay homage to the man who ushered in a new age of German superiority. Fritz had known the scorn of a woman who had chosen to be his rival. Charlotte would show him the support of a woman who wanted to be his wife.

A cunning smile slipped over her mouth as she counted off the days since her last cycle. Timing was everything. The cat knew this. The most opportune moment had to be identified before pouncing. That is, if one really wanted the prize.

She rapped lightly on the door of his study. "Fritz darling?" He was inside, she could hear him muttering incoherent formulas. The man had been in a daze all day, babbling about some impossible task that the kaiser had given him.

"Fritz?" She knocked again, twice, then stepped back as the white door swung open.

He blinked at her as though he had forgotten she existed. "Charlotte?"

"May I come in?" Leaning forward on her tiptoes, she kissed the thin lips beneath his cropped mustache. He had lost weight and his bald scalp glistened with a sheen of sweat. Apparently, his work for the kaiser was not going well. "Let me in, my love. Problems shared are problems solved."

He hesitated, making the pasty skin of his sagging face jiggle as he scratched his right cheek. She knew at once that he was thinking of his wife.

"Fritz." Charlotte laid a gentle hand on his chest. "I'm not your rival. I'm the woman who loves you. Please?"

He hesitated again, then with a slow nod, he stepped aside.

Charlotte clucked her tongue as she entered the large room. Papers littered the ground. Moldy, half-eaten sandwiches lay discarded on his worktable while incomprehensible writing scrawled across a dark blackboard. She was about to lay her coat on his worktable but thought better of it at the last moment.

"How do you even think in here?" She crinkled her nose.

With a shrug, he said, "I know it seems like a mess but it's actually a very systematic method of organization."

She took a deep breath, stifling her urge to throw everything in the trash. *Timing, Charlotte.*

"Right. So, the kaiser wants you to develop a . . . what is it again?"

21

"A-an antidote to a gas attack." Fritz wrung his hands together. "It's impossible! How can I take life and save it at the same time?"

She frowned. This wasn't like the man she had once known. He still hadn't come fully back to his old self. "Things are only impossible because we haven't done them yet."

"You don't understand. It is *impossible* to develop an antidote to gas." Haber's shoulders drooped. "Once inhaled the body reacts immediately."

"No, no, my love." She cupped his face in her hands and made him look into her eyes. "You mustn't think like that. You can . . . you *will* do this."

Gently prying her fingers from his face, he held them in his own. "You are good to me, Charlotte."

"Now, think back to the moment you discovered how to turn chlorine gas into a weapon. You once told me that it took months of failure before you succeeded." She stepped back, gingerly wiping her fingers on a discarded napkin. "What did you do differently?"

He turned to his board and sketched unintelligible symbols. "I switched from one element to another then burned—"

"Burned?" She tilted her head to one side. "Does burning something change its . . . " She faltered, gesturing helplessly. "I don't know, it's shape?"

"I must remember that you are not a scientist. Forgive me."

She pursed her lips. "What if you were to burn something you've already made? Would that do anything?"

"Well, no, I—" The words died on Haber's tongue. He gaped at her, then blinked several times.

"Burn?" He whirled toward the blackboard, chalk in hand and scrabbled at the surface like a madman. "Burn!"

"Burn nitrogen."

She caught only fragments of his mumbles.

"Muscles, poison used . . . Greeks, no Egyptians . . . invert the formula . . . "

Haber sucked in his breath and stepped back from the board. "Charlotte!" He pivoted toward her, eyes round. "It might work."

Her eyebrows hiked together. "What might work?"

"Y-your words. They made me think." He rattled off a convoluted scientific explanation, concluding with, "it just might give me an antidote!"

"You've done it?" A surge of adrenaline coursed through her veins. She was as thrilled by the animated energy that suddenly pulsed from him as the fact that he may have stumbled across the answer to his chemical problem. "You've actually done it?"

Turning back to the board, he stood with shoulders back and legs spread apart. "Nothing is impossible. Nothing!"

Charlotte gazed at the back of his rounded shoulders for several moments before easing toward the door. *This* was the man she remembered. *This* was the man she needed. For the moment he was lost in the arms of molecules, poison, and death but soon—perhaps in a few days or even a few weeks—he would lose himself in her arms. And then, everything she had always wanted, everything she had been denied as a child would be hers. *Timing.*

"Good night, Fritz." She slung her overcoat around her shoulders. He did not reply. Tossing her head, Charlotte shut the door, leaving him to bask alone in the rays of self-importance that surely shone upon his mind. Tonight, Fritz would climb back on the altar of his pride. This small discovery made him secure in the knowledge that he could not fail. *Soon.* Her lips curved in a victorious smile. *Soon he will be ready to rule.*

23

JP ROBINSON

Chapter 3

March 1917. Etaples, France.

Malcolm rolled onto his back, folded his hands behind his head, and stared up at the brothel's ceiling. *So, Leila, I've kept my word.* His mind flitted to the last time he had seen his wife. After hearing about the severity of his wounds, Leila had travelled with his father, Thomas Steele, to visit him at a hospital at Etaples. The reunion had been anything but happy.

Malcom's lips curled back in a sneer. The traitor. At that fateful encounter, Leila had revealed that she was a former German spy, recruited by Abteilung 3B to elicit secrets from the son of Sir Thomas Steele. As a personal friend to both the Prime Minister of England and the head of British Intelligence, Thomas was too tempting a target for Germany to ignore. *And I was the gullible errand boy.*

He slammed his eyelids shut. Eight months after he had learned the truth, he was still unsure of what hurt worse—the fact that he had just been a necessary tool to get to Thomas, or the fact that Leila had deceived him at all. Her beauty had blinded him to reason. As impetuous as she was beautiful, he had believed Leila was his soulmate. They had married in secret a few weeks after their first encounter despite his father's firm orders to never see her again upon penalty of disinheritance.

With a groan, Malcolm buried his face in his sweaty palms. After learning of their marriage, Thomas had banished the pair from his home at Northshire. Too late, Malcolm had discovered a duplicitous side to his golden-haired beauty. Furious at her betrayal, he had fled to the Front where the battles were physical and not of the heart.

For his part, Malcolm had sworn to Leila that he would replace her with other women as soon as he recovered from his injuries. He slid his hands down his face as he glanced at the auburn-haired prostitute beside him.

Leila betrayed me. She deserves no better. Why then did he feel sick with shame?

The woman yawned and stretched. "Mmm . . . " Her eyelids flitted open. She reached for him, but he pulled away, sitting up and jerking on the tan pants of his uniform, then ramming his feet into his boots.

"Leaving so soon?" She sat up, pouting. "I'm insulted."

He reached into his pocket and tossed a few bills onto the bed. "Thanks. Keep the change."

She arched a pencil-thin eyebrow, then slid out from beneath the sheets and she minced toward him. "Oh." She intertwined her bare arms around his neck. "I've seen this before. Men always act strange the first few times they step out on their wife. You kept calling her name in your sleep, you know." Her lips, covered with smudged paint, curved upward. "Don't you see? I'm better than this Leila could ever be."

Rage, irrational and unexpected, surged in Malcolm's gut. "Don't you dare sully her name!" He shoved her backward, resisting the impulse to slam his fist down her throat.

She fell onto the bed then pushed herself onto her elbows. "Not man enough?" Her lips twisted in a sneer. "Well, there

26

are a hundred more waiting outside for what you got last night. Get out of here!"

Blinking, Malcolm stared at her then snatched up his hat and staggered to the door. Outside, he sucked in a lungful of the crisp air. Dawn had just grayed the horizon, but the town of Etaples, which bordered the vast British military camp already stirred. As the prostitute had predicted, dozens of Allied soldiers waited patiently in long lines to gain access to the brothels. The nausea struck him again. *Why?*

He walked slowly along the railway tracks that connected Boulogne and Paris, his tramping feet beating out a dismal rhythm on the dusty street.

Malcolm, are you happy? An image of Eleanor Thompson, the nurse who had saved his life, floated through his mind. She had asked him the question eight months earlier, but those five words clanged about his skull day and night without reprieve. The answer was simple.

"No." His voice was hard. Guttural. Hard like the ground over which he marched. Hard like the iron tracks that forced their way across a barren landscape.

Life had made him hard. Two years of war had transformed a spoiled, angry boy into a calloused, bitter man. Whereas he had once been disgusted at the thought of mud on his boots, he could now snap a man's neck without a second thought.

Are you happy?

Malcolm slammed the heel of his palm against his forehead, wishing he could drive the nerve-wracking question from his mind. Eleanor maintained that forgiveness was the path to happiness. According to her, he had to forgive Leila if he ever hoped to find peace. He had to admit his own wrongs then seek the forgiveness of God.

Mercy. That was the key to his redemption.

As if Eleanor herself could ever forgive the wrong I've done to her.

A muscle ticked in his jaw. Eleanor and her husband, Will, had been ripped apart by the chaos of war. Neither knew the other's location but Malcolm had known the whereabouts of both. In a fit of jealous rage, he had lied to Eleanor, swearing that he had witnessed her husband's death.

Months later, Will, acting on some instinctive suspicion, had almost carved the truth out of Malcolm with the unforgiving edge of his trench knife. Malcolm had confessed to Will that Eleanor was alive, waiting for him at Etaples only moments before Will had been captured by the Germans.

Badly wounded, Malcolm had been brought back from the brink of the grave by Eleanor's healing touch. But though he had escaped both the Germans and death, he could not escape the guilt that plagued him each time he thought of Eleanor or her husband.

If Eleanor knew what I've done, all her talk of God and forgiveness would disappear like smoke through a chimney.

Malcolm expelled his breath in a deep sigh. He wanted to confess. Eleanor deserved to know the truth. But the thought of losing her friendship . . .

Malcolm squinted as a gleam of light streamed into his eyes. The sun. No matter how many times the sun rose, his life would remain shrouded in darkness. After his recovery, British command had refused his request to return to the Front, opting to post him to non-combatant duties for a few months.

Malcolm shrugged. What did it matter? He had lived so long in the night of jealous hatred that he could not imagine what it would be like to see the sun rise. He shoved his hands in his pockets, slowing his steps as his mind rolled back to his childhood at Northshire.

I was happy then. When Mother was alive. Catching sight of his reflection in a puddle, he stopped. Dull blue eyes stared out of a narrow face, tinged with the beginnings of a scruffy beard. The Victoria Cross, earned for bravery in the face of the enemy, dangled loosely from his neck. A tan uniform, decorated with the stripes of a Sergeant, hugged his wiry frame.

Time blurred in his mind and the face in the puddle morphed into that of a ravishing young woman whose flowing, golden hair framed a heart-shaped face, accentuating emerald eyes that sparkled with life. *Leila.*

A distant buzzing reached Malcolm's ears but, lost in the mist of the past, he ignored it.

Their relationship had violated the rules of propriety, scandalizing his father and ruining his prospects of inheriting the estate.

But I was happy then. I was happy when we were together.

He blinked twice at the disconcerting thought. Her face disappeared, replaced by his own sullen countenance. *Why was I happy then but not now?*

"Could it be that I still . . . love her?" At first, he almost laughed at the thought. But a quiet voice in his heart argued that, if he dared to look past his pain, he would find that some part of the love he once held for Leila still lived.

The buzzing in the back of his mind swelled into a mechanical drone, hammering its way to the forefront of his thoughts. Malcolm turned toward the east, shading his eyes against the glare of the morning sun. There was something about that noise that he recognized. Something that was out of place here in Etaples.

His stomach wadded itself into a ball of iron as recognition sunk into his mind. *Planes.* The metallic taste of fear tinged the edges of his tongue. He pivoted to his left, craning his neck upward. *War planes. Lots of them.*

Malcolm's feet were moving before he could think, pounding down the dirt road toward the military encampment, toward Eleanor. Those were not French or British aircraft.

The steady hum of Fokker engines, coupled with the black crosses painted all over the gray frames, shouted more clearly than words that—"The Germans! The Germans are attacking!"

———————————— ◆◆●◆◆ ————————————

"Here, take these bandages with you." Veronica Coughlan, head of a small team of volunteer nurses called VADs, handed a bundle of bloody strips of cloth to her friend, Eleanor Thompson.

Eleanor tossed them into the large, wooden tub at her feet. "I can't believe I've been doin' this for almost two years."

"Me neither. It feels like I've been doing it for fifty!" Veronica grinned at her. "Although you don't look the worse for wear, despite everything you've been through."

She stretched out a clean sheet onto the empty mattress. "Could it be that the handsome Sergeant Steele is responsible for that spring in your step?" She slanted a wink in Eleanor's direction.

"What?" Eleanor stared at her friend, slack-jawed. Veronica's insinuation could not be farther from the truth. Eleanor had performed an emergency operation, saving Malcolm's life, and had helped him reacquire the skills he needed to learn in the long months of his recovery, but that was as far as their relationship went. "Veronica, my husband just died!"

Veronica began to pound a worn pillow back into shape. "That was two years ago, El." She faced her friend, all trace of humor gone. "Sometimes the heart plays tricks on us."

"Not *my* heart. It's tied, now and forever, to Will." Eleanor folded her arms across her chest. "In any case, Malcolm's *married*."

"Good point." Veronica pursed her lips. "That could be a problem. Hey, don't worry. I know that there's nothing between you two. I'm just saying don't be afraid to move on. That's all."

"Have *you* moved on?" Eleanor bent and picked up the tub. "Since your fiancé was killed?"

"I've tried El. I've tried, and tried again, but always I've failed. There's no hope. I'll love him till I die—which, given the way things are, will probably be soon."

"Then you understand what I mean. We're both hopeless romantics." Eleanor turned toward the door but paused as Veronica's last words sunk into her mind. "What do you mean, you'll probably die soon? What kind of joke is that?"

Veronica shrugged. "Oh, nothing." She tossed a pair of bloodied scissors and other surgical instruments into a sterilization bowl. "Just some weird feeling. Happens to all of us every so often, I guess." She shrugged. "It's only natural, given that we work on the edge of a war zone."

Eleanor eyed her for a long moment, noting the dark circles under Veronica's eyes. This melancholy atmosphere wasn't like her flippant friend. Despite Eleanor's best efforts to convince her of God's reality, Veronica purposed to face eternity as an agnostic.

"Hey." Eleanor pushed the screen door open with her body. "If you want to talk, I'm here for you."

Veronica threw her a tight smile. "I know that. Thanks, El."

31

The bright morning light glinted in Eleanor's eyes as she made her way toward the disinfection room where the linens would be washed or burned if they were unsalvageable, pressing through the crowds of soldiers and medical personnel that brushed past her. The British military camp of Etaples was a massive conglomeration of tents, military training grounds, soldiers' barracks, and hospitals. Sprawling outward in all directions, it had been her home for the past two years.

Veronica had persuaded her to join the war effort after her baby had been killed in a German raid on London's East End. Eleanor had followed, believing that she would be reunited with her husband, Will, who had also been sent to Etaples for training. Unfortunately, Will had been transferred to a different regiment and his paperwork had been misplaced. Any letters sent to their home had never reached her, leaving her in complete ignorance of her husband's whereabouts.

Then Malcolm broke the news. She had run into Malcolm at the train depot near the village of Etaples just before he had been deployed to the Front. He had informed her that Will had been killed in a skirmish. Eleanor winced as the memory of that horrific moment ripped through her. In less than three months, she had lost both her baby and her husband. The foundations of her life had been unhinged. Faith was the only thing that had pulled her through the bleak slough of despair.

Now, Veronica urged her to move on. *How can she say that when—*

A thunderous roar from above drowned out the alarmed shouts of the crowds around her. She jerked to a halt and craned her neck upward, shading her eyes against the morning light. About a dozen planes darkened the morning sky. They flew low, strafing the ground with machine gun fire.

IN THE MIDST OF THE FLAMES

Eleanor stared, transfixed by the sight. The Germans had never attacked Etaples before. Here, surrounded by thousands of British troops, she had fallen prey to the illusion of security. It was an illusion that had just been shattered by cold reality.

Run! Her mind screamed the order, but her legs refused to move. She gaped with wide eyes as glass windows yielded to the impact of a hail of bullets. The planes rose like graceful birds in flight as they doled out death to those who scurried about in the dusty streets below.

"Eleanor!" Malcolm's voice jolted her from her reverie. "Get out of the way!" Grabbing her arm, he pulled her forward, and together they ran for the shelter of the nearest building.

⸺⸺⸺◆●◆⸺⸺⸺

"Get down!" Malcolm shoved Eleanor into the side of Saint John's hospital then crouched in the shadows.

"Are they leavin'?" Eleanor craned her neck toward the skies.

"I don't think so." Malcolm shook his head. The planes hovered in a tight circle over the camp. They were like vultures, preparing for a second pass. "They'll want to do more damage before our own planes can get in the air."

At his words, the enemy warplanes dropped downward, guns blazing at indiscriminate targets. But this time, Malcolm saw something falling from the underbelly of each aircraft. *Bombs.* "They're bombing us. They're targeting the hospitals!"

Whoomp! Whoomp! The bombs exploded some distance away, but the concussion threw both of them backward. Malcolm was the first to scramble to his knees.

"We should make a run for it!" Eleanor grabbed his arm.

Malcolm pulled her down. "No." He pointed toward three planes that had veered off from the main body and flew directly

33

toward them. "They've turned in our direction. If you move now, you'll be dead in under a minute. Stay down!"

The chatter of Allied anti-aircraft missiles mixed with the thunderous explosions. One of the German planes spiraled downward, leaving a trail of smoke and flames in its wake.

The remaining two planes ripped through the sky. Malcolm licked his lips. Those still in the open scrambled to get to some sort of shelter, presenting easy targets to the invaders. Others, doubtless hearing the noise but unaware that Etaples was under attack, rushed from the relative security of the buildings into the streets.

Malcolm sneaked a glance at the woman behind him. In a few minutes, they would both be dead. His eyes flitted back to the dark planes that drew closer, ready to send them both into oblivion. Thomas's face flitted through his mind. How many times had his father warned him that to die with sin unconfessed was to ensure safe passage to hell?

His breathing came heavier. This might be his last chance to tell Eleanor the truth. He doubted he would make heaven, but, without confessing, he had no chance at all.

Bratatat! Bratatat! The bullets that striped the ground came closer. Out of the corner of his eye, Malcolm saw a woman slip out of the hospital near where they crouched.

"Veronica!" Eleanor waved her arm in a frantic attempt at getting her friend's attention. "Veronica, get back inside!"

Veronica glanced up at the sky, recoiled at her first sight of the plane that swooped toward her, then acted on her instinct to run.

Bratatat! Bratatat!

"God, no!" Eleanor clapped her hands to her mouth as the body smashed into the ground. Carried by its momentum,

Veronica's corpse tumbled over once in the dirt. Then she lay still, spread-eagled in the dust with her sightless eyes staring at the sky.

"Oh, God." Eleanor sucked in deep breaths, eyes wide. "T-this can't be happening. Not now!"

"Shh!" Malcolm grabbed Eleanor's arm, eyes darting from her stricken face to the aircraft. "Don't even think of moving or you'll die too."

Adrenaline coursed in his veins and his mind hummed with indecision. At that moment, the two warplanes pulled upward, preparing for yet another assault. *This is it. I'm going to die.*

The German aircraft streaked downward, pulling together in tight formation as they roared toward the hospital where the pair cowered in the shadows.

Malcolm's mouth went dry. "Eleanor . . . "

Confess!

He glanced at her bloodless face. Her eyes were still locked on the body of her friend. Would she even hear a word he said?

Confess!

"Eleanor, I-I've got to tell you something."

The planes were almost overhead. He could swear the noise of their engines would split his eardrums.

"Eleanor, listen to me!" He turned her to face him, cupping the back of her neck with his broad palm.

"Are you listening?" He stared into her wet, brown eyes.

She gave a mute nod.

In his peripheral vision, Malcolm saw the first bomb begin its descent. It was literally now or never. The words tumbled out of his mouth as he shattered the lock on his long-held secret.

"Eleanor, it was all a lie." He was shouting at her, bellowing out the guilt that he had sworn he would carry to his grave.

"I'm sorry. I lied to you. Will's not dead. The Germans captured him. He's alive. Will's alive!"

Her brow crinkled as she jerked away. "What? What did you just say?"

"Your husband. Will. He's alive."

"Will's alive?"

Then the world exploded in a hurricane of dust and smoke.

Chapter 4

April 1917. Prisoner of War camp near Münster, Germany.

Will Thompson hunched his shoulders and shuffled out of the long wooden barracks that had been his cage for the past eight months. The crisp morning air tinged his face as he loitered about the large, dirt courtyard of the camp built for prisoners of war. He inhaled deeply then coughed as the pungent odor of tar filled his lungs. The exterior of the barracks walls was coated with the stuff.

His eyes darted to a dark sign with white bold print that hung on the side of an adjoining barrack.

Mannschaftslager. He had learned enough German to know that it meant "other ranks' camp," a term used for prisoners of war who were not officers. It was yet another gut-wrenching reminder of the shame that burned in his chest. Will covered his face with his hands as he slumped onto a wooden bench. He was a captive of the enemy, and no one in his home country knew where he was.

He sat up and stared with disinterest at the faces of the people who marched by, their individuality lost in a sea of monotonous dark blue prisoner uniforms. Thousands of captives were interred at the camp. Thousands of men who, like himself, faced the constant humiliation of menial chores, forced labor, and fences topped with barbed wire. They were lost souls, condemned to work for their captors until either death or the end of the war set them free.

The guards were mostly local men—farmers, businessmen and the like—who had been pressed into mandatory service by their government. They patrolled the area, eyes peeled for any attempt at escape or rebellion. A thick post jutted upward in the center of the camp as a visual reminder of the penalty for non-compliance. Those who broke the rules faced the *anbinden*—a sentence of hanging by the wrists from the pole for long periods of time . . . sometimes until they died.

With a grunt, Will fished in his pocket for his Bible. Overall, the treatment he had received thus far was not harsh. Many of the guards spoke English and most were decent, if not friendly, with the inmates. He had expected worse, maybe torture and starvation, but thus far, all his torment had been internal.

After his capture, Will had been brought to a temporary camp where he had been stripped of his clothes, his identity, and all personal items, except his pocket Bible. But they had taken his wedding ring. It was the loss of this final link to his wife that had driven him to the brink of madness. Throughout the entire two-day railroad trip from the battle lines to Münster, his thoughts had been consumed by two things: Malcolm's betrayal and the knowledge that Eleanor was alive at Etaples.

His face twisted in a grimace as Malcolm's face rose in his mind. *The snake! The stinking, pampered snake!*

Will wanted to scream his rage, to slam his fists against a wall, but reason held him in check. Escape was impossible if he were injured. And he *would* escape. Of that he was sure.

Will flipped open the tattered book in his hand, but his mind was too busy plotting to notice the words on the page. Germans were the masters of rote punctuality. In about ten minutes, he and the other men of his prison squad would receive their scanty lunch ration.

Twenty minutes later, all thirty men in his squadron would be shipped back to a farm to work for the remainder of the day. There they would work for the rest of the week on the farm, sleeping in a village hall while being guarded by a patrol of armed Germans. At the end of the week they would return to the prison camp, so the prison commanders could be sure that no one had gone missing.

Will rolled his shoulders. The physical labor was not too difficult; it was the patient waiting that was unbearable. Each second wasted in this camp decreased his odds of finding his wife. Malcolm's information had already been a year old. What if Eleanor had left Etaples? What if, thinking he was dead, she had married again?

The sickening thought made the words on the page swim before his eyes. *I've got to get out of here.* But the timing had to be perfect. He needed a plan and an opportunity. Thus far, fate had not delivered either.

"*Hallo!*"

Will started at the unexpected voice. He swung his head to the right as a guard sunk down on the bench next to him with a contented sigh. His bronzed face, dark breeches, and cream, mud-flecked shirt hinted at a hands-on trade, perhaps farming.

"I am sorry I startled you." The guard tossed his hat on the bench, revealing a head of wavy, silver hair. "I am Burkhard." He hitched his rifle back over his shoulder and then gestured at Will's Bible. "You are a Christian, *ja?*" A wide smile touched the crow-feet that marked the corners of his eyes. "Me too."

Throwing his head back with a snort, Will slapped the Bible down on the bench beside him. "There's no such thing as a

German Christian." He stood up and hooked his fingers in the pockets of his uniform. In just two blows he could turn this soft, mouth-wagging civilian into a twitching corpse.

And then what? He'd be just another dead prisoner, unable to go back to his wife.

With a snarl, Will spat on the guard's feet. "You're all a pack of murderers. Child-killers, that's all you lot are."

For a moment, Burkhard said nothing. Then he cocked his head to one side. "What is your name?"

Will hesitated. Revealing his name could compromise his plans. Then his eyes drifted to the string of numbers that had been sewn across the chest of his uniform. He had lost his identity when he had passed through the barbed wire that ringed Münster's gates. But he was more than just a set of numbers. This German needed to know that. *All* Germans needed to know that.

Thrusting his chest out, he squared his shoulders and jerked his chin upward. "Will Thompson of the British Expeditionary Force, 83rd Division, Northumberland Fusiliers, 7th battalion." He snapped out a sharp salute. "God save His Majesty, King George."

Burkhard propped an elbow on his knee. "I suppose I should say something patriotic about the kaiser in return, but I'd rather talk about our similarities than what drives us apart." He gestured to the Bible. "May I?"

Will grabbed it and shoved it back into his pocket. "Push off! No filthy pig will touch this book."

The guard leaned back in his seat, arching an eyebrow. "As a farmer, I know a thing or two about pigs, *ja?* They are more like humans than you might think." He scratched his head. "Pigs fight over a stupid scrap of mud in a manure pile. Humans fight over a piece of land that was here before they were born and will be here after they die."

In a slow, dignified motion, he rose to his feet. "Your squad has been assigned to dig peat on my farm." His probing gaze searched Will's face. "I will speak to the commandant."

Will's jaw tightened. *I've gone too far!* Instinctively, he glanced over his shoulder at the vicious post where he would surely be whipped. But Burkhard spoke again. "I will ask him if I may invite you to dinner."

"D-dinner?" Will's gaze snapped back to the farmer. He must have misheard!

"Dinner." Burkhard pulled his hat over his head. "In case you haven't noticed, your rations are pitiful. We civilians do not have much food either, but I believe that somewhere in your Bible it says that 'if your enemy hungers, feed him.'" He pointed to Will's pocket from which the tip of the book protruded. "Your Bible is the same as mine after all."

Will stuffed his hands in his pocket, averting his eyes. "W-well I . . . don't—"

"That is, of course, assuming you don't mind having dinner with a pig."

Without waiting on an answer, Burkhard walked away. When he was sure the farmer had gone, Will looked up. For the second time in only a few minutes, his face was burning. But this time, the shame he felt wasn't due to his captivity.

He could've had me punished . . . but he didn't.

He felt the Bible in his pocket press tightly against his thigh. He eased it out and ran his thumb over its worn cover then looked up at the overcast sky.

God had once been such a reality for him and Eleanor. But somewhere in the trenches of France, the God he once loved had faded into a dormant memory, replaced by the mounds of dead.

Why are you silent, God, in the middle of my pain? Where is my sin? His eyes slid from the Bible in his hand to the bench where Burkhard had sat moments before. *Where is my sin?*

Chapter 5

April 1917. Etaples, France.

Eleanor knelt before the altar in the empty chapel, wrestling with the storm of hate that battered at the gates of her heart. Despite the words she mumbled through clenched lips, her fury remained like an obstinate giant blocking her path. Finally, unable to concentrate, she pushed herself upright, wincing at the pain that burned in her side.

A month had passed since the deadly attack on the military camp that had claimed dozens of lives. While she had survived, heat from the explosion had scarred her abdomen with burns and prevented her from hearing or seeing clearly. In time, her senses had been restored but the bitter pain sparked by Malcolm's words lingered on. *I lied. Will is alive.*

"God!" Eleanor wrapped her arms tightly around her chest and faced the altar. She wanted to scream. She *had* screamed. But nothing was enough to vent the raw emotions that threatened to choke her. The news that Will lived, following so closely on the heels of Veronica's death, still ripped the breath from her lungs. A million questions howled within her mind but they all fell silent before the pulsing, overwhelming rage that burned within her.

"I thought I'd find you here."

She bunched her hands into fists. *Think of the devil and he'll come runnin'.* There was no avoiding him. Not here.

Turning slowly, Eleanor kept her face impassive as Malcolm limped down the aisle of the chapel. He had come through with nothing more than a few bruises and a dislocated shoulder, but Eleanor couldn't say that she was happy to see him alive.

Life was simply unfair. Malcolm, who deserved to die, had escaped a bombing relatively intact while Veronica, who had shown her only kindness, had been snuffed out by a few German bullets.

"Well?" He came to a halt, shoving his hands into the pockets of his khaki pants. A dirty white shirt hung open at his neck beneath his unbuttoned uniform jacket, revealing a mass of purple welts. "Aren't you going to say something? Or will you keep on ignoring me like you have for the past month?"

She sniffed and turned her back to him. Malcolm had often tried to look in on her during her recovery, but Eleanor had refused to see him. For if she did see him, Eleanor knew that she would kill him.

Malcolm released a deep sigh. "Eleanor, I-I don't know how many times I can say I'm sorry. I—"

Something snapped in her mind.

"Sorry?" The word came out as a screech. Whipping around, she planted her fist in his gut, blind fury overriding the pain in her side. Malcolm bowled over and staggered backward. Then he straightened, keeping his arms limp at his sides.

"You're sorry?" *Crack!* Her right palm connected with his cheek. "Do you have any idea how much pain you've caused? Do you know how positively *evil* you are?" Flecks of spittle flew from her mouth. "I thought my husband was dead because

44

you told me you saw him die. For two years, I've mourned him because I trusted *you*."

"Eleanor, listen to me." Malcolm stepped toward her, rubbing his jaw.

"No!" She jerked a pistol from her apron pocket and pointed it at his head. "You listen!"

Fury made her chest tight. She gripped the gun with both hands and focused on this man whose lying tongue had ripped her heart to shreds, and—when it had finally begun to heal—had done it all over again by confessing the truth. "What if I had remarried?" Her voice hitched. "W-what if I had given some other man children?"

Malcolm froze, his eyes shifting from the gun to her face. "I know it's not what you want to hear, but what more can I do than apologize?"

"Why, Malcolm? Tell me why." She cocked the hammer, her pulse beating a rhythmic tattoo in her ears. "For three weeks I've been prayin' for strength to resist the temptation to blow your brains out. Right now, I think I'm about to lose the battle. You've got to help me. Tell me why you did it!"

He grimaced. Some part of her mind dimly registered that it was not fear but regret that flitted across his face.

"I . . . I was jealous." Looking straight into her eyes, Malcolm said, "I saw that you and Will had a bond that Leila and I never shared. It seemed unfair, especially since you were poor and we, well, we could have had everything."

He looked away. "I wanted what you both had. When I realized I'd never have such happiness, Eleanor, I . . . I'm ashamed to say that I lashed out. I didn't want anyone else to be happy either. Not even you."

He sunk to his knees before her, craning his neck upward. She started at the glistening tears that streaked down his cheeks. "You've every right to pull that trigger."

He shrugged off the brown jacket of his uniform and spread his arms wide. "Here, I'll make it easy for you. All I ask is that you say you forgive me before you do. Please! Forgive me."

In the stillness of the sanctuary, Eleanor heard a faint whisper, a voice that was more a memory than her imagination.

Save my son. It was a fragmented memory—an echo of a distant dream.

"Eleanor . . . I beg you . . . forgive me!"

Rage flooded Eleanor's mind. This was the sanctuary. It was the judgment seat of God.

Her mind cried out for justice. Malcolm's cruelty had shattered her life. He deserved no less than death. There could be no place more fitting for him to die than here, kneeling like the hell-bound creature he was, before the altar. God was his judge and she would be his executioner.

Her finger curled around the trigger.

My son. Save my son.

This was the sanctuary. It was the place where God offered mercy. Her shoulders shook as hot tears blurred her vision.

"Eleanor. Please!"

Justice. The gun quavered in her hand. "Malcolm . . . I—"

Save my son.

"Forgive me. That's all I ask. Say it!"

An image of Will's face sprang into her mind. "I-I . . . ."

"Forgive me!"

Eleanor screamed as the gun roared to life in her hand. She sunk to her knees, her shoulders heaving as sobs wracked her body. The revolver dropped from her nerveless fingers.

"I'm sorry, Malcolm. I'm so sorry!"

———— ◆◆●◆▶ ————

Malcolm crawled toward her, his eyes flitting from the woman he had wronged to the hole her bullet had carved out in the chapel wall.

"I'm sorry, Malcolm. I'm so sorry!"

He heard her words, but they made no sense to his tortured mind.

"Eleanor." He stretched out a trembling hand, like a drowning man. For he was drowning, sinking into the abyss of his guilt. "You once said 'nothing is too hard to forgive.' Do you remember?"

She jerked her head downward in a sharp nod, cheeks wet. "I remember."

"Did you mean that?" Malcolm grabbed her arms. "Or was it all just words?"

She flinched, drawing back. "It's hard, Malcolm. You're asking me to . . . I'm human, God help me. Human!"

His heart lurched. He could face anything if he could be free of this guilt that weighed him down. *I'm sorry. So sorry.*

He had to try again. "But . . . can you forgive me?"

How could he make her understand? He was condemned in her eyes and in the sight of his own conscience. He choked on his own shame. Now that his sin was exposed, without her pardon he could not go on living.

"Please!" He clasped his hands before him, rocking back on his heels.

Eleanor stared into his eyes for a long moment, mouth twisting wordlessly as though she was praying within. "Forgive you?"

He followed her gaze as it turned from him to a looming wooden cross on the far wall. "Father, forgive them. They

don't know what they're doin'." The words she whispered were
barely audible.

That was him! He hadn't known the hurt his words would
bring. She was right. He was evil. But he wanted, oh, how he
wanted to change.

At length Eleanor faced him and he saw that the hard glare
in her eyes was gone, replaced by a deep sorrow. He waited
and something inside him trembled as he willed her to say the
words he longed to hear.

"Y-yes." Her voice was soft, so soft that he barely heard her.
She shifted closer to him, chest heaving as though she had run
a marathon that ended at the top of a mountain. "I . . . forgive
you, Malcolm."

"You do?"

"I do. I-I'm furious with you, to be honest. I can't forget
what you've done. But today," she whispered, breathing in deep
through her nose, holding her breath a moment, then releasing
it, "I *choose* to forgive."

"How?" Malcolm felt as though the ground beneath him
had given way. The words themselves were incredible, but they
made no sense. "How can you forgive . . . me?"

Eleanor leaned forward, clasping his hands in her own.
"Because I see now that *this* was why God brought me here."
She swallowed. "All the hurt and despair of the past two years
has been pushin' me here, toward this moment."

Twisting, she pointed toward the cross that hung on the
wall behind her. "Forgiveness. It's a choice, Malcolm, not a
feelin'. Don't you see? Everythin' comes down to our choice.
I'll either choose to forgive and conquer my bitterness, or I'll
be destroyed by it."

Eleanor swung back toward him. "As God forgave me, so I forgive you." She lowered her voice. "And so, you must forgive your wife."

Malcolm recoiled. "Forgive Leila?" The awe of the moment faded before her words and the bitter memories that crowded his mind. Leila using him for her own purposes. Leila lying to his face when she said that she loved him. "You don't understand. She lied to me. She *used* me."

Eleanor spread her hands wide. "Has she wronged you any more than you've wronged me?"

Her words slammed into his mind. *She's right.*

"But I'm not you. You're an angel, a saint. I'm . . . " His protests sounded feeble when compared to the naked truth of his guilt.

Eleanor's mouth flattened. "No, I'm not. A few minutes ago, I wanted to kill you. It's what's in our heart that counts." Her head drooped. "I'm as guilty as you are."

Shifting to his side, she pointed again to the rough-hewn cross. "Malcolm, accept the forgiveness Christ offers. He alone has the strength to forgive the unforgiveable."

"No, no." Malcolm shrank back. "I've gone too far. I-I've even spit on His love."

She reached out a hand. "But that's just it, Malcolm. That's the power of forgiveness. Even when we've rejected His love, even when we've left home and rebelled against what we *know* to be true on the inside, Christ still offers us a new beginnin'."

A new beginning. He closed his eyes, relishing the spark of hope the words unleashed. How many times had he run from the past, wishing he could undo his litany of crimes? Images of his past flashed through his mind.

Reviling Thomas and mocking his God. *How could I have done it?*

Trying to drown his latent anger in the slime pits of alcohol and lust. *I was so wrong.*

Abandoning Leila and running from his responsibilities. *I'm sorry. God! I'm sorry.*

Cringing, Malcolm's hands flew to his face. At each stage in the journey, his path had grown darker, more twisted. Life, once so rich and full of promise, had become a burden, something he wanted to escape.

"God, there's no hope for me!"

Telling Will he didn't know the whereabouts of his wife.

Lying to Eleanor, telling her that Will was dead.

Sleeping with prostitutes to eke out petty revenge.

He clenched his teeth, unable to hold back the choked cry that escaped his lips.

What would his father say? Surely, he didn't deserve to be called the son of Thomas Steele. He slumped forward, slamming his fist against the wooden floor. "I'm evil. Evil! I have so many regrets, s-so many wrongs. What can I do?"

Words once spoken rolled like a fog around his mind.

The path to redemption is long and often difficult to perceive, but those who have eyes to see will find it.

Greyson. The butler had said that just before Malcolm had left home. He struggled to his knees, arms outstretched to the cross. "Even the servants in my father's house can find peace! Why can't I? What's wrong with me? Where is my happiness?"

Malcolm crawled forward, eyes intent on the object before him. One thing and one thing alone consumed his thoughts. "Is there hope for *me*?"

"Yes, Malcolm." He started as Eleanor's voice penetrated the fog in his mind. Lost in the whirlpool of his thoughts, he had forgotten she was there. "He offers a full pardon, one none of us deserve."

"T-tell me. What must I do?" His head swiveled toward her, eyes red from weeping.

"Forgiveness was His choice too. Accept what Christ has already done."

Shame made his throat constrict. "Father!" He croaked out the word. "I've nothing left. Forgive me!"

He beat his fist against his chest, conscious of a presence that he could not see, could not explain but *knew* existed. "I'm not worthy to be called Your son."

An image of Greyson, always steady, always serene, flashed through his mind. *A servant.* "Let me just be Your servant."

He had wronged God too many times to be considered a son. He had spit upon his love and rejected his mercy but now, when all had seemed lost, faith, sparked by Eleanor's words, brought the possibility of a new beginning.

"Can you do this, Malcolm? Do you believe?"

Thoughts swirled through his mind like leaves before a hurricane. *Who saved me on the battlefields? Who brought me back from the brink of death? Who protected me when the hospital exploded?*

Realization made him cringe. He had missed the obvious expressions of God's love time after time, blundering through the evidence that had surrounded him all along. Blinded by his own selfish greed, he had mistaken them for nothing more than coincidence when they were, in fact, signposts pointing him to a Father who had never abandoned him.

"Father, forgive me!" An image of Thomas's pained face flashed in his mind's eye. "Forgive me."

"He has, Malcolm. Do you believe?"

Thomas's face faded and only the cross remained visible. He reached upward, grabbing hold of the gnarled timbers.

"I-I believe." Malcolm whispered the words, recognizing only as they rolled out of his lips, the unseen power they contained. "I believe."

Clinging to the cross, he pulled himself upright. "I believe."

It was not a whisper this time but a shout. A cry of victory, a scream of triumph. Guilt melted before the power of forgiveness. Doubt vanished as light, streaming in through the stained-glass windows, illuminated his soul.

Malcolm turned and faced her, seeing in her eyes a reflection of the sudden, powerful, and totally unexpected joy that welled up within him. "Eleanor?"

She tilted her head to one side. "What is it?"

"I believe."

———————◆◆●◆◆———————

"All aboard!"

Malcolm Steele gripped his suitcase in his gloved left hand and extended his right toward Eleanor. "This is where our paths separate. I'm going home to Northshire and you—"

"I'm goin' to find my husband." With a smile, she gripped his hand. "He's out there somewhere, waitin' for me."

Malcolm grunted. "Looks like we're both going to need a few miracles."

"Me more than you, I think."

His smile faded. "I don't know about that. I can only hope my father will forgive me. It's as if my eyes have been opened and I see just how selfish I was."

"Don't look back, Malcolm." Eleanor interrupted him. "Remember, God makes everything *new*. Look to the future. Look to a reunion with your wife."

"I'll try to remember." He released his breath in a sigh. "It's the first time I've taken leave in three years of service. It's hard to imagine life away from the chaos of the battlefield."

"No matter what happens, Malcolm, remember that God is with you."

His heart lurched, and he pulled her into a quick embrace. "If it weren't for you Eleanor, I would never have known that."

"Hmm . . . " The corners of her lips turned upward. "If it weren't for me, you'd be dead."

He grinned. "I'm in your debt."

"Perhaps I'll come to collect it from that grand castle of yours someday. With interest!"

The shrieking whistle reminded him that he had only seconds left.

"Be safe, Eleanor. You remember what I told you about how to find Lieutenant-Colonel Stewart?"

"I do. Pray for me?"

He spoke past the lump that formed in his throat. "I will. Everyday. Thank you. Thank you."

He boarded the train and waved, keeping his eyes on her until she was no more than a speck in the distance. Heaving a deep sigh, Malcom leaned out the window. The train sped east, toward Calais, where he would board a steamer and cross the English Channel. A mixture of anticipation, mingled with fear, made his spine tingle.

Home waited for him. Leila waited for him. His father waited for him. A shadow crossed his brow. He was leaving the war behind, but would he find peace when he entered Northshire's gates?

Eleanor's train chugged west toward the Front. It was an armored coach, better suited to carrying soldiers than civilians. Despite the cramped quarters and throngs of soldiers around her, she felt a settled peace as though this decision was not one of her own making.

Save my son.

She closed her eyes, pondering the words that had first haunted her dreams over a year ago. She had saved Malcolm's life in a risky operation. Now, in a different way, Malcolm had found salvation with her at his side. But still the words echoed in her heart as though they held a greater meaning yet to be fulfilled.

Her eyes flickered open and she caught sight of the French countryside that sped by. Burnt out hulls of armored tanks littered the barren landscape with not a speck of green to be found.

Every cord that had tied her to Etaples had now been severed. First Will, then Veronica, and now Malcolm. As a volunteer, she was free to leave her post when she desired, but instead of leaving altogether, Eleanor had requested transportation to the frontlines of the conflict.

Malcolm had made it clear that Will had been captured by the enemy when on duty and had given her the name of Will's former regiment commander. She would speak with the man, a Lieutenant-Colonel Stewart, and learn what she could. If nothing else, there'd be plenty for her to do so close to the battle lines, of that she was certain.

She steadied herself on a metal handlebar as the train chugged onward, taking her toward the unknown. What waited for her in the trenches? News of her husband? Perhaps death itself? There could be no doubt that the danger would be infinitely more real.

Her mind called her every sort of a fool for leaving the relative security of Etaples and choosing to go where bombs turned men into human puddles. But her heart urged her onward, pushed by a quiet voice of steady reassurance.

"Father." Eleanor closed her eyes as she tipped her head toward the train's metal roof. "Help me find Will. Help me find Your son."

JP ROBINSON

Chapter 6

April 1917. Meier Farm near Münster, Germany.

Burkhard Meier pulled back the lace curtain that lined his kitchen window and angled his body, so he could observe the swarm of laborers that worked the land of his farm without being seen. From this distance, he could just make out the sweating faces of the squadron of British, French, and Romanian prisoners-of-war who were forced to labor under the watchful eyes of at least three dozen German soldiers.

Burkhard's gaze drifted down the line of men, seeking one face in particular. The farm's once-beautiful landscape had been ravaged by intersecting lines where the prisoners' mattocks carved neat squares of peat from the loam. They reminded him of the horrific trenches in the photographs that his son, Markus, had taken at the Front. The farmer's chest tightened, and his eyes shifted from the men outside to the framed photograph of his son that rested on a wooden shelf in the corner of the kitchen. A red rose lay before the image of the smiling man who would never grow a day older.

"Husband."

Burkhard forced his eyes away from the photo as his wife, Adele, entered the kitchen. Dark hair, streaked with swaths of silver that only enhanced her beauty, was curled up in a prim bun behind her head. Though wreathed with wrinkles that time and sorrow had carved on her face, in his eyes she was as beautiful as the day he had first called Adele his *frau* or wife. While her eyes brightened at the sight of him, the frown that darkened her brow remained. Perhaps it would never go away. Not now.

"*Mein Leben.* My love." He extended an arm to her.

Slipping into his embrace, she turned back to the window. "Are you certain this is wise?"

Burkhard pulled her closer. "You mean bringing a British prisoner to dinner?" He shook his head. "*Nein*, I am not sure it is wise at all."

"But you are going to do it." The matter-of-fact tone in her voice did not surprise him. Adele knew him as no other woman could.

"Yes."

"Which one is he?" She pulled back the curtain.

Burkhard hunched over and squinted out the window. Then, "There he is." He pointed toward a figure that stood apart from the rest.

Adele followed his finger with her eyes. "He looks about our son's age."

Burkhard was quiet for a long moment. Then he placed both arms on his wife's shoulders and turned her toward him. "Markus would have been thirty last week."

Tears glinted in her honey-brown eyes. "You don't need to explain yourself to me." She patted his weathered cheek. "I understand."

Burkhard grabbed her hand and held it. "I need to explain, Adele. I need to say it to someone . . . to you." His eyes probed her face. "The war killed Markus, not the British or their allies.

Our son"—his voice hitched—"our son could not live with what he had seen or . . . with what he had done."

Markus had been home on leave, but his son's mind had still wandered the barren terrain of no-man's land. Starting at sudden noises, responding with extreme violence to the slightest provocation, Markus had never truly left the war.

His mind flew back to that fateful morning. One morning, Burkhard had found his son lifeless on his bed, a gun in his right hand and a bullet in his brain. The few lines he had scribbled onto a paper confirmed the worst—Markus had taken his own life.

"I-I never noticed Will Thompson until I saw the Bible in his hand." Burkhard squeezed his eyes shut for a moment, trying to stop the flow of tears that his eyes let fall as though they had a life of their own. "When I spoke with him, I realized that he was another one, just like our son—lost in the pain and turmoil of a pointless war." He released a ragged breath. "I just can't let him slide into that void without trying to pull him back from the brink. *Verstehen*?"

She gave a slow nod. "I understand, husband. But what about the risk? You said that the commandant agreed that he could be fed in our home, provided you assume full responsibility. What if he tries to escape? You could be jailed or worse."

"Have faith, Adele." He turned her palm over and gently kissed it. "God holds our destiny in His hands. Do not worry."

Adele studied him for a long moment then reached up to brush a stray lock of his gray hair back into place. "I *am* trusting God. And I trust you." She pressed a slim finger gently against his chest. "But you are not only placing *us* in jeopardy. You must also think of our daughter, Katja."

Burkhard turned back toward the window. Will swung the mattock into the earth like a man possessed. Bringing such a violent man into his home was dangerous, there was no doubt about that. Was his desire to help such a man worth the risk?

"If he does anything foolish," he said, glancing sideways at his wife, "you have my permission to kill him."

Adele narrowed her eyes. "Believe me, Burkhard, I will."

<hr/>

Will ducked his head as he passed beneath a low-hanging wooden beam that made up the archway of a door and followed Burkhard into a spacious but sparsely decorated kitchen. His eyes darted around the room. Drawings of multicolored roses on bright yellow paper lined the walls. Beams of sunlight, only partially obscured by white lace curtains, floated in through several large windows, and landed on a large round, wooden table in the center of the room. A whistling kettle on a cast-iron stove evoked the memory of an emotion he hadn't felt in a long time—peace.

He sucked in a deep breath and his mouth watered as the scent of fresh-baked bread filled his nostrils.

"Welcome to my home." Burkhard bowed as he turned around. "Please, come closer."

Will shuffled forward, the illusion of peace vanishing as quickly as it had appeared. This had to be some ploy to gain information about the British army. He had heard of these kinds of tricks before. The enemy pretended kindness so soldiers would lower their guard. Well, such conniving foolery would never work on him.

"Allow me to present my wife, Adele." Burkhard gestured toward a far corner of the room. Will turned as a door opened and a short, middle-aged woman in a simple but elegant dark skirt and white top came forward.

"*Wilkommen.*" Her smile was tight and her gaze watchful. Apparently Burkhard's wife suspected Englishmen as much as he distrusted Germans.

Well, we have that in common at least. The thought was oddly comforting.

"And this is my daughter, Katja."

Will caught his breath as a young woman stepped lightly into the room. Her auburn hair was tucked neatly into a bun. High cheekbones graced her heart-shaped face, and her neck rose in a graceful curve above a trim figure. Her chestnut eyes were warm, but her gaze, like that of her mother, was cautious.

"Welcome." Katja dipped her head in greeting, the bottom of her green dress making a soft *swishing* sound as she glided forward. Will remained immobile, then realizing that he was staring, forced his eyes away from the daughter to her father.

Burkhard moved to stand beside his wife. "Both Adele and Katja speak English. Before the war, I exported peat to British farmers. I thought it prudent that my wife and children be as educated as I in these uncertain times."

"Children?" Will cocked his head to one side. "You have another daughter?"

Burkhard ignored his question. "Please, sit." He pulled a chair back from the table. "Here we are neither German nor English. We are only human beings, made in the image of God."

There were five chairs and Will noted that Burkhard positioned himself so that his daughter was across the table from Will.

So, the old fox doesn't trust me around his daughter. He didn't blame the man. If Abby had been alive, he—

Will closed his eyes as a tremor ran through him. The fact was, his daughter wasn't alive. She had been killed, crushed to death by a German bomb that had been released by German hands. Like those around this table.

"Are you all right?"

His eyes flew open. It was Katja who had spoken. Her voice had a musical quality, like the throaty sound of a flute as it lilted the notes that made each song unforgettable.

Will blinked several times. There was no denying the girl's beauty. It was a fact that contradicted his belief that nothing German could be beautiful.

"I'm a prisoner in a dirty German war camp." He gripped his fork in a clenched fist, jaw clenched. "I've lost my pride, thanks to *German* soldiers. You lot have ripped away my identity and stolen my freedom, so, no, I am *not* all right!"

A slight smile played about her full lips. She seemed unmoved by his outburst. "But you have a meal before you, which is more than many men—German or British—can say." She propped one elbow on the table. "You are alive. And you are in the home of friends."

Will's face reddened. "Friends? You're a bunch of stinking Germans!"

"Germans who can see past the mask of hate to the real man below," she shot back, her eyes narrowing. "What more could you want?"

Burkhard cleared his throat. "It is bad for the digestion to quarrel before a meal."

Will's angry retort died on his tongue, and he dropped his gaze to his large, rough fingers.

"As our guest, Will, I ask you to bless the table." Burkhard extended both his hands. Katja joined hands with her mother and father. Will's eyes darted from the eating knife on the table to Burkhard's outstretched palm. With one blow he could maim the man and sprint out the door toward freedom.

Burkhard followed his gaze. "We are about to bow our heads and ask the same God to bless the food that we will all eat. If we cannot be friends, can we at least agree to not be enemies while we pray?"

Have we not all one Father? Has not one God created us? The words rippled across Will's mind, triggering a niggling sense of unease. His hatred was justified . . . wasn't it?

He gave a terse nod, feeling the weight of Katja's steady gaze upon him. *What is she thinking?* The question gave him pause. It didn't matter what she thought, only what his conscience demanded. With obvious hesitation that left no doubt of his reluctance, he clasped Burkhard's hand and bowed his head.

JP ROBINSON

Chapter 7

May 1917. Northshire Estate, Great Britain.

Leila Steele slipped the book *The Pilgrim's Progress* from its place on the massive bookcase that lined the walls of Thomas's study and inserted a slim, golden key in the small lock that the book had concealed. She turned the key and leapt back as an entire section of the bookcase slid outward on concealed pulleys to reveal a dark passage.

Hurrying over to the unlit fireplace, Leila pressed on a wooden pane under a portrait of Isabella, Thomas's late wife. The panel retracted to one side to reveal a small drawer in which she replaced the key. She was about to turn around but paused, mesmerized by the sight of the woman in the portrait. *What would it have been like to know her?*

Dark eyes, that spoke of compassion and humor, smiled down at her from the wall. The strong set of the narrow chin, which Isabella had obviously passed on to her son Malcolm, indicated a strong resilience to which Leila could relate. A simple face, framed with straight, cinnamon-colored hair, bespoke both practicality and the quality of an inner beauty.

"It's hard to believe that this place has become my home." Leila smiled back at the woman, convinced that, were Isabella alive, they would have been good friends as well as mother and daughter-in-law. She had little doubt that Isabella would have forgiven her crime against her family as Thomas had done.

Two years ago, she had infiltrated the Steele estate under orders from German High Command. But neither the kaiser's clandestine forces nor Leila herself had considered the incomprehensible quirks of the heart. While she had met Malcolm with the intent of eliciting secrets, she had ended up loving him as she could love no one else. At his insistence, they had married in secret after an impetuous courtship of only a few weeks.

Her brow furrowed as darker memories surfaced. One night, Malcolm had found her meeting a male German contact and had wrongfully assumed that she was unfaithful. Leila had been unable to reveal the truth without compromising her identity. After a public altercation, Malcolm had abandoned her, leaving to join the tide of British soldiers heading for the Front.

Leila closed her eyes, reliving the pain of those interminable weeks. She had continued to spy for the Fatherland until some intelligence she had unearthed had placed Malcolm's life in jeopardy. Her handler, General Werner Jaëger, had grown suspicious of her loyalty and sent an agent to bring her back to Berlin. A violent struggle had ensued, and in desperation, she had shot the man, killing him.

She let her forehead slump against the marble hearth, relishing the cool comfort it provided. With both Werner and the British government on her trail, her only recourse had been to seek sanctuary from the man she had both loathed and feared: her father-in-law, Thomas Steele.

She lifted her head and considered the woman's acrylic eyes. "Thomas accepted me despite knowing my past. Northshire is my home now, Isabella. I'll safeguard it for you. I won't let you down."

"I know you won't."

Leila whirled around as Thomas entered the study. A smile gentled the stern set of his jaw, and she could not help but smile in return.

"Lady Isabella is good company." She gestured toward the portrait.

"Ah . . . " A faraway look crept into Thomas's eyes as he gazed upon the image of his wife. "She is indeed. I have missed her company sorely these past ten years. I look forward to our reunion."

Leila wrapped him in a quick hug. "For all our sakes, may that reunion be many years away." Then Leila pulled back and eyed him, a worried frown on her brow. "You're headed to London."

"And how did you deduce that Mrs. Holmes?"

She refused to respond to his attempted levity. "You're wearing a brown plaid suit and matching tie."

He arched a silver eyebrow. "I always wear a suit."

"*And* you're wearing a waistcoat." She pointed to the vest that framed his neckwear. "You only do *that* when attending a very formal meeting."

"Ah!" Thomas gave a grudging nod. "I should have known better than to question your powers of observation."

"Thomas." She laid a hand on his arm. "London is a dangerous place for you. What if Hughes arrests you?"

"Why would he?"

"Why would he?" She stepped back and stared at him. "We found two of his agents dead on your property after the fire last year."

"I contacted the local law and in no uncertain terms explained that I didn't know the men. As you know, the chief inspector did a thorough investigation after removing the bodies. I'm sure Hughes had them confiscated. The entire village fought the fire with me that night, so there was no shortage of witnesses." Thomas shrugged. "The chief inspector felt there were no grounds for charges and rightly so."

"All the same, what if Hughes thinks you had them murdered?"

"I have no easy answer, Leila." Thomas tugged on his brown gloves as he spoke. "The truth is, I fear you're right. The circumstances do paint a very grim picture of my loyalty."

"So, you'll—"

"But I am a soldier." Thomas interrupted her, setting his shoulders. "I cannot win my battles if I run from them. The Prime Minister contacted me the day after the fire, urging me to take all the time I needed to straighten things out here before coming to London."

He shrugged. "It's taken almost seven months to recover from the damage on the Estate, during which I have been in constant communication with Joseph Mara, my right hand at the Bank. However, much longer away and Hughes will paint my absence as proof of my guilt. No, it is high time to face the enemy."

"What do you plan to do?" She spoke in a quiet voice. Fear for his future gripped her heart. Thomas was Northshire. If anything happened to him...

"I will fight." He took her hands in his. "And I will win."

"And what should I do in the meantime?"

"You must fight in your own way." He gestured toward the secret passageway. "Find out what the Huns are up to while I'm gone. You have installed enough radio and satellite equipment in your listening tower to hear what the kaiser is taking for tea!"

"I'm worried Thomas. Worried for you." Leila folded her arms across her chest.

A warm smile crossed his face. "I have a solution." He paused as she looked at him expectantly then said, "Pray."

She let out a pent-up breath as she nodded. "Right. Pray. The most important thing that I always forget to do in moments of crisis."

"It's alright. You wouldn't be the first to do that." Thomas bowed his head. "Will you start?"

Leila closed her eyes, gathered hold of her frazzled emotions, and poured out her heart to the God she knew was listening.

<hr/>

Prime Minister David Lloyd George leaned against the marble ledge of his fireplace, glanced at his wristwatch, then ran a moist hand over his short-cropped white moustache. "He's late."

"Your watch is fast." The voice belonged to Robert Hughes, head of British Intelligence. "We're talking about Thomas. He is never late."

The two men waited inside David's office at Whitehall Court for a meeting that was certain to be unpleasant. Hughes, however, seemed almost eager for the upcoming encounter. The reticent, one-legged spymaster reminded the Prime Minister of a pirate ready to pounce on an unsuspecting ship. True, he wore a pressed navy-blue suit and a starched white shirt instead of baggy breaches and a loose jersey, but the glint in his blue eyes and his erect posture created an atmosphere of anticipation that set the Prime Minister on edge.

"I don't like it, Hughes." David fidgeted with the back of his collar. "I realize that I told you to proceed, but I've had the chance to think things through. Now I'm not certain we should continue with this assault on Thomas's character. Our evidence is . . . circumstantial. I can't arrest a peer of the realm based on coincidental speculation."

"Prime Minister." Hughes ran his fingertips over the wooden stump that protruded from his blue pant leg. He leaned back in one of two white cloth armchairs that sat on either side of a wooden circular table. "Evil runs rampant, like weeds, throughout the world. It is our duty to ferret out the evil in our midst, and when we have done so"—Hughes flicked a hand upward and a switchblade appeared in his palm—"we must cut it out!" He slammed the blade down into the stump.

David blanched, a sick feeling rising in his gut. "Oh, dispense with the theatrics, man! I need solid evidence before bringing Thomas in, not drama."

Hughes leaned back in his chair, a slight frown creasing his brow. "Very well. Allow me to guide the conversation."

It was David's turn to frown. Despite the looming German threat, Great Britain was far from united concerning the global conflict. Antiwar sentiment ran high, with different minorities seeking to turn the struggle to their own advantage. The Irish, for example, continued to seek opportunities to overthrow the yoke of their colonial rulers. Protests had sometimes turned violent, leading to sharp crackdowns and reprisal raids from the authorities.

Thomas was one of Great Britain's most respected citizens, and to date, his bank had funded a large portion of the war effort. If he were accused of treason and later proven innocent, an invasion by the Germans would be the least of the Prime Minister's problems. The various antiwar factions within the country would unite, and making Thomas a martyr of British injustice, would spawn riots across London that would bring the country to its knees.

"What do you have in mind?" He shifted in his chair, then tugged at the sides of his black suit jacket.

"A test." The spymaster leaned forward, a tight smile on his lips. "Nothing more."

David considered this. "What sort of test?"

Hughes clenched his fist and the switchblade retracted with a sharp *click*. He pushed himself out of the chair and held David's gaze. "The kind of test that will yield . . . solid evidence. Do I have your permission to proceed?"

David's mind weighed the implications of Hughes's proposal. Thomas had been David's childhood friend. Worse still, Thomas had saved his life while on a foreign campaign. David owed him his loyalty. However, he also planned to run for reelection as Prime Minister. If he refused to allow Hughes to proceed with his absurd test of Thomas's loyalty, the spymaster could interfere with the coming election by planting reports of his reluctance to proceed in the ears of his political opponents.

More than likely, Hughes would use David's hesitation to launch his own political career. After a lifetime spent in the shadows, no doubt the man was itching for a chance in the spotlight.

Ultimately, the choice was simply a matter of priorities: was he more loyal to his friend or to his career?

"Proceed." The word had scarcely left David's lips when his secretary knocked, then opened the door.

"Beggin' your pardon, Prime Minister. Sir Thomas Steele has arrived."

"Ah." Hughes shoved himself upright, then sniffed as he glanced at his watch. "Right on time."

Thomas marched into the Prime Minister's office, shoulders set and head erect. He removed his hat, tossing it onto a wooden table in the center of the room.

"Welcome, Thomas." David reached over his small paunch and grasped his arm, a meaningless smile plastered on his pasty face.

Thomas turned to Hughes and jerked his head downward in a stiff nod but kept his hands at his side.

"I'm very glad to see you, Thomas." Hughes lifted his monocle to his left eye, peering at him as though he were an insect that had blundered its way into a glass bottle. "It's been far too long. About seven months, I believe?"

"You know, that's the odd bit, Hughes." Thomas tilted his head to one side. "I feel as though I've seen quite a lot of you despite my time away from London."

"What do you mean?" Hughes's narrow face remained impassive. Clearly the man thought he had him trapped.

"Don't be coy with me, Robert." Thomas took a step forward. "You had two men—spies—posted on my property." He clenched his jaw. "*My* property."

David interrupted the growing tension by gesturing to one of the plush seats. "Ahem, gentlemen. Perhaps it would be better if we all sat down?"

"With respect, Prime Minister, I prefer to stand." Thomas's eyes didn't leave Hughes's face. "Explain yourself!"

A smile twisted the man's thin lips. "I think it is you who should do the explaining, Thomas." His wooden leg clunked ominously on the carpeted floor as he moved closer. "Explain why it is that two of *my* men died—as you say—on *your* property."

He lifted his monocle and peered at Thomas through the lens once more. "Who killed them, Thomas?"

"I suspect a German agent." Thomas had anticipated this question.

Hughes started, obviously not expecting such candor.

"A *German*?" This from the Prime Minister.

Thomas swung his head sharply toward him. "Yes. I suspect that a German agent planted explosives on my property as a diversion with the intent of rifling through my home."

He jabbed a finger against Hughes's chest, keeping his eyes on the Prime Minister. "Hughes's men must have been in the way."

"Ridiculous. You expect us to believe that—"

Thomas whirled back to the spymaster, cutting him off. "I suggest you train your lads better. *Two* highly-trained British agents downed by a single German? Embarrassing."

Hughes colored.

"He does have a point." David reached in his breast pocket and pulled out a cigar.

Hughes shifted the focus of the conversation. "Who is the woman, Thomas?"

"What woman?"

"The blonde, quite a beauty by all accounts, who lives in your home."

So, he knows about Leila. Thomas didn't hesitate. "Family."

"I wasn't aware that you had any family." Hughes stroked his chin slowly. "This is rather sudden isn't it?"

Thomas snorted. "Your interest in my genealogy is unhealthy, Robert. If you must know, my son secretly married the girl before he went to war."

"Really?" David lit a match and held it to the cigar. "Congratulations, old boy. Why the secrecy?"

Thomas sucked in a deep breath then released it. He would have to phrase this carefully. "She wasn't my first choice."

"Ah!" David nodded. "Young men are always rebellious at that stage." He barked out a laugh and spoke around his cigar. "I know I was."

"So . . . you are sheltering your daughter-in-law?"

"Yes, I am. Has that also become an act of treason under the Defense of the Realm Act, Hughes? If so, speak plainly and be done with it."

Hughes frowned but did not reply.

"The point is"—Thomas hardened his voice—"why me? Why do you persist in suspecting that I am collaborating with the enemy?"

"DORA gives me the right to collect information in any way I see fit." Hughes leaned upon his cane. "It does not require me to justify my actions to you."

Thomas bunched his hands into fists. "And neither does it require my bank to fund the government's expenses."

There were two frozen statues in the room.

"W-what did you say?" David found his voice first.

"Do you honestly expect me to finance your operations while you persist in insulting my honor?" Thomas shifted his gaze from one man to the other. "I have dedicated over three decades of my life to my country." He scoffed. "Now you want to accuse me of treason?"

Silence.

"Your organization is funded by *my* money." He glowered at Hughes. "Call off your dogs or the next financial request made by the government of England will be denied by the *Bank* of England."

"I-I am sure this is all a simple misunderstanding." David bent to pick up the cigar that had fallen from his pudgy fingers. "Erm, Hughes was only doing a routine inspection, that's all. Making sure everything was in . . . tiptop shape out there in the woods. Now that is over, I am sure there'll be no need to monitor Northshire any further. Wouldn't you agree, Hughes?"

The spymaster's knuckles went white as he gripped his cane. "Yes." He spat out the word through clenched teeth. "It was routine reconnaissance, Sir Thomas. My apologies for the inconvenience."

Thomas nodded, feeling the same sense of grim satisfaction at an enemy's defeat that he had often experienced on the battlefield. "Then, unless there are other matters the Prime Minister wishes to discuss, this meeting is adjourned."

Without waiting on a response, he picked up his hat, slammed it onto his head, and pivoted on his heel. He was halfway to the door when Hughes's words pulled him to a halt.

"Two months ago, our agents intercepted a note from the Germans to Mexico encouraging them to invade the United States. The Americans are outraged. But that game works both ways. As we speak, my men are laying the groundwork for a British invasion of Germany through Denmark."

Thomas shook his head. *The clever fox.*

He turned and stared at Hughes's sallow face. "Why do you tell me this?"

The head of the Secret Intelligence Service bared his teeth. "Why not? We three have often discussed such matters in the past. As we have just established, your loyalty and discretion are beyond question." He shrugged. "I see no reason why things cannot continue as they always have. I'm actually quite chuffed to know I can rely upon you implicitly."

Thomas held his gaze for a long moment. "This is war, Robert. Nothing will ever be the same again."

Then he turned and slammed the door shut behind him.

"What was that about?" David spoke around the cigar in his mouth. "An invasion of the Rhineland from a neutral territory? I hope you're not keeping secrets from *me*."

Hughes thumped his way to the window and watched as Thomas's driver opened the door of the Vauxhall. Thomas turned and looked up at the window from which Hughes observed him, tipped his hat in an exaggerated bow, then entered the car.

Hughes gritted his teeth. *How does he anticipate my every move?*

"As I said, it is a test." He let the curtain fall back into place.

"To what end?"

"The preservation of the British Empire." Hughes raked his hand through his silver hair, expelling a breath through puffed cheeks. "If Sir Thomas is a traitor, he will tell his German contacts about the alleged invasion. I will have my agents monitor all cable transmissions to Germany. If there is significant chatter about an invasion from Denmark, we will know that Saint Thomas is really a Judas."

"And you really believe he fell for your little charade?" David shook his head. "The man is a master of strategy."

"The key to the plan is the bait. Germany cannot afford to open a third theatre of war. Even if Thomas suspects this is a trap, he will be compelled to transmit whatever information he knows. Once that is done, I will have my proof."

The Prime Minister contemplated this in silence.

"You called him a master of strategy." Hughes slanted him a humorless smile. "Well, so am I."

Chapter 8

May 1917. London, Great Britain.

Werner Jaëger tilted a glass of water to his lips and sneaked a glance out the window of London's prestigious Red Lion restaurant. Dusk enveloped the city. By the light cast by the lampposts that lined the cobblestone streets, he watched as throngs of pedestrians scurried like cockroaches on their way to their miserable tenements or to the pubs.

Life had disappointed Werner, tantalizing him with the possibility of revenge only to snatch it out of reach at the last moment. A muscle twitched in his jaw, an imperceptible movement that expressed the bitter rage that swirled within his heart. When Leila Steele had pulled the trigger on his agent, the man she knew only by his codename Charles, she had unknowingly snuffed out the life of his son, Christophe.

Determined to avenge his son's death while preventing Leila from divulging the dangerous secret she carried to the British, Werner had left his post to personally hunt down the rogue agent.

He shifted in his seat, his dark eyes probing the scarlet sky. After months of fruitless searching, he had discovered that Leila had surprisingly taken refuge in Northshire Estate. As such, Werner had launched an all-out assault on Northshire, certain that he could capture Leila and be on his way to Germany by dawn.

But he had failed, miserably. His attempt at infiltrating the home of Thomas Steele had been born of desperation, not cold logic and careful planning. As a result, he had been forced to kill two British guards and had nearly lost his life in the process.

Recovery had occurred over an agonizing seven-month period, but while Werner's body mended, his mind had been busy laying the groundwork for his next assault. This past March, the kaiser had given him another chance and sent him back to London with orders to eliminate Leila, the one person who could possibly derail his nefarious mission Project Herkules. *Now called Hubris.*

Werner's fingers drummed lightly on the table. This time, he would rely on his cunning to take down his prey. Since his return from Berlin, he had discreetly studied Northshire's infrastructure, memorizing the layout of both the estate and the nearby village. But his surveillance had been limited.

After his attack last year, the estate's owner, Sir Thomas Steele, had doubled the number of guards on the property, making it almost impossible to do anything but analyze the grounds from afar with his high-powered binoculars.

The town itself maintained an atmosphere of perpetual vigilance, which was not surprising given their recent experience. Even the children had looked at him crosswise when he had passed through the town.

And so, Werner had once again adjusted strategy. This time, his target would not be Leila but her father-in-law, Thomas Steele. The corners of his lips lifted in a feigned smile as his eyes slid from the window to the face of the talkative secretary who sat across the table from him.

"So, Elaine, do you miss your hometown?"

The brunette tipped her glass of champagne to her lips before answering. It was her fourth glass. Werner leaned back, amazed at how unattractive the woman was. In fifty-four years of life, he had never seen so many warts on so pale a face. Her short, stubby neck led onto a pair of thick shoulders that were better suited for a man than a woman. Add to this forty pounds of excess fat, and in his mind, Elaine was the top candidate for London's ugliest.

Based on their conversation this evening, Elaine had never enjoyed a suitor's attentions. Were it not for the fact that she was Sir Thomas Steele's secretary at the Bank of England, Werner would have never given her a second glance.

"Me?" Elaine hiccupped then pressed her pudgy fingers to her lips. "Miss little Devonville?" She shook her head then giggled. "No, George. There's nothin' there but cows and cornstalks."

George. Werner had chosen a common British name as his alias. His English was flawless with barely the hint of an accent, but one could never be too careful. If anything did go wrong, with a name like George, he would be untraceable.

"No." Elaine hiccupped. "London's the place for me. Lot's more to do here."

It was the third time in four weeks that Werner had asked her to join him at the Red Lion and it was obvious that time, and the intoxicating prospect of a suitor, had made the woman lose some of her earlier inhibitions.

His eyes flickered over their surroundings. Tapered candles on their table enhanced the low lighting of the Red Lion. Somewhere in the corner, a singer crooned out a love song, making the entire atmosphere nothing short of romantic. But it was not a woman that he sought; it was information.

"What brought you to London?" Werner refilled her glass with champagne.

"Um, I was lookin' for work." Her eyes on the glass, she shook her head with another giggle. "No more for me please, George. I've never drunk so much of the stuff in my life."

"No more? Are you sure?" His voice was intentionally soft, letting her feel that she was in control.

"Well." She licked her lips. "Maybe just a little. Mr. Steele will be wonderin' what's come over me tomorrow!"

At last. Werner smoothly shifted the course of the conversation, pushing her glass toward her. "What's he like, your boss?" He swirled the water in his glass.

"Oh, he's a real gentleman." Elaine's eyes roamed from his combed peppered hair to the white suit and vibrant red tie that hung around his neck. "Like yourself. I've worked for him for over five years now."

A waitress approached the table, carrying their meals on a tray. Werner waited until she had left before he spoke again.

"Does he live in London as well?" Disgust filled him as Elaine tore into her meal with the decorum of a ravenous bear.

"Oh no." Speaking around a mouthful of crab, Elaine said, "He lives on an enormous estate called Northshire." Despite her protest, Elaine reached again for the glass of champagne then dabbed at her mouth with a scarlet cloth napkin. "Rumor has it that Sir Thomas kicked out his own son." She leaned forward and winked.

Werner drew back. "No!"

"'Tis true!"

"But you said he was a gentleman?" He neatly sawed off a piece of steak. It was rare and the distinct flavor of blood made him salivate.

"That's the point." Elaine's pale forehead gleamed in the candlelight. "His son ain't"—she frowned, struggling to correct herself—"*is not* like his father. Sir Thomas couldn't stand his way of livin' and so he kicked him out." She lowered her voice. "But I think he's shelterin' his son's wife."

She stabbed the fork into a piece of broccoli and popped it into her mouth.

"Why would he do that? Surely, if he's a man of honor as you say, he would just wash his hands of the woman altogether." Werner chewed slowly, savoring both the meat's juices and the tingle of anticipation that slid up his spine. His internal hunter's instinct warned him that this woman held some vital piece of information, something that he *needed* to know.

"Well." Elaine swallowed. "At least I'm sure there's a woman in the house."

Werner arched an eyebrow. "Really? Do tell."

She glanced around and leaned forward . . . opened her mouth wide . . . then drew back. "No. I-I really shouldn't."

Werner wanted to howl with frustration, but instead, he calmly dabbed his lips with the napkin and smiled. *Give her the illusion of power.* "As you wish. On no account would I want you to feel that you had compromised your employer's honor. I want you to feel comfortable with me." He dropped his voice to a seductive whisper and slid his left hand forward so that the tips of his fingers brushed hers. "Especially as I am so very interested in you."

Elaine just ogled him, sucking in deep breaths. For a moment, Werner feared the girl would keel over like a hyperventilating cow!

Then she slid her fingers forward, intertwining them with his own. "I-I'm sure that it would be all right, if I told you."

She's mine.

Werner replaced the victorious smile that threatened to break across his face with a look of consternation. "No, please don't Elaine. Don't do anything that could jeopardize your employment. I'd feel horrible if I were to cause you any trouble."

"No, really, it's nothin' important." She slid her plate to one side and leaned over the table. Dropping her voice to a whisper, "This afternoon, Mr. Steele asked me to send a telegram to his home. It was addressed to a woman—a Leila Steele."

"Do you remember the message?"

"Hm?" She stared at him, her nostrils twitching. Evidently Elaine found the musky scent of his cologne captivating. Unfortunately—or, rather, fortunately in this case—he had no time for distractions and so, Werner pulled away. "Was the message anything interesting?"

With a sigh, Elaine dropped her head and picked her fork up once more. "Nothin' important, just that he'd be in London for a few weeks and not to worry." She crinkled her brow. "Oh, and somethin' about bein' careful to listen closely because friends will soon become enemies."

Friends will soon become enemies? A chill settled in Werner's gut as his mind spun through the implications of Elaine's words. To an ordinary woman like the one across the table, the message was nothing more than practical, if slightly odd, advice—especially in times of war. But Leila was not an ordinary woman and Thomas was no ordinary man. They were both highly-trained military personnel and, as such, nothing Thomas said could be taken at face value.

Werner's mind dissected each syllable, probing for any sign that would bring his quarry within reach. *Listen.* Listen to what? For what? What if Leila had constructed a listening post somewhere on Northshire's vast acreage. She had been

82

trained to do exactly that with little more than a ball of wire and a primitive radio.

It makes sense. The girl was isolated from the world in her fortress of stone. Her natural instinct would be to monitor the actions of the country she had betrayed. Perhaps Leila was even decoding messages she intercepted on shortwave radio. The knot in his stomach tightened.

Friends will soon become enemies.

Perhaps Thomas was referring to his relationships with Britain's political heads of state. Was Thomas himself the victim of a betrayal? *Possibly.* But what if he hinted at something more? What if he hinted at pending attack?

With another winning smile, Werner complimented her on her choice of clothing. "That shade of purple unleashes the passion in your eyes." He let her blush and simper while his mind chipped away at the mystery before him.

Based on over a year of careful observation, Werner knew that Thomas Steele was not a man to take lightly. His strategic mind was formidable, and his every word contained significant meaning. He was connected to the most powerful men in Europe and, as such, knew things that others did not. Why send such an abstract message to a former spy like Leila unless there was something she should know? Something that she would learn by listening on whatever radio structure she had presumably built?

Werner signaled the waitress and collected the bill. He included a generous tip and winked at the awe-struck Elaine. *Friends will soon become enemies.* It was possible that Thomas hinted at an invasion of Germany by a neutral party.

The thought gave him pause and he considered his options carefully. He had no concrete proof that his speculation was correct, but even the slight possibility of an unexpected invasion was too much of a risk to keep quiet. If a friend of Germany, or a neutral territory, opened up a third Front the war would quickly be over, and his country would be the loser. In his quest to ensnare Leila, he had stumbled across information that could prove vital.

Werner made up his mind. He would send an encoded message to Berlin tonight, warning them that the possibility existed of an invasion by a neutral territory. What High Command would do with such a warning, he could not control. But his duty as a patriot was clear.

Rising, he helped Elaine with her coat then bowed and kissed her hand. "It has been an unforgettable evening, Miss Blair."

With another hiccup, she swayed, steadied herself on his arm, then shrieked out another giggle. "I do hope we can do this again, George. It's been a *perfect* evenin'. You really are such a gentleman."

He walked with her to the door, noting that the evening had melted into a foggy night. Werner waved goodbye and turned away, glancing at his watch. *Half-past six.*

His eyes rolled to Elaine's receding back. The girl lived about fifteen minutes from the Red Lion and the poison he had slipped into the bottle of champagne would take its time in working through her system. Werner believed in leaving no evidence, nothing that could possibly incriminate him. Elaine would reach her home and have an hour or two to go to bed. Then, in the dead of the night, Elaine Blair would pass away.

Werner placed his white top hat on his head, pulled on his matching gloves and walked into the lamplit mist, letting the swirling fog enshroud him. By morning, Thomas Steele would find himself in need of a new secretary.

"He's done it. Thomas has done it." Despite the late hour, Hughes's voice contained no trace of fatigue.

David Lloyd George massaged his temples with one hand and clutched the telephone to his ear with the other. "Are you sure? Think carefully, man!"

"My men intercepted the message and I have examined the document myself. It warns of the possibility of an attack from a friendly nation. He even referred to Germany as the 'Fatherland.'" His tone sharpened. "There were three of us in that room, Prime Minister. Unless you or I have suddenly developed a love for the Huns, there *is* no other possibility. Thomas has sent the information to Berlin."

Silence, broken only by static on the line, stretched out for several long seconds. Then David spoke.

"I need more proof Hughes. There's too much at stake to risk botching this up."

"With respect, Prime Minister, how *much* proof do you need? Two of my men were killed on his property and now, classified information has been intercepted while on its way to the kaiser! Thank God, it was false information. Were it real, British interests would have been compromised."

He released his breath in an exasperated sigh. "I will not allow anyone to hazard the security of our nation. Not even the prime minister is above suspicion."

"Have you gone barmy, Robert?" David bared his teeth, almost choking with indignation. "You *dare* threaten me?"

"I only wish to be sure you understand—"

"No, Hughes. I want *you* to understand. Understand that *I* am the prime minister of this nation. I will not be dictated to, bullied, or manipulated to accommodate your own political schemes."

"Political schemes? I assure you sir—"

"Oh, shut your laughing gear, you numpty." David paced the hallway floor as far as the telephone cord would allow, gripping both the receiver and base between whitened knuckles. "I've played politics for far too long to be blind to your little charade. If I don't follow your lead, here's your plan: you'll drop a hint here and there that I'm not fit for office. You'll tell your pals that I've gone soft because Thomas is my friend. Then, when my political backers are effectively divided, you'll step in as the hero of the day—giving yourself a strong platform on which to launch your own political career."

"I-I assure you, Prime Minister, that was the furthest thing from my mind."

David released a humorless chuckle. "You're an excellent spy, Hughes, I'll grant you that. But if you want to win at politics, you need to learn to lie without stuttering."

Silence.

"Now"—David released a tightly-held breath—"while the evidence regarding Thomas is compelling I need something more definite. I need something that will *unite* the Empire around an accusation of Thomas Steele . . . should it come to that. At present, what you're offering will have us all at each other's throats. Until you have proof that *I* consider indisputable, you will take no direct action against him. Is that perfectly clear?"

"Yes, Prime Minister."

David grunted. *That's the way it should always be.* "Then we have nothing further to say on the matter."

Without waiting on a response, he slammed the receiver onto its cradle and marched back to his bed.

Chapter 9

June 1917. Meier Farm near Münster, Germany.

Smack! Adele Meier rolled her shoulders then punched her fists into the dough that she kneaded on the flour-coated counter. She was a lean woman, toughened by years of hard living and grief. Jerking the dough back toward the counter's edge, she slammed the heels of her palms into it.

A warm summer breeze passed through the open windows of her bright yellow kitchen, bringing with it the voices of men— prisoners of war—who worked her husband's farm.

Smack! She gritted her teeth and punched the dough again. What she would give to have Will Thompson beneath her fists instead of the doughy paste!

Adele paused to wipe sweat from her forehead with the crook of her elbow, then glanced at her daughter. Katja stood by the open window, hands coated with flour, but her own wad of dough lay neglected before her. Her mother grunted and slammed her fists into the mixture. In the three months since Burkhard had first brought Will inside their home, she had watched as her daughter's attitude toward the beguiling enemy had shifted from a hostile interest to romantic fascination.

Her husband, meanwhile, remained oblivious to what was happening to their daughter. Adele threw back her head with a snort. *Burkhard is willfully oblivious.*

"Mother." Katja's eyes were glued on the line of working men, but Adele was certain she saw only one of them. "Do you think that English women are more beautiful than we are?"

At first Adele chose to remain silent, weighing the implications of Katja's words while considering the impact that the angry retort, which burned in her throat, could have upon her daughter.

The war had claimed her son, Markus. The wrong words now could alienate her daughter.

And nothing can slip between a girl and her family as easily as a strong, handsome foreign man.

Wiping her hands on her apron, Adele moved to stand next to her daughter. "I think,"she said, slipping her arm around Katja's waist,"that a better question would be, 'What plan does God have for my life?'" She pulled her daughter close. "You are special, Katja. And you have a special purpose."

"Mother, I have to tell you something." Katja's voice held a note of excitement that made Adele curl up within herself. "I-I think I've found that purpose."

"Is that so? Well . . . what is it, *Tochter*?"

Katja spun toward her, face flushed and eyes gleaming. "Wi—"

"Ah, the two loveliest women in the world!" Burkhard burst into the kitchen, stooping slightly to catch both Katja and Adele into his wide embrace.

Adele pulled herself free and eyed him askance. "You are only saying that because it is lunch time." She jabbed his stomach.

With a chuckle, Burkhard lifted his hands in a gesture of surrender. "I am guilty, my love." He turned to Katja who had watched the exchange with a strange wistful look in her eyes.

"Daughter, would you please inform General Klein that we wish our guest to join us for the midday meal."

Panic wiped the faint smile from Adele's face. "Can't you go, Burkhard?"

"Oh, I think some air will do her good. It is a beautiful day, isn't it, Katja?"

"Absolutely, Papa." Katja hurriedly peeled off her striped apron and scrubbed her hands clean in a bowl of water, taking care to rub each fingernail free of dough.

"Won't you go with her, Burkhard?"

Her husband shook his head. "There's no need, *mein leben*. Will has shown remarkable improvement over the past months. True, he is British, but he is also a gentleman at heart. We must show him that we trust him."

"Trust him?" Adele struggled to keep her voice calm. "He's the enemy!"

Burkhard's eyebrows furrowed together. "He is our *guest*." He gestured to the window. "Besides, it's a straight walk from the fields to the house, there are guards posted along the way, and we can observe everything from this window." Shrugging, he said, "Why not?"

Wiping her hands, Katja leaned on her tiptoes and kissed his cheek. "Of course, you're right, Papa. Will is a guest now. I'll go at once." She threw him a smile then danced from the room.

It was Adele's turn to frown as the door slammed behind Katja. "I don't like what you're doing, Burkhard. Not at all."

"She's a good influence on him, Adele." Her husband positioned himself next to her at the window. "Look at how much Will has changed since he first arrived. We have Katja to thank."

Adele glared at him. "It's not the change in *him* that concerns me. It is the change in our daughter."

"What do you mean?"

"She is falling in love with him, husband." Adele spoke in short clipped tones that left no room for doubt as to how she felt about the matter. "Our daughter loves this *Englishman* of whom we know nothing. She feels that he is somehow connected to her purpose in life."

Burkhard was silent for a long moment. His eyes shifted to a photograph of a little girl in a white dress, matching shoes, and ribbons in her hair. Then he gazed through the window at the young woman who hurried toward the line of forced laborers.

"She's growing up Adele. We cannot stop the future."

"Yes, but he is not a part of her future."

"Would it be such a bad thing?" His arm curled around her waist. "To have a man in the house again?"

She pulled away, a heavy feeling settling in the pit of her stomach. "What are you saying? You would replace our son, our Markus with this man of whom we know *nothing*?"

Grabbing her husband's arm, Adele spun him toward her. "Have you noticed that he never speaks about his past? He may have a wife and ten children for all we know! The man is a-a bomb, waiting for the right moment to explode, Burkhard. And I won't have our Katja hurt—not by him. Not by any man."

"I won't let him hurt her Adele." Burkhard caressed her cheek with his fingertips. "Don't forget, she's my child too."

"But you're not only happy with a daughter." He flinched, and she knew her words were true. "You once had a son. Now you seek to fill that void with a man who needs rescuing"—her voice hitched—"as Markus once needed rescuing."

"Adele—"

"Hear me Burkhard." She thrust a finger in his face. "If that man harms one hair of Katja's head, I will never forgive him . . . and I will never forgive you."

The summer air carried the heady scent of roses in bloom. For Katja, the season had also awakened a sense of curiosity— curiosity in what was, as well as what could be. She would turn twenty-three in a few weeks and had seen a decent share of handsome men. But none had intrigued her like the broken soul that both she and her father felt compelled to heal.

"*Guten Tag.*" Nodding, she greeted the sentries that lined the path to the prisoners' working area with a smile. They were good men, mostly fathers from neighboring farms that she had known all her life. While they were not fit for active service, the kaiser had found other ways to make use of Germany's aged manpower.

Katja wiped her moist hands on her skirt then furrowed a brow as she glanced down at her outfit. A simple cream shirt, a drab brown leather belt, and a dingy brown skirt. So plain. English women probably wore brighter colors. *Will he find me attractive?* The thought, disturbing as it was, led to another thought that was equally troubling. *What do I think of him?*

It was hard to define her feelings. At first Will's brutal anger had shocked her but time and patience had taken the edge off his hatred. Now, he seemed lost in a pool of perpetual sorrow, sorrow that she longed to soothe.

"General Klein." Katja approached the older man who dipped his graying head in a courteous gesture at her approach. "My father asks for Prisoner Will Thompson to join us at our table."

"Thompson?" The general crinkled a brow. "We don't use names here, *Fräulein.*"

"Right." Katja colored then hurriedly added, "Prisoner 11321, please."

91

The captain nodded, then turned and bellowed in English, "11321, report!"

Katja's eyes flitted through the crowd, her heart thundering an erratic rhythm. Over two hundred men swung mattocks into the long rows of peat moss, separating the peat from the soft loam below. Under the watchful eyes of their captors, the prisoners had carved long, straight rows into the green earth then stacked the peat onto wooden horse drawn carts. After leaving the quarry, the peat was divided into smaller stacks for drying. Ultimately, it would be sold as a source of fuel.

Klein's command was repeated by several other officers further down the line and, after several minutes, a disheveled man came forward, sloshed water onto his face and chest, then shrugged on a shirt.

Will.

He came closer. Then his eyes met hers and Katja felt her heart stop.

———————————◆◆●◆▶ ——————————

Will's eyes roamed over the woman before him. Slim, dark-haired, and gifted with dark eyes that brimmed with a subtle sense of mystery, she carried herself with a poise that made her unforgettable. The simplicity of her clothing bespoke an emphasis on character instead of charm, a quality he could only appreciate.

His brow furrowed. *Watch yourself, Will.* He had a wife that he loved, a wife to whom he would return.

And if Eleanor's dead? Or if she's remarried?

He flinched. He couldn't afford to think like that. Not if he wanted to preserve his sanity. The Germans had stripped him of his wedding ring, his last physical tie to his wife. All he had left were his memories.

But how long can I survive on memories?

Gravel crunched under his booted feet as he stepped toward her. In many ways, Katja reminded him of Eleanor. They shared an ability to see to the heart of the matter instead of being distracted by appearances. Was that why—despite his best efforts to prevent it—a smile tugged at his lips even now?

"Return in forty-five minutes." The guard scrawled his signature on a slip of paper authorizing Will to leave the immediate area and thrust it against his chest. "While you are inside, you are the responsibility of *Herr* Burkhard."

Will nodded, took the paper and turned back to Katja.

"Fräulein Meier." He dipped his head and fell into step beside her. It was the first time she had come to him alone. He didn't know whether to be honored or suspicious of Burkhard's trust. In either case, he had to be on guard.

"Are they treating you well?" Katja slowed her pace, and of necessity, he did the same. A slight accent tinged her words.

"I'm a prisoner, but as you've said before, I have food and I am alive. So yes, I am well."

A small chuckle escaped her lips. "I suppose I should be flattered that you have taken my words so much to heart."

"It took me a while to see your point, but I admit now that they were true words. Forgive me." Will ran his hands over his bearded chin. He was only allowed to shave once a month and then, with a guard holding a rifle to his temple. The Germans knew that in the right hands, a razor could become an effective weapon. "I suppose I should thank you. I-I do thank you. But I still don't understand why your family is so . . . interested in me."

For a moment, silence claimed them both. Then Katja came to a stop. "May I tell you something?"

"Yes," he said after a moment's hesitation.

She turned her warm brown eyes upon him, and he noted with surprise that they were moist. "A year ago, my brother . . . took his own life."

Will sucked in a sharp breath. "Why?"

"He couldn't live with the guilt of what he had done. War made him a monster, eating at his mind until he became consumed by violence and guilt. The war destroyed him." She laid a soft hand on his forearm. "I . . . that is, my father, doesn't want the war to destroy you."

His mind reeled under the impact of her confession. For months, he had suspected Burkhard's motives were subversive, that the farmer wanted to elicit information about British defenses after wooing him with kindness. But Burkhard had never asked any questions about his personal or military life. If Katja spoke the truth, then the man was interested in *him*, not in what he knew!

But can she be trusted?

Again, his eyes drilled into her face, taking in the sincerity in her eyes, the furrowed brow, and the tears that still glinted in her eyes at the mention of her brother. His mind flew back to the extra chair at the table, the photograph of the young man on the wall and he knew, beyond any doubt, that this woman spoke the truth.

"Katja . . . " It was forward of him to use her first name. But, after sharing such a personal part of her family's history, to address her in any other manner seemed frivolous. She would never have spoken so freely if her father were present. Perhaps he too should take advantage of the opportunity.

"Yes?" She did not sound offended.

"Thank you. Thank you for telling me."

THE MIDST OF THE FLAMES

IN THE MIDST OF THE FLAMES

She held his gaze. "The war has stolen from us all, Will. British, German, French"—she shrugged—"it doesn't matter. The only way anyone can win is to move beyond hatred . . . and embrace the power of love." She averted her eyes. "T-the love of God, I mean. The kind of love that makes us forgive. Unless we forgive, we will never be forgiven."

The words swirled around his mind. *Unless we forgive, we will never be forgiven.* He was oblivious to the remaining steps they took toward the house and remained quiet throughout the meal. He had refused to see the Germans as human like himself, demonizing them into a symbol of all that was evil.

Hating the killers of his baby had kept him alive in battle. Hating Malcolm, who had ripped the heart out of his chest, had given him a reason to live. But Katja's words showed that he had already lost the war for his soul. If forgiveness was the price of his redemption, then he was doomed indeed.

———————————◆●◆———————————

The afternoon sun beat down upon Will's bare shoulders as he shuffled back into position alongside a long, snakelike line of prisoners that coiled around the peat farm. Mattock in hand, he began to mechanically chop at the peat, his mind still probing Katja's words. The prisoners were segmented in clusters of thirty over a span of about ten acres of farmland, with each group laboring under the watchful eyes of twenty armed guards.

"Enjoyed your lunch?" A sniggering voice broke through his troubled thoughts. Will looked up to see a fellow prisoner sneering down at him.

"Yeah, Jack, I did." Will's mattock bit deep into the earth.

"Well, ain't that fine." The surly prisoner grunted out a mocking laugh then swung the sharp edge of his mattock near

95

Will's foot. "You eat in the big house, with your fancy lady, while we sweat it out in the heat!"

Straightening, Will glanced around. The nearest guard was about a hundred yards away. *Safe.* He slammed the mattock back in the loam and pulled hard on it, sending a spray of dirt into Jack's face.

"Watch it, bucko!" Jack spit a mixture of peat and mud onto Will's back. "Keep it civil if you want to look good for your lady. That is, assumin' she *is* still a lady. Like as not, you've fixed that little problem!"

The back of Will's neck began to burn but this time not from the summer heat. Ramming the edge of his mattock into the ground, he thrust his face inches from Jack's.

"Just what are you saying?"

The workers around them began to slow in their labors, sensing the tension of the moment. Out of his peripheral vision, Will saw General Klein rush toward them, blowing his whistle.

"I'm sayin'"—Jack dropped his mattock, bunching his hands into fists—"that you're either collaboratin' with the enemy or you're a lucky dog that's sniffed his way into a loose woman's bed!"

"Shut your mouth, you fool." Will shouted the words and dropped into a crouch. He could land at least two blows before Klein arrived. "Don't you dare insult Katja!"

"Katja, is it?" Jack rolled up his sleeves. "Someone's on familiar terms."

"Traitor!" Jeers rose from the crowd of onlookers. Apparently, more than a few men were on Jack's side. "Land him one, Jack!"

"Oh, look at him!" Jack rolled his shoulders. "Defendin' his little Katja." His tone oozed sarcasm. "Fightin' for his precious Hun. Maybe because she's his *hunny* bun!"

Will saw black. His right fist shot out, catching Jack square on the jaw. "Shut your filthy mouth!"

Jack reeled backward but recovered, lowered his head, and with a roar, charged forward. His head connected solidly with Will's gut.

"*Ugh!*" Will landed hard on his back. The rough stones, unearthed by the men's mattocks, dug into his skin. Above the jeers of the crowd, Will heard the shouts of approaching guards.

Then Jack's fist shot out of nowhere and connected with his nose.

Crunch.

Will cried out as pain sparked across his face. Bursts of sticky blood gushed from his nose and trickled down his chest.

Jack had pulled his arm back for another blow when he was hauled off Will's prone body.

"What is this?" Klein waved his revolver first at Jack then Will. "Stop at once!"

The cords in Jack's neck throbbed. "He's a German-lovin' traitor!"

Shouts of agreement from the crowd ripped through the air. Klein had been followed by more soldiers who forced Jack to the ground, pinning his arms behind his back.

"Order!" The general pointed his revolver to the sky and pulled the trigger. As the shot faded, silence claimed the riotous prisoners.

"Now." His eyes narrowed. "Our rules are clear regarding riots. Those who start them are shot at once. Those who participate in them are flogged at the *anbinden*."

Not even the wind stirred.

"I could ask who began the fight but that is simply asking who wants to die." Klein threw both hands in the air. "Up! Both of you, get up!"

German soldiers grabbed the arms of both men, pulling them upright. The captain eyed them both for a long moment then raised his arm, pointing the pistol between Will's eyes.

"You!" He cocked the pistol. "I saw you strike first."

God. Will's chest rose and fell like the bellows of an organ. *Not now. Not like this.*

A thin smile snaked over the general's lips. "But, lucky for you, 11321, I also heard both of your words. You struck this pig while defending the reputation of Burkhard's daughter."

He turned in a slow circle toward Jack. "That leaves you."

Jack's face paled. "P-pardon, sir. I didn't know the penalty for brawlin'." He jerked a grubby thumb in Will's direction. "Me and him, we was just havin' a bit of fun." Glancing at Will, "Weren't we, mate?"

His eyes pleaded with Will to speak up for him. Will ignored the dizziness brought on by his loss of blood. "Begging permission to speak, sir." Pressing his hand to his nose, he stepped forward. Despite everything, Jack was British, like himself. Had Will known the brawl would have cost the man his life, he would have ignored his crude insinuations. "Please spare him."

"Defending the enemy? How admirable." The general's eyes hardened. "How foolish. Discipline must be maintained." His gaze swept over the silent crowd of spectators. "Let this be a lesson to you all!"

The gun's report barked loud across the farm.

"You are prisoners of war!" The general's voice rang out across the clearing as Jack's body thudded against the hard earth. "You follow orders and maintain discipline. Do this and

you will live. Break the rules, and you will share this idiot's fate."
He nudged Jack's body with the tip of his boot.

Turning to his men he pointed to Will. "Bring him." They dragged the prisoner to a long pole that protruded from the earth in a clearing near the farm's gate.

Strapping his wrists to the post with leather thongs, the soldiers stepped back.

"Twenty lashes," Klein said. "Be glad I am in a merciful mood."

Will's head rose to the sky above. *Why did I do it?* Defending a German woman against a fellow prisoner. Now the man was dead.

"Eins!" One! He stiffened as the lash bit into his skin but refused to cry out. Pain exploded in his skull.

"Zwei!" Two! Will sagged against the post. From this moment on, he would be an outcast among his own people. Despite his efforts to save Jack's life, they would see him as a traitor. Nothing would ever be the same again.

"Drei!"

◆◆●◆◆

Burkhard Meier rammed his hat onto his head, and heaving a sigh, he opened his front door. The afternoon sunshine had given way to a rainy evening. Even now, sheets of rain fell from gray skies, turning the verdant peat fields into miry bogs. The prisoners had all been herded into open-backed lorries and shipped off to the village hall where they spent each night under guard.

Tonight, he would join the other members of the kaiser's watch guard ensuring, on his honor and his life, that no one escaped.

He twisted around to plant a kiss on Adele's cheek. "I will see you tomorrow morning, my dear."

She nodded stiffly then wrapped her arms around his neck. "Watch well, husband. Be safe."

Burkhard held her a moment longer, knowing that Adele's concerns for their daughter still preyed upon her mind. He agreed that Katja should not be encouraged to love a man of whom they knew little. All the same, a part of him rebelled at the thought of abandoning a young man with so much potential to a life of solitary hatred. Not when a little love on their part could help him heal.

Burkhard winked, tipped his hat to Katja, then, opening his umbrella, he stepped outside. As he gripped his old rifle and shuffled down the lane that led to the village hall, the setting sun revealed a scene with which he was unfortunately familiar. A stout wooden post, called the *anbinden*, jutted up from the ground as a deterrent to would-be insurgents. Normally the post was empty, but tonight his keen eyes picked out the form of a man, left to suffer until nightfall.

Burkhard squinted, trying to make out the identity of the perpetrator. It was the first time such a punishment had been meted out on his property. After his noonday meal, he had left immediately to oversee a shipment of peat into a neighboring village. Evidently, something had taken place during his absence. What could possibly—

The farmer froze, eyes riveted on the man who hung, unmoving, from the rough post.

"Will!" His voice was a hoarse shout. Lying half-naked in a pool of congealed blood and grime was Will Thompson. He hurried forward and knelt beside the body.

"Burkhard."

He straightened and turned around, eyes probing the falling shadows. From underneath the shelter of an overhang, General Klein hailed him.

With a parting glance over his shoulder at the still form, Burkhard crossed the clearing in long strides.

"General Klein!" He slung his rifle over his shoulder then saluted.

The soldier gestured toward the man hanging from the post. "That is the one you've taken under your wing. 11321. I caught him attacking a prisoner today after he came back from your home."

Burkhard stared at him, slack jawed. "Are you sure?"

"Hmm, yes." Klein pressed a lit cigarette to his mouth. "He and another fellow, swinging fists and breaking noses." He shook his head. "You would think that, since they're all on the same side, they would get along, eh?" He barked out a laugh.

"W-what was it all about?" Burkhard struggled to understand. His wife's words echoed in his mind. *He's a bomb, waiting for the right moment to explode.* But Will had begun to change, he was sure of it. He prayed with them now, he even smiled at times, he—

"He was defending your daughter's honor."

Burkhard felt his pulse quicken. "Her honor?"

"*Ja.*" The captain flung the spent cigarette to the floor and ground it under the heel of his black boot. "The other fellow—I had him shot by the way—insulted *Fräulein* Meier. Pointing to Will, "This one took it upon himself to defend her."

He shrugged. "The English are a strange breed, but I must confess, it was admirable. For his trouble, he earned a broken nose and twenty lashes while strapped to the *anbinden.*"

Burkhard staggered backward, stunned by the realization that he had been right. Will had seen past the blindness of his hate and put his own life at risk for the daughter of an enemy nation. But now it fell to Burkhard to set things right.

"General, he will die if those wounds are not treated." He motioned to the sky. "Especially in this weather. With respect, I request exemption from my duty tonight, so I may treat his wounds. We are too far from the main camp of prisoners to send him for treatment."

Klein shook his head. "*Nein.*"

"But—"

"The sun will set in fifteen minutes. Then his time at the *anbinden* will be complete. You may take him to your house and treat his wounds, but within two hours you must report for guard duty."

"Must I bring him with me?" Burkhard tossed his umbrella to one side.

Again, the general shook his head. "I do not think that he can go anywhere. Besides, if you bring him to the barracks tonight, his own people might kill him. Given his rash action today, I doubt they will welcome him with open arms."

Burkhard considered this, his brow furrowed as his mind digested this information. Will was a prisoner of war, but in addition to his inclination to care for the young man, Burkhard now owed him a debt of gratitude. An idea shoved its way to the front of his mind.

"Might it be possible . . . " he faltered. What he was about to propose was so unusual, he hesitated to voice it. *Adele will be furious.* But there was no other option . . . was there?

He cleared his throat. "You are the kaiser's regional commander. You oversee all prisoners of war in this area. Might it be possible for the prisoner to remain in my home, working under my direct supervision, for the duration of the war?"

"What?" Klein blinked several times.

Burkhard hurried to explain. "You and I have been friends for a long time, General. You understand my position. This is a matter of honor. The prisoner defended my daughter's good name, putting himself at considerable risk. Knowing this, how can I stand by and do nothing?"

"He is British, Burkhard." Klein lifted a spiked helmet from his head and ran his fingers through his graying hair. "They have no honor."

"But he is also human." Burkhard stepped closer, intent on his purpose. "Besides, you know that every death of a prisoner must be accounted for to the kaiser. The international community already accuses us of brutally mistreating the prisoners in our care. Help me ease my conscience and prevent a catastrophe by allowing the prisoner to remain at my home. He will work, as do the others, but away from the general corps of prisoners."

Klein tugged at his bearded chin. "You raise a valid point. In any case, perhaps it is wiser to prevent a problem than to fix one. Should he rejoin his compatriots, there will only be more trouble."

Ramming his helmet back onto his head, "If you assume responsibility, he may remain at your home under your direct supervision. But I warn you, Burkhard, that it is his life for your life." He thrust a finger upward. "If he escapes, I will not be able to save you from the kaiser's wrath. If he escapes, you die. Do you accept the responsibility?"

A smile slipped across the farmer's face. He nodded and thrust out his chest as he saluted. "*Jawohl!*"

103

"Adele! Katja! Open the door, quick!"

Katja threw open her bedroom door at the urgency in her father's voice. He never yelled; he never had a need to. She hurtled down the staircase to the house's main landing and pulled the door open as her mother walked in.

"Burkhard? What is it? Why are you still here?"

Her father did not answer but backed into the room, dripping water all over her mother's homespun carpets. "Katja," he shouted over his shoulder, "get Markus's room ready."

"For who, Papa?"

"Does it matter? Be quick!"

She started to leave but paused at her mother's voice. "Burkhard what are you carrying in your arms?"

Her father turned around and Katja forgot to breathe.

Her mother gasped. "What . . . ?"

"Is he dead?" In an instant, Katja was at her father's side. "Is Will dead?"

Burkhard shook his head. "No, but he's badly hurt." To her mother, "Adele, boil some water." To her, "Find some cloths for bandages and prepare the room."

Her mother was the first to recover. "Burkhard, this has gone far enough. Before you bring that man into our house, you must tell me what is going on. Are those *whip lashes* on his back?" Her eyes drilled into Burkhard's face. "He was punished like a criminal and you want to take him in as a guest? You want to put him in our *son's* bedroom?"

"Mother—"

"Be quiet, Katja!" Her mother's eyes blazed like lightning in a summer storm. "This is between your father and I."

"Adele, he was whipped"—Burkhard held her gaze for a moment, then his eyes shifted to Katja—"because he attacked a man who insulted our daughter's good name."

Silence claimed the small group, a silence broken only by the sound of water that pooled from Will's body. Katja's hands flew to her mouth as she gazed at the battered man whose arms flailed helplessly in her father's grasp.

Adele lifted her chin. "Well don't stand there gawking, daughter. Move! Get the bed ready." She turned to march up the stairs but paused at the landing to catch Burkhard's eye. "A service for a service. We always pay our debts, but this doesn't mean I trust him."

Her husband's grin was his only reply.

JP ROBINSON

Chapter 10

June 1917. Meier Farm near Münster, Germany.

"**H**e's still unconscious?" Adele deposited a bowl, pitcher of water, and razor onto a small table in the room that had belonged to her son, Markus. He had been born in this room. He had died in this room.

Adele's eyes darted around and, as always whenever she entered the small space, she had to force herself not to cry. Blue had always been Markus's favorite color. Throughout the nigh-on thirty years of his life, the wallpaper had been replaced several times, growing darker as he matured from toddler to adulthood.

But it had always remained blue. The color was constant, unchanging. Just like her son. Markus had been the stable rock in their family, thoughtful and considerate until he had gone to war. He had returned a haunted shadow of the man he had once been, struggling against himself until evil had squeezed the trigger of the gun that had snuffed out his life . . . in this very room.

"*Ja*, Mama." Katja's voice shook Adele from her reverie. "He keeps slipping in and out, probably because of all the blood he's lost. I'll have to set the bones in his nose when he wakes."

Adele's gaze drifted back to the walls. She had once loved to paint. A watercolor of Markus hung on her left. *His first birthday.* She reached out a trembling hand toward the painting. Will Thompson could sleep here, but this would always be her son's room.

"Mama, are you all right?"

Adele pivoted, jerking her hand back against her chest as though the canvas had burned her fingertips. The atmosphere had suddenly become too poignant for her to bear. She needed to leave—now.

"Y-yes. I'm fine, *danke.*" Wiping her hands on her apron, she turned on her heel. "I-I have to do some weeding in the garden. Wake me"—she sucked in a deep breath—"wake me as soon as he's conscious."

Breathe, Adele. Breathe. She shuffled toward the door but paused as fear for her one remaining child coiled around her heart.

"Katja." Adele turned to catch her daughter's eye. "Protect your heart. Do not give it away easily for, when the reason for your love is gone, you will be left with nothing. Nothing."

Then, stifling a sob, Adele closed the door.

———————◆◆●◆◆———————

Alone, Katja was free to admire the wounded warrior who lay on the bed in need of her healing touch. Jagged lines snaked across Will's chest, each one a silent witness to his courage. *But is there more than courage in his heart?*

Katja poured some of the tepid water into the bowl, soaked the cloth then, hesitantly, laid it upon his broken skin. Will must have known that, by defending a German, he would commit an unspoken act of treason. He had crossed the line between prisoner and traitor as far as his people were concerned.

"Why, Will? Why do it for me?"

Some of the cuts had reopened and trickles of blood seeped onto the fresh white sheets that she had spread out on the bed. Katja continued to clean his wounds, looking for signs of returning consciousness and trying to understand the storm of emotions that raged within her heart.

At first, it had been Will's pain and the aura of mystery that shrouded this intriguing, handsome foreigner. In many ways he had reminded her of a young grounded hawk she had found a few years ago. With fierce determination, the bird had refused to allow her to set its broken wing. But with time she had won its trust and the bird had soon flown once more.

What if I have to let Will go too? Katja flinched as the unexpected thought burrowed itself in her mind. She was drawn to hurting souls. But it was no longer Will's pain that made her want to stay at his side. It was something more, something she was not ready to admit existed. Katja didn't know if she loved him, but if the feeling that pulsed within her was not love, she was willing to bet that it was something very close.

Her brown eyes shifted to Will's bloodied face. An unkempt chestnut beard curled around his chin and cheeks. His nose was bent at an odd angle and his breathing was shallow but steady.

"For me, Will?" Katja wiped the clots of blood from his mouth and nose. She was flattered and confused by his actions. What had caused such a drastic change? Just a few months ago, he had hated all things German—including herself. Now, in a moment of crisis, he had put his own life at risk . . . for her. Could it be that he felt as she did?

Katja leaned over his prone body. "Come back to me, Will. Come back."

Will drifted toward consciousness, drawn by a sweet voice that whispered his name. Through the haze of his half-open eyes, he saw Eleanor's face floating inches above his own. "Come back to me Will. Come back."

Eleanor?

The world swirled around him. "My love?" Disoriented, he slowly lifted his head, cupped her cheek tenderly in his right hand and pressed his lips against her own.

A startled gasp filled his ears at the exact moment that pain fractured his semi-conscious state, shoving him into full awareness. He felt as though a swarm of hornets stung every inch of his chest while someone slammed a sledgehammer into his nose.

"Ugh!" Will sat up slowly in the bed. Blinking, he pressed his hands against his swollen nose. As his eyes cleared, he realized that the woman above him was not Eleanor but . . .

"Katja?"

She jerked away from him, face burning, and pressed her fingers to her lips. "What are you doing?"

"I-I'm sorry. I thought—" He covered his face with his hands then looked up at her in horror. Her back was stiff, her posture rigid. He had offended her. The realization made him nauseous.

"You thought that, just because you attacked a man who insulted me, you have the right to *kiss* me?" She took another step back. "In our home, a man marries a woman first!"

"No. It was a mistake. I—" He gritted his teeth as a wave of pain swept over him. "I'm sorry."

Katja let him sit there, suffering for what felt like an eternity, before she edged closer.

"Hold still." She picked up two pieces of wood and some sort of adhesive bandage and leaned over him. "And *do not* touch me."

Depositing the items on the bed, she placed a finger on both sides of his nose. Her brow furrowed. "This will hurt." She pushed the bones back in position, ignoring Will's sharp cry. Reaching over, she placed a thin piece of wood on each side of his nose and secured the rough splint with adhesive.

"There." She stood up, wiping her hands on her apron, and took a few steps back. "Don't touch your nose and try to breathe through your mouth for the next week."

Will frowned. His last memory was the sting of a whip across his back. "How did I get here?"

She told him in clipped, terse tones while cleaning up the utensils and concluded with, "Father has been granted permission to shelter you."

"For how long?"

"Indefinitely."

An awkward silence filled the room. Will eyed her for a long moment, torn between the desire to clarify his mistake and the very shame that admitting it would cause. What kind of man mistook another woman for his own wife? Then again, he wasn't sure how much of his past he wanted to reveal.

She shared a family secret with you.

His face reddened at his conscience's rebuke. He was not obligated to tell her about Eleanor. Or was he?

"Well"—she loaded the pitcher and utensils onto a tray—"Mother will be in here soon to shave you."

"Katja—"

"I think it would be better if you addressed me as *Fraulëin* Meier." Katja thrust her chin forward then turned and stalked out of the room.

━━━━━━━━◆◆●◆◆━━━━━━━━

Early the next morning, Burkhard sat at the breakfast table sipping a cup of steaming *kaffe*. The aroma of his wife's freshly-baked bread wafted over to his nostrils, tantalizing him.

"I don't know how your mother does it." Burkhard tossed the newspaper onto the table, spread a tad of butter onto a slice, then turned to his daughter. "The Allied blockades have reduced our country to the point of starvation"—he gestured at the newspaper—"but still she manages to make bread from thin air."

Katja replied with a tight smile but said nothing as she lifted her own cup to her lips.

Chewing, her father eyed her carefully. His daughter had her moments of melancholy, but this was different. This was new. There could only be one thing on her mind.

"You know"—Burkhard wiped his fingers on a cloth napkin—"it is harder to be the object of a selfless act than to be the doer."

He dragged his chair closer. "It can be rather uncomfortable, really. You don't know if you should feel gratitude, embarrassment or something else."

Katja looked up at him. "I-I don't know what to feel, Papa. He seems so lost, there are times I want to hold him, to comfort him. I don't understand why he did it."

"Then why not ask him?" Burkhard shrugged.

"Because," Katja said, hesitating as she set the cup down, "I'm afraid of the truth."

He covered her hand with his own. "Yet you know that truth is the only thing that sets us free."

"Papa." Katja's eyes dropped to her plate then rose slowly to meet his own. "I think Will"—she swallowed—"may be interested in me."

With a sigh, Burkhard leaned back in his chair. He was glad that Adele was busy with the laundry. Katja loved her mother but he doubted she would have voiced such thoughts in his wife's presence. Despite their differing perspectives, Burkhard respected Adele's intuition and agreed that no relationship was possible without complete transparency.

"And how do you feel about this possibility?"

"Me?" Katja's hand flew to her throat. "I-I would think that you would have something to say. I thought you'd be horrified at the very idea! He's *British*."

"I am your father. Your happiness is my only concern."

"I love you, you know?" She slid closer and wrapped her arms around his neck.

Warmth stole through Burkhard's heart. He held her close, patting her back. "It seems to me that you are avoiding what must be, *Tochter*. Since the Americans joined the war, things have become very difficult for us. The good news is that one day it will end, and all prisoners will be released."

"And then?"

"Then he will have to decide which place he wants to call home: Germany or Britain." He pulled back and smiled at her. "Speak with Will in the garden. Find out what is in his heart. Only then will *you* be free."

———————————— ◆◆●◆► ————————————

Will shuffled out of the bedroom toward the kitchen, each step shaking and careful. Adele had told him last night in no uncertain terms that he must remain in bed to minimize the chance of infection. But he refused to be obligated to anyone. He would pay his debt to Burkhard.

Someone had slipped into his room during the night and left a pair of loose, black trousers and a white cotton shirt at the foot of his bed. They were a little small but fit well enough. He could only assume that they had belonged to Burkhard's son, Markus.

He limped into the kitchen, pulling up short at the sight of Katja. She sat next to her father. Her auburn hair hung down her back, spilling over the collar of a pale-yellow dress. Her dark brown eyes flickered over him.

"*Fraul*ein Meier." Will dipped his head, but not before noticing a slight furrow of her brows.

He turned to Burkhard. "*Herr* Meier, good morning."

The farmer returned the greeting, then stood, and walked around the table toward him. "But why are you out of bed?"

Shaking his head, Will did his best to straighten his stooped shoulders. "You welcomed me into your home, sir, and for that I am grateful. Were it not for you, I might not be alive." He held Burkhard's gaze. "But I refuse to be in any man's debt. Let me know what work you want done and I will see to it."

"Very well." Burkhard lifted his head, slipped his hands in his pockets, and rocked back on his heels. "It is a beautiful day. The sun is shining outside and the birds are singing God's praises as though the war did not exist."

He pointed toward the back door. "Here are your orders for today. Walk outside and sit on the bench that is in the sunlight and have a conversation with my daughter."

"Papa!" Katja sucked in her breath.

"A conversation?" Will blinked. "A-about what?"

114

Burkhard hiked his shoulders together. "How should I know? I am an old man. Talk about whatever interests young people. That is what I ask you to do for me."

"And then, sir?" Will heard a slight quaver in his own voice. *I'm afraid.* The notion struck him as preposterous but, on the heels of the absurd, came an awareness of reality. He had been away from his wife for three years which was longer than he and Eleanor had been married. Not once in that time had he visited the brothels frequented by the men of the British army.

He feared the power of the emotions Katja triggered because a subtle voice warned him that the compassionate beauty who now glided toward him, would unwittingly incarnate the ultimate test of his devotion to Eleanor.

"Then . . . " The sudden steel in Burkhard's voice brought Will back to the moment, all trace of friendliness gone as though it had never existed. Burkhard's eyes bore into Will's skull as though he wished to peer inside the depths of his soul. "Then I will know what must be done."

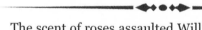

The scent of roses assaulted Will's nostrils as he shoved the heavy door outward and limped outside. A series of slate tiles formed a sort of path on the verdant grass that formed a natural carpet leading up to the rear door of the farmhouse. A white fence, along which multi-colored roses climbed upward, cordoned off both sides of the garden area, providing privacy from the rest of the farm. In the corner of the garden, a flowing waterfall emptied into a large pool filled with some sort of yellow-and-black fish.

Will clenched his jaw. He should see this area as a sort of sanctuary. God knew it was paradise compared to the brutality and stink of no-man's land. But he had not left the war in the trenches. It was still with him, dogging his every step.

Will stiffened at the sound of the door slamming shut behind him. The soft *clack, clack,* of Katja's shoes echoed like gunshots in his mind. But she was not the enemy—*he* was.

He closed his eyes, trying desperately to envision Eleanor's face. Her hair was a peculiar shade of brown. *Like Katja's.* Her eyes were mesmerizing twin pools of honey. No, that was the woman who now stood beside him. His brow furrowed, and he felt like weeping. *What is happening to me?*

He knew the answer but was afraid to even think it.

"We should sit down."

His eyes flew open. Katja pointed at a stone, crescent-shaped bench at the base of the pool. In silence Will followed her, wrestling with a growing sense of shame that roiled in his gut.

"*Fraulëin* Meier." He dropped onto the bench, keeping as much space between them as possible. "I owe you an apology."

"You've already apologized." Katja shifted so she could see his face. "What you owe me is an explanation."

She wore a dress he had never seen before. It was pale-yellow and fell just below her knees. A thick black belt encircled her waist. Hunger ravaged Germany but skipped meals and food shortages could not hide her beauty.

"What is there to explain?"

She arched a thin eyebrow. "Quite a lot actually. Let's start with this: why does a British officer—who hates everything German by the way—assault another prisoner when he insults a *German* woman?"

Will glanced at the pool.

"This same man is beaten unconscious and left to hang on a post." Her voice softened. "All for a woman he barely knows. Yet he is not bitter or angry toward her or her family. Why?"

Katja cleared her throat. "Then he awakens and the first words out of his mouth are—"

"I remember." Will's head flew upward. "And I'm sorry."

Eyes drilling into his own, she leaned toward him. "And he emphasizes his words with a kiss." Her fingers touched her lips, exactly as she had done yesterday in the room. "Why?"

Will heaved a sigh. Her nearness brought his self-control to the breaking point. There was only one way to save himself; one way to fight back. He had to reveal the truth. And yet he hesitated, somehow sensing that the truth would either hurt or disappoint her.

"I'm a mystery, *Fraulëin*. I volunteered to fight but, at first, I cringed at the thought of killing a man." He barked out a dry, humorless laugh. "Do you know how many I've killed since then?" He answered without waiting on a response. "Forty-five."

She did not react other than asking, "What happened?"

"Two years ago, something happened that I cannot forget." Emotion choked him, bringing his words to a pause. It was the first time he had spoken about Abby since the fateful afternoon when Malcolm had broken the news. "M-my daughter was killed."

This time she did react.

"You have a daughter?" The sudden paleness of her face showed him at once that the unspoken implication had hit home.

"I did." Tears rolled down to the bandage that swathed his nose. "My little Abby. She was killed in a Zeppelin strike on London's East End."

Katja grabbed his hand. "Will, I'm so sorry. That's . . . that's terrible!" Then she caught herself and released him.

"Since you had a daughter, you also"—she faltered—"have a wife?"

Her voice was small, so small that for a moment Will's every instinct urged him to surrender the fight, to clasp her in his arms.

"Yes." His voice was clear, filling up the space between them. "Her name is Eleanor."

"I see." Katja closed her eyes for a moment.

"When I kissed you, I mistook you for her. My mind was confused and—"

"It's all right." Katja held up her hands, palms turned outward. "I understand. Really."

An awkward silence fell between them, broken only by the sound of the trickling waterfall. Then she asked the question to which he had no answer.

"Why stand up for me if you . . . love someone else?"

He ran his hand over his smooth chin. "I don't know. I just couldn't let him talk about you like that. Not when your family has been so good to me."

"Will." Katja moved closer but still kept a wary distance between them. "Thank you. What you did was decent."

"It was stupid." He shook his head.

"Maybe a little." A sad smile tugged at her lips. "But it shows you for what you are—a good man."

Katja sucked in a deep breath, held it, then released it slowly. "What is your wife like?"

Will hunched forward, gripping his skull between clenched fingers. "I-I can't remember!" The admission was the hardest blow he had faced since Abby's death.

"I don't understand."

"We were only married for two years before the war started. It's been three years since I left home. I could never afford to have her photograph taken and I've no letters. The only thing I had was my wedding ring and the Germans took that before I reached the camp at Münster!"

She absorbed this in silence then said, "Tell me what you *do* remember."

"I remember the basics. She has brown hair and eyes, but as hard as I try to keep them, the memories are starting to fade." He straightened, turning toward her. "When I try to remember the details all I can see . . . is you."

Katja touched his face, then jerked back as though she had been burned. She stood up, turning away from him and clasping her hands behind her back. "You need to go to her. There's no other way for you to survive."

"What?" He struggled to his feet.

She whirled around and he started at the sight of twin wet streaks glistening on her pale cheeks.

"Will, you've been three years without your wife. The war stole your child and now"—her voice cracked—"it is robbing you of your heart!"

"My heart?"

Shaking her head, Katja approached him. "My father is right; this is no time for pretense. We can only be free if we're honest with each other."

He didn't reply.

"Can't you see what's happening to you?" Katja dashed the tears from her eyes and pressed her hand to her heart. "To *us*?"

Will's mouth went dry as the message behind her words sunk into his mind. Her words bared her own heart and challenged him to do the same. *We're both fighting the same enemy.*

"We . . . we are attracted to each other."

She nodded then bit her lip. "And it's wrong, Will. It's totally wrong."

He recoiled, shaking his head. "But I love my wife!"

"I know you do." Katja wrung her hands together. "And I respect you even more for it. But your mind is replacing me with her and I"—she looked away—"I will not be guilty of parting what God has joined together." Her voice dropped as she confessed, "No matter how much I am tempted to do otherwise."

Will gaped at her. Something akin to relief curled within him. Their conversation had brought them to the brink, but he saw her now as an ally instead of temptation personified. At length, he found his voice.

"Where do we go from here, *Fraulëin*?"

"Oh, call me Katja! You owe me that at least." She made a weak attempt at a smile. "We move forward, Will." She pointed to his borrowed clothing. "The war destroyed my brother. I won't let it destroy us."

"What do you mean?"

"None of us knows how long this war will last." Her voice was dull, as though the life that had energized it had somehow been squeezed out. "It could be months or even years before you see Eleanor again. To be here with you all that time . . . " She let the unvoiced reality hang in the air for a moment then spoke again.

"No, there's only one way for us to win this fight." Katja's chest heaved as she pulled in a deep breath. "You must go to your wife."

"But how?" Will gestured toward the distant fields. "I'm a prisoner and there are guards all over this place."

"I know, but all the same, you must leave." Katja squared her shoulders. "It might take a few months, maybe even a year.

But I swear to you, Will, that someday you're going to escape. And I am going to help you."

JP ROBINSON

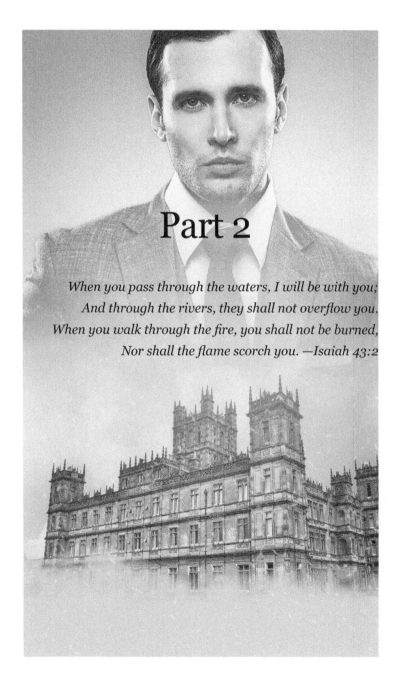

Part 2

When you pass through the waters, I will be with you;
And through the rivers, they shall not overflow you.
When you walk through the fire, you shall not be burned,
Nor shall the flame scorch you. —Isaiah 43:2

JP ROBINSON

Chapter 11

June 1917. Northshire Estate, Great Britain.

Gravel crunched underneath Malcolm's feet as he
trudged to the top of the hill overlooking the village
that bordered Northshire Estate. Puffs of dust, rising
from the parched ground, threatened to choke him. But it was
more than dirt that clogged his throat. It was a conglomeration
of longing, hope, and fear. Ripped at last from the senseless
nature of his selfish pride, he was a returning prodigal. A prodigal
brought to his senses by a singular encounter with a God that
was strong enough to forgive.

He squinted, straining to see through the waving green
branches of the arboreal sea that separated the estate from the
village. In the distance, the hot afternoon sun glinted on the
tallest of the castle's spires.

Malcolm's grip tightened around the butt of his rifle. Over
three years had passed since he last set eyes on his childhood
home, and his parting had been all but idyllic. His eyes fell to the
dilapidated tan uniform that covered his body. Like his dreams,
it had once been new and full of promise. Driven by his jealous
hatred, he had renounced all ties to Northshire, including his
wife. His sole purpose had been to achieve a greater glory on the
battlefields of Europe than his father, Thomas, had ever gained.

He idly fingered the loose threads of his shirt. Now, the glory that had once seemed so alluring, had proven to be nothing more than dust in the wind. Fidgeting, Malcolm shifted his rifle then wiped his moist hands on his pants. At last he was ready to come home, but was home ready to receive him?

Just beyond those trees, his father ruled Northshire with an iron fist. His word was law, a law against which Malcolm had rebelled.

You stupid, stupid man. I'll hate you till I die.

The memory of the insult he had once slung in Thomas's face made him cringe. How could he face his father now? With just one word, Thomas could have his men remove Malcolm from the Estate. He had done it before.

Despair coiled around his heart like a serpent. There was no way the proud general could forget the dishonor Malcolm had cast upon the family name. Thomas would never forgive Malcolm's outright denial of his bloodline. Thomas—a professional soldier himself—could never trust a son who had once threatened to kill him.

Malcolm's shoulders drooped. His own self-indulgence had brought him to this moment of crisis, spawning a litany of consequences he could never undo. What good could possibly come of his return?

He thought to turn back, to flee the pain of Thomas's certain recriminations. But there was another who waited at Northshire, a woman that he had wronged and the hold she maintained over his heart kept his feet rooted to the ground.

"Leila."

He had run from her once, realizing too late that a life without her was no life at all. A puff of wind ruffled his hair, bringing a memory of Eleanor's words with it.

IN THE MIDST OF THE FLAMES

"Don't look back, Malcolm. Remember that God makes all things new."

He spoke the words aloud, trying to hush the relentless voice in his mind that promised there was no place for him on the Estate. His father had removed his status as a son, true. But Malcolm had to consider his future. Sooner or later the war would end, and, if he survived, where would he go?

"I could leave it all."

He could abandon his wife and start over, maybe in America. Malcolm scoffed, spitting to one side. The thought wasn't even worth considering. Three years ago, he had run from his wife, yes, but he had been a boy then. War had made him a man. Christ had made him a *new* man. He wouldn't run again. Not from his wife, not from his home, not from himself.

He lifted his chin. If Thomas couldn't accept him as a son, perhaps after the war he could find it in his heart to let Malcolm live on the premises, working like one of the hired help.

And Leila?

He heaved a deep sigh. Perhaps they had gone beyond the point of reconciliation. "But I won't give up, not without a fight."

Breathing a prayer with every step he took, Malcolm began the long journey down the hill, across the bustling village, and through the woods that lined the winding path which led home to Northshire.

━━━━━━━◆◆●◆▶━━━━━━━

"Right, so, is everything set to continue as normal in my absence?" Gripping the handle of his simple black briefcase, Thomas Steele arched an eyebrow at his daughter-in-law, Leila. She, who had once been an enemy, had grown to become an indispensable member of his household, proving herself more

127

than capable of handling the myriad of responsibilities that came with running a massive estate.

"Don't worry, Thomas." Leila's emerald eyes sparkled as she smiled up at him. "Everything's under control."

"Hmm, with you at the helm, I'm sure it will be." The corners of Thomas's mouth turned upward. "Your new housing complex for widows and war orphans is set to open soon, isn't it?"

She nodded, sobering. "I met with the project manager this morning. We're on schedule and, within a week, all the bereaved mothers and children of Northshire will have access to free, clean housing on the premises."

"I don't know if I ever told you that your vision is simply ingenious as well as compassionate." Thomas set his briefcase down. "By training the women to fill the positions their husbands held before they left for war, you've reduced the estate's personnel costs. You've also provided a way for them to keep the majority of their widow's pension while having a beautiful place in which to live."

"And that's not all." Leila leaned forward, smiling. "While the mothers work on the estate, their children will be educated in our own school, a Christian school, which will open on the same day!"

"I am proud of you, daughter. Your growth into this responsibility has been simply marvelous." Stepping closer, Thomas gave her a quick hug, hearing a note of wistfulness in his own voice. "Naming you my heir was a wise decision."

Leila pulled back. "We comb through the casualty list every day, Thomas. We both pray for him each night. He's alive and someday he *will* come home."

Thomas frowned. "That's what I keep telling myself but, even though I watch for him each evening beneath the family crest"—he gestured through the open door at a golden eagle perched atop a massive pillar in the courtyard—"after three years without just one word, there are times when even my faith is challenged."

"What about me?" Leila touched his arm gently. "I'm his wife. Three years without a woman? Malcolm?" A sad smile crossed her lips.

Then she tossed her head, sending wisps of blonde hair across her face. "But we're soldiers, Thomas. Soldiers locked in a war against bitterness and despair. My husband will come home, and when he does, God will give us both the strength to move beyond the pain of the past."

Thomas cleared his throat, blinking back the tears that stung his eyes. "I-I don't know what to say. You . . . "

She laughed, picked up his briefcase and turned him toward the door. "Say goodbye. The president of Switzerland is expecting you. Don't keep him waiting."

They stepped outside, and Thomas squinted as his eyes adjusted to the bright afternoon light. Greyson, Thomas's butler, waited alongside the smoke-gray Vauxhall with the driver.

"Your valise, sir?"

"Here you are, Jamison." Leila handed it over to the driver as Thomas beckoned for Greyson to join them. The tall butler stepped forward, arms clasped behind his black swallowtail coat.

Thomas waited a few moments then said, "I'll be gone for about a month. Hughes may be planning something so both of you be sure to be watchful and trust no one."

"Understood, Your Lordship." Greyson dipped his head. "The Lady Leila and the estate will be secure, have no fear."

"I don't doubt you, my friend." Thomas scanned the perimeter of the property where armed guards patrolled in small teams.

"But Hughes is up to something. We may have as much to fear from him as we do from the Germans."

"Is the situation so grave, Your Lordship?" Greyson stroked his chin.

"I am afraid the situation is grave indeed. First, Hughes laid a rather obvious trap in giving me confidential information." Thomas snorted. "Doubtless, he expected me to radio the kaiser and tell him that Germany is about to be attacked."

"Well, you would have no choice," Leila observed. "Not if you were a traitor. Information like that would be critical for Germany. The main thing is you *didn't* send the information along. No one did. So Hughes's little scheme will come to nothing."

"True, but that won't stop Hughes." Thomas's mouth thinned in a firm line. "The next day, I learned that my secretary was dead, most likely poisoned but there have been no suspects and, as the poor girl had no family, the case will likely be closed without being solved."

"We don't know that Hughes was behind the girl's death. What would he gain by it?"

"True, Leila and I find it hard to believe myself but, all the same, just be very careful while I'm gone. The man's dedication to his work has driven him to the point of obsession."

"Understood, sir." Greyson opened the door.

Thomas turned to enter the vehicle but paused. "One moment, Greyson."

He glanced back at Leila, who gave him a slow, understanding nod, then turned toward the eagle, whose outstretched wings were set ablaze by the setting sun. Thomas moved to stand at the base of the pillar from which he would have a clear view of the treelined path that wound its way from the village to Northshire Estate.

Why bother looking? Doubts riddled his mind. *Today will be as every other.* He closed his eyes as he moved forward, knowing that he could not escape the loneliness, the longing that surged within him each time he thought of his son.

Malcolm. Malcolm. Where are you?

Although his son had sworn he would hate him to his dying day, Thomas could not resist the pull to watch for him tonight as he had each evening for the past three years.

Why?

Because perhaps this night would be different from other nights. Perhaps tonight, the rays of the setting sun would fall upon a returning prodigal instead of an empty road that mirrored the hollowness of Thomas's heart.

My son.

Only a father could understand the agony of such rejection. Only a father could sustain such a fragile tendril of hope in the face of continued disappointment.

Perhaps tonight...

His eyes flickered open.

Movement.

Thomas started, not daring to hope.

Can it be . . . ?

Taking a step forward, he shaded his eyes with his palm.

A man, familiar yet unknown, shoved his way past a guard who challenged him at the gate.

Who—

The stranger moved up the path, each motion hesitant but purposeful, eyes fixed upon him.

Thomas's breath came faster, matching the wild crashing in his chest. His mouth opened but only an unintelligible choking sound escaped.

Then he ran.

He ran like a madman toward this vision, this unbelievable reality that every part of his soul had ached to see for countless heartbeats. He ran, oblivious to the stunned gazes of the estate tenants, guards, and spectators.

He ran like a man possessed, seeing one face and one face alone—that of a child he had believed lost to him forever. A son who, against all odds, had come home.

━━━━━◆●◆━━━━━

Malcolm Steele moved ahead, followed closely by the armed guard who held a loaded rifle between his shoulder blades. But he barely noticed the soldier behind him for, pounding down the dusty path toward him, was his father.

Thomas Steele. Legendary warrior. Commander of Britain's army. Honored Peer of the Realm. The man who had never run from an enemy but had snatched victory from the very jaws of defeat countless times. That man was now running . . . toward him.

Malcolm's own knees turned to water. He stumbled forward, letting his rifle and pack fall to the ground.

Will he forgive me?

"Malcolm!" He was close enough now to make out his father's words.

Have I gone too far? Run away for too long?

The questions hammered at his skull but, before he could take conscious thought, Malcolm's own feet propelled him toward the man that he had once reviled.

He skidded to a halt a few feet from his father and Thomas closed the gap between them, clasping him in his arms.

"Malcolm?" Thomas said the name as though he doubted his eyes, doubted his arms, doubted everything that his senses declared.

"Father!" Malcolm slid to his knees, grabbing hold of Thomas's feet. He felt no fear now, only the knifelike pain of remorse. Thomas blurred before him as he blinked back tears.

"I've been wrong." Memories of his callous words, his misdeeds, flashed through his mind with merciless clarity. "So . . . so wrong!" He cringed within himself, disgusted by the pride he had once cherished.

"Blind. I was blind." Desperate now, Malcolm clutched at Thomas's arms. He had every right to banish him once more and, if he did, Malcolm wouldn't blame him. "I don't deserve to be your son!"

"My son." Strong arms slipped underneath his own as Thomas pulled him to his feet and clasped him to his chest. "Do you know I still love you?"

The words washed over Malcolm, unlocking a wellspring of emotion. "Can—can you forgive me?"

"No, I can't." Thomas pulled Malcolm still closer. "I can't because I already have forgiven you." His voice broke. "A long, long time ago."

———————◆◆●◆◆———————

Leila moved next to the pillar on which the golden eagle rested. Thomas's unprecedented display of emotion left no room for doubt as to the identity of the man who walked beside him.

All the same, her breath caught in her throat when Malcolm came into view. He was lean, well-muscled and tanned, the same height and build as when she had last seen him a year ago in Etaples. But the aura around him was radically different.

This was not the unprincipled womanizer she had married nor was it the bitter, egocentric villain who had sworn to kill her if ever he laid eyes on her again. His shoulders were slightly slumped, his mouth straight and brow furrowed. Malcolm carried himself like a man who was filled with regret, a man who sought mercy from those he had wronged.

"Leila?" His voice broke as he called her name.

She clung to the pillar, hesitating. *What is this?*

Though she also was to blame for their broken relationship, it was Malcolm who had chosen to abandon her, dicing her heart into small bloodied chunks before leaving her to rot! She loved him, but could she trust him enough to place the power over her heart in his hands for a second time?

Malcolm moved toward her then faltered. For what felt like ten years, but was in reality less than a minute, they stared wordlessly at each other, oblivious to the murmurs of the servants and tenants that crowded around them.

Then Malcolm sunk to his knees and reached for her hand. Leila's breath hung in her chest but, trembling now, she placed it in his. His eyes shone with unshed tears as he pressed her hand against his lips.

"I've wronged you. In my anger, I abandoned you when you needed me most. When you came to me, I rejected you. I'm can't say how sorry I am."

She waited, numbed by his confession.

"There's more." Malcolm heaved a deep sigh. "You need to know the truth. All of it. I-I broke my pledge of fidelity and I know I don't deserve your forgiveness." He glanced at the cobblestones beneath him, wiped his nose on the back of his sleeve, then reclaimed her gaze. "But I'm a different man now." Malcolm swallowed. "Christ made me a different man."

Leila's heart clenched as a tidal wave of emotions surged within her heart.

Pain, spawned by his confession of infidelity.

Joy, birthed by the sight of her husband and the news that he had met God.

Fury that he had abandoned her in the first place and taken so long to come to his senses.

Love . . . *why?* She didn't know. But as sure as she breathed, Leila knew that she still loved him.

Leila released a breath she didn't know she had been holding as she touched his cheek. "Get up, Malcolm."

He rose and took a step back, waiting in obvious tense anticipation. She could feel the heat of Thomas's gaze as he observed the scene. He would understand the thoughts that churned through her mind, the turmoil that raged within her.

Leila studied Malcolm through narrowed eyes. Whatever she said now would determine the fate of their relationship, one way or another. She could give in to the hurt and tell him to leave, that it was too late for them. But what was life without him? Then again, could she condemn him when she too had been to blame?

Bad blood. It ran throughout the entire human race, tainting all with an instinctive evil that none could escape. She had deceived him, playing upon his emotions for her own twisted purpose. He had wronged her, abandoned her, and betrayed her.

Yes, she could reject him. Hurt him as he had hurt her.

Or she could yield to the irrational but compelling love that swelled within her and give him a chance to prove the truth behind his words.

A quiet hush fell over the muttering crowd.

Her mouth dry, Leila moved closer then pulled him into her arms as she whispered, "We were both wrong, Malcolm. But we've been given a second chance."

"Can you forgive me?" He clung to her as though she were a lifeline and he was a drowning man.

Leila closed her eyes as her own tears escaped her lashes and rolled down her cheeks. How long had she prayed for this moment? Now that it was here, she had no idea what to say.

"Yes." She gasped out the word, feeling sobs wrack both his body and hers. "Malcolm, I do."

She held him for a moment longer, then, pulling away, she cupped his face in both her hands. "But trust is a fragile thing, difficult to rebuild. It won't be perfect, not right away."

"Maybe not. But if we're in it together, we'll make it work." The ghost of a smile flitted across his face.

A choked, relieved chuckle bubbled up within her. It seemed that his transformation was, like her own, something more than words. "Yes, yes I think we will."

"Greyson!" Thomas's voice boomed over the gathering as he cast an arm over both their shoulders. "Prepare Lord Malcolm's best clothing and tell Cook to make a feast out of whatever food we have on the premises."

"A feast, Your Grace?" The aged butler wiped his eyes. "But you are supposed to be *en route* to Switzerland. W-what shall I tell the Swiss president's secretary?"

Thomas threw back his head and laughed. "Say that my son, who I thought was dead, is alive." Sobering, his eyes lingered on Malcolm's face. "My son, who was lost, has come home."

Chapter 12

June 1917. Northshire Estate, Great Britain.

The gray light of dawn found Malcolm awake and dressed in a tan plaid suit, white collared shirt, and maroon tie. He fidgeted with his collar. Jenny had absconded with his discolored uniform shortly after his arrival and a part of him wondered if he'd ever see it again.

He glanced at the blue quilt that he had pulled around his shoulders before going to sleep last night on the hardwood floor. Civilian life was radically different from everything he had known for the past three years. The comforts of civilization left him feeling disoriented. Uneasy.

Malcolm strode over to the glass doors that separated his spacious bedroom from a veranda. Pressing down on the handles, he stepped out onto the white tiles and made his way toward the stone railing. A warm summer breeze, tinged with the scent of roses, ruffled through his dark, shaggy hair, bringing a sense of comfort—comfort that he sorely needed.

He clasped his hands together behind his back and took in the vast fields of wheat that formed this part of the estate.

I'm home.

Thomas had welcomed him when he feared rejection. But, although his father, Leila, the village tenants, and even the servants had celebrated his return late into the night, Malcolm knew that he could not assume that everything was as it had once been. As was to be expected, both Leila and Thomas were willing to give him a second chance but both expected proof that he was indeed a changed man. And therein lay his greatest challenge.

Thrusting his hands into his pockets, Malcolm rocked back on his heels. He wanted—no, *needed*—to live up to their expectations. He craved Leila's touch, longed to see her eyes light up when she saw his face just as they had when he had first married her. And his father? Malcolm wanted to prove that he was worthy of inheriting the estate that he had once spurned.

Footsteps sounded behind him. On instinct, Malcolm pivoted, one hand reaching for the pistol that normally hung at his side. Of course, his fingers brushed only the side of his pants.

"At ease, soldier." Thomas smiled at him, dipping his head as he passed beneath the doorframe and joined his son on the veranda. "I thought you would be awake."

"I had forgotten how beautiful Northshire is at this time of year." Malcolm turned around, resting his palms on the cool stone railing. In truth, he had never taken time to appreciate the beauty of his home. His pursuit of pleasure had always left him grasping for the next thrill, finding only jaded disillusionment in what he already possessed.

Thomas moved to stand next to him and set his black briefcase down. "There's no lovelier place this side of heaven. Much has changed in your absence." He pointed toward a picturesque row of small quintessential English cottages whose brown roofs sloped down over whitewashed walls. "That is the newest addition. We're offering free housing for the war widows and orphans from the village."

"Free? But can the estate afford to give housing at no cost?"

His father slanted a thoughtful glance in his direction. "It can if the women take on the trades their husbands used to perform. Work in exchange for housing and minimal wages. It was your wife's idea, you know."

Malcolm faced him, one eyebrow arched. "Leila came up with this?"

"Hmm . . . yes." Thomas held his gaze, his face serious. "Leila's become an irreplaceable part of both the estate and the village. She's gone so far as to start a school for the children." He fell silent for a moment then spoke again. "You should know, Malcolm, that I've named her my heir."

Silence, broken only by the warbling cry of a whippoorwill, fell between them. Thomas folded his arms across his chest. "I hope this news will not cause any problems between you both. I felt it only fair that you heard it first from me."

"No." Malcolm shook his head. "It is the right thing to do." He motioned toward the village. "I'm ashamed to admit it, but she probably knows these people better than I do."

He breathed deep, nodding. "She's clearly capable. Besides, if anything happens to me, Leila will already have a place to call home."

Thomas absorbed this in momentary silence. "It was not chance that brought you both together, son. God's hand was in it."

"I hope she sees it that way." Malcolm glanced toward the house.

Pursing his lips, Thomas said, "Did I ever tell you about the time I almost lost a skirmish in India?"

"You? Lose a fight?"

"I said *almost*." Thomas's eyes took on a faraway look. "My men and I were in the Arhanga Pass near the Tirah Valley. Our mission was simple. We were to escort twenty prisoners back to our base. Our scouts had reported no insurgents on the route home, so I sent half my men on ahead, thinking they wouldn't be needed."

He snorted. "Stuff and nonsense, really. Needless to say, we were attacked by rebels that had somehow gone undetected by our scouts. The prisoners escaped. My men and I found ourselves facing an enemy twice our size."

"What happened?" Malcolm leaned forward. His father had never talked about his past.

Probably because I never asked.

"I told half my men to provide a blistering barrage of covering fire while I led a handpicked few down a narrow pass and around to the enemy's side. We stripped a few corpses, infiltrated their camp, then captured the rebel leader." Thomas shrugged. "After that, the battle was over in moments, our prisoners were recaptured and we apprehended a wanted criminal."

His gaze became focused. "My mistake could have sparked a series of disasters. Risking everything was the only way to save anything."

Thomas laid a hand on his son's shoulder. "Picking up the pieces is never easy, but you must keep the objective in mind. You're a soldier. You're a Steele. Most of all, you're my son. I believe in you. Risk everything and you'll save more than you ever thought you could."

For a moment, Malcolm couldn't get any words past the lump in his throat. The simple story revolutionized all the assumptions that he had made about his father. He was human after all! Even more surprising was the thought that Thomas *wanted* him to understand his humanity.

"Thank you, Father."

140

Thomas clasped him in his arms then stepped back. "I'm afraid I have to leave for Switzerland. Greyson informs me that the Swiss president accepted my excuse once, but he might not be so congenial the next time. How long is your leave?"

"Three weeks. They're a little more generous when it comes to us officers than with the regular squaddies."

"I should see you before you return," Thomas said. "I'm in the middle of some technical negotiations and will be away for about two weeks."

He pointed to a dilapidated shack near the far end of the wheat field, just visible from this angle. "If you're looking for her, Leila normally starts her mornings there."

"In a shed?" Malcolm did a double-take. The Leila he had married prized sensual luxury. The run-down hovel across the way would be the last place on Northshire Estate that he'd expect to find her. "Why?"

"That," Thomas said as he stooped to pick up his briefcase, "sounds like a very good way to begin a conversation."

◆◆●◆▶

He shuffled through the grass, letting his hands brush lightly against the maturing stalks of spring wheat that grew alongside the path. Beads of dew soon covered his palms. A clinging mist that cloaked the verdant earth rose toward the sunlit sky. Overhead, flocks of sparrows spiraled through a set of aerial acrobatics in perfect formation.

Malcolm contrasted the lush greenery around him with the barren wastelands of the trenches. Each sprig of grass, each trilling bird, was a sight from a forgotten world.

There were no birds near Ypres.

Or the Marne.

Or Verdun.

141

No grass or trees grew anywhere near the places where men butchered each other with bullets and clouds of poisoned gas.

His eyes shifted from the acres of wheat to the distant sheep pens in which women, the wives and widows of Northshire's soldiers, toiled despite the early hour.

Malcolm hailed them and received a cheerful wave in return. Despite the grim realities of war—hunger, fear, and grief—the tenants maintained a plucky optimism that he admired. Northshire itself was a paradox; it was an island of peace in a storm-ridden sea.

As his father had inferred, Malcolm suspected that Leila was largely responsible for the positive attitude of Northshire's tenants. A wheedling inner voice tempted him to jealousy, but he immediately silenced it. Leila deserved every ounce of credit that had come her way. She had been here, earning the respect of those who lived on the estate, while he had pursued a path of self-aggrandizement.

The path ran in the general direction of the main gate but, instead of leading straight to the eastern border of Northshire, it curved upward along a slight hill on the other side of the row of trees that lead to the castle courtyard. At its end, Malcolm glimpsed the decrepit shed.

Rotting shingles, half blown off by some sort of explosion, hung at odd angles and the sagging door seemed ready to fall off at any moment. As he drew closer, Malcolm felt his pulse spike. Inside this derelict building was the woman who embodied his happiness. But how to earn her respect? He licked his lips. Approaching Leila took more courage than charging a regiment of Huns!

He slipped off the main path and wound his way around the corner of the building. Leila had been reserved, perhaps even cool toward him during last night's celebration. He knew she was happy to see him, but her stiffened back and rigid posture had shown him that she was as uncertain about their future as he was.

He had saved her from embarrassment by announcing that he wished to sleep in his old room and asking Greyson to see that it was ready. The past was still too fresh in both their minds to allow them to think about the future. Leila had thrown him a look of silent gratitude which, for the moment, had made his heart sing.

Stealthily making his way forward, Malcolm peered through a jagged hole in the wall. His breath caught in his throat. Leila knelt with her back toward him. Her hair tumbled over her shoulders like a mane of golden silk, set ablaze by the caress of the morning sun. He couldn't make out the words that left her lips, but he distinctly heard her murmur his name.

She's praying for me. Warmth spread throughout his chest. After a few moments the flow of words stopped, and Leila rose, her back still toward him.

"Will you join me, Malcolm?" Her voice was low and soft.

His heart thumped out an irregular rhythm as he picked his way around the debris, stooping to pass through the broken door. "How did you know?"

Turning around, Leila shrugged. "I'm a spy." She ran her hands down the front of a simple teal dress that subtly enhanced the mesmerizing allure of her green eyes. He noticed she wore no jewelry, not even—he swallowed—her wedding ring.

She followed his gaze to her hands. "I . . . still have it. If that's what you're wondering."

"I wish I could say the same." Hunching over, he shoved his hands in his pockets. Before abandoning her in London, he had pulled the ring off, spit on it, and trampled it underfoot. Now, he would give anything to have that small band of gold in his hands once more.

"So, what is this place?" He tried to fill the silence that claimed them both. "It looks like someone tried to invade!"

"Someone did." Leila motioned toward a rickety bench in the corner.

"What?"

"At least one German agent acting on behalf of my former handler, Werner Jaëger, attacked the estate last autumn."

He dropped onto the bench at her side and grabbed her hands on impulse. "Were you hurt?" Fury made his chest tight. "Where can I find him?"

She didn't answer, but instead let her eyes rest on their interwoven fingers. Malcolm started to draw back, but she stopped him with a whisper. "No, Malcom. Don't . . . don't pull away."

"Leila." Malcolm placed a finger under her chin and tipped her head to look into her eyes. "There's so much to say, but I don't know how to begin."

"That's because I'm the one who has the most to tell." She licked her lips. "It's hard for me to share secrets, Malcolm so please, don't press me. I'm still learning how to trust."

"I won't. Share what you like, when you're ready. I'll still be here, waiting for you."

The brilliance of her unexpected smile robbed him of breath.

"Thank you." She hesitated then began slowly. "There's something you should know about our family history. I, um, discovered the truth when I first came to Northshire."

"All right." He held her hand, savoring the warmth of her touch. It wasn't much but it was a beginning. And a new beginning with Leila Steele was something he wanted very much indeed.

"This is a new beginning, O'Malley, the beginning of a new era for Ireland." Werner Jaëger squared one ankle over his knee, fixing his gaze on the burly Irishman who slouched across the table and glared at him as though he were death itself. A bulbous nose sat square in the middle of a pockmarked face, right between a pair of shifty brown eyes. The man's square face was framed by a thick beard the color of fire.

In addition to being a notorious thug-for-hire, Aengus O'Malley was a vociferous critic of the British government. He didn't believe in words alone, however. In his view, democracy worked best when it was spurred along by exploding pipe bombs in Paddington Station and other acts of terror—all done with the goal of obtaining a free and independent Ireland. For years the London police had tried to infiltrate his tight network of criminals and thieves. For years they had failed.

Now, Werner sat in the gang leader's inner sanctum, the murky cellar of a rat-infested pub in the heart of London's criminal district. He was ready to unleash the final phase of a carefully-woven plan that could not fail to bring Leila Steele within his grasp.

"Argh, I dunno." O'Malley yawned and scratched his armpit. "My boys are good for a wee fight in the back alleys o' London, but to take on a mess o' trained soldiers? We'd be smashed to *drobes*."

"No, you would bring London to its knees." Jaëger leaned forward, tapping the table. "By challenging a trained group of Britain's best, you will show Whitehall that the Irish *cannot* be defeated. What better way could there be to prove to a corrupt government that your country is strong enough for total independence? For home rule free of British interference?"

145

He let the tantalizing words soak into the burly giant's mind then spoke again. "Imagine, a successful attack on British soil launched by a militant branch of Ireland's separatist party, the Sinn Féin." He spread his hands outward. "You'll have the Prime Minister trembling in his boots whenever your name is mentioned."

"He already trembles." O'Malley glowered at him.

"So you say, but I ask you only one question."

"Yeah, an' what is that?"

"Is Ireland free?" Reclining, Werner stroked his salt-and-pepper goatee and let a thin smile play about his lips. He had him. Despite his reservations, O'Malley was not a man to back down from a challenge. Werner could have rallied support from British citizens of German descent, but such a ploy might draw unwanted attention to the few German spies that had managed to establish themselves in England. Attention from Robert Hughes's counterespionage units would hinder Werner's own operations.

No, it was far better to get the Irish to do his dirty work. They were a proud, impulsive people who had tried for years to overthrow the yoke of British colonialism without success. He would use O'Malley's pathetic zeal for Ireland as a tool to destroy Thomas's small army at Northshire. While the guards were busy with O'Malley and his men, Werner would take care of Leila Steele.

"Of course, O'Malley, if you think your men will turn and run . . . " Werner made a flippant gesture.

O'Malley threw back his head with a snort. "It's not a matter of courage, just practicality. Besides, what's in it for yerself?"

"Revenge."

"Huh." The Irishman slanted him a glance, obviously expecting more, but Werner maintained an impassive silence. Vengeance was the blood that pulsed through O'Malley's criminal body. The man would understand.

"Revenge for you and Home Rule for Ireland." O'Malley pulled at his beard. "An intriguin' notion. But the gentleman in question is a man o' some reputation. How does killin' him help our cause?"

"I would think it obvious," Werner said. "How do you think Thomas Steele acquired his reputation?"

O'Malley threw a baleful stare in his direction. "*Ach*, an' I wouldn't know, now would I? Seein' as I've never had the pleasure of askin' him?"

Werner ignored his sarcasm. "By enforcing colonial rule upon countries just like yours. India. Africa. Ireland. Wherever his government ordered, Thomas Steele went, working to enslave the masses. Whitehall sees him as the perfect servant. By destroying Steele—and his precious home at Northshire—you will tell the world that Britain's days as a colonial power are over. The Irish are and always will be *free*."

"That's right!" O'Malley's eyes blazed and the wooden table quaked as he thumped it with a meaty fist. "A free Ireland for a free people. I knew I had a reason for lettin' ye into my circle. I have to admit"—he wagged a thick finger—"I like yer style."

Werner concealed the thrill of anticipation that pulsed through him. Last fall he had launched an ill-fated raid on Northshire, giving in to the urge to avenge his son and preserve his status as a revered spymaster in Germany.

He had almost died that night.

This time, he had taken precautions, forging a rather unconventional alliance with O'Malley and his gang over the past three months. This time, he was not making some desperate gamble but a calculated partnership that held every promise of success.

He could care less about the future of Ireland. All that mattered now was avenging his son's murder and silencing the elusive blonde-haired wraith who held a secret that could unravel his country's government. To that end, when next he came to Northshire, he would bring an army of his own.

"And you, O'Malley." Werner dipped his head. "You are a man of vision. When will you be ready?"

"Oh, for a job like this, I'll need to reach out to me friends in Sinn Féin." O'Malley's Irish brogue was as thick as his crimson beard. "'Twill be about a hundred of us *aul* told. Gettin' the *eejits* scattered about Northshire woods while keepin' 'em out of the coppers' sights will take some time." He screwed his ruddy face into a ball, thinking. "Mebbe three weeks."

Three weeks. Enough time to put the finishing details on a plan that must not fail. The muscles of Werner's stomach tensed. Failure would mean the death of his son's soul, the decease of his name, and the demise of three decades of unflagging service to Germany.

The grating sound of his scraping chair filled the small room as Werner pushed himself upright. "Do we have an agreement?"

O'Malley lurched upright, spit into his hairy paw and thrust it forward. Masking his distaste, Werner clasped his hand.

"Congratulations, laddie." The Irishman bared several gold teeth in a twisted leer. "Ye've got yerself an army."

Chapter 13

June 1917. Northshire Estate, Great Britain.

"So . . . what do you think?" Leila could hear the tension in her own voice, as though Malcolm's next words meant the difference between life and death. Perhaps they did. She had exposed her heart, revealing a web of secrets that had entangled her soul for years. Now he knew everything. Whatever he said now would either prolong the life of their relationship or kill it outright.

Resting his elbows on his knees, Malcolm massaged his temples. "What do I think? Well, I think it's incredible, really. If your ancestor hadn't been abandoned by his own father and taken *my* ancestor's place in that French prison then"—his eyes rose to meet her own—"I wouldn't be alive." A momentary hush filled the little shack. "Four generations later, our two families have been united by our marriage. That's a gift, Leila. One we can't afford to waste."

"And what about the rest?" Her stomach quivered as she waited for his response. "There've been so many secrets between us. My first husband, my handler Werner, the German spy I killed." She drew a deep breath. "The very reason I came to Northshire in the first place was dishonest. A-are you sure you're able to look past it all and start over, Malcolm? I won't blame you if you don't. Just know that, while it's true I came for the wrong reasons, I truly loved you. I *still* truly love you."

He slipped his arm around her waist. "Do you remember Eleanor?"

"Hm?" How long had it been since she had felt so loved, so safe? She rested her head on his broad shoulder.

"Eleanor, the nurse you met in Etaples." His voice was a low murmur she found mesmerizing. "Do you remember her?"

An image of a young woman, slightly shorter than herself, with dark brown hair and a no-nonsense attitude flitted through her mind. "I think so. Why?"

"The last thing she said to me was, 'look to the future.' I think that's what we both must do." He turned toward her, then tenderly cupped her face between his large hands.

A slight gasp escaped her lips as a tingling sensation sparked across her skin. Blood coursed through her veins, pulsing in her temples.

How long has it been since we kissed? Three years. *That's far too long.*

"Despite the wrong I did to Eleanor, and her husband Will, she urged me to look to the future."

Leila forced herself to concentrate. "And what is our future, Malcolm?"

"Northshire." He answered without hesitation. Releasing her, he rose and strode to the sagging door. Her shoulders slumped a little at the loss of his touch.

What would it feel like to be in his arms again?

Malcolm wheeled around. "Since you're sure that this German agent was targeting you then we must assume that he's still after you. No body was found, right?"

Leila reluctantly disentangled her mind from her amorous thoughts. "Only the bodies of Hughes's spies."

"The question is, why go through so much trouble to get rid of you? I mean, yes, a rogue agent could be a problem but honestly Leila, people defect all the time. On both sides. Why go to such lengths to silence you? After all, since you were a German spy, it's unlikely that the British government would believe anything you would have to say, not without explicit proof."

"Malcolm, there's something you should know."

His brow furrowed. "What is it?"

"There is something that I haven't told anyone, not even Thomas." Standing, she moved to the center of the small room.

"Leila, if you're not ready to confide in me, it's all right. I'm not going to force you."

"No." She turned and placed both hands against his chest. "I want no more secrets between us, Malcolm. Not now, not ever." She held his gaze. "That's the only way to build trust. What one knows, the other knows also. Do you agree?"

Again, he did not hesitate. "I do."

"Look behind my right ear." Leila tilted her head and brushed aside the hair that covered a vicious scar. It was the mark of her loyalty to Germany, a loyalty she had broken.

"This . . . this is a knife wound!"

She nodded.

"Who did this?" His voice became hard as granite. Malcolm placed a hand on both her shoulders. "Tell me!"

"Werner. Werner Jaëger."

Malcolm took a step or two backward, face twisted. "The swine!"

"It was part of my training, a test to see if I would break under torture." She held her chin high. "I didn't give in, and Werner knew he could trust me with the kaiser's darkest secret."

His eyes narrowed. "What do you mean?"

"The project was called *Herkules*. It was a contingency plan that only a half-a-dozen people knew about, at most." Leila licked her lips. Even now, despite her promise, revealing the truth was difficult. She forced the words out, not only because he needed to know, but because confiding in him would add another layer of strength to the fragile bond that joined them together. Malcolm had shared the details of the wrong he had done to Eleanor and her husband Will. Now, it was her turn to confide in him.

"If it becomes clear that Germany has no hope of winning the war, the kaiser will launch *Herkules*. German agents, of which I was one, will infiltrate the designated meeting place prior to the signing of the official treaty. The heads of state from all the warring nations will all be in one place."

Malcom's face paled. "What an opportunity."

"An opportunity the kaiser is determined not to miss. While the leaders of Europe and beyond are putting ink to paper, they will have no idea that they are signing their lives away."

"But how?"

"Gas," she said with a shrug. "Fritz Haber's work at Ypres was only the beginning. I don't know the details, but some sort of gas would be smuggled in beforehand. It would be unleashed during the final signing, killing everyone unless they have an antidote supplied by Haber himself."

Malcolm stood rigid. "But the world would be thrown into chaos!"

"A chaos that the kaiser will turn to his advantage. Germany's troops are not defeated on the battlefields; they are still strong while it's obvious that the Russian army on the Eastern Front is crumbling. Russia will soon leave the Allied war effort."

"If that happens"—his voice went hoarse—"the rest of Germany's army will be able to launch a massive assault on the Western Front."

"Exactly." Leila nodded, relieved that he understood so much so quickly. Their minds followed similar paths, grasping potential problems with alacrity. "While it will seem that Germany is disarming in the months prior to the treaty being signed, a core group will be kept not too far from France's border. Like lightning they'll push over the border once the assassination has taken place. At the same time, the rest of the army will remobilize."

Her husband clenched a fist. "Within a few weeks he could have half of Europe!"

"This is my listening post." Leila knelt, pushing aside a thick motley throw-rug that lay to her right, exposing the iron ring of a trap door.

"There's a radio down there?" Malcolm knelt beside her.

Pulling hard on the ring with a grunt, she threw him a quick smile. "Come and see."

Despite its decrepit condition, the trapdoor slid easily back on well-oiled hinges. Bunching the hem of her dress in one hand, Leila placed one foot on the first rung of a barely visible ladder and climbed downward.

She cupped both hands to her mouth. "Come on!" Then, she turned on the lights that cast a yellowish hue over her subterranean office. The room was an abandoned cellar that she had stumbled across while helping with repairs after the attack on Northshire last year. Cement walls enclosed three tables that were covered with a jumble of radio equipment. Wooden beams, strung with electric lights, crossed the ceiling above her head and, in the corner, she kept a small supply of canned food, bandages, two handguns, and some ammunition.

Malcolm released a low whistle when his feet hit the ground. His eyes darted around the room, then focused on the equipment on the table. "You built this?" A trace of awe tinged his voice.

"Well, yes, actually." Leila stepped forward in slow, unhurried movements. "It's small but it's clean and dry." Gesturing toward the table, "Part of my training focused on radio communication. Werner wanted his agents to be able to transmit information in all circumstances when in the field. Thomas bought the parts and"—she shrugged—"I put them together."

She touched a green, square box covered with dials and switches.

"This is an airplane radio." She pointed at three other contraptions. "These are a number station, a transmitter—in case I need to send a decoy message of my own—and a recording device that stores everything I can catch off stations commonly used by the *Abteilung* 3B, which is German intelligence, while I'm elsewhere on the grounds."

Noticing the wrinkle in his brow, she laughed and explained. "Shortwave radio allows us to transmit messages for hundreds of miles." She traced the path of a thin metal wire with her finger. "I've run an antenna through the ceiling and to the top of the roof. Because we're on a hill in the open, the signals actually come through quite clearly."

Malcolm shook his head. "I didn't see an antenna outside."

"Well, I wouldn't leave it in plain sight, now would I?" Leila arched a playful eyebrow. He was visibly impressed by her skills and the realization sent tendrils of pleasure throughout her entire being.

"What's this?" Malcolm gestured toward rolls of paper, covered with numeric symbols and letters. "Some sort of code?"

"Oh that." Leila groaned as she shifted closer to him. "That's a nightmare. The numbers are recordings from a number station—a shortwave radio transmission on which strings of digits are read off. Each number corresponds to a specific letter, word, location or series of letters."

Malcolm just stared at her. "And you can decipher this?"

"Only in part. The code changes but some of the base roots remain the same." Leila pursed her lips then said, "I can pick out bits and pieces but nothing definite." She shook her head. "All I can do is wait and see if something, some clue, comes up that will give me more information."

Leaning over, she grabbed a small stack of slim, nondescript books that lay next to the recorder. "These are code books issued by the *Kriegsnachrichtenstelle*—the espionage center in Antwerp where I underwent my training. Last night, the recording caught a short message, a string of numbers, that must have been intended for German agents in France."

"What does it say?" Malcolm peered over her shoulder at the long sequences of numbers underneath which she had inscribed neatly written letters.

"I don't know. It's some chatter about something called *Hubris* but I don't know anything about it. It seems to be something about the Palace of Versailles in France, which is rather odd since Versailles is far from the Front."

Malcom glanced around the room. "Right, well, we won't figure out anything down here. Let's go above ground and put our heads together." Standing aside, he let her climb up first then flicked off the lights and followed.

"Since we've no proof that the man who attacked Northshire is dead"—Malcolm closed the trap door and slid the rug back into place—"we must assume that he'll strike again in a different, maybe more devastating, way."

"They won't stop until I'm dead, Malcolm."

He reached out and pulled her close. "That won't happen, Leila. I swear it. Not while I'm alive."

She was silent, unsure of what to say, and Malcolm once again withdrew. Turning, he leaned against the warped doorframe and gestured toward the village. "He might strike at the tenants. We need emergency plans for the people should he, or any Germans for that matter, attack Northshire again."

Leila's mind churned like a wind-tossed sea. The man before her was not the self-gratifying boy she had married. His first thought was for her welfare. His second was for the people. His people.

"You *have* changed."

"We both have. For the better, I hope." He faced her, his warm eyes roaming over her body. Leila curled her toes in her shoes as heat crept up her neck and spilled into her cheeks.

"What is it?" Her voice was weak.

"You are exquisite."

"Malcolm—" She felt positively dizzy and placed a hand on the wall for support.

In an instant, he drew back. "I'm sorry. I . . . don't mean to offend you."

"No!" She moved closer and placed a hand on his cheek. "It's not that at all. It's just . . . been a long time since anyone has shown me that kind of attention."

156

Their eyes locked in a wordless embrace, slowing the hand of time to a crawl.

"I love you, Leila. You know that, don't you?" Malcolm's eyes were sincere, and his voice left no doubt that he was in earnest. "I always will."

"I—" her breath hitched. Love and desire battled with the memory of his confessed infidelity.

But this is a new beginning, for both of us.

She had to find a way to push past the hurt of the past in order to be a wife. To be *his* wife. Perhaps it all came down to a conscious choice. Choosing to put his adultery out of her mind, choosing to let the love she felt override the pain of his abandonment. Just as he had chosen to move past her wrongs. It would be difficult but not impossible.

The words had to be said. Said and meant. "I love you too, Malcolm."

He held her gaze a moment longer then withdrew. "Have Greyson assemble the staff. I want every man, woman, and child on the estate and in the village gathered in the Northshire Commons within two hours." Then he stooped underneath the doorframe and disappeared into the morning light.

———————◆◆●◆▶ ———————

Harold Greyson slid onto one of the rough-hewn benches near the front of the Northshire Commons, a simple but elegant structure that also served as a chapel in which the village pastor, Elijah Farrows, held weekly services. Greyson shifted on his seat, pulling his black swallowtail coat out from underneath him. He had been butler to the Steele family for over forty years and, in that time, had witnessed much change within the Estate.

He had been present at Malcolm's birth, had supported Thomas when his wife, Isabella, had passed away, and had tried to console the grieving father when Malcolm had rebelled against his authority. But now it seemed that he was destined to witness yet another transformation—the greatest that he had yet seen in his fifty-six years.

Malcolm strode to the pulpit on the raised dais at the center of the room, flanked by Elijah Farrows and Captain Leonard, commander of the security force that Thomas had hired to protect Northshire. With an approving nod, Greyson leaned forward, eyes intent on the young Steele.

Malcolm had wisely chosen to appear in uniform. Epaulets on his shoulders designated him as a ranking officer and, dangling from his breast, hung a gold cross. Greyson knew from his own years of military service that the Victoria Cross was given for bravery in the face of the enemy. It appeared that the prodigal-turned-warrior was ready for battle against the greatest threat he faced at home: the distrust of his own community.

He leaned over to Leila who sat with hands folded primly in her lap beside him. "I didn't know that your husband had received the Victoria Cross, did you?"

Leila's eyes twinkled as she leaned toward him. "My husband, Greyson, is full of surprises." Then, suppressing a smile, she faced forward.

Elijah Farrows stepped to the pulpit. "Thank you all for comin'. Today, as you all know, Lord Malcolm has asked to speak to everyone."

Hooking his thumbs in his suspenders, the preacher cast stern eyes on his congregation. "Now, to those among you who might be tempted to cast stones at the young lord here, I'd like to remind you of Christ's words." Thrusting his arm forward, Farrows pointed at the entire assembly. "'He who is without sin among you'"—he swung his arm from one side of the congregation to the other—"'let him cast the first stone.'"

Greyson estimated that about two hundred people, including children, were present. Yet Elijah's words brought utter silence to the room.

Nodding, the preacher stepped back. "Let's listen as the young master speaks." He dipped his head in Malcolm's direction then gestured to the pulpit.

Malcolm walked to the podium with wide steps, shoulders back, chest thrust out, and chin high. "Thank you, Mr. Farrows. I won't avoid the truth of those words. You all know me for who I was: a selfish, cowardly reprobate unworthy of the Steele name." His gaze swept the crowd. "I'm not proud of my past but, as I said, that is who I *was* not who I *am*."

Greyson's gaze flickered to Leila, and he noticed that her cheeks were damp. *So love will once again ultimately conquer all.* A smile tugged at his lips, then he turned his attention back to the man behind the pulpit.

Malcolm pointed over his shoulder at the looming cross that hung from the wall behind him. "The man who died on that cross has given me a new beginning, another chance to right the wrongs I did to my father and to you." He spread his hands outward as though he wished to embrace them all. "Northshire, I ask you to follow His example. Give me another chance. Trust me as I seek to lead us to a better future."

For a moment, the silence that had gripped the audience at Elijah's words continued. Then one man to the far right stood to his feet, clapping. "We're with you, Lord Malcolm!" He was joined by another, then a few more. Soon, the entire crowd stood, applauding the young leader.

Malcolm bowed his head for a moment then, wiping his eyes, he looked back up and raised a hand. When the audience had quieted down and regained their seats, he spoke. "Thank you for your trust. It is one that I shall not break. Now, we must think about the defense of Northshire and the village."

He turned to the captain who stood beside him. "Captain Leonard, how many men do you have?"

Saluting, Leonard stepped forward. "Eighty-three, sir. With a property as large as the Estate, that's barely enough. To include plans to protect the village would be next to impossible." He shuffled his feet.

"I understand, Captain." Malcolm again lifted a hand to silence the angry mutters that rifled the crowd at Leonard's reply. "But the lives of the villagers are as important as those in my home."

"'Tis true!" The lone shout was echoed by others.

A woman's voice rose over the murmurs. "Protect our children!"

Malcolm's voice took on a sharp edge. "I insist that some of the men be deployed to the village, even if it means reducing those on the Estate itself."

"Beggin' your pardon, sir." Leonard licked his lips. "I was hired by Sir Thomas. I am only authorized to accept orders from His Lordship or the Lady Steele."

Greyson tilted his head to one side as he considered the woman next to him. Leila could either support her husband and, in doing so, acknowledge his claim to Northshire or publicly undermine his authority. If Leila did the latter, she would show that she alone, deserved both the Estate and the trust of its tenants.

Over the past two years, Leila had earned their confidence. She had sought their interests and even worked alongside them in the fields. While the people had vocalized their support for Malcolm, if forced to choose between the untested prodigal and the faithful lady of the house, Greyson knew that Leila would carry the day.

More importantly, this moment spelled the future for Leila and Malcolm's relationship. There could be no doubt that, if Leila publicly undermined Malcom's image by refusing to support his initiative, their relationship was doomed. The moment of decision had come. The power was in her hands.

Leila rose slowly, her gaze sweeping over the audience, then shifting to the captain. "Captain Leonard." Her voice was firm and decisive. "The man before you is my husband."

A collective gasp ran through the crowd. Until this moment, only Greyson and Jenny had known that Leila Steele was wife to Malcolm. Thomas had introduced Leila as "a member of his family." As Malcolm and Leila had been married in secret, most of the Estate's tenants assumed she was a cousin or some other distant relative brought to Northshire by the turbulence of war.

In only a few, well-chosen words, Leila had announced what most of the villagers had never considered. But she was not finished.

"My husband's will *is* my will. Do as he says and send men to safeguard the village."

The crowd erupted in a roar of cheers and applause. Leila, flushed and radiant, glided forward. The hem of her simple teal dress brushed lightly on the ground as she mounted the platform and stood next to her husband.

"And in case there is any lingering doubt as to where my heart lies"—she turned Malcolm toward her—"let me remove it now."

With those words, she took a deep breath, leaned forward and kissed him. They remained locked in their embrace until Malcolm pulled away.

"Reverend Farrow." He turned to the minister. "I have no ring but, would you renew our vows, right here and now before all these wonderful people?"

Elijah's deep voice boomed over the congregation. "It seems to me that the lady is more than willing!" Laughter swept through the hall as the minister brought the two in front of the platform. With words more powerful than time, Leila and Malcolm pledged themselves to each other afresh.

"You may, Lord Malcolm, kiss your lovely bride."

Chuckling, Greyson covered his ears to dull the raucous noise of those present as the couple leaned into each other with arms intertwined. Somehow, he doubted they even heard anything louder than the thunder of their own hearts.

Pushing himself upright, he shuffled through the cheering throng and made his way to the door. Sir Thomas Steele was due to ring him this evening from Switzerland. He would surely want to hear about this!

"Truly God." Greyson slipped his black fedora on his head as he glanced over his shoulder once more at the loving couple. "Truly, You make all things new."

—◆◆●◆◆—

Later that evening, Malcolm hunched over a walnut-stained desk in his room, poring over a map of Northshire in hopes of identifying any possible weaknesses in the lines of defense that he, Leila, and Captain Leonard had drawn up that afternoon. The last glimmers of the setting sun glinted through the glass doors leading onto his veranda. Stretching, he glanced down at the black, silk pajamas that fell loosely around his ankles. "Much more comfortable than a uniform."

A soft knock sounded on the door.

"Enter!"

There was a moment of silence, then the door creaked open. "Leila?"

Malcolm's heart lurched as he caught sight of the vision before him. A gold robe of silk covered a cream nightgown. Her hair fell loosely around her shoulders.

Stepping lightly into the room, she closed the door behind her. "I have a gift for you, Malcolm."

"What—"

She interrupted him by pressing a slender finger against his lips. "Shh . . . " Then, with her other hand, she dangled a small, black box before his eyes. "Open it."

"All right." Taking the box, he flipped it open, then jerked his head back at the sight of a wedding ring. *His* ring. It was battered and scraped but it was here, intact and in his hand.

"How, Leila?" His eyes darted from the ring to her upturned face. He had thrown the ring on a street in London the night he had abandoned her. "I thought this was gone forever."

"That's what I thought about our marriage." She held up her left hand and he caught sight of her own ring, glistening on her finger.

"You kept our rings?" Emotion made his voice tight.

Leila nodded then wrapped her arms around his waist, pulling him toward her. "I couldn't bring myself to get rid of them."

Malcolm held her close. "You're a treasure, you know that?" He skimmed his fingertips along her jawline. "I'm so sorry for ever hurting you. I should've recognized that you had changed when you came all the way to Etaples to see me, instead of pushing you away."

"But look at us now," Leila said softly. "Together, when we thought there was no hope for us. Or for our marriage."

With a contented sigh, she snuggled closer. "You are my husband and I . . . think it's time that we acted as a husband and wife should."

He tensed, and she lifted her head from his chest.

"What is it?" She threw a wicked grin in his direction. "Malcolm, are you getting cold feet?"

He stepped back, holding her by the elbows. "I'm just surprised."

"At what?" Leila wrapped her arms around his neck. "You married me today for the second time. Isn't a wedding day always followed by a wedding *night*?"

"What I've done . . . to you." He faltered, not wanting to bring up something so painful yet needing to know she wasn't just doing this for his sake.

"Is done." She paused, looking steadily into his eyes. "It's behind us both."

Malcolm held her close, savoring her softness. "I'm only on leave for a few weeks. Then it's back to the frontlines. Anything can happen to me out there."

"Then let's not waste a minute of the time we have left."

"A-are you saying..."

"Malcolm." She breathed his name through parted lips. "Stop talking and kiss me."

With a low chuckle, he swept his bride off her feet and made his way toward their bed, heart throbbing under the impact of love, desire, and victory. He had left the battlefields of France to fight for his marriage and now, he knew that he had won.

He crushed Leila's lips with his own, tasting the sweetness of her caress.

After a few moments, Leila broke away, cradling his face between her palms. "It's *our* new beginning, Malcolm." The light of innocent hope shone freely from her face, sparking a warm glow that spread throughout his chest. "Nothing from the past will ever come between us again."

JP ROBINSON

Chapter 14

July 1917. Kaiser Wilhelm Institute. Berlin, Germany.

The air inside Fritz Haber's laboratory was a pungent mixture of chlorine, silicone, and death. Karl Schmidt, a close friend and colleague of Fritz Haber, scarcely noticed the chemicals, but the last ingredient—death—held his undivided attention.

The portly, middle-aged man peered through a two-foot-thick window at two young German soldiers. They lay prone on steel-framed cots in an observation room with metal bands strapping them to their beds. Stripped to the waist, these men would be the rats fated to test a supposed antidote that had been spawned by an ill-fated encounter between Haber and his lover, Charlotte Nathan. Wrinkling his nose, Karl pulled off his gas mask to better observe the two subjects in what could be their final moments of life.

The kaiser had demanded an antidote to gas inhalation if it became necessary to execute the nefarious Project *Herkules*, now dubbed *Hubris*. A few months earlier, Haber had approached him with a wide grin announcing that Charlotte had helped him discover the elusive answer. Since burning pesticides produced a lethal gas, in Fritz's twisted mind, reversing the convoluted chemical formula while adding a few new ingredients, should produce a viable antidote.

After weeks of futile analysis and failed tests Karl had been ready to abandon Fritz's idea, but the frenetic chemist had refused to accept the fact that, like his relationship with Charlotte, this approach was doomed to fail. Desperate for some sign of progress, he had concluded that the problem was not his supposed *antidote* but the lab rats that had so far been his subjects. An antidote for humans demanded *human* specimens. Despite Karl's vehement protests, Fritz had obtained official permission for his dark scheme.

Karl shook his head, muttering under his breath. Three years ago, before Haber had unleashed the madness of chemical warfare upon the world, Karl had been approached by a British intelligence officer who had attempted to turn him to the Allied cause. He had strongly considered the matter, as the very thought of using science to kill was offensive. But, out of loyalty to Haber and in the hope of pulling him back onto the path of true science, Karl had sent one message warning the British government of an impending gas attack then dropped all contact.

He swallowed hard, eyes darting from the prostrate men on the other side of the glass wall, to the bald, perspiring chemist who smushed his face against the window, waiting with bated breath for the fatal gas to be released.

Perhaps I made the wrong choice after all. Perhaps there was no redemption for men like Haber.

An image of Clara, Fritz's late wife, flashed through his mind. She too had tried to change the man beside him. Now she was dead, allegedly killed by her own hand.

Sighing, Karl rubbed the back of his neck. He knew Clara well enough to question the official story. He also knew that, in the months prior to her death, the entire team had been under surveillance by a counterespionage unit of the German military.

Had his government somehow discovered London's attempts to turn him? *No. If they had, I would already be dead.*

Karl slowly rubbed his jaw, thinking. Had they wrongfully suspected that Clara was in league with the enemy and had killed her in his place?

The suspicion was implausible, he was ready to admit, but the fact that the head of the military had forbidden an autopsy on Clara's body made him uneasy. Why the secrecy? Since he was the real culprit, was he to blame for Clara's death? A slight groan escaped his lips.

"It will work, Karl, don't worry." Haber's own voice contained the unmistakable note of anxiety.

The older chemist rested his gas mask on a steel lab table. "Fritz, these are not prisoners. These are loyal Germans—men with families. I beg you to abort this test!"

"*Nein!*" Fritz jerked off his mask with a snarl as he swung his head in Karl's direction. "It *will* work, I say. It has to."

"Do you mean your relationship with Charlotte or your supposed antidote?" Gentling his tone, Karl laid a hand on Fritz's shoulder. "They're not the same thing, you know."

The *hiss* of gas as it was released from a pressurized valve passed through the window, but neither scientist noticed. Neither did they see the erratic twitches of the two men as they inhaled the deadly air.

"Karl . . . Charlotte's pregnant." Fritz wiped his dripping brow with the back of his sleeve.

Karl recoiled as he would from an open canister of biohazardous material. "Pregnant!"

Again, an image of Clara rose in his mind's eye. She had been one of the finest women he had ever known, with a mind that had been rich with potential. Seeing only his selfish pride,

Fritz had openly reviled his wife by pursuing an extramarital relationship with Charlotte.

Now that Clara was out of the way, instead of feeling remorse, his colleague seemed determined to extinguish the feeble light of whatever morals remained in his dark mind.

"So, you see"—Fritz gestured toward the window—"this *must* work. My reputation depends on it." He wrung his pudgy hands together. "Charlotte wants a man that the world admires. It's the only way she'll be happy. I failed a woman once, Karl. I cannot endure the guilt of failing another."

Numbed by his friend's folly, Karl turned back to the window. What he saw made the blood run cold in his veins.

"Fritz, get the antidote!"

Haber pivoted back toward the window, eyes bulging from their sockets. The two soldiers jerked wildly, thrashing on their cots as though the devil himself was clawing at their throats.

With a shout, Fritz slammed his gas mask onto his head. Karl had only just pulled on his own headgear when Haber yanked the door open and staggered into the room. Grabbing their antidote—a clear liquid in two syringes—Karl slammed the door behind him and rushed to the closest victim. "Hold him still!"

Fritz appeared not to have heard. He remained immobile in the center of the room, head swinging from one writhing patient to another, mouth agape.

"Fritz, hold him!"

With a shudder, Haber grabbed the prostrate man's shoulder.

"I've got to get it right into the muscle." Karl positioned himself near the man's heart, held the needle just above the gray cloth of the victim's uniform, and stabbed downward, emptying the vial.

He spun toward the other soldier. "Now this one. Quickly!"
Once again, he plunged the needle downward, mentally calling Haber every sort of a fool for gambling with these lives.

"Success." Fritz grabbed his arm. "Glory. It will all be ours!"

Karl shook his head, barely able to speak past the nausea that clogged his throat. "Not like this." It was more a growl than intelligible speech. "Not like this!"

He lifted a trembling hand in the direction of the first patient. Convulsions had given way to immobility. A few minutes later, the man stopped breathing.

"No." Haber slammed a fist in the soldier's gut. There was no response. "It's not possible!" He swung to the other man, shaking the body then recoiled, letting it drop back onto the cot. "They're . . . they're . . . "

"Dead." Karl's voice was detached but inwardly he was seething. "We've failed. *You* have failed." He deposited the glass vials on the cot next to the dead man then looked at Haber through narrowed eyes. "I've stood beside you for many years, but this is where we part."

"What?" Haber grabbed the front of Schmidt's white lab coat and stared at him with wide eyes.

"I am no murderer," Schmidt said simply. "That is precisely what your ambition has spawned. Murder. Consider this my resignation, *Herr* Haber." He pried the man's fingers off his lab coat, spun on his heel and marched out the door.

"You cannot abandon me, Karl." Fritz's howl was frantic. "This is our work. *Ours!*"

Karl paused. "No, Fritz. This, like your unborn child, is solely the product of your evil desire. It has nothing at all to do with me."

Ignoring Haber's enraged bellows, he closed the door. Outside, Karl jerked off his mask and lab coat, tossed them into a corner, then strode down the hall in short, brisk movements. Haber, the prodigal scientist, was beyond redemption. *I should've stopped him three years ago.*

But perhaps it was not too late. He could still contact the British agent. One discreet telegram alerting the man of the kaiser's plot could put a stop to the madness that brewed in Fritz's lab.

His heart clenching, Karl darted outside the institute's brick walls. He would do it! For Clara's memory. For his own conscience. Hurrying now, he stepped outside the building, leaving Haber surrounded by corpses and broken dreams.

Chapter 15

July 1917. Berlin, Germany. Dahlem suburbs.

The Haber residence was a rather drab little hovel. True, many would call the sprawling white stucco house, expansive gardens, and lavish courtyard a mansion, but to Charlotte Nathan, the place stood in need of dire transformation.

Charlotte stood in the main hall, one finger on her pursed lips and the other hand resting lightly on her left hip, considering just what changes she would make once this place became her own. Of course, first she would need to make *Fritz* her own.

A sly grin snaked across her face and her left hand slid from her hip to the flat plane of her stomach. She could be no more than a month along but the child she carried had already become an invaluable tool. Fritz knew that marriage was an inevitable conclusion. It was not a question of *if* he would marry her . . . only *when*.

"Timing is everything." Charlotte chuckled, catching sight of her reflection in an antiquated mirror, a relic from the Victorian era. Her brown hair had been neatly cut and curled at the sides into a style that was all the rage nowadays. A loose, black blouse with sleeves cut off at her elbows was neatly tucked into the waist of a pair of white slacks. The pants were a daring touch,

173

one that only a few women in Berlin had embraced as of this moment. Pants were a man's domain.

But that would change. As would the ridiculous decorations in this house.

She crinkled her nose, eying the mirror once more. What *could* Clara have been thinking?

"Servants!" She clapped her hands twice, a sharp sound that cracked through the air with the force of a whip. "Come at once." She hadn't bothered to learn their names.

Within moments, a heavyset matron puffed into the room then leaned against the doorframe as she struggled to catch her breath. Charlotte's lip curled at the sight of the red-faced woman. *Woman? She's a walrus!* This one would be the first servant to go. She would be replaced by someone much more pleasing to the eye.

"You called, ma'am?" The walrus attempted a bow and Charlotte barely stifled a giggle as she almost fell over.

Pointing to the mirror, "Remove that atrocity."

"The mirror?" The servant stared at her, maw agape. "That was a wedding present to Lady Clara!"

Charlotte's nostrils flared. "Yes, well Lady Clara doesn't need it anymore, does she?" She closed the distance between them in two long strides. "Lady Clara is dead!" Thrusting a finger toward the mirror, "Remove it. Now."

The servant's dough-like face shifted from red to a sickening pale but, lips set in a firm line, she waddled over to the mirror and, with a grunt, lifted it off the wall. As she watched the woman's ungainly motions, Charlotte had a thought.

Replacing the walrus with a more attractive female servant would be to invite trouble. She knew well enough that Fritz had a wandering eye. Why put temptation in his face? It was his weakness that had first lured him into her net. But, now that the tables were about to turn, she must choose her staff carefully while insisting her future husband knew that she would tolerate no nonsense. Charlotte refused to endure the same humiliation she had inflicted upon Clara.

"Will there be anythin' else, ma'am?"

As Charlotte's attention returned to the waddling crone, she gave in to a fit of laughter. "No, my dear walrus, you may go." She let her moment of hysteria linger then, catching her breath, she made a dismissive gesture with her fingers. "Shoo, Walrus. Shoo!"

The servant's face turned a shade darker, but she waddled out of the room without another word. After a few moments, Charlotte turned and stalked through the front door to examine the mansion from the outside.

Reaching into her black purse, she withdrew a slim, Overstolz cigarette, lit it, and inhaled. Then, folding one arm across her belly and propping the other elbow on it, she released her breath in a cloud of smoke. "Now, what's next?"

◆◆●◆▶

Fritz jerked his door open before the driver brought the vehicle to a complete stop. Aside from his gas mask, he was dressed in the same attire that he had worn an hour ago in his lab. Just as he started to swing his feet outside, he noticed Charlotte.

The woman stood outside his home as though surveying a property she was about to acquire. She turned toward the car, a look of smug satisfaction plastered on her face and a decidedly unfeminine cigarette in her hand. Smoke plumed out of her mouth like a dragon and the red of her painted lips reminded him eerily of blood.

175

Slinking back into the leather seat, Fritz pulled the door shut. He didn't fear Charlotte, but he did fear the consequences of not meeting her expectations. Charlotte was counting on him to initiate her into the highest echelon of German society. But if he did not provide what the kaiser demanded, every door that was now open to him would close as quickly as the one he had just slammed shut.

He hunched over, burying his face in the flesh of his palms. Driven by an acute sense of guilt produced by Clara's suicide, he had purposed to revolutionize his attitude toward the female sex. His renewed relationship with Charlotte offered him a sort of catharsis, a means of self-redemption. Unfortunately, it seemed that redemption always came with a price.

"Is everything all right, *Herr* Haber?"

Fritz jerked upright at the sound of his driver's voice. *Is everything all right?* What good would it do to admit the truth? What good could come of confessing that he feared failing at a second marriage just as he had failed in the first?

He had eaten long and hard off the tree of knowledge. The result had been the death of his first wife.

Now, propelled by the kaiser's orders and Charlotte's dreams of grandeur, he bowed once again at the shrine of science, seeking a gift that would boost him to greater heights while obliterating the stains of his past. But what sacrifice would his god require this time?

Is everything all right?

Everything was wrong. So wrong. But in times like these, lies were the only truths worth telling.

Smiling, Haber nodded. "*Ja, danke.* Everything is fine. Just a long day at the lab." With these words he pulled the handle, sucked in a deep breath, and stepped outside.

Charlotte's eyes narrowed the moment Haber exited the car. His lab coat, wrinkled and stained by unknown chemicals, was something he never wore when at home. His eyes were red and puffy, as though he had been weeping and he dragged his feet as he moved toward her.

Her first thought was that she had asked for too much too soon. Her brow crinkled as she mentally rehearsed their conversations. To date, Fritz had said nothing that indicated she was being too demanding.

Is he tiring of me already?

Her frown deepened. No, she refused to consider such a possibility. Whatever bothered Fritz now, probably centered around his research.

"Darling." Charlotte minced toward him, eyes wide. "You look *so* tired this evening." She tapped her cigarette lightly with a slim finger, sending a flurry of ashes spiraling downward. "Why not join me in the bedroom?"

Haber shook his head. "No, I'd prefer to go into my office." Without another word, he pushed past her and lurched inside.

She followed him, the frown creasing her brow once again. Fritz hadn't taken her up on her unspoken offer and that troubled her.

When in his office, Haber shrugged off his coat, then faced her. "Karl is gone. He refuses to help me find the kaiser's antidote. Without him, the project is doomed."

"Why?" It was more a gasp than a question but, through her surprise Charlotte perceived a window of opportunity. Fritz was vulnerable now. The trembling mouse had come running to the cat for consolation. If ever there was a time to reveal her predatory nature, to sink her claws into his heart . . . it was now.

177

In a rush of words, Fritz related the incident in the lab, concluding with, "There must be something wrong with the formula, but I *can* fix it. The problem is Karl's morals won't let him gamble with human lives!"

"But," Charlotte spoke in a quiet, unyielding voice, "what makes you so certain that Karl's scruples are the problem? What if the problem is the man himself?"

Haber grew still. "Are you implying that Karl is working against me? That's preposterous!"

"Think of it Fritz. This man has stood with you when the gas bomb seemed a hopeless cause. Together, you made the impossible reality. Your weapon has already killed thousands. If his conscience was the issue, why didn't he speak up then?"

She slipped closer. "Karl Schmidt would never quit on the kaiser's work. Why," she scoffed, "that would be an act of treason, wouldn't it?"

He was silent.

Charlotte allowed a few seconds for her words to sink into his mind, then pressed her point further. "No, Karl intends to *steal* your research and unveil an antidote without you."

His eyes bulged out like those of a dead fish. "You mean . . . "

She drew on the cigarette. *How easy he is to manipulate.* "Karl will steal the glory that belongs to you and you alone." Her voice hardened. "Your work, *your* research but the credit goes to him."

Haber wrapped his arms around his belly. "B-but I've known him for years. He's never done anything like this before!"

"Exactly the point, darling." She moved around the desk to stand next to him, noting the slight grimace that tugged at his pudgy face as his eyes drifted to the still-burning cigarette in her hand. Fritz did not approve of a woman smoking. She had never smoked when in his presence. Until today.

"The ones closest to us are the best equipped to betray us." Charlotte lifted her thin shoulders in a small shrug. "Wasn't Judas close to Christ? Look at how that ended."

He squeezed his eyes shut. "I'll give him another chance. I'll go visit him and then—"

"And have him deny your accusations or, worse, flee the country?" Scorn tinged Charlotte's voice. "Strike first. Strike to kill!"

"But how?"

She cocked her head to one side. "This is the kaiser's special project. Contact the head of military operations and explain that *Herr* Schmidt has hindered your plans. No doubt they will give the fool his just deserts."

Frowning, Fritz rubbed the back of his neck. "I don't like it, Charlotte. What if he is innocent?"

Charlotte carefully deposited the cigarette onto a nearby table then shifted closer, wrapping her arms around his neck so the heady perfume she wore would tantalize his nostrils. Fritz was all about chemical reactions and she was prepared to spark the right one.

"Innocent Fritz?" She cupped his rotund face between her palms. "Who among us is truly innocent?"

His eyes widened and she brushed her lips against his own then pulled back.

Time to pounce.

"This is what I've been saying all along. You need someone who will stay with you always, a woman who will protect your interests." Pulling his hand to her belly, "A woman who will ensure your genius lives on."

179

Haber stiffened. "I'm not prepared for that, Charlotte. My studies, my work. I barely have time for my son Hermann, let alone a wife."

Charlotte grew still. Very still. Then she unsheathed her claws. Shoving him backward she said, "It's too late for that, Fritz. I'm pregnant and we both know who the father is."

"It's not as if I alone am to blame. It takes two to father a child!"

She ignored his jibe. "You see, I read the papers every day. I know that members of the international scientific community find your work with the chemical gas to be positively criminal."

He flinched.

Slinking closer, Charlotte ran her fingertips up his shirt. "What would happen, I wonder, if the papers carried a story that you, the celebrated Fritz Haber, seduced an *innocent* woman while you were married?"

She paused, enjoying the way beaded perspiration suddenly dotted the top of his mustachioed lip. What power a woman could wield if only she knew a man's weaknesses. "You know those reporters; always out for the next 'scoop' as the Americans say. How would it look if the world knew that, after your wife was buried, you refused to marry this same woman, knowing she carried your child?"

"What are you saying?" His hands trembled. It crossed her mind that he might strike her, but Fritz was too cunning for that. His status in the public eye was precarious at best.

The threat of negative publicity would bring him to heel and she would keep him there. Fritz would learn now that *she* was no Clara who stayed whimpering in a home while her husband trotted all over the country.

Charlotte flicked his tie into his face, then pulled away. "I'm saying that I've always thought October is a beautiful month for a wedding."

She retrieved her cigarette, sucked in a lungful and breathed it out slowly, letting the smoke wrap around his sallow face. She had pandered along, pretending to love him but the time for pretense was over.

"Your path is clear, my love." She spoke in loud, firm tones, tones that reflected the emotions that pulsed in her heart. "Destroy Karl. Find the antidote. I've put too much into this to see it all fail now."

Fritz just stared at her, mouth agape. No doubt he had expected her to coddle him, commiserating as he launched into a pitiful diatribe about the unreasonable nature of his colleague. Better the mouse learn now that the cat was mistress of this castle.

Blowing him a kiss, Charlotte turned and sauntered from the room. October was only three months away.

I'd better order my wedding dress.

JP ROBINSON

Chapter 16

July 1917. Spandau Prison, Berlin, Germany.

P aul Hindenburg despised traitors. As a man who held the enviable position of military Chief of Staff, he had every reason to hate the rodents whose treachery made light of the sacrifices endured by millions of loyal Germans. But the pudgy man before him who stood, blinking like an owl without his glasses, was unlike any traitor Hindenburg had seen to date.

Karl Schmidt had been one of Germany's elite scientists, a man who was respected almost as much as Fritz Haber himself. Yet this man, this brilliant scientist, had been caught sending a telegram to a British contact. This then was the mole which Werner Jaëger had sought. Hindenburg's fist clenched around the incriminating piece of cream paper. Written in a code that had taken less than a day for his cryptologists to decipher, there was no doubt that Schmidt was the turncoat.

Which means that Clara Haber died in vain.

Hindenburg's scowl deepened. At Jaëger's insistence he had prohibited an autopsy of Clara's body, confident that the master spy could not have made a wrong move. Now, with the proof quaking in the chair before him, Hindenburg realized that Werner Jaëger was no longer the man he had once been. Not only had Jaëger failed to eliminate the elusive Leila Steele, but his case of mistaken identity had led to the death of one of Germany's leading citizens.

"You are ready to die?" He glared at Schmidt, not bothering to mince words. There would be no mercy, no attempt at a parole. Not for this one. Even now, a firing squad assembled in an open plaza just outside the subterranean interrogation center.

The condemned man's Adam's apple bobbed wildly. "Yes." It was more a croak than a sentence.

Hindenburg sneered and spit on his victim's face. It hadn't taken much to break the man—two crushed fingers and a few blows to his expansive gut had been more than enough. Schmidt was no hero.

"*Warum?* Why did you do it?" He dangled the crumpled telegram beneath Schmidt's nose. "Do you know what you could have done?"

"Why did . . . Clara Haber die?" Schmidt's eyes were round pools of glassy terror but behind the fear Hindenburg sensed a trace of remorse.

"Shut up!"

Schmidt wheezed out a wet cough. "She was killed . . . in my place, wasn't she? You thought she was . . . the spy."

"Because of you, scum, an innocent woman was killed." He leveled his face inches from Schmidt's eyes. "You die with her blood on your hands."

Schmidt slumped forward, tears mingling with the flecks of blood on his sagging jowls. Hindenburg was about to slam his fist into the traitor's gut again when the doors to the chamber flew open and Fritz Haber, backed by several guards in black uniforms, stormed into the room.

"I came as soon as I received your message." Rushing forward, Haber faced Schmidt. "You idiot!" His mouth flapped wordlessly. "I trusted you. And you were working for the enemy?"

The prisoner gave a barely discernible shake of his head. "You are your own enemy, Fritz."

"You dog!" Haber's palm connected with the man's battered face, whipping Schmidt's head to one side.

Groaning, Schmidt looked back at him, his face a battered mass of welts and bruises. "You're no scientist; j-just a murderer."

"Death is death, no matter how we make it happen." Haber glared at him with fists clenched and chest heaving. "What right have you to question me?"

"To question is the birthright . . . of a true scientist."

"General Hindenburg!" Fritz turned to the Chief of Staff, pointing a trembling finger at the prisoner. "He does not deserve to live."

"Soldiers!" Hindenburg shoved his way between the two men. "Take him." The guards unbound Schmidt then dragged him by the arms toward the execution grounds.

"One day your evil will destroy those you love, Fritz." Karl's voice rose above the sound of his shoes as they scraped the concrete floor. "Just as it has . . . already destroyed you!"

"Get him out of here." The veins in Fritz's neck bulged purple.

"*Herr* Haber come with me." Hindenburg gestured toward the door. "I would like you to witness his execution."

Haber stalked toward the door, fury written in every inch of his rotund body. Outside, a gray sky hung over the small courtyard. At the far end, Karl Schmidt was strapped to a tall stake then offered a blindfold which he refused.

"Ready!" At Hindenburg's call, the eight soldiers that made up the firing squad drew their rifles into position.

"Take aim!"

Hindenburg turned to the chemist, struck by a sudden burst of inspiration. There was a sort of poetic justice to Haber's presence. "*Mein Herr*, you have been the most hurt by his treachery. It is therefore only fitting that you be the one to issue the final command."

Haber nodded and stepped forward. Across the courtyard, Schmidt locked eyes with the younger man—his colleague turned executioner.

"I f-forgive you, Fritz. May God . . . forgive you too."

Fritz's lips pulled back in a snarl as his fist chopped downward. "Fire!"

Chapter 17

July 1917. Whitehall, London. Great Britain.

Robert Hughes tapped a green pen against the wooden prosthesis that jutted from his left pant leg. The stump, like the green-ink pen in his hand, was a quintessential aspect of his personality. Both were unique elements that had made him a legend in the eyes of the British people.

Tack, tack, tack. The tapping continued as his mind shifted to the problem at hand. In the interests of his government, he purposed to take down another legend, a man whose very greatness had made him vulnerable to German corruption: Thomas Steele.

Hughes's eyes rolled to the world map that splayed across the wall opposite his desk. A blizzard of red dots—drawn in false locations of course—represented the international branches of the British intelligence network that he had established. His agents intercepted messages from both Britain's allies and enemies, filtering through thousands of encoded messages with the same dogged persistence that had transformed his country from a backwater island into a mighty empire.

Crossing his arms and leaning back in his chair, Hughes let the pen drop onto the desk. The Navy had once described him as 'unfit for service' due to his poor health.

He sneered. "Balderdash!"

The demeaning verdict had fueled his inner flame of ambition, changing a flicker into a carefully contained inferno. While others slept, Hughes worked, capitalizing on his innate ability to drill into the hearts of men and extract their darkest secrets.

Determination. Vision. A thirst for justice. These were the tools with which he had scaled the political mountains of British society, coming to rest like Noah's ark on the lofty peaks of government. From this viewpoint, he could see clearly that Thomas Steele had something to hide. And, despite the Prime Minister's objections, Hughes would not rest until he knew precisely what that *something* was.

His head swiveled to the ebony telephone that sat on his desk as its shrill cry filled his office. It rang five times then fell silent.

"Hmm . . . " The ring pattern meant that the caller was from a rural area near Sussex County. *How curious.*

Hughes glanced at his watch. Forty-three seconds later the telephone rang again, twice this time. *The police near Northshire Estate.*

Pulse quickening, Hughes leaned forward, eyes no longer on his watch but on the telephone receiver. It rang once and he immediately picked it up. As expected, the husky voice of Sussex County's chief inspector sounded in his ear.

"Sir, as you requested, I'm just callin' to report some unusual activity around Northshire village."

Hughes waited in silence despite the surge of impatience that swelled within him. Phones, even lines as secure as his own, could be tapped. He never spoke unless necessary.

After a moment, the chief inspector continued. "One of my men was near the Estate trainin' some dogs to track scent yesterday. The hound picked up a trail and led him to a stockpile of weapons in the forest. Rifles, shotguns, clubs. Even grenades!"

He paused, obviously expecting a reaction of some kind. There was none.

"Well, it was gettin' near evenin' and my man was afraid to stay around. He came on back to the office straight off and made his report. We're goin' in to investigate. I'd normally not mention anythin' but since you ordered me to contact you with any incidents involvin' Northshire—"

"Well done." Hughes muttered the words then disconnected the call. Lacing his fingers behind his head, he leaned backward, closing his eyes and imagining possible outcomes of the plan that mushroomed in his mind.

Instinct declared that whatever Thomas had been planning for the past three years was about to come to a head. *Grenades?* Something was brewing on Northshire Estate and *he* needed to be there. True, the Prime Minister had forbidden any direct action against Thomas, but now much more than one man was at stake. British lives were on the line. If he remained idle, national security could be compromised. And such a thought was unthinkable.

Hughes's eyes snapped open. He pulled open his desk drawer, retrieved a slip of carbon paper, then scrawled out an order.

With a flourish, he signed his name in green ink, then picked up the phone.

"Connect me to General Wilbert," he said to the operator. One minute later the retired general who headed the armed division of British Intelligence was on the line.

"Wilbert, I'm invoking the emergency powers provided for under article nine and section three of the Defense of the Realm

Act. I want sixty armed men ready within the hour, under my command. You will receive the signed order presently."

Wincing, Hughes held the phone away from his head as the general's voice barked in his ear.

"It's highly irregular?" Hughes threw back his head with a snort. "Yes, I suppose it is. But think, man! What about me is regular? One hour."

Hughes hung up, silencing the general's continued protests, then lurched around his desk. Leaning on his walking stick, he stared up at the map. It all came down to this moment. He had sacrificed much in service to his country over the years. Most Britishers loved him. But now he was about to risk everything in a calculated gamble aimed at destroying another man the country idolized.

If he was right and Thomas was aiding the enemy, the nation would applaud his insight. Equally important was the fact that another threat to his country would be eliminated.

His nostrils twitched. If he was wrong, his reputation and all that he had built would be torn down by the vociferous sharks in Parliament who already protested the Secret Intelligence Service's intrusion into their personal lives.

The Prime Minister would claim, honestly enough, that he had no knowledge of the coming raid and would doubtless leave Hughes alone to bear full responsibility. The ensuing scandal could cause him to resign in ignominy. He pursed his lips.

Instinct. Always trust instinct. Hughes shook his head. Whatever the outcome, his duty was clear. He would root out whatever evil lurked in the woods that Thomas Steele called home and leave the consequences of his actions in the hands of the gods.

The cheerful warble of larks, wafting through Northshire's languid summer air, seemed oddly out of place to Werner as he contemplated the violence he was about to unleash. The German spymaster crouched in the dense undergrowth on a slight rise overlooking the gate that marked the entrance to the estate's verdant acres.

Pressing his binoculars to his eyes, he glared at the blackened remnants of the shack from which he had launched his ill-fated invasion ten months earlier. The corpse of a building taunted him, wordlessly shouting his failure to avenge his son and fulfill his obligation to the kaiser.

A failure I will soon rectify.

He clenched his jaw, lowering the binoculars. It was as though Sir Thomas and Leila had purposefully left the shack as a sign that they would not be intimidated. More than likely, Thomas had simply not had the time to rebuild, but Werner felt a surge of bile rise in the back of his throat all the same. He shifted his gaze to more relevant considerations.

About thirty yards away, just beyond the screen of trees, a long, gravel road wound its way to a circular courtyard. At its center, the gleaming wings of a golden eagle perched on a marble pillar could be seen even from this distance. A low whistle from his left indicated that O'Malley too had laid eyes upon the treasure.

"Would ye cast yer eyes on that pile o' gold? And I thought we Irish were the lucky ones!"

"I'd rather cast my eyes on those men at arms, if it's all the same to you." Werner nudged him with an elbow then pointed to the small clusters of black-clad guards that lined both sides of the road about every sixty yards.

191

O'Malley grunted then spoke in rapid, hushed undertones. "Whoever organized these defenses knew what he was doin'. There's only one way into the Estate and that's through those men." Drawing a long-bladed knife, he scraped away some dead leaves then began jabbing at the ground.

"Here we are." He drew a rough "X" in the dirt. "Linin' the road with fifty men behind us."

A cross materialized a few inches away from his first mark. "Here's the village, where about twenty more of our'n are minglin' with the locals, waitin' on our signal. On the other side of the road is a clearin' bordered by some sharp bluffs and here"—the blade flung a clod of dirt into Werner's face as O'Malley carved a small circle in the ground—"here's the castle itself."

Werner tapped the village. "We stick to the plan. We lure the guards into the village. There's no way we can fight our way through." He shrugged. "Rushing through the clearing would be suicidal."

O'Malley glared at him, teeth bared in a snarl. "Don't forget that I am in charge here! Sinn Féin thinks and acts for the good of Ireland."

"What are you talking about? We've already laid out our plans."

"I'm talkin' about gold!" The gang leader's eyes gleamed as brightly as his gilded teeth. "Melted down, that pile of beauty could pay fer the resistance in Ireland for years to come."

Werner scoffed. "Or line your pockets! You'll die trying to get to it."

"Do ye think I've called my brothers in arms together to *run* from a fight?" O'Malley brandished the dagger, blade inches from Werner's heart. "Ye might think that we can't stand up to these vermin, but that's because ye don't have the blood of

Erin runnin' through yer veins. Those men might be soldiers but they're not *expectin'* a fight, now are they? Their surprise will be their undoin'."

For a moment, Werner was sorely tempted to knock the silly toothpick out of the Irishman's hand and ram it down his throat. The arrogant fool would be dead within six seconds. But his mind rolled to the men behind them—also Irish—who were watching the interplay with avid interest.

One false move and he would not leave here alive. Besides, O'Malley wasn't his concern. The Irishman and his lot of pathetic numbskulls were only a diversion, a means of keeping the guards busy while he took care of Leila

"As you wish." Rising slowly, Werner slid his revolver from its holster and verified that the chamber was loaded. He had been given a deadline of six months by the kaiser. Time was almost up. Jaëger breathed deeply, tilting his head to the sky, as a sense of calm flooded his being.

He had taken all precautions, planned for all contingencies. This time, there would be no surprises. A detailed report on the Estate's defense had been delivered to him by Captain Leonard, the leader of Thomas's guards. Leonard was a German agent who had infiltrated British Special Forces before the outbreak of the Great War.

When Thomas had doubled the size of his small army, he had unwittingly brought a viper into his nest. Leonard had responded to the advertisement at Werner's behest. Now, ten months later, Werner was ready to strike again.

As expected, Leila had planned well. But the beautiful defector had never known the true strength of his international network. This was her weakness.

His eyes flickered open. "Do what you like with your men, O'Malley, but remember, I am *not* under your command. Your men know what to do if they find the woman?"

With a grunt, O'Malley straightened. "Yeah, if they see a pretty blonde puttin' on airs they'll fire the flare gun." He slipped two cartridges into his shotgun then pumped the slide backward, a lustful leer twisting his mouth. "Ye can have her. Or whatever my boys leave of her!"

Werner followed the Irishman with wary eyes as he turned toward the silent fighters behind him. They were a mix of O'Malley's thugs and Sinn Féin members who had managed to slip into the mainland from Ireland. All told, they were a hard-bitten group, men who had fused their penchant for violence with a justly deserved thirst for freedom. Dressed in cotton breeches and dingy shirts, they were armed with rifles, pistols, and grenades, most of which O'Malley had managed to have hidden in Northshire's dense woods beforehand. A few clutched the orange, white and green flag on which the words *Sinn Féin*, or "We Ourselves," were scrawled in ink.

Today, Leila. It ends today. A wolfish smile tugged at the corners of Jaëger's mouth. He was once again the hunter, ready to rip the throat out of his prey.

"Get ready boys." O'Malley's hoarse whisper mingled with the breeze that ruffled the maple leaves above Werner's head. "Today, we strike a blow that England will never forget. Today, we strike for freedom!"

───◆◆●◆►───

"Do you think Lord Malcolm will be pleased when he finds out?" Jenny grabbed Leila's arm as the two women ambled down the road that bisected the heart of Northshire Village.

"Excited? He'll be speechless, Jenny. Having his portrait mounted on the family wall is a priceless moment for the men of the Steele family." With a throaty laugh, Leila slipped her hands into the pockets of her loose, caramel-colored skirt. "It's a sign that Sir Thomas acknowledges him as his heir, that Malcolm has the full right to act on his father's behalf."

"All that?" Jenny's fingers flew to her parted lips. "I never thought I'd see his portrait hangin' alongside his father's." She reddened, then shot Leila a sidelong glance. "Beggin' your pardon ma'am."

"Granted." Leila looped her arm through Jenny's. They were about the same age and, if truth be told, she thought of her lady's maid as more a sister than a servant. Leila herself did not come from a lineage of aristocrats and, as such, adopted a more practical view of Northshire's staff. Jenny had played a pivotal role in helping her understand the varied demands of running a household. If anyone deserved the right to voice an opinion, it was her.

Jenny waved at a group of children that played tag in the street. "So, you sent a photograph of Lord Malcolm to Sir Thomas. But why is His Lordship havin' an artist in Switzerland do the portrait?"

"Well," Leila said as she ruffled the dark hair of one of the boys that zoomed by, "this man apparently was commissioned by Sir Thomas's father to paint *his* portrait and he feels that no one else—"

She froze, gripping Jenny's arm.

"What is it?" The maid's eyes darted around. "What's wrong?"

Leila turned slowly and, pulling Jenny along, moved in nonchalant motions into the shade cast by the overhang of a stationary shop. "That man on the bench with the paper," she made a slight motion with her chin while stooping down as though she had dropped a coin on the sidewalk, "I've never seen him in town before, have you?"

Licking her lips, Jenny cast a glance over her shoulder. "No, now that you mention it. I mean, I can't say I know everyone in the village but . . . "

"That man neither." Leila felt her pulse quicken as her eyes shifted to various corners of the village square. She counted at least six strangers scattered across the plaza. They were doing nothing noteworthy—one walked casually down the street while others talked with shop owners or the local women. But, despite their visible calm and simple clothing, they all carried an aura of violence, an aura that only someone trained to kill would notice.

The man on the bench flipped his paper over then lifted his eyes to hers.

He's watching me. The realization made her scalp prickle.

"Maybe they're visitin' family?" Jenny's voice was hopeful, but a subtle inner voice whispered of danger. What was it Werner had always said? *A well-tuned instinct for danger is the difference between a good spy and a dead one.*

"Jenny," Leila spoke in a rushed whisper. "I want you to listen to me carefully. I need you to go to the Northshire Commons and ring the alarm bell."

The maid's eyebrows shot upward. "Another drill?"

"This isn't a drill, Jenny." She paused, letting the words sink into the woman's mind. "Ring the bell, then get to the castle as quick as you can. Tell Lord Malcolm that I'll evacuate the village, bringing everyone to the outside of the castle's secret entrance. Do you understand?"

Jenny stared at her with widened eyes then jerked her chin downward. "Y-yes."

"Go now but, whatever you do, do *not* run."

Leila watched until her maid disappeared around the corner. Then she pivoted on her heel, shoulders back and head high, going in search of Captain Leonard, leader of Thomas's hired guards.

A tingle of anticipation slid down her spine. Such an organized but subtle invasion presence could only be the work of one man. She and Malcolm had prepared for this eventuality, spending countless hours devising ways to minimize the risk to Northshire's tenants then putting those plans into motion by holding massive drills involving every person on the Estate or in the village.

Today it all ends. Lifting her chin, Leila felt a surge of confidence. Northshire was ready.

━━━━◆●◆━━━━

"Captain Leonard!" Leila moved briskly toward the soldier. "A word if you please." Ten of Leonard's men were scattered across the square, gazing languidly at passersby with rifles in hand.

"How can I be of service?"

"It appears that the village has some unexpected guests." Leila lowered her voice. "Has there been any sign of trouble?"

"No, Lady Steele." Leonard hooked his thumbs into the waist of his black uniform. "I see nothing unusual." He shrugged. "So, we've got company. A few visitors, maybe. Pacifists out for a day in the country?"

"They're not just visitors. They're here for a purpose and it's not a good one."

Leonard eyed her. "Forgive me, Lady Steele, but what makes you so certain?"

Leila didn't bother to answer. She wasn't about to tell anyone of her past, least of all this idiot of a man who couldn't see what was staring him in the face.

The strangers were of military age, but they were here, not at the Front. The thought that they were pacifists was ludicrous given their surly appearance and smooth, well-coordinated movements. They were men used to handling weapons, men who could only be hired killers. She hadn't been close enough to listen for the hint of an accent but, based on appearances, she doubted they were of German origin. Jaëger had sent some sort of special force, maybe a neutral party, to carry out his will.

But only six? Surely, whoever who had attempted to infiltrate Northshire last year would have informed Jaëger that there were armed men on the premises!

Why such a small party against such odds? There had to be more men, hidden somewhere no one suspected.

"How I know doesn't matter, Captain." She jutted her chin. "What *is* important is that your men are ready to evacuate these villagers as we planned."

"Evacuate?" Leonard smirked, folding his arms across his chest. "Because a handful of strangers decided to come to town? With respect—"

"If you respect me at all, Captain Leonard, you'll do as I say. Now!" Leila's pulse quickened, not because of the captain's arrogance, but because she knew there was some part of the puzzle she hadn't figured out. Jaëger wouldn't risk the humiliation of failure a second time. He must have a secret weapon somewhere, something she was overlooking.

Leonard's tongue flicked over his lips as he slithered closer.

"Lady Steele, evacuating the entire estate now would be a mistake. We cannot do that."

Beads of sweat dotted his brow.

Odd, given the cool morning temperatures.

"The only mistake I see is keeping you employed." Her hands flew to her hips. "I head this estate, and my explicit order is to start the evacuation, right n—"

"Now!" Leonard leapt forward, his fingers clamping around her arms like iron handcuffs. "Strike now!"

Leila writhed in his grasp. From the far end of the square, a pistol barked, and a flare snaked upward. It exploded in a blinding ball of flame and sparks and, at that moment, the square erupted.

The six men pulled revolvers from beneath their clothing and rushed the black-clad guards in a loose triangular formation. The first two, dropped to their knees, while those behind stood up and fired. Their synchronized attack felled three of the Northshire guards where they stood.

Screams rose on all sides as civilians scrambled to escape the onslaught of violence. At that moment, the piercing clanging of the Commons alarm bell split the air, alerting all of Northshire's residents that the Estate was under attack.

Leonard jerked his head upward at the unexpected noise and Leila, sensing his distraction, planted her feet on the ground and threw herself backward. The back of her skull slammed into Leonard's chin. As he staggered backward, she slammed her elbow into his side and wrenched herself free.

Bullets spattered the ground around her as the invaders streamed toward the black-clad guards who gawked, first at their commander, then at her.

"Stand down men!" Leonard snarled while keeping his eyes on Leila.

"What are you doing?" Leila screamed, backing away. *I've got to get the villagers out of here.* "Shoot them!"

The soldiers fell into a ragged formation, one line on bended knee while the second line stood behind them with weapons at the ready. "Sir? Permission to engage?"

"He's a traitor, don't you see? Shoot them!" Leila's unbound hair flew into her eyes and she scrambled madly to clear her vision. She sensed, rather than saw, Leonard's movement and shifted to one side.

Reaching out, she hooked her arm into the falling captain's belt, while twisting her body to one side, intent on using him as a human shield. A guttural cry ripped out of his throat as bullets from the attackers—that were meant for her—punched into his back.

Leila jerked the revolver from Leonard's belt, then let his corpse collapse onto the ground. Sighting down the short barrel she pulled the trigger. The man in front flipped backward, arms flailing. Following her lead, the soldiers to her right began to pour bullets into the approaching fighters but by this time, the attack had stopped.

Crouching, Leila's eyes darted from Leonard's corpse to the four remaining men who fled toward the woods lining the village. Two of the attackers lay stretched out on the ground and she shifted closer, gun at the ready.

Leila prodded the first corpse with her foot, then stooped by it. The dead often said more than the living. Catching sight of a chain around the man's neck, she ripped his shirt open. A small tin harp hung from a loose chain around his neck. The word *Erin* was tattooed across the skin below his collarbone. Her mind whirled as she made her way to the second body and found the same. *Erin.*

Erin was an ancient name for Ireland. She frowned, trying to connect the pieces. The Irish had no quarrel with Thomas, but they did want independence.

Jerking the chain free, Leila focused on the small harp. The Sinn Féin, Ireland's militant political party, had adopted the harp as their emblem when they began their rebellion against British rule two years ago. The dead man before her had obviously been a member of the Sinn Féin.

Early on in the war, the Germans had tried, with little success, to incite the Irish to rebellion against their British oppressors, hoping to destroy the empire from within. That plot had failed but Werner had clearly used his connections, as well as the Irish hatred of Great Britain to his advantage. Was there no end to the man's ruthless cunning?

Grabbing her revolver, Leila pushed herself upright as the pieces fell into place.

"Lady Steele." The voice of Leonard's second-in-command brought her back to the moment. "What are your orders?"

Leila hesitated. Leonard had obviously been a German plant, which explained why he had protested Malcolm's decision to send troops to guard Northshire village in the first place. But if he had been disloyal, could she trust any of his men? Then again, did she have a choice?

Pressing her lips together, she motioned to the streams of villagers who moved past her to their meeting point. "Everyone in the village knows to meet at the church. Now we need to get to the castle. Line up alongside the people. If anything moves in those woods, shoot it."

He nodded, then spun on his heel issuing crisp orders to his men.

Leila sucked in a deep breath then sprinted for the church. Something else was coming, she would stake her life on it. During the action she'd have to fight, protect her people, watch everyone and trust none.

Clenching her teeth, she stormed ahead as a surge of raw fury swelled within her. "So be it."

Chapter 18

July 1917. Northshire Estate, Great Britain.

Malcom was in motion as soon as the first echo of the clanging bell reached his ears. It was the last day of his leave and as such, he wore his tan uniform, freshly washed and pressed by Jenny's skillful hands. He was scheduled to take the 15:00 train to Calais, but now it appeared that the war had come to his home.

"Greyson," Malcolm shouted over his shoulder as he snatched up his rifle and dashed for the door, "that's the evacuation signal! Get the secret passageway open for the villagers."

The moment his feet hit the courtyard cobblestones, Malcolm's eyes flew to the road that led to the village. Leila had left early this morning on what she had dubbed a "secret mission," and had insisted that only Jenny accompany her. He had pushed aside his reservations but now he called himself every sort of a fool for letting her go.

The bell tolled again, but this time the sound was eclipsed by a thunderous roar that rolled out from the trees. A fusillade of smoke and bullets burst out of the woods on the left side of the road, felling five of his guards in the first volley.

A chill swept through him as a tidal wave of sound spilled over the courtyard. The noise was followed by swarms of men that leaped from the trees and smashed into the foremost row of Northshire's black-clad guards. Taken by surprise, the defenders fell back before the furious onslaught, harried by shrapnel and exploding grenades. Despite their reckless charge, the attackers moved with a coordinated professionalism that he could not fail to notice. Within moments, the first division of twenty soldiers that he had installed at Northshire's gates had fragmented, leaving behind a swath of broken bodies.

"Men, to me!" Malcolm barreled forward, eyes intent on an Irish flag that fluttered in the hands of one of the invaders. *Irish?* Fury made his gut tight. He didn't care who they were. They were attacking his home and therefore, they were the enemy.

In a few seconds, he reached the right side of the second division of twenty men. "First division fall to the rear. Second division, prepare yourselves!" The defenders rallied around him.

"Let them have it. Fire!" The veins in Malcolm's neck bulged as he screamed out his defiance. A volley of brutal fire belched from the guns of the men at his sides, punching holes in the advancing Irish lines.

"Reload!" He lifted his own Enfield to his shoulder. "Fire!" He pulled the trigger, sending a man screaming to the ground. Malcolm was about to shout out another order when two hand grenades detonated simultaneously in the middle of his group. Bodies were tossed into the air like matchsticks and knocked him off his feet. Malcolm staggered upright, ears ringing.

With a roar, the Irish surged forward, engaging the defenders in furious hand-to-hand combat.

"For Ireland!" Some screamed, slashing downward with clubs, rifle stocks, and bayonets. "*Erin* forever!"

Hacking and thrusting, they beat his men back inch by inch. "Third division, split ranks!" Malcolm threw himself into the fray. Ducking under an Irishman's savage downswing, he blew a hole in the man's chest then shoved the falling body out of the way. This was his home. There could be no better place to die.

------◆◆●◆◆------

From the shadows of the trees, Jaëger watched as the Irish charged Northshire's defenders. O'Malley's men had done unexpectedly well, using the advantage of surprise with deadly efficiency. Unfortunately for the Irish, their legendary luck was about to run out.

He focused on the man in the tan uniform who had seized command as though he were born to it. No doubt this was Thomas Steele's son, Malcolm. With a shake of his head, Jaëger slipped through the shadows toward his prey who had been spotted in the village. There was no need to remain to see the outcome.

The Irish had decimated two of Malcolm's three divisions while losing less than a quarter of their own men. But that was about to change. Malcolm's decision to split his third force in half was an excellent strategy. It would divide the attention of the invading force, allowing him to maximize inflicted casualties while minimizing the killing power of the Irish grenades. The battle for Northshire was as good as done.

But the real battle wasn't one of flesh and bone; it was an unseen struggle between two powers that sought to shape the destiny of mankind. While some might condemn what he was about to do, today's events were a key part of history's march.

Jaëger halted, molding his body into the shadows as the first line of fleeing villagers spilled past the iron gate at the end of the road. Leila, holding two children by the hands, led the group in a running crouch. Releasing them, she glanced over her shoulder, directing the human flood away from the fighting and around the edge of the clearing toward the far side of the castle.

Jaëger slipped closer to the edge of the tree line, moving with sinuous grace toward the refugees. By this time Leila was almost out of sight but he was not worried. Why chase after her when she would come to him? When the crowd was almost within reach he froze, waiting for the perfect moment to pounce.

His lips curved upward in a vicious smile as a little girl, who wandered a few steps behind her mother, came into view. With one grubby paw in her mouth and clutching her teddy in the other, she could neither fight nor scream. Jaëger's gaze flickered to the harried mother who staggered ahead, carrying an infant on each arm.

The woman glanced over her shoulder. "Hurry Edna, keep up with Mummy!"

The little girl tottered faster and the mother turned around, shifting to protect her screaming babies from the flying shrapnel and bullets that sped by.

A whisper of wind.

Two swift movements.

"Keep up, Edna. Come on!" The woman's head whipped over her shoulder. "Ed—" Her eyes bulged in their sockets as she shrieked her daughter's name. "Edna? Edna, where are you?"

Cloaked in the shadows, Jaëger watched as those around the frantic woman dragged her away, still screaming, toward Leila, the castle, and safety.

"Shh." He clamped his hands firmly over the wriggling child's mouth, then pressed his lips against her ear so she could hear him above the thunder of war. "Shh . . . "

With a contented sigh, he withdrew a length of rope from his inner breast pocket, looped it around the child's waist, then glanced at his watch.

3:10 p.m. He closed his eyes, jerking the leash tight around the whimpering child. Within twenty minutes, his son would be avenged.

———————————◆◆●◆▶———————————

Seen from above, the battle unfolding on Northshire reminded Hughes of a painting he had once seen that depicted Napoleon's defeat by the outnumbered British navy near Cape Trafalgar. Then as now, the invaders had advanced in a crushing line, depending on numbers and surprise to bring victory. Then as now, the plan was not working.

Hughes stood on the summit of the hill overlooking an empty Northshire Village. Behind him, sixty British special forces had been joined by ten officers from Sussex County police. They waited in military lorries, guns and small field cannons at the ready.

Through high-powered glasses, Hughes, his second-in-command and the chief inspector, surveyed the butchery below. Thomas's son, Malcolm, had effectively split his outnumbered army in half, sandwiching the men between them and forcing the invading Irish to fight on two fronts. Now, the ground was littered with dead—mostly Sinn Féin from what he could see.

"Sir, permission to advance?" The request came from his lieutenant.

"Advance but do not engage the Irish."

"Do not engage?" The soldier stared at him. "Sir, they are attacking loyal citizens!"

Hughes snorted. "Loyal?" He pressed the binoculars to his eyes, while leaning on his walking stick. He was certain he had seen her. There! He zoomed the lens in to the maximum. A young woman with blonde hair, directed civilian traffic around the side of the castle. She turned, and he caught full sight of her face.

"Loyalty means obeying orders." Grunting, he lowered the lens. "Now, I repeat, advance but *do not* engage the Sinn Féin. If there are any survivors, I want them arrested and brought in for questioning. Drive me in and have thirty men form a perimeter. No one goes in or out. Is that understood?"

"Sir!" His lieutenant snapped out a salute.

Hughes stumped to the car and dropped into the seat. Coming to Northshire had been a gamble but, despite the obvious attack on national security, the Irish invasion couldn't be used to justify his claims that Thomas was collaborating with the Germans. He needed indisputable evidence. If he could prove the blonde woman was indeed his former maid . . .

He ran his fingers over his beardless chin as the car rolled down the hill toward the gate. This time, it would take more than a lucky stroke to bring down a giant. But, like David of old, he *would* succeed.

◆◆●◆◆

"Come on ,Martha, we're nearly there!" Leila grabbed the old woman's arm, pushing her through the side entrance of the ancient castle. Inside, Greyson waited, a benign smile on his peaceful face. "Come in, come in!" His voice was cheerful as though he were welcoming the entire village to a picnic instead of helping them escape a wholesale invasion. He directed them up the narrow, winding staircase that led to the heart of Thomas's study through the secret passage.

"Keep them moving, Greyson." Leila drew her revolver. "I need to be with my husband."

Her heart hammering as loudly as the crackling firearms, Leila swung around the side of the castle and stole forward. The grassy open area bordering the cobblestone courtyard had become a killing field. Bodies littered the ground and holes, gouged out by the deadly grenades, stared up at her like empty eye sockets.

She heard Malcolm's voice ringing out over the clamor of battle before she saw him. "Regroup!"

Mud and gore spattered his uniform. A flash spouted from his rifle and she saw another invader fall. "With me!" He flung the rifle to one side and jerked his revolver from its holster. With a roar, both halves of the remaining Northshire guards streamed forward, following Malcolm as he drove the Irish back down the long lane.

Is this what he's like in battle? Leila stood with stalled breath. He was magnificent.

She moved forward, wanting to be with him, but stopped short. Malcolm needed this victory, not only to show the tenants of Northshire that he was worthy of their trust, but also to prove to himself that he was worthy of his father's name.

She breathed a prayer, turning to rejoin Greyson. "God, protect him. Be his shield."

As she rounded the corner, a keening wail grabbed her heart. "Edna, m-my Edna!" A woman from the village staggered out of the castle, clutching two squalling infants to her chest.

"What's happened?" Leila hurried over.

"Please you must help me! My daughter." The woman jerked her chin toward the woods. "S-she was there one minute and then she just disappeared!"

Leila glanced over her shoulder, frowning. "Go inside quickly with the others. I'll go search and let you know what I find." She spun the woman around and pushed her gently toward the butler.

"If Malcolm returns before I do, Greyson"—she slipped a few cartridges into her Luger—"tell him what's happened."

"As you wish." Greyson dipped his head, but then laid a restraining hand on her arm. "Will you not take someone with you? The men from the village, perhaps?"

She hesitated then shook her head. "I can't." Leila leaned closer and whispered, "Leonard was a German agent. I don't know who else I can trust." Straightening, she forced a smile. "I'll be fine, Greyson. Don't worry."

Then, without another word, she slipped through the door then glided into the woods.

———◆●◆———

The black Rolls Royce slid through the wrought-iron gate, followed by the rumbling lorries that were crammed with soldiers. Hughes's eyes narrowed as he spied the remains of a burnt-out shack. This had to be where the alleged German had launched his one-man invasion of Northshire last year, burning much of the estate to the ground. Once again, violence stalked Thomas's estate.

Coincidence? Hughes snorted. There was no such a thing in his world.

"Stop here." He opened the door and struggled upright. *What if Thomas was trying to conceal something in this wreck of a building?*

The man was a master strategist. It would not be too much of a stretch to conceal condemning evidence beneath the wreckage of a building supposedly attacked by the enemy.

Hughes motioned for his second-in-command to join him. "It sounds like the battle is coming this way. Have your men form a defensive line there"—he gestured with his walking stick—"then a second line of defense outside the gate in case any try to escape through the woods. I want every man jack of them taken. Is that understood?"

"Understood, sir."

"Right then, have two men accompany me inside this wreck, sharpish." Without waiting on a response, Hughes moved inside the shack, his wooden prosthesis scraping on the ground. He ducked as he passed below the sagging door.

"Why, Thomas?" The spymaster glanced around the room. Aside from a bench and a few pieces of farming equipment, it was largely empty. "Why not destroy it all and rebuild?"

Hughes stepped forward, eyes probing every corner of the room. He turned at the scrape of boots on wood behind him. "You lot. Help me look and be quick about it."

The soldiers exchanged puzzled glances. "Look for what, sir?"

"Evidence, you blithering idiots!" He pulled in a deep breath, forcing an atmosphere of calm. They had no idea how much he had at stake. "Anything out of the ordinary, anything remotely suspicious."

With raised eyebrows and ridiculous shrugs, they moved off.

A small window let some light into the tiny shack. Hughes ran a finger over the sill, noticing that the dust was minimal. Someone had been here and recently. His frown deepened. "What are you hiding from me, Thomas?"

Moving slowly, he stepped into the middle of the room. *Pock, pock.* Hughes froze then looked downward. His wooden leg had produced a hollow sound when it struck the floor, not the solid tone that would accompany wooden slats on the ground. Were it not for the prosthesis, he would have noticed nothing.

"Of course!" He gestured to a faded rug that covered a large portion of the flooring. "Move this rug."

When the rug was pulled back, Hughes pointed to a barely visible trap door. "Open it."

The first soldier tugged hard. "It's locked, sir."

"And that is a problem?" Hughes leaned forward with a snarl. "You're a British soldier. Get it open!"

One minute later, the opening revealed the dim outline of a stairway.

"You." Hughes gripped the shoulder of the man nearest him. "Get down there."

He waited for precisely thirty-five seconds, a sheen of sweat dotting his brow. "Well, what do you see?"

"Equipment, sir." The surprise in the soldier's voice was obvious. "Radio equipment and . . . writing in some sort of code!"

"Ah!" A smile cracked Hughes's thin lips. "Tell me, what language is it in?" He knew what the answer would be before the soldier's voice wafted up the stairs.

"Sir! I-it's in German!"

Malcolm lifted his fist as the retreating Irish pounded down the path toward Northshire gate.

"Halt!" He thrust a hand in the air. Shading his eyes, he peered down the lane. At the end of the path waited more soldiers in black uniforms, like those worn by the panting men behind him.

A shiver slid down his spine.

Irish reinforcements?

But the remaining Sinn Féin who fled from his troops seemed just as confused by the sudden appearance of the black-clad militia as he was.

"Sinn Féin, surrender your weapons or die where you stand!" Dozens of rifles swung upward toward the defeated Irish.

Malcolm wiped at a stream of blood that dripped from a gash above his eyebrow. None of the Irishmen moved.

"I repeat!" A thin officer stepped forward, gun at the ready. "Lay down your arms or die. Now!"

"Sons of Ireland." A burly giant stepped forward, clutching a shotgun in his hands. He turned, and Malcolm caught a glimpse of his face. Blood from gashes along his bearded cheek and massive chest did nothing to hide the pride that shone from his eyes. "Today we've struck a blow for freedom that'll not be forgotten." He swung his arms wide. "Who'll stand up for us?"

"Sinn Féin! We ourselves!" The answering cry was exhausted but still fierce. "Sinn Féin!"

"Then follow Aengus O'Malley once more. For the glory of Erin!" Pumping his shotgun, the Irishman charged the waiting soldiers, followed by the ragged remnants of his band.

"Fire!" The officer chopped downward.

Malcolm watched in mute horror as British machine guns ripped the advancing line of rebels to shreds. *Ratatat! Ratatat!* Dark blood spattered the brightly colored Irish flag as the last of the Sinn Féin poured his life out upon the ground.

An eerie silence hung as heavy as the gun smoke that drifted across the long stretch of road. It was the silence of men who faced the evil of their deeds. Malcolm advanced cautiously, his revolver dangling loosely between his fingers. "I am Sergeant Malcolm Steele, sir."

"Yes, Steele, we know who you are." This voice came from within the shack.

Malcolm pivoted to his right as an old man with a wooden leg stumped toward him.

"Robert Hughes, head of British Intelligence."

Malcolm stiffened.

"Ah . . . I see my reputation precedes me. Well, well." Hughes shuffled closer. "Today is quite a day, isn't it? Your last day on leave and your castle is assaulted by rebel Irish."

"How—"

"How do I know that you're late for your 15:00 train to Calais? Because I take great interest in your family, boy." Hughes rapped the side of the closest lorry. "And, now that I've obtained evidence of your father's collusion with the Germans, my interest in your family has grown by leaps and bounds."

"Collusion?" Malcolm felt the back of his neck begin to burn. "You call Thomas Steele a traitor? In his own home?" He took a threatening step forward and found himself confronted by a row of cocked rifles.

"But of course," Hughes said simply. "Perhaps you'd prefer another word? Rebel? *Judas*?" A cold smile tugged at the corners of his lips. "What else would you call a man that transmits secret information to the enemy? What else would you call a man who *murders* British military personnel in the line of duty? What else would you call a man who knowingly shelters a German spy? Oh, did I mention that the spy happens to be his daughter-in-law?"

A rush of fear made Malcolm's throat tight. "Where's my wife? What have you done with her?"

"Nothing. At least, not yet."

Hughes pointed toward the castle. "Lieutenant take one full brigade of soldiers and find her. Hold someone hostage if you must."

"Don't come any closer!" Panic coiled around in Malcolm's gut. This cretin had somehow discovered Leila's decoding lair and mistaken it for a tool to collaborate with the enemy. How could he explain? Anything he said would only further incriminate his father or Leila. "Stand down!"

Hughes scoffed. "Do you honestly think that the men behind you will fire on their own? Have a care, Steele, before you too end up arrested. Let my men do their duty."

He jerked his chin upward and his soldiers filed past Malcolm at a jog.

Jabbing Malcolm's chest with his stick, Hughes said, "What I saw today was rather impressive, I must admit. You've obviously earned that Victoria Cross."

Malcolm was silent.

"Somehow, I doubt that your self-control is as impressive, however. Your reputation with the ladies makes me doubt your ability to collaborate with your father. You couldn't keep a secret from the first harlot who crossed your path. All the same"—Hughes motioned to a nearby soldier—"restrain him."

Malcolm lashed out, but resistance was futile. Within moments, his hands were secured behind his back and he was shoved against the lorry with a rifle pressed against the base of his skull.

A few minutes later, the lieutenant returned. He saluted crisply then said, "The suspect is in the woods sir. One of the women said she'd gone to look for a lost child."

Malcolm let out a muffled groan.

"Lieutenant," Hughes spoke in terse, clear tones. "Take fifty men and comb through these woods. No matter where she is, I want her found!"

She was coming, wending her way through the brush with the skill of an accomplished hunter. And, in a sense, that is what Leila had become: a woman who sought to escape the righteous punishment for her crimes. But the sins of her past were too powerful to flee. There was only one escape, one absolution. And he would give it to her. He was her accuser, her judge—and her executioner.

Jaëger peeked over his shoulder, squinting as the afternoon sunlight blazed through a gap in the canopy of trees. He then leaned backward, waiting with a patience born of experience. He had chosen the site for his trap carefully. The afternoon sun would be in Leila's eyes, preventing her from seeing the rope that coiled around the child's waist until it was too late.

Leila paused, scanned the woods, moved forward three paces, then paused again. He could not help but admire the finesse of her movements. The soldier in him almost regretted eliminating such talent. But the father in him held up a mental image of his son, lying sprawled upon the ground with two bullets in his chest.

"Mummy's waiting, little one." He pulled off the gag that bound the child's mouth, then as her wails filled the air, Jaëger stealthily circled off a hundred yards to the north, pausing when he stood to Leila's right. He breathed deep, calming the surge of adrenaline that flooded his being.

Come, Leila. Time to die.

Her head jerked upright at the noise, then she took a few steps forward, crouching low in the brush. The sobbing child staggered forward, arms outstretched, and Leila straightened.

"Come, Edna." She held out her arms, but the girl remained where she was. She had gone as far as the cord would allow and stood, bleating like a lost lamb.

Leila laid her Luger on a rock and picked her way around the loose tree roots. "It's all right, it's all right. Come on, I'll take you to Mummy."

"I'm afraid you'll find that rather difficult to do. The dead don't go very far."

As expected, Leila didn't freeze or look behind her. She threw herself to one side in a roll, hands reaching for her gun.

But Jaëger was there before her. Detaching himself from the shadows, he planted one foot on the weapon while pointing his own between her eyes, eyes that were wide with incredulity.

"Werner?" Leila scrambled to her feet, backing away until she stood next to the little girl. She pushed the child behind her, offering her body as a shield. "W-why you?"

Jaëger scooped up her gun and closed the gap between them in two strides. "Who else? Didn't I warn you of the penalty of failing me?" The smile faded from his face. "You betrayed us. You *murdered* one of your own."

Leila's eyes blazed. "You mean Christophe? He tried to rape me. I had no choice!"

"And neither do I." His shout rang across the clearing. Chest heaving, he pinned her with a glare. "Christophe was my son!"

She staggered backward, as though he had already shot her. "Your son?"

"Murdered. By your hand."

"I didn't know—"

"Does that make a difference?" He slapped her hard, whipping the pistol across her face. "Does it?"

"Of course!"

"You know too much to live. You have done too much evil to be forgiven."

Leila pressed a palm to her bruised face. "Let the child go, Jaëger. She has nothing to do with this."

"As if I care. Kill two for the price of one." He pressed the revolver in his right hand against her forehead. "How fitting. This is how we met. You were my prisoner and I had a gun to your head." His lips curled in a feral snarl. "If I could have seen the future, I would have pulled the trigger."

"You'll never win." She held his gaze. "You know it's true. It's taken too long to bring me down. The kaiser will never trust you again."

He made a choking sound. "In the name of His Imperial and Royal Majesty, Wilhelm II"—his finger curled around the trigger—"I sentence you to death!"

Chapter 19

July 1917. Woods bordering Northshire Estate.

The men prowled through the woods, picking their way through the undergrowth with professional silence. Hughes's lieutenant had spread his men in a wide arc in hopes of picking up their quarry's trail sooner. They had not gone more than half a mile when the gleam of light on metal caught his eye.

He lifted his hand, signaling a halt, then motioned for three of his men to accompany him. Wending their way forward in a half-crouch, they climbed up a small hill that overlooked a narrow clearing in the trees then pressed their bodies against the damp earth. Sunlight streamed through a hole in the tree line, glinting off the barrel of a gun—a gun pressed against the forehead of a young, attractive blonde.

Exchanging a glance with the men who lay on either side of him, the lieutenant lifted his rifle, an Enfield equipped with a sniper's scope, into position, pulling the well-oiled bolt into place. The men on either side of him did the same.

"Follow my lead." He whispered the words, pressing the scope to his right eye.

"I sentence you to death!" The executioner's voice rang out across the clearing and, without another second's hesitation, the lieutenant pulled the trigger.

Werner lurched forward with a sharp cry as a bullet plowed into his right thigh. Seizing the unexpected distraction, Leila threw herself to one side as Werner's own bullet bit into the bark of the tree where her head had been a second before. Landing hard on her side, she lashed out with her right ankle, hooking it behind his heel and kicking outward just as he pulled the trigger on the second gun.

He flipped backward, crashing to the floor, and the bullet flew wide. Werner twisted with a muted cry of rage and bit off another shot. Leila rolled to her right, letting the ball fly over her, then grabbed the hysterical Edna and crawled behind the tree trunk. The rope that tied the screaming child to the tree was just long enough to reach the other side.

"Shhh." Leila kissed the top of Edna's matted hair. "It's all right, love."

"Drop your weapons!" The cry rang across the clearing from the ridge. "Now!"

Leila sneaked a peek around the tree to see dozens of uniformed men pouring into the clearing, guns pointed toward the German spy who staggered to his feet. Werner whirled toward her, guns in hand, but another shot rang out, laying him prostrate on the forest floor.

She pulled Edna close. The soldiers' black uniforms identified them as British Special Forces, the same branch of military that Thomas had hired to guard the Estate. But none of these men looked familiar and it was obvious that she, not Werner, was the one they sought. *Why me?*

There was only one possibility. Her breath came heavy as though someone had dropped an invisible stone on her chest.

"Don't cry, Edna." Smudges of dirt covered the child's wet cheeks and Leila wiped them away with her sleeve. "I'll get you to your mother, I promise."

Then, swallowing hard, she stepped around the tree with hands upraised. Into the ring of rifles.

———— ◆◆●◆▶ ————

Jenny moved through the rows of displaced villagers that crowded the inside of Northshire's ballroom, offering watery soup and words of comfort. But, although she offered smiles of reassurance, the knot inside her stomach seemed to grow with every minute that ticked by.

"Don't fret, Jenny. She'll be back soon." Greyson's soothing voice sounded behind her.

Turning, Jenny bobbed out a quick curtsey. "Um, could I have a word Mr. Greyson?"

He took her elbow, leading her out of earshot of those nearby.

"Somethin' is wrong, Mr. Greyson." Jenny wrung her hands together, throwing aside the mask of calm. "Soldiers brought that little girl, Edna, back to her mum, but Her Ladyship wasn't with them. Cook says she heard shots being fired from the woods. What if she's been hurt or . . . ?"

Greyson sighed. "I share your concerns, Jenny, however it will do no one any good to rush into the fray armed with only anxiety."

"What are you sayin', Mr. Greyson?" Jenny blinked at him. "That we should attack the lot of them? Soldiers?"

"No, I'm saying that we must have faith. You remain here and take care of these good people while I investigate."

Jenny's brow furrowed. "With respect I'm Her Ladyship's personal maid. If she needed anythin', women's things I mean, you would be rather uncomfortable. Besides . . . " She fell silent as heat flooded her cheeks.

"What is it?" Greyson's eyes probed her face.

Jenny cleared her throat. "I-it's not my place to say. Just that, as a woman, a-a lady's maid, I mean, you notice certain things."

"Certain things." Greyson leaned forward, placing his face only inches from her own. "What kind of things?"

"Well, erm, things that only a . . . woman would understand, Mr. Greyson." The maid cringed, hoping he wouldn't ask her to say more.

"Are you saying . . . ?"

"I can't say for sure. It's too soon for anythin' definite. I doubt she's even certain herself. She hasn't told me anythin' and if she'd said aught to Lord Malcolm, no doubt we'd all have heard about it by now."

"Dear God!" Straightening, Greyson rubbed his hand over his mouth. "Right," he said after a moment. "Go to the gate and see if she needs you. There are a lot of soldiers outside, so do be careful."

With a nod, Jenny squeezed his arm. "Thank you."

Hughes tapped Malcolm lightly on the shoulder with his walking stick. "I believe that woman in handcuffs is your wife." To the soldiers that guarded Malcolm, "Turn him around."

When he saw her, Malcolm's heart lurched. "Leila!" Pale and spattered with mud, she was surrounded by fifty men who held rifles at the ready, as though she alone had the power to destroy them all.

A purpling bruise across her face made him lunge forward, struggling against his bonds. "Let her go, Hughes. She's done nothing to deserve this."

Hughes ignored him, waiting until the platoon of soldiers shoved Leila forward before speaking. A dozen trained rifles on her while the rest secured another prisoner, a man.

"Well, well." Hughes forced her chin upright with the end of his stick. "Leila Durand, Leila Steele, Annabelle Durand . . . no matter what name you use, there's only one word to describe you—spy."

Leila did not respond.

"What? Nothing to say?"

"Why is my husband bound?"

"Ah, yes, the husband." Hughes's lips curved up in a smile. "Tell me, Leila, was he your accomplice or was he really just stupid enough to marry you without knowing what you really are?"

"He is neither stupid nor ignorant." Her green eyes flashed like lightning in a summer storm. "But he is innocent of any wrong."

"So, you admit that you are guilty?"

"Guilty? If love is a crime, then yes, I am the worst of criminals. I am guilty of loving my husband and"—her breath caught in her throat—"the people of Northshire."

Hughes thrust his face inches from her own. "We'll see just how strong that love is, my dear." Pivoting, he turned to the other prisoner, a middle-aged man whose weight was supported by two officers. His teeth were clenched and both legs of his pants oozed blood.

"And who is this?"

Hughes's lieutenant spoke up. "We found him in the woods, sir. He was about to execute this woman."

"Really?" Hughes's gaze shifted from one prisoner to the other then he slithered closer to the wounded man. "And why would you do that?"

A slight groan escaped the prisoner's lips, but he did not respond as he glared at the Englishman.

"Your name." Hughes leaned closer.

No response.

"Answer me!" Bracing himself, Hughes whipped the back of the prisoner's wounded legs with his walking stick.

Another groan passed through gritted teeth.

Pivoting back to Leila, Hughes said, "You obviously know who and what he is. Talk."

"I will say nothing unless my husband is released."

"You are in no position to bargain!" He pulled a gun from his pocket and held it level with Malcolm's eyes. "Who is the man?"

"Don't say anything, Leila." Malcom struggled against his bonds. He would not have her condemn herself for his sake. "Just keep silent."

"Shut it!" Hughes shoved the muzzle of the gun underneath Malcolm's chin then glared over his shoulder at her. "Three seconds . . . two seconds . . . " He cocked the revolver. "One s—"

"Stop!" Leila staggered forward, cuffed arms outstretched in a pleading gesture. "Just . . . stop! His name is Werner Jaëger and he is the head of Abteilung 3B."

The spymaster's eyebrows hiked together. "German military intelligence?" He strode toward Werner and stared deep into his eyes. "Operating under my very nose. How daring of you."

"It wasn't even . . . difficult." The German spymaster's voice was a haggard rasp.

"Since you're in chains, old chap, I'd say it was difficult indeed." Releasing his hold, Hughes sniffed and backed away. "Why did he want to kill you?"

"Because my love for my husband is greater than my love for my country."

Pressing his monocle against his eye as though the brass-rimmed eyepiece would better enable him to see the truth, Hughes studied Leila's face for several moments. Then he scoffed. "Do you take me for a fool? You expect me to believe your little love story?" He released the monocle, letting it catapult downward and spin on its chain like a condemned man at the end of a noose. "Our interrogation team will ferret out the truth. Lieutenant!"

"Sir!"

"Bring the prisoners back to London. We'll hold them in separate cells in the Tower."

"And this one, sir?" He thrust Malcolm forward.

"This tomcat?" Hughes flicked his hand in a dismissive gesture. "Let him go back to the killing fields where he can actually do something useful."

As soon as his bonds were removed, Malcolm shoved his captors aside. "You're making a mistake, Hughes. My wife is innocent. I won't rest until she's free."

"Is that so? Then I'm afraid you'll never sleep again." The spymaster bared his teeth in a snarl. "She is an enemy agent, captured while operating on British soil. I'm going to interrogate her. A jury will try her." He thumped his stick against Malcolm's heaving chest. "And then a firing squad will kill her."

Malcolm lunged forward but Hughes's pistol, jabbing hard against his belly, pulled him up short. "Easy, easy, young man. I'm being rather generous in sending you back to die. I could just as easily kill you here. But our country needs you. Take your anger out on the Huns." He spit on Leila's feet. "After all, it's their fault we're at war."

Every fiber of Malcolm's body itched to tear the man in front of him to shreds. But that was madness. And as long as she lived, he couldn't afford to die. He pulled in a deep breath, trying to regain a sense of calm. "At least give us time to say goodbye."

Hughes backed away, slipping his revolver into its holster. "Two minutes." He snapped his fingers. "Lieutenant, keep your guns on them."

The soldiers panned out in a large circle with Leila and Malcolm at its center. Their cocked rifles were trained on the couple who, only three weeks ago, had celebrated their love and the rebirth of their marriage.

Malcolm shuffled forward, eyes locked on the woman he loved more than life. Her hands were still bound and her hair, knotted and snarled with twigs and branches, spilled around her face. She had never looked more beautiful.

Reaching out, he clasped her in his arms, tenderly kissing away the tears that pooled down her cheeks. "I won't stop fighting. I'll find a way—a lawyer, an army, something."

"Don't, Malcolm." Leila leaned against his chest, her fingers gently pressing against him. "Don't give them a reason to kill you too."

His muscles tensed as he wiped the corners of his eyes with the heel of his palm. "I can't let them murder you, Leila. What good is life without you? It took me years to realize that." His eyes misted. "I love you."

"And I love you too, but what good will your death do to any of us?" She leaned her forehead against his own. "Northshire needs you, Malcolm. The tenants, the land, they'll need you more than ever now."

"Leila." His voice broke as he whispered her name. "Tell them everything. Tell them about the plot. Maybe they'll pardon you or put you on some sort of parole."

She shook her head, cradling his chin between her manacled hands. "It's no use, Malcolm. This isn't about justice. It's about Hughes's reputation. He can't afford to have me free. Think of what could happen to his status if the people knew that the head of Secret Intelligence had been duped into hiring an enemy agent as his maid! He'd lose everything."

"But—"

Looping both hands around his neck, Leila silenced him with a lingering kiss. Then she pulled back. "You're the best thing that's ever happened to me."

Emotion choked him. "This isn't the end, Leila. I-I don't know much, but I can't believe God would bring us together just to rip us apart!"

"We'll never be apart, Malcolm, not anymore." A frown appeared on her silken brow. "But promise me you won't worry."

"I can't promise that!"

"You need to focus on staying alive, Malcolm. You know that on the battlefield, distractions can be fatal. Please . . . " She pulled him closer. "I can't be the cause of your death."

He traced her chin with the ball of his thumb. "This is the way it should've been the first time I left for war."

"But we made it here at last." A faint smile tugged at her lips. "No regrets. No looking back."

Breathing deep, he inhaled her scent, treasuring it as though it were life itself. "I'll write to you as often as I can."

"I doubt they'll let me get mail in the Tower."

"No." He gripped her arms, his eyes boring into her own. "I'll write to you here, at Northshire. One day you'll come home and you'll see a pile of letters waiting for you in our bedroom. It's a sign that I believe in miracles."

Leila traced his face with her fingers. "I—"

"Time's up!" Hughes's harsh voice sliced through Malcom's heart. Two of his men held Malcolm back while they dragged Leila into the lorry.

"Let her go." He writhed in their grasp. "I said, let her go!"

Hughes's laughter mocked him. "I really don't care."

"Lady Steele!"

Hughes slammed his cane against the ground, then threw his hands in the air. "What is it, now?"

He whirled around as Jenny hurried toward Leila. "Who are you and what do you want?"

Jenny glared at him, fingers splayed against her chest, as she struggled to catch her breath. "I-I'm her Ladyship's personal servant, Jenny Edwards." Her eyes widened as they flew to the shackled Leila. "You can't take her anywhere without me."

"She's going to die." Hughes's voice was as flat as the ground on which he stood. "You wish to join her?"

Blanching, Jenny raised her chin. "She's done nothin' wrong."

"So I keep hearing. Unfortunately, madam, I don't share your opinion."

"You don't understand." Jenny glowered at him. "There's somethin' you don't know!"

"Really? Do tell."

"I—" Jenny hesitated. "I can't say, not out loud at least."

"Look, woman, I have no time for this excessive display of devotion. Either tell me what you have come to say or get out of my way!"

Malcolm felt the ball of dread in his gut tighten as Jenny stood on her tiptoes and whispered something in Hughes's ear.

What Jenny could possibly have to say to that vicious beast, he couldn't imagine. He only hoped that whatever it was, it would keep his wife alive until something could be done.

"You don't say!" Hughes straightened, his eyes flickering from Leila to Malcolm. "How fortuitous."

"Fortuitous?" Jenny stared at him, mouth agape. "But—"

Hughes silenced her with a hard glare. "Your usefulness has expired. Leave. Now!"

The maid staggered backward as though he had slapped her. "I don't understand. You're still going to take her?"

Ignoring her, Hughes stumped toward his vehicle. "We're done here. Lieutenant, you know your orders."

"Leila." Malcolm's shout rang out across the space between them as the rumbling lorries followed the gleaming black Rolls Royce out of the gate. "I won't stop fighting. I won't—"

Then the butt of a rifle slammed into his temple and it seemed that the ground leapt up to meet him. He felt himself falling as though his legs could no longer bear the weight of the grief that pressed upon his shoulders.

God, save my wife.

Black.

Chapter 20

July 1917. The London Tower, Great Britain.

Werner sat with hands bound, glaring up at his captor, the British scourge, Sir Robert Hughes. It had been three days since Hughes had dragged him to the London Tower, a notorious prison that overlooked the River Thames. Not that he had been able to enjoy the view. It had been thirty-six hours of brutal interrogation, sleep deprivation, and endless pain. His tongue gingerly probed the bloodied mass that lined his jawline.

"I see that we'll get nothing from you." Hughes spoke slowly as though admitting defeat was something he had never done until this moment. "But I don't want to kill you. I'm sure we'll have better luck with your minion, Leila."

Werner guffawed, a low, pain-soaked sound that passed through broken lips. "Good . . . luck."

"What do you mean?"

"She will never b-break."

Hughes eyed him for a long moment. The two men were alone in the room, but Werner knew from the relaxed posture of the cripple before him that, on the other side of the door, soldiers waited, ready to kill him at a moment's notice. He was somewhere deep underground. At times the gentle *slush* of flowing water echoed through his subterranean cell, leading him to believe that a part of the river had been diverted into the prison itself.

There were no windows and a solitary electric bulb was the only source of light in the small, cramped room. He sat backward on a chair, with both hands and legs handcuffed and bolted to the cement floor. Hughes was confident, that much was obvious, but he was also careful which meant that he considered Werner a threat.

Werner's eyes flickered closed. He would not survive this defeat. As much as it galled him to admit it, Leila had been right. Even if he did make it back to Germany, the reputation he had cultivated over three decades was now ruined beyond repair. He had only one goal now. To destroy the woman who had destroyed his world.

At all costs, he must convince the man who scrutinized him as though he were a three-headed horse, that Leila was still a loyal German agent instead of one who had defected. If he could achieve this last victory, Hughes would execute Leila instead of recruiting her for the British cause.

Leila had to die. Only then could he die in peace. Only then would his son be able to rest in peace.

"I assume there's a reason you believe so much in the girl." Hughes narrowed his eyes. "You know, we are alike in some ways. We are both good judges of character, both loyal to the death. And we both understand that one mistake could lead to the collapse of our government."

He gestured toward Werner's chains. "Yet you misjudged her. Misjudged her to the point that you felt compelled to come and execute her yourself." He tutted as he moved closer, the strands of his gray hair barely visible in the dim light. "What's that all about, eh?"

Werner was silent. The cards had to be played perfectly to defeat a mind as cunning as the one before him. Hughes needed to believe that he was in control of this little charade.

"Nothing to say?" He withdrew a revolver from the inner pocket of his blue uniform and lined it up with Werner's eyes. "What about now?"

"Kill me," Werner growled, "and the truth dies with me."

"Understood." After eyeing him for another moment, Hughes put the gun away. "So what would a man like you fear more than death?"

Silence filled the small room, a silence that was abruptly broken by the *snap* of Hughes's fingers. "Failure. That is what you fear. You failed to kill her and, in so doing, failed your Kaiser."

Werner waited, anticipation hammering past the pain that wracked his body.

"Since you won't give in to torture, you're of no use to me. At least not here."

"What do you . . . mean?"

Hughes slid a small chair, identical to the one to which Werner was bound, from the corner of the room. "I mean," he said, sinking into the chair with a sigh, "that your government will pay dearly to have you back. Alive."

A surge of genuine fear momentarily drove the pain from Werner's mind. If he were killed here, the kaiser would never learn the true extent of his failure. He would die alone and forgotten. But if he were handed over to his own people, his death would be one of humiliation and torture.

He felt a muscle jerk in his jaw, a subtle movement that betrayed the one emotion he could still feel.

"Yes." Hughes leaned forward, eyes boring into Werner's face. "You're afraid of that, aren't you?"

"I fear nothing." Werner spit the words out, knowing before they left his bloody lips that Hughes would see through the lie.

"Of course not." A dry laugh escaped the Englishman's lips. "I'm sure old Willy would be more than happy to give up a hundred British prisoners of war in exchange for his top dog." He shrugged. "You failed him, so it is only right that you face the consequences in Germany. Don't you think so, old chap?"

Despite the fear that clouded his thoughts, Werner sensed the glimmer of opportunity. Hughes knew he was afraid. With the threat of repatriation hanging over his shoulders, whatever Werner confessed now would be much more believable.

He blinked, his agile mind piecing together a story that was credible yet incriminatory, a story that would be enough to send his former protégée to her death. "Unless?"

"Have you gone barmy? Unless you tell me why you were after one of your own, of course!" Hughes patted the pocket that held his revolver. "The truth now, mind you. If you tell me, I'll be merciful and kill you with a clean bullet. If not, I'll give you up to your own people in exchange for a hundred of my own."

"I . . . " Werner stalled, sensing that the moment wasn't just right. Not yet. "No. I can't say." He let his head sag.

"Very well." The scrape of the chair told him the British spymaster had risen. "I'll have the lads send you to the hot house below then. Tell old Satan that his son, the kaiser, looks just like him, will you?"

"Wait!" Werner looked up.

Flicking his walking stick against his palm, Hughes paused at the door and turned back toward him. "Change of heart?"

"I want your word. You will not give me up."

"I give you my solemn oath." Hughes's eyes were like flint.

Werner met his gaze. Could he trust him? *No.* Did he have a choice? *No.* But none of that mattered now. His one objective goal was to manipulate this man so that Leila would be destroyed. He would take her down with him. Whatever else happened was moot.

With a slow nod, Werner sucked in a breath and spun his lie. "I am no longer head of Department 3B. Two years ago, the kaiser replaced me with another. He felt that . . . I would be better placed in the field." He paused, catching his breath. Speech was an effort. "The execution that your men saw . . . was all an act, a charade so you would think that Leila betrayed us. We . . . wanted you to use her as one . . . of your own agents so we could destroy you . . . from within."

"By feeding us false intelligence." Hughes gave a slow nod. "And Kaiser Wilhelm was willing to sacrifice you to make this happen?"

"Wouldn't King George do the same with you?

Hughes did not respond. "Go on."

"The truth is . . . " Werner clinched his jaw, ignoring the pain the action produced. Hughes had to be convinced that this pseudo-confession was born of desperation—which in fact it was.

"Leila, Thomas Steele, and some of his servants are involved in a much larger plot, one that will ensure my country's victory. Leila's father-in-law sheltered her to win the kaiser's favor. He expects land and power in exchange."

"I see." Hughes stroked his chin.

The prisoner's chains rattled as he wiped his brow. "Leila is . . . one of the best I have ever trained. Not even her husband knows . . . the truth."

Hughes considered this for a long moment. "Sir Thomas is involved, you say. Who else?"

"No one. No one else knows." Werner shook his head. "I have kept my promise. Please." He lifted his shackled wrists as though praying. "Keep your promise. Kill me."

"I'm afraid that's not possible." Turning, Hughes rapped on the door with his stick. It flew open and teams of soldiers poured into the room, guns trained on the chained prisoner.

"What are you doing?" Werner's eyes darted from Hughes to the men who unshackled him and pulled him upright.

"You may no longer be the head of German military intelligence but your kaiser is very keen on having you back. You see, his general and I have been negotiating terms. We reached an accord last evening. One hundred prisoners of war will be released in exchange for your sorry face."

Chills coursed through Werner's body. "B-but your word." He strained against the men who held him tightly. "You gave your word!"

"Really?" Hughes scratched his temple with his finger. "Can't seem to remember that, actually. But, even if I did, who could trust the word of a spy?"

He snapped his fingers and the men surrounding Werner shoved him forward. "Get him ready to travel. The exchange takes place in the Netherlands in a week."

Chapter 21

Meier Farm near Münster, Germany. July 1917.

The sweltering rays of the summer sun beat down on Burkhard Meier's broad back as he hefted another block of harvested peat onto the bed of his white, open-backed lorry. He called it a lorry, but the well-used vehicle was nothing more than a farm tractor to which he had attached the carriage of a sturdy wagon. In times like these, he counted himself lucky to have any kind of motorized vehicle on his property at all. Everything with mechanized wheels had been commandeered by the kaiser's hordes and carted off to the war zones that zigzagged across Europe.

Burkard had only been able to keep this relic by convincing Uther, the captain of the local militia that, without it, he couldn't supply his local customers with peat—a key source of fuel.

Grunting, Burkhard straightened, arched his back, and stretched, rolling his shoulders to loosen the knots in his joints. After three years of dehumanizing conflict the majority of Germany's civilians had lost faith in the army's ability to win the war. But Burkhard knew that, whatever the outcome, neither side could truly claim victory. Not when the body of his son, and the bodies of millions of other sons, rotted in mangled pieces on the barren grounds. Death would be the only conqueror.

Shaking his head, the farmer pulled off his hat and ran a hand through his damp, graying hair. His gaze fell on the young man who carved peat out into the square bales that were to be loaded onto the lorry.

Using his sleeve as a towel, Burkhard wiped beads of sweat from his brow. Normally, he wouldn't take such an active role in harvesting the peat. But his real purpose this morning was not to work but to discover the reason for the unspoken tension that simmered between Will and his daughter.

Folding his arms across his chest, Burkhard considered Will as he jabbed a spade into the earthen loam then edged it out into a cube. A blind man could see that Katja and Will were drawn to each other. If he knew more about Will's past, he might be willing to entertain the idea of a relationship between them. God knew he loved the boy like a son. But Will was reluctant to discuss his life in England, and Burkhard, sensing the issue raised painful memories, had never pressed him.

"I think we'll finish this patch today." Burkhard waved to catch Will's attention as he meandered forward. A month ago, he had urged Katja to have a frank conversation with their guest. Something had changed that day.

Perhaps he said he wanted to go home. That was only natural. To a man, being a prisoner was shameful, no matter how comfortable the surroundings. His daughter refused to discuss their conversation but, in the weeks that followed, he had noticed that she avoided speaking to Will—a change that delighted Adele.

Straightening, Will thrust his hoe into the ground and rested his arms on the tip of the smooth wooden handle. He stood a good two inches taller than the farmer and wore dark brown workpants and a loose-fitting cotton shirt that had belonged to Burkhard's son. The only difference between their clothing lay in the suspenders which, for some reason, the younger man refused to wear.

"I don't know." Will shaded his eyes with his palm. "I'd say it'll take at least another day. Those clouds from the west look like they're bringing a thunderstorm."

Burkhard nodded. "There are a lot of storms in the west these days." He let silence fall between them, then added, "But there is hope."

"The Americans?" Will slanted him a curious glance. "I would think that you'd rage at the thought of their entry into the war."

Burkhard affected a pained grimace. "Will, when have you ever known me to 'rage' as you say?"

A smile cracked Will's tanned face. "Not too often. Only when the lorry stops working."

Burkhard chuckled and let an affectionate silence grow between them. Perhaps Will himself was a victory. The corners of his mouth tipped upward. After almost eighteen months as a prisoner of war, Will had managed to put aside his rancid hatred of all things German and understand that evil contaminated all humanity that was as yet unreached by Christ.

Burkhard tugged at his suspenders then let them snap back against his loose, sweat-stained cotton shirt. He suspected that he couldn't take credit for a large part of Will's redemption. That honor belonged to his beautiful daughter, to Katja.

"Look at us! A German and Englishman working together, *laughing* together. That's the hope, Son. Looking to the future." Burkhard jerked his head in the direction of the gathering clouds. "After every storm comes the sunshine."

Will didn't answer, and Burkhard laid a hand on his shoulder. "But that can only happen if we're willing to let go of the past.

Otherwise, we will forever carry our storms in our hearts. We will never experience the power of a new beginning."

"I've changed a lot, I admit it." Will spoke slowly as though each word were carefully weighed in his mind. "I was a prodigal in my own right when I came here."

"You believed in God."

"Yes, but . . . " The soldier's gaze dropped to his calloused hands. "I let hate cloud my judgment, rebelling against the Father's plan of love and brotherhood." He jerked his head up, pinning Burkhard with the intense stare of his brown eyes. "In the end, there's only one true enemy—evil itself."

Burkhard pressed his lips together in a firm line. Yes, here was a victory indeed. But what then was the source of the conflict between Will and Katja?

"So, now that you understand this, are you ready for a new beginning?" Burkhard knew the true meaning of his question would not be lost on Will. There was more at stake here than inspiring words and camaraderie. His daughter's heart hung in the balance and that was a treasure with which he would allow no man to play games.

"I—"

"*Herr* Meier!"

A sour taste filled the back of the farmer's mouth as he recognized the voice of General Uther Klein. The kaiser's regional commander checked in with him each day, holding him accountable for Will's whereabouts. Klein always staggered the times of his visits, allowing Burkhard no time to prepare.

Releasing Will's shoulder, Burkhard turned around slowly and saluted. "General Klein, *guten tag*."

"I am not so sure it *is* a good day, Burkhard." Thrusting his chin upward, Klein clasped his hands behind his back. "You there! Prisoner! Get back to work. This is not a charity, you know."

Twisting to one side, Burkhard watched as Will slammed his hoe into the ground again, cutting into the thick loam as effortlessly as if he were slicing through butter.

"I do not like what I am seeing." Klein cocked his head to one side, indicating that Burkhard should follow as he stepped out of Will's hearing.

"And what is it you see, General?"

"A fellow German—a friend—who is forgetting the natural order of things."

"Natural order?" Burkhard's forehead crinkled. "Of what?"

Klein leaned forward as he tapped the medals decorating the front of his olive-green uniform. "Of war. That man is our prisoner, yet you treat him as though he were your son! He eats with you, sleeps in your home." His eyes took in Burkhard's appearance. "You even dress alike!"

"I have shown him basic kindness, nothing more. He came to my daughter's rescue and I took him in with your permission. Courtesy is still permissible under the law, is it not?"

"Courtesy that he has not refused." Scowling, Klein gestured to the house. "I cannot help but wonder if he is playing some sort of game. Deceiving you, preying upon your emotions in the hope of escaping."

Burkhard fell silent for several long moments. When he spoke, his voice was tight with suppressed anger. "You said that I am your friend, General. If that is the case, why do you question my loyalty to the Fatherland?"

"It's not your loyalty I question; it is your ability to see what's happening before your eyes. *Think,* Burkhard. This man risks his life for your daughter—an enemy. In so doing, he obligates you to open your heart and home to him. He is smart and knows that you will be grateful, *ja?* He is using you, my friend."

"With respect, General Klein, you are wrong if—"

Klein continued as though Burkhard had not spoken, emphasizing each point with a jab of his right index finger into the palm of his left hand.

"You feed him, treat him with respect. You remove his prisoner's uniform and dress him like one of us. Every day he gets a deeper hold over your heart until the day comes where he escapes. Do you even lock his door at night?"

"No. There is no need. I trust him."

"Trust?" Klein jerked his head back. "He is an enemy!"

"He is a good man, Uther. British, yes. Flawed, yes. But a good man nonetheless."

Klein barked out a dry laugh. "I doubt your wife would agree. Does Adele know the risk you are taking?"

"I have told no one of our agreement." Burkhard pulled in a deep breath, held it, then released it slowly. "There is no need to cause my wife any concern."

Clamping his jaw shut, Klein stared down at him. Then he said, "I think, given the circumstances, that it is best I return the prisoner to the common ward."

Burkhard's mouth went dry. "Return him?"

"You are not yourself, my friend. You are blind to the danger he has become. It is best for us both that he be taken off your hands."

Burkhard stepped closer, the sour taste in his mouth evolving into an ache in his heart. "But they'll kill him. When your men aren't looking or during the night, his own people will execute him!"

"And if he escapes, I will have to execute you!" Klein jerked the spiked helmet off his head and slammed it into the curve of his armpit. "Have you thought about what *that* would mean? How could I face Adele or Katja again, knowing that I was responsible for your death?"

"I—"

"It is decided, *Herr* Meier. As regional commander, I am responsible for all prisoners of war near Münster. Yes, the prisoner may die. But I would rather answer to the kaiser for the loss of an enemy than answer to my conscience for the death of a friend."

Burkhard swallowed rapidly, flooded by a growing sense of unease. None of Klein's words had persuaded him that Will was skillfully manipulating his situation to his own advantage, but he was powerless to resist the General's authority. Yet, to send Will back to a certain death would, in itself, be a betrayal. He would need time to broach the subject. To prepare Will for what lay ahead.

"One more week." The words came out as a garbled croak and he had to repeat himself to be understood. "Give me one week. I beg of you."

Klein hesitated a moment, then gave a slow nod. "One week." He turned so that he stood alongside Burkhard, his glare focused on Will who, oblivious to the die that had just been cast against him, continued to stack cubes of peat into neat piles for loading. "It's too bad he's not in the camp near Worms. I hear that the kaiser has agreed to release a hundred British prisoners in some sort of exchange."

Burkhard didn't bother to answer. Whatever was happening in Worms had no bearing on the immediate problem. In his mind's eye he imagined Katja's face when he broke the news.

243

God, what will happen to her if he dies?

"Well, every man must meet his fate." Turning back to Burkhard, Klein said, "There's no guarantee he would've been chosen anyway, even if he was in Worms."

"Yes, yes, you're right. I'm happy those men at least have a chance in surviving this madness."

Klein raised an index finger. "One week, Burkhard. I will check on him as always until that time. If he disappears, you pay with your life. Is that understood?"

Burkhard met his gaze. "Yes."

<hr />

The clucking of hens, made nervous by the coming storm, filled the barn. Katja shooed them into their coop, then turned to grab at a stubborn spotted white pullet who ran past her.

"You too. In with you now." She scooped the squawking bird in her arms then pushed it inside the coop and slid the latch into place. The rumble of distant thunder reverberated through the spacious, hay- strewn barn. Katja picked up a basket of warm eggs and made her way toward the barn's entrance.

The thunder spoke again, louder this time and, as though answering its call, Will stepped through the barn doors. He held a set of tools in his hand—hoe, spade, and shovel—and he set them down in one corner while keeping his eyes on her.

"Hello, Katja."

Whenever she saw him, her first response was always an instinctive glance at her clothes. The toes of dark black boots peeked out from beneath a cream checkered dress whose front was slightly stained from the blackberries she had canned earlier that day.

"Hello, Will." Clutching the basket of eggs to her chest like a shield, she dipped her head and swished forward, giving him as wide a berth as possible.

"Katja, please." Will's hand shot out as she passed him, catching hold of her wrist. His touch was gentle, but she jumped as though she had been burned. "*Talk* to me."

She closed her eyes, shutting down the maelstrom of emotions that swirled within her. When she spoke, her voice was quiet and tight, like a spring coiled under intense pressure. "Let me go, Will."

"Seeing you like this bothers me. You jump like a nervous cat every time I walk into a room. As though something was wrong."

Her eyes snapped open. "But that's just it, Will. I do not want . . . " she faltered. "*We* do not want there to be anything wrong between us."

The soft clucking of the hens seemed deafening in the sudden silence. After a moment, she spoke again.

"This is hard for me—"

"—for us both." He finished her sentence.

"So, please. Just let me go."

Stumbling back a step, Will released her forearm. "Can't things ever be normal between us? I value our friendship."

"Normal?" Katja smiled despite the tears that pricked at the back of her eyes. "I seem to remember your first conscious act being a kiss."

He flushed but returned her smile. "We argued the first time we met. Are things supposed to be that way?"

She laughed despite herself then sobered. "We should stop talking like this. It's dangerous."

Will nodded. "Right. You, um, you better go inside. I'm just going to finish cleaning up before the storm breaks."

"All right." Katja turned but paused at the door. "Will?"

"Yes?"

She pulled in a deep breath. It was so hard to put into words the thoughts and feelings that surged through her mind. The past month had been a nightmare, a living torment in which her mind and body yearned for a man she knew could never be hers.

Each moment with him had seemed a century of self-denial while each moment away from him was an eternity. Life had become a crucifixion of the heart instead of the body. God demanded purity but there were times when all she wanted was to give in to the dark desires that threatened to obliterate all she knew to be right.

She prayed—God knew she prayed—to be free of this relentless temptation. At times she raged at the injustice of it all. Why would God let her feel so strongly for a man beyond her reach?

Will could have preyed upon her emotional vulnerability. She didn't know if he felt as strongly as she did, but so far, he had neither done or said anything that could cause regret. "Thank you."

"For what?"

She breathed out slowly as she turned to face him. "For fighting *with* me and not against me. It's agony to be with you but it would be worse to be apart from you. I-I just want you to know that I'm grateful."

Then, with a tight smile, she turned and fled the storm that threatened to overtake them both.

Adele Meier's heart pounded as she dipped the bristles of her round-tipped paintbrush into the sky-blue glob of paint that quivered on her palette. To be more precise, it wasn't the paint that quivered but her hands.

Her hands, always cool and stable, now had the steadiness of an earthquake. She closed her eyes a moment, willing herself to be calm. But closing her eyes was a mistake, one that opened a floodgate of memories, foremost of which was the last time she had worked her magic on a canvas screen.

Markus had been the subject. She had wanted to capture the rugged beauty of his profile when he had last returned from battle. Even now, maternal pride swelled in her breast, pushing back the pain sparked by the memory of the following morning.

"I-I'm sorry, my son." Propping her elbow on her knee, Adele let her forehead fall against the heel of her palm, the wooden handle of the brush dangling between clenched fingers. "How did I not notice? I should've seen the pain in your eyes. I should have . . . I should have noticed the hurt in your face."

Adele let the tears slip down her cheeks and drip off the tip of her nose, wishing that she could be free of the guilt that still plagued her. Could she have prevented her son's death? Burkhard always said no but . . .

Wiping her cheeks with the back of her hand she focused again on the incomplete portrait before her. Markus stared back at her from the canvas, eyes that had once sparkled now lifeless and vacant.

Licking her lips, Adele dipped the brush into the paint. *Blue. His eyes were blue.* She curled her fingers around the crimp of the brush, moving her wrist in a tight circular motion. How many times had she wished she could repaint the last two years of her life? But she could not. Time was an unusual brush that only painted in shades of gray and black.

Burkhard might have found healing by pouring himself into Will Thompson's spiritual rescue but she needed something more tangible. She needed to finish the work she had begun.

Changing colors and brushes, Adele melted into her work, coaxing life into the image of her son who would never live again. The trembling in her hands faded and her rapid breathing yielded to a steadier rhythm as the memories within flowed through the brush onto the off-white canvas. She leaned forward, as much engrossed by the fruit of her hands now as she had been the morning Markus had drawn his first breath.

"I never thought you would finish it."

Adele started as Burkhard's voice pulled her from her silent reverie. She hadn't heard him enter the room, a small closet really, that was illuminated with electric lamps. As she jerked backward, the tip of the brush grazed the side of her cheek, striping it with paint the color of Markus's hair.

"Oh, I'm sorry, *mein lieben*." Burkhard stepped around the easel. Wincing, he knelt and pulled a clean handkerchief from his pocket then wiped her cheek. "I thought you knew I was here. I called you twice."

"I didn't hear anything." She laid the brush and palette on a round wooden table beside her and pressed his warm, firm hand against her lips. "You're working too hard."

"Nonsense. Only old men work too hard!"

Ignoring his attempted humor, Adele wiped her cheeks then threw a mock glare in his direction. "Were you working with Will again?"

With a stifled groan, Burkhard straightened then sank into the empty seat of the faded couch on which she sat. "I wanted to see if there's a problem between him and Katja. Will has improved but he is still a soldier—a captive soldier. It is only natural for him to want to go home."

"And is there a problem?" Chewing her lip, Adele forced herself to tear her gaze away from the portrait.

He slipped his arm around her shoulders. "I didn't get to discuss it properly. Uther's sense of timing is . . . unfortunate."

Adele put the brush down and folded her hands together in her lap. "I'm sure he doesn't approve of your generosity. This is a dangerous game you're playing, Burkhard. Uther is your friend, but he is also a powerful man. What would happen if Will escaped?"

Burkhard studied her carefully for a long moment before answering. "Would it be a Christian act to chain him up? To stand outside his door each night with a loaded rifle?"

"No, but if something *did* happen"—her voice dropped—"I'm afraid for you. I cannot believe that Uther would let us go without some kind of penalty."

His brow furrowed, and she knew that her point had struck home. "He's said something about that to you, didn't he?"

"Yes. My life for Will's." Her husband's lips pressed themselves together in a thin line.

Adele's hands flew to her mouth. "And you've had him here all this time?" She gestured wildly toward Markus's portrait. "Isn't one death in this family enough?"

Burkhard leaned forward, elbows propped on his knees. "No one's going to die Adele." His head sagged, and when he spoke again, his voice was heavy with sorrow. "No one . . . except for Will."

———◆◆●◆◆———

Katja pushed open the kitchen side door and eased her way inside. Outside, the thunder rumbled, and the first drops of rain misted the kitchen windows. After depositing the basket of eggs on the counter and washing her hands in a bowl of sudsy water, she left the kitchen and slipped down the short corridor to the staircase that led to her room.

Her bedroom had become a sanctuary, a place of prayer in which she drew the strength necessary to fight life's battles. Katja didn't know if she could honestly say she was *winning* the conflict, but at least she was still fighting.

She had made it halfway up the stairs when she noticed the door to her mother's studio hung partially ajar.

Odd. Mother never paints anymore.

The staircase rose in a straight line, bordered on one side by a wall covered in a canary-yellow paint that was embellished with intertwining red stenciled roses, and a dark wooden railing on the other. Her mother's studio lay on the right-hand side of the landing at the top of the staircase.

Katja inched her way upward, the light tread of her feet muted by the thin pad of cream carpet. She was about to peek around the corner when her father's voice, heavy with unspoken grief, made her heart stop.

"No one's going to die, Adele. No one . . . except for Will."

Katja's blood turned to ice.

What is he talking about?

Her mother voiced the question that burned in her mind. "What . . . what are you saying?" Her voice sounded shrill as though, despite her previous misgivings, the thought of Will's death drove a spike through her own heart.

"Uther's taking him back to the general prison compound. By now, word of what Will has done has surely spread. You can imagine what the other prisoners will do to him."

Katja clutched at the railing to steady herself. *Die?* Guilt gnawed at her heart. Will had earned the enmity of his fellow prisoners when a dirty-minded Brit had slandered her reputation. Will had barely escaped death that day and now, months later, it appeared that he had not escaped at all.

"If he were at Worms he would have a chance." Papa heaved a sigh.

"Why is that?"

"Uther mentioned that a hundred prisoners from the prison camp near Worms are being released in some sort of an exchange. But it's no use even talking about it."

"Surely the guards will protect—"

"The guards are old men, Adele." The frustration in her father's voice was almost tangible. She imagined him sitting stiffly on the bed, scrubbing a hand over his face. "They cannot be everywhere at all times. Sooner or later, he will be murdered. A pillow over Will's head in the dead of the night or a blow from the sharp end of a mattock when no one's looking. One way or another, he'll die and I . . . " His words faded off into a groan.

Katja's breath came in short bursts as the world seemed to spin around her. She needed to get to him. Now. Prickles of anticipation skittered up and down her spine as the audacity of what she contemplated sank into her mind.

Escape. The word flitted through her head just as a clap of thunder roared overhead. *The camp near Worms.* For weeks, she had tried to contrive a plan that could get Will back to his own people. For weeks, she had failed. This one morsel of information that her father had unwittingly revealed was the key she needed.

The lights in the hallway flickered as she spun on her heel and silently dashed down the stairs.

An exchange of some sort, Papa said.

It was a slim hope, frail at best, but it was all they had. Making her way to the kitchen door, she shoved aside the niggling thought that, if Will did escape, she would never see him again.

That doesn't matter. Not now.

There could be no more waiting, no more deliberating. If Will did not leave tonight, he would not leave at all. Without a backward glance, Katja shoved open the kitchen door and threw herself into the heart of the storm.

———————— ◆◆●◆◆ ————————

Adele pulled her husband into her arms, cradling his head against her chest. "You brought Will here to save him from himself, yet I believe he was sent to save you."

Burkhard lifted his head, cheeks glistening. "Why, Adele?" He turned toward the portrait of his son, mouth twisting into a grimace. "If he dies, I will feel I have lost another son. Why?"

Her heart clenching, she pulled him to her once more. "I don't know, my love. But I know that you can't stop this any more than . . . " She faltered then forced herself to continue. "Any more than I could stop Markus from . . . taking his own life."

Burkhard inhaled a sharp breath, eyes glistening as he focused on her face.

"You told me that, and at last, I see it. Neither of us is to blame." She placed a palm on both of his moist cheeks. "You've taught Will the most important lesson of all. That is to love. Maybe he wasn't ready to meet God before, but now he is. Either way, there's nothing you can do."

For a moment, Burkhard didn't reply but his lack of a rebuttal meant that he believed her words. Then he raised the question that hounded both their thoughts. "Should I tell our daughter?"

After a moment, Adele shook her head. "It will do her no good to know beforehand. She's been struggling with her heart, and that is good."

"She told you this?" Burkard crinkled a brow.

"I'm a woman, *mein Leibling,* or have you forgotten? Trust a woman to understand a woman. Your daughter is fighting very hard to avoid loving this Englishman. I am proud of her. Given the circumstances, it is the right thing to do. Telling her that he is doomed could cause her to do something rash."

With a sigh, Burkhard gestured toward the image of the young man that stared out at them from the canvas. Mottled streaks of gray and black formed the background while, surrounded by a streaked cloud of burnished red, their son met their gaze with his piercing blue eyes.

He held his head high, defying the despair that had claimed his life. A few tendrils of his dark auburn hair forked over his wide forehead. He had his father's nose, straight and domineering. The shadow of a beard clung to his proud chin. A snug black tuxedo fit his broad chest under which a starched white shirt and matching bowtie were clearly visible.

"It is beautiful." Burkhard swallowed. "So much like him I . . . "

Adele smiled through the haze of sudden tears that misted her eyes. In her own way, completing her son's portrait mirrored the struggle that now confronted her husband. It brought to her the same sense of peace that Will's presence had offered Burkhard.

Loss. Grief. Acceptance.

Like paint on a palette, each phase added its own layer to the canvas of life, creating a somber background that only made the brilliance of brighter moments more visible. It was the darkness of the background that brought out the radiance of her son's eyes. And it was the somber reality of her loss that made the memories of Markus's short life infinitely more brilliant.

"Yes." She wove her hands, now calm and steady, into his own. "It is . . . beautiful."

Chapter 22

Meier Farm near Münster, Germany. July 1917.

Will crouched beside the entrance to Burkhard's barn, shrouded in a veil of darkness that was split by jagged streaks of white lightning. The peak of an overhang that arched a few feet over his head protected him from the torrential downpour. Now, as he waited for Katja to join him, it seemed that time itself had become as immobile as he was. For tonight, after a year as a prisoner of war, he would escape.

Only an hour earlier, Katja had found him still at work in the barn. Gripping his arm, she had said in no uncertain terms that he must leave tonight or be returned to the main camp of prisoners. Will held no illusions as to what awaited him if he were sent back to the *Mannschaftslager*. In hushed undertones they had thrown together a plan, urged along by a mutual sense of desperation.

Adrenaline pulsed in his veins, bringing with it a sense of clarity that had evaded him for months.

Eleanor.

A week ago, the thought of a reunion with his wife had seemed a remote fantasy. But now that hope, as unexpected as the lightning, had once again streaked across his path, his life had slipped back into focus. Eleanor was the reason he needed to escape. Together, they had to face the bitter losses of the past and lay the foundation for their future; a future that transcended the insanity of war.

A bolt of blazing energy pulsed overhead even as a flicker of movement caught his eye. Katja, swathed entirely in black, slipped around the side of the house then darted across the gravel path toward him.

Katja.

Tentatively, Will explored the varying emotions that stirred within him. She had brought him back from the brink of self-destruction, illuminating his darkest hours with her words and with her presence.

His lips flattened. Katja was also a source of temptation. His departure would hurt them both. But as Will peered into his heart, he was relieved to find that, now that a possibility of reuniting with his wife existed, the haze that had smothered his mind had grown weaker. But though his mind was clear, the fact that he was drawn to the woman who now motioned for him to follow her into the barn, was undeniable.

Rising, he followed her then eased the heavy door back into place. She pulled out a flashlight and flicked it on. Her cheeks were pale and wet; he could only hope it was from the rain.

"Ready?"

Will pointed at Burkhard's antiquated lorry. "I filled the lorry with petrol earlier and there's a spare can in the back in case we need it."

Her dark hair, normally tucked into a tight bun, now tumbled loosely around her shoulders but was covered by a black scarf. A few loose tendrils curled up at the scarf's edges and Will pushed aside the urge to smooth them back from her face.

"You understand our plan?" She slung a dark backpack off her shoulders and offered it to him, holding his gaze.

He took it and slipped it on his shoulders. "Yes. We'll drive through the village to the edge of the forest on the other side where you'll drop me off. From there, I'll make my way through the woods, going south-west toward Worms. The rest I'll make up as I go."

Their eyes met in a spate of wordless conversation. This was the defining moment in their complex relationship. Once they slid the lorry through the barn's double doors, there would be no turning back. The magnetism of this shared betrayal pulled them together like iron to lodestone.

Katja was about to commit treason for him and he was about to betray Burkhard's trust.

"We'd better go." His voice was firm, a little too firm perhaps, but given the emotional energy that crackled through the dimly-lit barn Will felt it was for the best. The most dangerous of enemies always struck when the defender was weakest. At this crucial moment, Katja's enemy was her own heart.

"Yes." Blinking, she backed away. "We'd better."

Will turned and strode to the door. He pulled the pin that bolted it to the ground with his booted foot. The cords of muscle lining his shoulders clenched as he bent forward and pushed both doors outward, letting a spray of cold rain dash against his face.

Thunder roared overhead, making his pulse spike with anticipation. But, just as quickly, Will realized that a storm of this intensity wouldn't stay in one place for long.

He pivoted on his heel and jogged back to the lorry, pulling open the passenger's door and tossing his rucksack inside. If they hoped to use the storm's noise as cover, they had to leave now.

Katja slid behind the driver's seat. "Crank the engine. Quickly."

He moved to the front of the lorry, then pumped the wooden handle that protruded from the engine five times before it sputtered to life.

Waving, he stepped to one side then jumped back as the lorry lurched forward. Will closed the barn doors then jogged to the waiting lorry. Pulling himself inside, he said, "I didn't know you could drive this monster."

The lorry had no electric headlights and Katja inched her way forward guided only by the momentary flashes of lightning overhead.

"There are a lot of things about me you don't know, Will." She accelerated slowly. "And a lot you'll never know . . . now."

Silence filled the small cabin and Will shifted his attention to the bag that bounced between his feet. He felt for the metal clasp then thrust probing fingers inside.

Katja must have heard his rustling above the engine's wheezing. "Inside, you'll find some food and water, a compass, bandages, a revolver, and six bullets."

"You gave me your father's gun?" Will stared at her, slack-jawed.

The lorry lurched as it rolled heavily into a pothole. Katja pressed lightly on the pedal, murmuring encouragement under her breath. Finally, the struggling engine coughed twice then, with a low growl, rolled forward.

"The gun is mine." Katja gently patted the steering wheel. "Good girl."

His eyebrows hiked together. Clearly, she was right. There was more to her than he realized. This thought led him to another, more sobering question. "Katja, I don't want you or Burkhard to suffer because of this."

Katja was quiet for a moment. When she spoke, her tone was crisp. "My father won't be punished, Will."

"What about you?" He whirled toward her, the crackling lightning playing games of light and shadow across her pale face. Her brow was creased and her knuckles white as they gripped the steering wheel. "What if you're caught, Katja? I won't be the cause of your family's ruin!"

"You must go, Will. General Klein and my father are good friends. Everything will be fine."

Will sucked in a sharp breath, lost in a vortex of conflicting emotions. When he had been stripped of his uniform, he had lost sight of who he was—a soldier in the British army on a mission to frustrate the enemy at all costs. Katja's news had rekindled that spark of determination, but while he ached to rejoin his wife, he was no longer the unfeeling killer he had once been. Concern for the caring family that had saved him from himself crammed his mind.

"If anything happens to you, I—"

"You'll what? Storm Munich prison and rescue me?" Her words were sharp, and her tone biting. "Assassinate Kaiser Wilhelm himself?"

"Katja . . . "

"You *can't* do anything Will. Neither of us can. That is why you have to leave."

He knew she wasn't just talking about his captivity. The fact that nothing could come of their relationship was eating at her. And she was right. He could do nothing.

Nothing will happen." She slowed the lorry to a crawl as they rolled through the outskirts of the village then lowered her voice and spoke again. "At least, nothing unbearable."

Shaking his head, Will stared out the window, straining to see through the gloom. Not a single light burned in any of the houses they passed. Fear of attack from the British Royal Air Force had caused many villages to enforce blackout periods after sunset. But the flickering lightning revealed the straight outlines of houses, standing erect like disapproving sentinels who were powerless to prevent the escape of a fugitive.

"You know enough German by now to get by," Katja said, "and you're dressed like one of us which should help you avoid attention."

Will rubbed his palms on the legs of his trousers then looped Katja's holstered revolver around his waist, noting idly that the storm had passed on. "Do you know anything about Worms?"

"I've travelled there with my father several times. It's about five hours away by auto."

Will's mind did some rapid calculations. On foot, through the woods as a fugitive, he should make it in about three days. Of course, the prisoner of war camp was not *in* the city. He'd have to find that on his own.

Can I do this? He balled his fists. As an officer of no rank, if he were recaptured the penalty would be severe indeed. For himself, he didn't fear death but the thought of leaving Eleanor alone in this cruel, dark world seemed somehow obscene.

Closing his eyes, he let his thoughts drift to the challenges ahead. Perhaps he could—

Kupugh! The sharp sound rang out from beneath the lorry's hood and echoed like a gunshot off the nearby buildings. With a deafening metallic screech, the lorry ground to a halt, dragging Will's heart to a stop with it.

Katja whirled toward him, face ghost white. "It's dead!"

Their eyes met in wordless horror.

"Try the gas." Will rolled down the glass window, straining his ears for shouts or the sound of running boots.

God help us.

He had a few minutes at best. There was no way trained soldiers would sleep through that commotion.

Katja pumped the accelerator up and down. "Nothing." She spun back to him. "You have to get out of here, Will!"

"But—" He couldn't just abandon her. Not now! An image of General Klein putting a bullet through Jack's brain flashed through his mind.

What will he do to her?

Katja grabbed his arm. "If you don't leave, it'll all have been for nothing. Go!" Her voice broke. "Go back to Eleanor, Will. Live. For my sake, please live!"

"Katja . . . "

"No more words! If you ever cared for me, even a little, just go."

He hesitated.

"Will, I'm begging you!"

A light flickered on at the far edge of town, then two more. Distant voices, harsh and alarmed, punched through the night air. His heart clenched as he gripped the door handle. What could he say? What words could express the gratitude that swelled within him?

"Thank you." The words seemed pathetically empty. Two words to summarize an ocean of feelings. Two words to atone for the torment that he had unleashed upon her. It was not enough. It could never be enough.

"Will," she shifted closer. Pulling the scarf from her head, Katja placed moist hands against his cheeks. "Just . . . just one kiss." Her chest heaved as she stared at him with parted lips.

"This time, you know it's me. Just one. T-to remember what might have been."

His mind went numb. *A kiss.*

Didn't he owe her this much at least? She faced imprisonment, perhaps even death, and all she wanted was a kiss in return.

What might have been.

His eyes fluttered closed. She would regret this. The storm that had passed was still raging in her heart. She wasn't thinking clearly.

But he was.

An image of Eleanor's face, beautiful and tender, floated through his mind, lingering like a long, sweet embrace. Details— her finely-arched eyebrows, her eyes that sparkled like diamonds, a mouth that promised heaven—all crowded his mind for the first time in a year, clinging to his thoughts with the persistence of a lover's caress.

"I can't."

Two words. Two words that would break her heart. Two words that would save them both. "I'm sorry, Katja, but I can't."

Katja pulled back, face aflame, then looked away. "No. Y-you're right. You're right."

Will jerked the handle upward and staggered out of the lorry. Katja turned back toward him as a soft breeze filtered through the window and tossed her disheveled hair around her shoulders.

She raised a hand, a sad smile working its way across her lips. "May you be happy, Will Thompson."

"I will never forget you." Closing the door, Will cast one more backward glance in her direction. She held herself like a queen, erect and in control once more. He stared at her for several long seconds, then tore his eyes away, slipped into the shadows, and took the first step of the long journey home.

The sun had just creased the eastern sky when Burkhard stepped to his front door, hurried along by the sound of a pounding fist. Behind him, Adele stood on the upper landing of their home, clutching at the wooden railing that ran the length of the stairs.

"In the name of Kaiser Wilhelm II, open this door at once!"

Burkhard knew the voice but why was General Klein trying to break down his door? He froze, one step suspended in mid-air.

"What is it, husband?" Adele's voice quavered, as though she too suspected the unthinkable, but was unable to articulate the horror that flooded both of their minds.

"Adele . . . " He swung his head slowly toward her, one hand clutching the wooden banister. Dawn always found the members of the family awake. Yet someone was missing. "Where is Katja?"

Adele's hand flew to her throat. "I-I don't . . . "

The unfeeling fist slammed into the door again, sending reverberations through the wood and into the core of Burkhard's soul. Burkhard knew, before he tottered down the staircase that waiting on the other side of the door was—

"Katja!"

His daughter blinked up at him with reddened eyes, hands cuffed behind her back. She stood between ten armed guards, dressed as though ready for a funeral. Her hair hung in a tangled mass around her shoulders.

"Wh-what is this?" Burkhard lurched forward. "Take your hands off my daughter!"

A long, thick, black walking stick swung upward, stopping his advance. Burkhard's eyes slid along the stick, to the rough hand that held it, and up to the scowling face of General Klein.

"Uther, what are you doing?" Adele rushed down the stairs.

"I apologize for disturbing your morning, *Frau* Meier." General Klein tipped his hat toward her without taking his eyes off Burkhard's face. "But that is a question only your husband can answer."

Burkhard's gaze swiveled back to Katja. *She didn't. God, she couldn't have.* His mouth opened and closed without a sound escaping.

"Daughter?" Adele moved to stand beside him. "What have you done?"

"She helped a prisoner escape."

"Will?" Adele's voice was tight. Shrill.

Burkhard shuddered. Only once in their thirty-five years of marriage had he heard such a note of panic in his wife's voice. They had lost their son that day. Now the wheel of time had come full circle.

"They were going to send him back to the *Mannschaftslager*." Katja lifted her chin. "He would've died there. Papa said so himself."

"The agreement was clear, Burkhard." Klein's voice was iron, slashing at his heart. "Your life for his. I should arrest both you *and* your daughter but, as you are the head of your home, I am choosing to spare your wife the pain of losing another child. The responsibility is yours." He nodded sharply. "Take him!"

"What?" Katja surged forward, voice cracking. "My father has done nothing. It was my plan. Mine alone!"

Klein stepped forward, face tight. "Your father has failed the Emperor. He has betrayed his country. He will be imprisoned and tried in court. If he is found guilty . . . "—Klein let the words hang in the air for a moment—"the penalty will be death."

"No, no!" Adele thrust herself past the general's stick and clutched at the black lapel of his coat. "We've already lost so much, Uther. A son, our hope! Now you would take my husband?" She sank to her knees, arms upraised. "I beg you to spare him."

The sight of his wife on her knees gave Burkhard his voice. "Do not beg for me, Adele." He pulled her upright. Then his gaze flashed to Katja. He couldn't be angry with her. She loved Will, that much was clear. He had never told her the condition of Will's imprisonment. But then again, perhaps it was a mercy that she had not known.

Had he told Katja that Will's escape would mean his own death, she would have been forced to choose the life of her father or the life of the man she loved. She had acted in ignorance and in that, Burkhard found a measure of peace.

He stepped toward his daughter, ignoring the guards' rifles that swiveled toward him.

"It was the right choice, Katja." He gently kissed her forehead, then bent to whisper in her ear. "He could never have been truly happy here. You have set him free."

"I'm so sorry Papa. I . . . I didn't know. Forgive me." Her eyelids slammed shut as silver tears slid down her cheeks.

He wrapped his arms around her, folding her into his embrace. "There is nothing to forgive."

She spoke again, her voice a ragged breath of undiluted pain. "I was the one that helped him escape. I thought that they'd come for me. Not you."

"*Herr* Meier." General Klein stepped back while motioning to his men. "You must come with us at once."

Rough hands grabbed him, ripping him from his daughter's frantic embrace.

"Wait!" Burkhard twisted around, craning his neck for a glimpse of Adele.

His wife lurched toward him, clutching both hands against her chest. Her hair, though streaked with silver, was a crown of glory on her head. Her eyes had never looked so beautiful, though they were bright with tears.

Burkhard swallowed. He could face anything, even death itself, if he knew Adele believed in him. Disappointing her would be in itself a punishment worse than death.

She moved closer, stopping only inches away.

"Do you regret taking him in?" He could barely speak past the lump in his throat. "Do you blame me for this?"

I need to know.

Adele shook her head, as she choked back a sob. "He made us whole again, if only for a little while." Reaching up, she stroked his cheek. "We must remember the bright spots of beauty we paint in the world instead of seeing the darkness of grief."

Burkhard crushed her to his chest, overcome by the renewed strength of his wife's resolve. In his own way, Will had brought healing to Adele as well. His presence had forced Adele to conquer the heartache that consumed her.

Burkhard's eyes misted as he gazed up at the sky. "Then that is worth any price, *mein Leben.*"

Chapter 23

Teutoburg Forest, Germany. July 1917

Will loped through the rocky mountain forest, eyes darting from side to side as he pushed past the prickly branches of pine trees that scraped his face and arms. The narrow game trail he followed ran in a rough southwesterly direction, allowing him to skirt around most of the smaller towns that stretched between Munster and Worms. He skidded to a halt and gulped down a lungful of crisp morning air as he glanced over his shoulder. *They're still following me.*

About a dozen German soldiers pursued him with the dogged persistence for which they were famous. Shifting the backpack on his shoulder with a grunt, he resumed his mad, forward dash. As he ran, his mind scurried through the events that had led up to this moment.

After leaving Katja, he had hidden in the cellar of an abandoned house near the edge of town, waiting until Kline's men had finished combing through the village. Sometime just before dawn, he had slipped into the forest but had been spotted just before gaining the shelter of the trees.

Desperate, he had crawled into a hollow log and covered up the entrance with dead leaves. There he had waited for a full day, ignoring the cold, damp rain that passed through the cracks in the log and dripped onto his face and chest. Finally deeming it safe to leave his hiding place, he had wriggled out of the log and began the trek toward Worms.

Unfortunately, after only a few hours on the path he had stumbled across the party of Germans on their way back to Klein's village. Then the chase had resumed in earnest.

Will shot another look over his shoulder. These men obviously knew these woods better than he. Most of the soldiers under Klein's command were older than him by at least ten years but, despite their age, they were gaining on him. Will ducked under a low-hanging branch, pulse hammering in his throat.

Katja had said that the prisoners would leave Worms within a week. He had lost a day in hiding and it would take at least three more days to find the camp of prisoners. What he would do when he arrived was still a mystery.

God will make a way. His mind simply refused to accept the thought that this could all end in failure. All he needed was a way to escape the hunters that hounded his trail.

The path ran along the edge of a rocky incline and, to his left, a narrow ravine sloped downward, parallel to the trail about ten feet below him. As he ducked to avoid another needled branch, Will lost his footing on the loose gravel and slid sideways over the edge. He grabbed at the branch, but his fingers clutched nothing but empty air.

Whoomp! He landed hard on his side, a small cloud of dust billowing around his head. For a moment, he lay immobile. Scrambling upright, he pressed his body along the side of the cliff, his back against the stones.

Shouts from above told him he had moved just in time. There was no telling if his pursuers had seen him fall but he knew now that he was out of their immediate line of sight. Should they choose to come down and investigate however...

He squinted against the brilliance of the morning sun and let his fingers drop to the holster that hung on his right hip.

God, make them move on.

After more than a year of captivity he had tasted freedom. The exhilarating elixir was not something he would relinquish easily. The shouts became a heated discussion and Will craned his neck upward as he strained to listen. Burkhard's family had taken the time to teach him the basic structure of their language and now, he was infinitely grateful.

"Go and check, Horst." The voice was harsh. "We can't take any chances. If he escapes, others will try to run too."

"He's gone on, I say." This voice was younger. "We should go straight."

"I outrank you. Now, stop wasting our time. What, you don't want to get your pants dirty?" Mockery tinged the first speaker's words. "Go and check!"

Will's heart sank lower than the ground on which he stood as the sound of boots sliding down gravel reached his ears. He pulled the pistol out of its holster and pulled back the hammer, knowing as he did so that the game was over. If he fired one shot, those above would split forces and come at him from two sides. He would be dead before his body hit the ground.

His thoughts of freedom mocked him, tantalizing him with the very brevity of their existence. He gritted his teeth, denying the disappointed rage that swirled within his soul.

The soft *cromp, cromp* of boots on crushed stone came closer, each step another beat of an executioner's drum.

"Eleanor." He breathed her name as he took a tight grip on the revolver. She would assume he had died a prisoner, never knowing the truth. They would never mourn the loss of their child together. They would never—

The barrel of a shotgun swung around the corner, aimed right at the center of his forehead. For a moment that spanned eternity, the two men stared, first at each other, then at the guns that were poised, ready to snuff out the other man's life.

"So." The German licked his lips. "We have a problem." His English was heavily accented but there was no mistaking his meaning. Sweat tinged his brow and the beard that curled around his chin was flecked with gray.

"I kill you and you kill me." A lopsided grin crossed his face. "We both end up dead, together. Sounds like fun, *ja?*"

"*Nein.*" Will shook his head. "No one needs to die today. All I ask is that you let me go on my way."

The German's brow clouded, eyes shifting from Will to the revolver that pressed against his chest, then back to Will again. "You! I remember you."

"What?"

"I see you fight other prisoner. You are the one who stood up for a German. *Fraülein* Katja."

Understanding flooded Will's mind. This man must have been one of the guards present on the day General Klein had executed Jack.

The German gave a slow nod. "I know her for many years. Good friend of my family. You"—he jutted his chin in Will's direction—"are *Ehrenmann.*"

Blinking, Will studied him carefully. His enemy had just called him a man of honor, implying that it was within his right to spare Will while retaining his own sense of personal integrity. Slowly, Will released the hammer on his pistol and slipped it back into his holster. Every military instinct urged him to keep the weapon drawn; to do anything else was suicide!

But a quiet voice in his heart commanded him to defy logic, to show that his fellow man was still worthy of trust. Everything was now in the hands of this German. The soldier could kill him and live to tell the tale of the foolish Englishman who was disarmed by a compliment or...

"You are too good a man to kill like a *Hund*." The German lowered his weapon and thrust out a brawny arm. "Good luck."

Will stared at him for several seconds, unable to believe that he was still alive and free. Then he clasped the man's hand. "*Danke*."

The soldier nodded then pivoted on his heel. "No one here." He shouted up at his comrades as he moved away. "He must have gone straight ahead, as I said!"

Will waited, the breath hanging in his chest, until the last of the voices had long faded away. Then, suppressing a chuckle, he shuffled off in the opposite direction.

He was free.

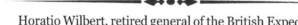

Horatio Wilbert, retired general of the British Expeditionary Force and current commander of the armed division of British Intelligence, scowled as the warship *HMS Poseidon* plowed through the dark waters of the North Sea toward the neutral city of Rotterdam in the Netherlands. Rotterdam might be neutral, but these waters were not.

Wilbert fiddled with the buttons of his navy-blue uniform as the dark sea slid by, spraying white foam as the prow of the ship ripped them apart. These waters were known to harbor underwater mines laid by the nefarious Huns. He would not hesitate to risk his life in battle but to court death while babysitting a German spy?

With a contemptuous grunt, Wilbert mentally reviewed his orders. He was to reconnoiter with his counterpart, a certain General Hindenburg in Rotterdam. Hindenburg would order his men to allow one hundred captured British servicemen to board the *HMS Poseidon* while he handed over the rat who knelt behind him. For his part, Wilbert would rather put a bullet in the prisoner's skull, but he could follow orders as well as give them.

After receiving the prisoners, the *HMS Poseidon* would immediately set sail for Etaples. The plan was simple enough, provided they weren't blown to kingdom come by a mine.

Wilbert jerked the pointed end of his short-cropped silver beard and turned to glare at the slight man who was cuffed and guarded by twenty armed soldiers. "I hope they rip the head right off your shoulders, scum."

The prisoner didn't reply, and his silence made the general's façade of calm crack. Wilbert stalked closer and slammed his fist into the prisoner's stomach. "If my orders weren't to deliver you alive, I'd shoot you now!"

A slight groan escaped the German's mouth. "That . . . isn't good form, General."

"Good form?" Wilbert sniffed then spat on the man's upturned face. "You know, I had two sons. Both were navy officers like me. They both drowned off the coast of Gallipoli thanks to your *German* mines." His lips curled back in a snarl. "Was that good form? Was it?"

The man was silent.

Wilbert grabbed his collar. "Do you have any idea what kind of pain a father feels when he outlives his son?"

"Yes." The prisoner's voice was hoarse and laced with pain. "I do." He paused then spoke again. "At least you will die knowing that you have not failed your sons. I will go to my death in shame."

The British officer stared down at his prisoner. The man before him was his enemy, true, but a broken one. He released his hold and took a step back. "You chose the wrong side in this war, German."

"Is there a right side? I cannot see one."

The silence was broken by the hum of the diesel engine and the rush of the waves. Finally, Wilbert spoke. "Get the German ready." He glanced at his men. "We land in Rotterdam within the hour."

The brown stone face of the Worms rail station or *hauptbahnof* rose in solemn grandeur toward the clear morning sky. To Will, who squatted on his haunches in the shadows of an empty warehouse, the building seemed to be a sprawling house with turreted roofs that rose in a welcoming, almost friendly manner.

The brown pointed overhang of the main entrance was the one through which he, like dozens of other passengers, would have to pass.

Keeping his eyes on the station, Will took a swallow of the lukewarm water in his metal flask, swished the brackish fluid around in his mouth, then swallowed. It was unlikely that anyone in the passenger area would notice him. Even if they did, his clothing was no different than any worn by the workers that bustled about the station.

He had spent the last two days hiding in the shadows and watching for any sign of the coming prisoner convoy while learning the layout of Worms. The time had been a gift, allowing him to better develop the plan he had outlined while trudging through Germany's woods.

Instead of trying to infiltrate a prisoner of war camp, he would simply go to the railway station at Worms then board the same train as the prisoners. Before arriving in Rotterdam, he would change into the prisoner's uniform that Katja had neatly folded and placed into his backpack then disembark, mingling with the others.

His brow furrowed as he took another swig of water, ignoring the metallic taste that burned as it slid down his throat. His time in captivity had instilled an abiding respect for the meticulous nature of the German army. Doubtless, they had counted the men they would exchange. They would probably count them again before letting them board the train. If he were among the prisoners, the count would be off by one.

"Which means I have to find another way on board." He rose slowly, eyes glued to a string of snorting well-muscled draft horses that were being led to the rear of the building. Will peered out around the frame of the door. The foremost stable hand clucked to the lead horse pulling the team across the iron tracks toward one of the last cars of a dormant train.

His gaze shifted back to the wide cobblestone pathway, covered with pedestrians.

Something is happening.

Instead of passing through the arch into the station itself, large crowds of civilians began to form a sort of gauntlet on either side of the walkway. First it was about a dozen on each side, then fifty, and within moments, the spectators had multiplied into a crowd of at least a hundred.

Will shrank back into the shadows. They were like children waiting for a parade to pass by, but instead of laughing and

274

giggling, they stood in eerie silence. His mind whirled at the implications. Were the prisoners about to pass through?

A cavalcade of large, dark green lorries rumbled over the hill, each gleaming in the light of the early morning sun. Their open backs allowed all spectators a clear view of the prisoners who were shackled to the wooden slats that formed the frame of each lorry.

Will counted twenty men clustered together in the center of the first vehicle. On both sides of them, bracing themselves against the sides of the lorry, stood six German soldiers with bayoneted rifles at the ready. Will's eyes shifted from the convoy to the crowd who watched until the growling lorries rolled over the tracks toward the rear of the station, stopping outside the same train into which the horses had passed.

That's it!

His grip on the wall tightened as an idea mushroomed in his mind. The soldiers' attention would be on the prisoners, which would give him the chance to slip aboard the animal transport car. No one in Worms was looking for an escaped prisoner, so he was unlikely to be challenged. Once in Rotterdam—assuming he reached the city undiscovered—he would disembark and follow the convoy from a distance.

There was only one problem. His eyes slid to the ranks of soldiers who lined both sides of the path to the train.

"It's like walking through a wall of fire and expecting not to get burned." The words sparked a memory of Eleanor reading her favorite passage from the Bible, a story of three men who refused to be cowed into submission and were thrown into a fiery furnace.

They walked through the fire and lived to tell about it, Will. He closed his eyes, remembering the last time she had read the passage. *Can you imagine that?*

Will grunted, reluctantly pushing the warm memory to one side. At this moment, he could more than imagine it; he was about to live it. Or at least, he *hoped* to live through it. His gaze shifted back to the soldiers who milled about the lorries, barking orders, and counting off prisoners as they shoved them into blocks of ten.

He ran his fingers through his dark hair. Once again, he was about to risk everything to return to the woman who meant more to him than life. But there was no alternative. Like the men who had defied the will of a barbaric king, only one path lay open to him.

He counted three heartbeats, and then, sucking in a deep breath, Will pulled away from the safety of the shadows and stepped into the midst of the flames.

Chapter 24

Rotterdam, Netherlands, July 1917.

"There are two things to avoid like the plague," General Wilbert said. He scowled, his narrowed eyes focusing on the black-clad German soldiers that surrounded a double-column of bedraggled British prisoners, nudging them with the butts of their rifles as they edged up the narrow cobblestone path.

Overhead, the squawks of seagulls filled the clear, afternoon skies, tossed about by the swirling winds that blew off the North Sea where Wilbert's ship waited at anchor. The silver-haired general stood on the road a few yards from the dock against which a dozen dinghies thumped as they were pushed by the gentle swelling of the waves. Those dinghies would transport the gaunt, manacled prisoners to the dreadnought once the exchange was complete. On the wooden dock behind him waited forty armed British soldiers, men whom he had trained for special operations such as this.

"Two things? And what would they be, General?" His lieutenant, a young man with sandy brown hair and matching eyes, lifted his chin as he contemplated the approaching enemy.

"One." Wilbert's hand dropped to the holstered pistol that hung from a black leather belt at the waist of his navy-blue uniform. "Retreat. Never budge an inch in the face of an enemy."

"Extraordinary strategy, sir. And the second?"

The general snorted, making his silver moustache quiver. "Politicians lad, politicians. Shun the vultures. They create dastardly situations like this one, where I'm forbidden from attacking the enemy unless I'm attacked first! It's a travesty, I say, a travesty."

His ears pricked forward as the sound of tromping boots intermingled with muttered curses from the soldiers around him rose on all sides. "Look at the blighters, prodding our lads along like rats in a cage. What I'd give to send a round of lead into the bunch of them!"

He pivoted and spoke in a low undertone. "If they so much as frown at us, I order you to treat it as an act of aggression. We'll not permit these villains to tarnish the honor of the Empire."

"Ah . . . I see, sir." The young soldier snapped out a crisp salute. "Very good, sir."

Wilbert's eyes probed the scene before him as he mentally reviewed the situation. Rotterdam's docks were built in the center of a series of tall buildings, tinged with roofs the color of blood. Before him sprawled a narrow cobblestone road. At the avenue's far end, he could clearly make out at least six open-back lorries. Approaching him, with rifles in hand, were about thirty of the enemy.

At Wilbert's signal, his own troops spread out into two neat battle lines on either side of him, bayoneted guns at the ready. Wilbert didn't think the Germans had treachery in mind—they needed to respect Dutch neutrality as much as Great Britain did—but experience had taught him to prepare for all possibilities.

He turned to his lieutenant but kept the advancing Germans in his line of sight. "Once the prisoners have been released, have the lads discretely hand them their pistols. I don't think the

Germans will try anything, but caution is always in order. That way, if things do get unpleasant, we'll have an extra hundred men on our side. Has the area been cleared of civilians?"

"Yes, General. My contact in the Dutch government at The Hague assured me that the area would be closed to the public from dawn until after the exchange is complete." He gestured toward a third group of mounted soldiers that approached from their right. "And here come the peacekeepers now."

Wilbert counted fifty armed horsemen, dressed in olive green uniforms and rounded helmets. The Dutch intermediaries were there to ensure that the prisoner exchange did not degenerate into open conflict on their soil.

His face twisted into a sneer. Remaining neutral when millions of men across the globe were dying because of German aggression made the term *Dutch* synonymous with *coward*.

"General Wilbert?" The leader of the Dutch forces struggled to pronounce his name. He rode closer then dismounted, and handing the reins of his horse to a subordinate, shook the British general's hand.

"I am General Velden. My Queen, Her Majesty Wilhelmina Helena, extends her greetings and urges you to respect the neutrality of the Netherlands."

"And I urge *you* to tell that to the Huns," Wilbert said, pointing to the Germans. They had stopped about twenty yards away from his own men. Shouts broke out from the prisoners at the sight of the red, blue and white Union Jack that fluttered on the breeze on the dinghies. For their part, the Germans shoved the men roughly back into line. Wilbert felt the back of his neck grow hot.

"*Guten tag.* I suggest we get this business over with as quickly as possible. I don't know how long I can stand the stink of your presence." The nasal whine came from the German lines. A tall, uniformed officer dropped from a snorting black stallion and slithered toward the pair of waiting men, the buckles of his black boots glinting in the afternoon light.

A set of overdone gold threads ran along the seams of his black uniform. At his side hung a ceremonial sword. A string of medals commemorating past victories covered the left side of his chest.

Victories? More like massacres.

Wilbert's eyes narrowed. This popinjay could only be the man he was supposed to meet—

"*Generalfeldmarschall* Paul Hindenburg." The arrogant sot pulled a helmet topped with a tuft of ridiculous white egret feathers off his bulbous head, and tucking it underneath his shoulder, dangled a pale hand in front of Wilbert's face.

"You expect me to touch you?" Wilbert growled out the words. "The only time I'll shake your hand, Bosche, is when you give me your sword, hilt-first!"

Hindenburg blinked rapidly then barked out a sharp laugh, making the angles of his grotesque mustache quiver. "You mean surrender? Germany?"

Letting his hand drop to his side, he stepped closer, a sneer on his face. "You Tommies are such . . . " He paused, searching for the word. "Such *dreamers*. That is why we are slaughtering you in Europe, Palestine, and everywhere else our armies meet. You can do nothing more than imagine impossible scenarios that never actually come to pass."

"Gentlemen." Velden stepped between them, pulling his brown leather gloves off his hands. "These insults will serve no purpose. Let us accomplish our mission with dignity and leave our fighting for *non-neutral* territories." His eyes swiveled from first one face to the other, waiting until both men took a step back.

"Now, General Wilbert, please produce the prisoner."

Wilbert snapped his finger and his lieutenant dragged the handcuffed German forward.

"Ah . . . " Velden turned to Hindenburg. "Is this the man you know as General Werner Jaëger?"

Hindenburg's jawline tensed as his gaze rested upon the prisoner who refused to lift his eyes from the cobblestone street. "It is."

"Very good." The Dutch general then took a step back. "General Wilbert, you will now hand the prisoner over to his own people."

With a nod, Wilbert also stepped back, allowing Hindenburg's men to take Jaëger into their custody.

"Make sure his bonds are secure," Hindenburg called over his shoulder.

"As agreed." He glared at Wilbert. "One hundred prisoners of war in exchange. Not that he's worth it." Turning to his men he shouted, "Unchain them and count them off."

"Watch how you treat those men, German." Wilbert thrust a thick finger in his pasty face. "They're no longer prisoners but free British subjects under international law."

Hindenburg ignored him. "Release the *prisoners*."

With a rattle of chains, the guards began unshackling the men who surged forward, their cheers ringing out over the water.

"Back, back!" German squadron leaders shoved the erstwhile prisoners into a rough line then began counting them.

"Is this really necessary?" Wilbert turned to the Dutch commander. "Didn't the Bosche think to count them before they got on the train?"

Ignoring his complaint, Velden said, "Commander Hindenburg, for the benefit of all parties, please have your man count in English."

"Of course." Hindenburg sneered as he gestured for his man to begin. "It's a pity that not everyone speaks *Deutch* but that will change, won't it General? Soon the official language of your country will be German." He cast a mocking smile in Wilbert's direction then skulked off toward his own men.

Twenty minutes later, the last cluster of prisoners stepped forward.

"Ninety-two, ninety-three . . . "

Wilbert's gaze roamed over the last set of men, coming to rest on the last soldier in the bunch. He cocked his head to one side, tugging at the sides of his mustache.

The last prisoner was tanned, like the others, but there the similarities ended. Whereas the others were haggard and seemed haunted by their experience, this soldier carried a different air about him. His face wasn't as gaunt, which probably meant he hadn't been fed scant prison rations for long and he didn't seem as though he had been worked quite so hard.

Wilbert knew that hunger stalked the prisoner of war camps.

"Ninety-six, ninety-seven . . . "

The general's mind spun through several possibilities. As an agent who worked under the command of Robert Hughes, he understood that German espionage units would go to any lengths to infiltrate British lines. The recent debacle at Northshire Estate had been proof enough of that!

This fellow's either a plant or an escapee who is sneaking his way on board. His eyes widened as he mentally counted the remaining men.

"Ninety-nine, one hundred . . . " The German soldier's voice melted into a question as he laid a hand on the last man's shoulder.

"One hundred one."

◆◆●◆▶

Will's breath hung in his chest as he locked eyes with the German whose hand lay like a mountain on his shoulder.

He had prayed—oh, how he'd prayed—that the Germans wouldn't recount the men before turning them over to the British. Once again, he hung on the brink, so close to a freedom that mocked him at every turn.

Silence, broken only by the squawking of the gulls and the rhythmic thumping of the boats, had claimed the docks. Will's gaze shifted around the man.

About thirty yards separated him from British lines. Thirty yards that might as well have been a hundred miles. To his left, at least twenty mounted Dutch soldiers ogled him while, to his right, about forty Germans did the same.

His lips curled back in a snarl. He had come too far, suffered through too much to be recaptured now. The soldier blinked, and at that moment, Will exploded into action.

He swung his left elbow in a vicious arch toward the man's chin, yanking the German's pistol from his waist before he crashed to the floor.

"Get back!" Sprinting forward, Will bowled over two stupefied guards. They wouldn't take him. Not now. Not ever.

He gained a few precious feet and hope flared within him. *Just twenty more yards.*

"Stop him!"

"Halt!" The German and Dutch commander's voices rang out as one and, at the sound of their leaders' voices, training overcame shock.

Like the coils of a python, both groups closed in around him.

He dodged left, slamming the hilt of the gun against a man's temple.

Jerking the barrel upward, Will pulled the trigger, sending a German spinning to the ground then careened around two more men in a zig-zag pattern.

Too many. There are far too many.

A jagged scream of frustration ripped out of his throat as he launched himself forward but, before he had taken three more steps, someone grabbed him from behind, pinning him to the ground.

Will writhed in his captors' grasp, but they jerked the gun from his hands and hauled him back to his feet. Chest heaving, he glared at General Hindenburg.

"So." The German cocked his head to one side. "What have we here? A stowaway?"

"What you have"—the harsh accusing voice of General Wilbert slid like a dagger between them—"is a choice."

Hindenburg rolled his eyes then turned around. "A choice? What—"

Will craned his neck to one side to see around the General's back. The entire corps of British soldiers and ex-prisoners had guns trained on both the Dutch and German soldiers. For his part, General Wilbert had his own revolver leveled with the man's face. He spoke around Hindenburg at Will.

"Identify yourself, soldier."

A slow grin slid across Will's face. "Will Thompson, sir. 28th Division, Northumberland Fusiliers regiment, 7th Battalion."

"Your cohort leader?"

"Lieutenant-Colonel James Stewart. Sir."

Wilbert grunted. "Stewart's still alive? You poor devil." He waved the gun under Hindenburg's eyes.

"That man is a soldier of the Empire. One hundred and fifty men behind me, including your *former* prisoners, say that he is coming with us. Now, you can either let him go or . . . " He pulled the hammer back.

"G-general." The Dutch commander, Velden, stepped forward holding his palms before his face. "What you're doing here is a breach of protocol. It is a violation of your government's respect for our neutrality—"

"Then have your government file a formal complaint." Wilbert pinned him with an angry glare. "I'll not leave a good man to be executed for serving his country. In fact, I'll see that he's promoted."

"We agreed to one hundred men." Hindenburg clenched his fists. "Not one more!"

"Lieutenant!" Wilbert's face twisted in a grimace that was meant to be a smile. "Let the record show that the Germans have threatened a British officer on neutral grounds. That is an act of war. As such, order the men to gun down the German prisoner we just handed over."

"Yes, sir!" The British officer turned to the grinning soldiers behind him. "Fire at will."

"Wait, wait!" Hindenburg backed away from Wilbert's revolver. He turned, and Will noticed the sheen of perspiration on his brow. *Odd.* He didn't think the thought of death would so unnerve a man used to leading on the bloody battlefields of Europe. It must be the thought of returning to his kaiser empty-handed that had Hindenburg on edge.

"Let not the world think that the Fatherland is a miserly country." The German stepped back, rubbing his hands together quickly. "As proof of our generosity, we offer you this extra prisoner."

Wilbert made a *humphing* noise in the back of his throat. "At ease, gentlemen."

There were a few grumbles, mostly from the prisoners who doubtless itched for the chance to strike back at their former captors.

Will stumbled forward, closing the open space between the three small armies to cries of "Huzzah! Huzzah!"

Tears dampened his cheeks as he knuckled out a crisp salute to the general. "Thank you, sir. Thank you."

Wilbert cocked his head to one side, eyed him a moment, then stepped closer. "If this is some elaborate scheme, you will be found out. If you are a German agent, you will be shot without mercy. Do you understand?"

"I understand, sir. Yes, I do." Will nodded, choking back his emotions. After more than a year of captivity, he was free.

"Good lad." Clapping him on the shoulder, Wilbert turned to his men. "Right, then lads, we have what we came for. Lieutenant let's get these worthy gentlemen aboard ship. Three cheers for England!"

"God save the king! God save the king!" The shouts punched through the afternoon sky. "God save the king!

Wilbert turned back to Hindenburg with a smirk. "Somehow, Hindy old dog, I doubt the lads will ever learn to say *that* in German."

The hood was ripped off his head, but Werner kept his eyes closed. This was it. This was the moment where he entered oblivion. After the exchange he had been hauled onto a train that had chugged steadily north toward Berlin under heavy guard.

Now, he knelt in a puddle of waste with his hands cuffed behind his back. It was a fitting position for a man condemned to die.

Humiliation burned like a scalding iron on his tongue. It was a foretaste of the black ignominy that would tarnish his name among the living and the torment that awaited him in the world of the dead.

Mosquitoes hummed around him, but he could do nothing to prevent them from landing on his forehead and drinking their fill of his blood.

Werner shrugged. *Drink up, little pests.* Soon, his blood would sprawl out in a puddle anyway. Perhaps through them a part of him would live on.

"Are you ready to die, Werner Jaëger?"

At the sound of the kaiser's sinuous voice, Werner's eyes flew open. Wilhelm stood with his back toward him, dressed from head to foot in a simple black military uniform, his crippled hand hanging limply at his side. At the kaiser's left, General Hindenburg slanted Werner a cold stare.

"I am, Your Excellency." Werner swallowed. He would not demean himself further by pleas for life or attempts at justifying his failure. Regardless of the cause, the result was the same. He had failed to kill Leila, failed to perpetuate the legacy of exemplary military service set by his ancestors . . . and failed to avenge his son. He could only hope that Hughes would act upon the web of lies that he had spun, and that Leila would follow him to the grave.

Wilhelm kept his back to the prisoner. "You disappointed me, General. Now you will die alone in an abandoned building in the back streets of our city. You will be forgotten, cast adrift into the world of the dead without even a tombstone to say you ever lived."

The kaiser paused, letting his words burn their way into Werner's mind. "Your body will be burned, and your ashes dumped into the Baltic Sea. Every mention of your name will be stricken from our history. Since you have no surviving children, it will be as though you never existed. A fitting end for a man who spent his life in the shadows, *ja?*"

Werner sucked in a deep breath through his nostrils. He did not fear death, but the knowledge that he had devoted the last thirty years to a king who refused to even look at him robbed him of a will to live. How many had he assassinated through the years to further the kingdom that now denounced him? How many secrets had been unearthed, how many lies had been told?

For nothing. All for nothing.

"I have a parting gift for you." Wilhelm bit off the words. "A tribute to your failure." He turned to General Hindenburg. "Bring them in, General."

"*Herein!*" Hindenburg barked out the order and Werner felt his stomach clench as two men and two women—all agents he had personally trained—entered the room. They were here for one reason. No matter how they felt about it, they had been taught to execute their orders.

Now their orders were to execute him.

His agents formed a line across from him, their expressions void and eyes flat. Werner's mind flitted through their names.

Johan. Hans. Annika. Yani.

"Do your duty." Werner locked eyes with each of them.

Wilhelm made a sharp chopping motion with his uninjured hand. "Begin!"

One after another, each agent spit on Werner's upturned face. Then the first man drew his weapon. A shaft of light glinted off the barrel of his silencer as he pointed his gun at the condemned man's left shoulder.

He pulled the trigger sending the ball through his victim's arm. Werner clenched his teeth, stifling a cry as the bullet bit into his flesh. A second shot from the second agent plowed into his right shoulder, sending him sprawling backward.

The two men stood to one side, letting each of the women take their turn. Werner cried out, writhing on the floor, as their bullets chipped away at his life, inch by excruciating inch. Hot bursts of blood spurted from his body, pooling in dark puddles beneath him.

They formed a circle, continuing the macabre execution by shooting at non-vital organs until his mind snapped under the tidal wave of pain.

"E-end it. Pleasshh!"

His voice was a mangled groan and it was then that Wilhelm turned around. His face held no pity as it took in the sea of blood and filth in which the once-peerless spy lay.

The kaiser closed the distance between them in two long strides. Jerking the prisoner to a sitting position, Wilhelm slid a gleaming revolver from his waist with his black-gloved hand.

Werner squinted up at him, seeing the world through a haze of blood. "F-forgive me?"

He didn't ask for life, only his master's absolution. But the cold look of utter contempt in Wilhelm's eyes forbade him even this final comfort. In the last seconds of life, his senses became surprisingly acute, as though they too wished for one final chance at redemption.

Werner heard the thin whine of the mosquitoes as they swirled about his head. He tasted the sharp tang of the blood that pooled in the back of his throat. His nostrils twitched at the sharp scent of his urine that mingled with the blood at his feet. He felt the slow *chug, chug* of his palpitating heart. He saw Wilhelm raise the gun to his forehead with startling clarity.

"I am the supreme leader of the Fatherland, Kaiser Wilhelm the Second. I never forget"—the kaiser cocked the revolver,—"and I *never* forgive."

Pough!

Chapter 25

Passchendaele, Belgium, July 1917.

Twilight's final rays filtered through the window of the makeshift hospital, coming to rest on Eleanor's cheek. She turned so that the light fell on the paper she clutched in her hand.

The day was dying. Like the soldier who lay in blood-soaked bandages on the bed before her, it was condemned to an irrevocable fate—a destiny more powerful than human will.

She bit her lip, her eyes dropping to the paper on which she recorded the patient's last words. His parents would receive a standard telegram from some unknown official, informing them in kind, but rather generic terms, that the light of their life had been snuffed out. The day after, her letter would convey his last thoughts to them. She could only hope that it would bring some measure of comfort.

"Tell Mother not . . . to worry." The soldier sucked in a deep breath as he struggled to form the words. "Tell her I made my peace with . . . God."

Eleanor willed her hands to stop their trembling. This letter would doubtless be the most important one his mother ever received. Every word had to be legible.

"And tell her—" His voice faded.

She looked up. "Yes? Tell her what?"

But his eyes were vacant, his mouth agape. Whatever else he wanted to say would remain secret until the Final Day dawned.

Eleanor put the letter to one side, buried her face in her hands, and wept. She had witnessed death more times than she could recall. Even now, as she cared for the wounded only three miles from the Front, the whine of falling shells and the resulting explosions, was a constant reminder that life was nothing more than a brittle thread which could be snapped at any moment.

Not only soldiers were at risk. Nurses too had died. German bombs did not discriminate. She was one of a hundred women who had volunteered to tend the wounded around the battlefields of Ypres. They were women who were willing to risk their own lives so that another could live to see the sun rise once more.

But something else drew her to Ypres. Malcolm's confession that Will had been captured by the Germans after a trench raid near the battlefields of Belgium had led her to volunteer to serve with Will's regiment, the 7th battalion of the Northumberland Fusiliers. In the month since her arrival, she had dressed wounds in the trenches, pulled men to safety under enemy fire and spent hours of each night praying for safety while the concussion from exploding bombs rattled the bed on which she lay.

Why Eleanor?

She couldn't say. Stewart had been unable to say anything more about Will's capture than what Malcolm had already told her. She could leave, admit that Will was dead, and go back to England. She could make some pathetic attempt at picking up the pieces of her life and start over.

But she was drawn to this muddy, blood-soaked battleground in a way that not even she fully understood. Somehow she felt closer to Will, as though Passchendaele had kept some part of his spirit even though he was gone.

The scrape of boots on the dirt floor made her look up. Lieutenant-Colonel James Stewart, the battalion's Scottish cohort leader, screwed his face into a ball as he looked at the corpse on the bed.

"Ah! Tim Sedgewick. A good man, if ever I've seen one. Got caught in an explodin' mine, more's the pity." He clucked and shook his head. "The lad had *gaisgeachd*. Courage. Much like you, lass."

Rising, Eleanor poured water into a steel bowl and began to wipe down the body. "I have no courage. Sometimes I can barely stop my knees from shakin' at night when"—she paused, waiting for the thunder of an explosion to fade—"when the shellin' is rattlin' my bunk."

"Aye, and to me that's the very proof of courage." Stewart gave a sagacious nod. "Much like your husband, you're willin' to stare the enemy in the face if it means savin' the life of another."

Eleanor put the bowl down slowly. "That's kind of you to say but there are times when my faith shakes as much as my bed."

"Oh?" Stewart arched a bushy silver eyebrow. "And how's that? You don't think your husband will come back?"

With a sigh, Eleanor wiped the blood from her hands and moved around the bed toward him. "I keep tellin' myself that we'll meet again but he's been gone over a year! I know you've tried to find him, and I'm grateful. But there are millions of prisoners in German hands now and tens of thousands more missin' and I–I..." She stifled a sob, pressing one hand against her face and the other against her hip as she turned away. "I know I should keep believin', but . . . I've never felt so alone."

"Alone?" Stewart cleared his throat. "I wouldn't quite say that you're alone, lass."

Wiping her eyes, Eleanor turned back to him. "I know. I'm needed by the soldiers. They're all that keep me going." She forced a smile. "They've started calling me 'Angel.'"

"And with good reason. You bring them comfort when they need it most. By the way uh," Stewart mumbled as he tapped his hat against the palm of his left hand, "there's someone else who's been askin' for you. A soldier you might remember."

"I, I'm afraid I don't understand."

"Oh, I've been approached by a certain young buck this evenin' who asked for you personally."

"Me?"

"Aye. The mongrel's been pesterin' me with requests for leave so he can go and spend time with his wife. Claims it's his due, although he hasn't seen action for about a year now." He scratched his head. "I suppose I'll have to give him about a week. 'Tis only human to do so given the fact that he'll probably get killed before too long anyhow." He cast a grim glance at the body on the bed.

"Colonel." Eleanor picked up the pitcher of water intending to refill the bowl. "What does this have to do with me?"

"Oh, I, uh thought you might know the fellow." He lifted his head and it was only then that she saw the glint of mischief in his eyes. The stark contrast between the gloom of the moment and the colonel's humor was not lost on her.

"Know him?" She realized she was echoing Stewart but nothing he said made sense.

"Aye. He's about six feet tall, brown hair, thin with a scar down his right cheek, and..." Stewart's voice trailed off for a moment. "He's your husband, lass. Will. He's waitin' for you outside.

The pitcher clattered onto the floor. Eleanor was a statue, staring at him with mouth agape. "Will? *M-my* . . . Will?"

Stepping toward her, Stewart took her by the elbow and gently led her to the door. "He's alive, lass. Escaped from enemy imprisonment and earned a Victoria Cross for his gallantry. He's been recommended for promotion. Just go outside, he's waiting . . . " Stewart's voice faded out of hearing as Eleanor slid to the door.

This is a dream. It had to be! She laid her hand on the door and pulled it open. How many times had she dreamed of the moment she would hear those words? She stumbled down the flight of stairs, breath coming in short gasps.

She no longer heard the concussion of exploding bombs or noticed the distant geysers of dirt that sprayed upward as shells burst into fragments. She no longer saw the bustling crowds that hurried by or felt their rough shoves as they jostled past her. She no longer tasted the iron tang of fear.

She only saw *him*, standing beside an empty lorry, resplendent in his tan uniform, his dark eyes locked on her own.

This is a dream.

But the feel of his powerful arms as they curled around her waist was real. The ardent crush of his lips against her own was real. The feeling of awakening that burgeoned within her heart, as though she were a spring flower receiving the sun's first caress after an endless winter—*that* was real.

Then he spoke and his voice, husky and choked with emotion, melted the last lingering doubt in her mind.

"Hello, El."

Will stooped as he placed a handful of pink primroses on his daughter's grave. "We'll never forget you, Abbey Thompson." Then, rising, he pulled his wife close and gazed up at the overcast London sky.

Conflicting emotions swirled within him. With each breath, he thanked God for the series of miracles that had reunited him with Eleanor. But, as he gazed at the small mound of earth under which their daughter slept, sorrow splintered his heart.

"Promise me somethin', Will." Eleanor turned him toward her, then reached up to touch his cheek.

He cradled her hands in his own then wiped away the wetness from her cheeks. "Anything."

"Against all odds, we've been given a new beginnin'." Her gaze flitted from their daughter's grave to his face. "Promise me that we'll not let anythin' of the past hold us back. I've told you about Malcolm, what he did and why he did it. You've told me about the German family and your struggles with . . . Katja."

Eleanor drew in a deep breath. "I know our love is real, Will. It's what kept us true to each other. I think you're the best man in shoe leather. Thank you for bein' true to me even when . . . " Her breath hitched. "But now, we're together again. Let's agree that we'll keep nothin' from each other. No secrets, nothin'. Together, let's move forward, makin' the most of every minute."

Shivering she wrapped her arms around him. "I learned that when Veronica died. We can be here, hale and hearty, one minute but gone in the next. I need you to hold me. I need you to promise me somethin'. Promise me that we'll not waste a second of our time together by lookin' back."

Will cupped the back of her neck and gently pulled her close, sensing her need for reassurance. There was no one he treasured more than this woman who laid claim to his heart. Whatever the future held, they would make it as long as they faced it with hearts full of faith.

"We won't look back, El. In any case, I've been promoted and reassigned to my original regiment, the Sherwood Foresters. I'm in a totally different part of the army than Malcolm. Like as not, I'll never see him again. So, yeah." He swallowed, feeling the power of the moment. "Yeah, we won't look back."

"You promise?"

"I promise." Cradling her in his arms, he pressed his lips against her own, savoring the warmth of her embrace. "I promise."

JP ROBINSON

Chapter 26

Prisoner of War camp near Münster, Germany.August 1917.

Adele shifted uncomfortably on the unforgiving wooden slats of the bench in the center of the spartan courtroom. It was here that the Münster regional commander played at being God, destroying lives and altering destinies with a few terse words.

Her aging eyes narrowed at the sight of General Klein, her husband's accuser. He too fidgeted in his black uniform, taking a few steps back under her censuring gaze while avoiding her eyes. The judge, a vulture in a spiked helmet, also wore black. It was as though the pair wished to announce by the somber color of their clothing that there would soon be a reason for Burkhard's family to mourn.

Adele suppressed a shudder and gripped Katja with a clammy hand. At her daughter's insistence, they had both worn white. Katja's words, spoken this morning, flitted through her mind.

Wear white as a symbol of resistance. Father has done nothing wrong. Why wear the colors of a mourner as though we ourselves doubted his innocence?

Now, her daughter smiled at her, but the warm brown of her eyes was unable to conceal the worry that plagued them both. Adele had wrestled with her emotions throughout the past two weeks. Worry for her husband. Fury sparked by her daughter's impetuous actions. Compassion brought on by the knowledge that, in Katja's place, she would have done the same. She had been reduced to an emotional ragdoll.

"It'll be all right." Katja shifted closer, slipping her arm around her mother's shoulder.

Aside from the judge and General Klein, they were the only occupants of the room. Military regulations had not allowed entry to the throng of neighbors and friends that had wanted to stand by Burkhard in his hour of need. They had written letters instead, letters that Adele hoped would somehow alter the situation in Burkhard's favor. Judging by the commander's stony face, that possibility was remote at best.

"Bring in the accused." The commander, a short, greying man with a sharp nose and hooded eyebrows who would preside over Burkhard's trial, spoke without preamble.

Klein saluted, clicking his heels together. "At once, *Kommandant.*" Marching to a door to the judge's right, Klein jerked it open and barked out an order.

Within moments, Burkhard shuffled into the room, chained and escorted by three guards. Adele gasped, stunned by the change that two weeks of imprisonment had wrought. His eyes, once so bright with life, were now dull pools. His pallid skin and sunken cheeks gave mute testament to the food shortages that plagued the country. She understood the government's logic. Why feed a man who would doubtless be condemned to die?

Burkhard caught sight of her and a spark of energy animated his eyes. "Adele." He started toward her, but the soldiers grabbed his arms, pinning them to his sides.

"Father!" Katja rose, but Adele quickly pulled her back onto the wooden bench. The last thing she wanted was to have another member of her family incarcerated.

"Burkhard Meier." The judge cracked his neck then peered down at the prisoner from his perch on the elevated platform. "I am General Oberlott, regional military commander under the authority of his Majesty, Kaiser Wilhelm II. You stand accused of treason. A prisoner of war escaped your care. How do you answer this charge?"

"Not . . . guilty." Burkard's voice was a shallow croak.

"How original." Oberlott rolled his eyes then shuffled through a sheaf of papers. "Do you deny granting the prisoner access to your home?"

"No."

"What precautions did you take to ensure he did *not* escape?"

There was a slight pause. "None."

"And did you, knowing the natural reaction of any prisoner is an attempt at escape, insist that he wear his prisoner's garb at all times?"

"Well, I couldn't—"

"Yes or no, *Herr* Meier, yes or no."

Burkhard dropped his head. "No."

"Ah." With a shake of his head the commander began to pace behind a rectangular wooden desk that separated them. "You see, General Klein has apprised me of the details of this case. Although he was your friend, he made it very clear that on several occasions you were warned about becoming too familiar with the prisoner. Is this true?"

"Yes."

"And despite these warnings, you persisted on treating the enemy as an equal."

At these words, Burkhard raised his head and threw his shoulders back. "I showed Will Thompson the love of God and for that, I have no regrets. It is you, the power-hungry leaders of Germany that drag this wretched war on!"

He ripped his arms free and lifted them in a pleading gesture. "If it were left to us ordinary citizens, this butchery would have ended long ago. English, French, German, what difference does it make? I loved that boy." His voice softened then broke. "Loved him like the son I lost. And if I had the choice, I would have set him free the moment he first entered my house."

There were six frozen statues in the room, each staring at the man who had cast aside whatever scrap of doubt remained of his guilt.

Adele was the first to find her voice. "Burkhard?"

He craned his neck in effort to see her then forced the corners of his mouth upward in a herculean attempt at a smile. "Be brave, my love."

"Well, if nothing else, I must thank you for your honesty." Oberlott gave the prisoner an appraising look. "You have made my job an easy one."

Adele stifled a sob. "No, please God, no."

"Wait!" Katja shot to her feet, arm extended. "My father had nothing to do with the prisoner's escape. I planned it. I did it. Me!"

"Sit down, *Fräulein*." The judge pinned her with an angry glare.

Katja ignored him. "I loved Will. I helped him escape but my father knew nothing of it."

"Katja, no!" Burkhard's cry mingled with her mother's muted whimpers and Oberlott's angry shout.

"I said to sit down!"

"If it is justice you want"—Katja sucked in a deep breath, balling her fists at her sides—"then you must punish me, not him."

Oberlott glared first at Katja then at Burkhard, whose face had gone deathly pale. "Is this true?" The question was directed at Burkhard.

"I . . ."

"Answer the question! Is it true? Is your daughter guilty of treason?"

"No." Clenching his jaw, Burkhard met the general's eyes. "My daughter is innocent."

"Papa!"

Burkhard raised his voice. "I gave the prisoner access to my lorry. I gave him the clothing and supplies. The fault lies with me."

"Papa, please, don't do this!"

Adele pulled her daughter down onto the bench and wrapped her in a tight embrace. "He loves you," she whispered into Katja's ear. "He'll do anything, *say* anything to protect you. Don't let it be in vain."

Oberlott held Burkard's gaze for several long minutes then nodded once. When he spoke again, his voice was tinged with a note of respect that Adele had not noticed until this moment.

"I see." Turning to the soldiers he said, "Secure the prisoner. General Klein"—he motioned to the man in the corner—"come with me."

<hr/>

General Klein followed his commander into a small, white antechamber that sat behind the courtroom, then closed the door firmly behind him. With each step, the aged general mentally cursed the moment he had allowed his friend to take Will Thompson under his wing. At the moment, it had seemed a kindness to do so.

Klein, like all who knew Burkhard, had realized that the farmer's grief over the loss of his son was destroying him. When Burkhard had approached him with the idea of helping Will recover in his home, Klein had pushed aside his misgivings with the hope that healing Will would also heal the wound that putrefied inside his friend's soul.

If Klein could have seen the future, he would have shot Will Thompson in the field the day he had been caught fighting. But honor had dictated that, given the circumstances of the brawl, he spare the prisoner's life. Honor had driven him to arrest Burkhard on the charge of treason when Will had escaped. And honor now compelled him to testify against Burkhard, knowing that to do so would devastate a family that had already suffered far too much.

"So." General Oberlott jerked off his helmet and tossed it onto a narrow rectangular table. "The daughter set the man free and her father is lying to protect her."

"The prisoner *was* his responsibility, *Kommandant,* regardless of the specifics." Klein thrust his hands in his pockets.

Oberlott raked his fingers through his silver hair. "Ah, yes, the specifics. We must not forget about them. In fact, the specifics of this case change everything."

"With respect, *Kommandant*, what do you mean?" Klein frowned. "Will not Burkhard have to pay with his life?"

"Pay with his life?" The regional commander barked out a harsh laugh. "Of course not!"

Klein stared at him. "B-but the law dictates that treason is punishable by death. This is treason."

"It is treason only if I *decide* it is treason." Oberlott's voice hardened. "These are modern times, General. Perhaps you do not see that the days of the kaiser are numbered, but believe me, it is the generals of Germany who will soon hold power. As such, our decisions must be governed by the realities of the battlefield, not by archaic notions of blind obedience."

He sighed then gestured toward a newspaper on the table. "The Fatherland is starving. Food shortages, fuel scarcities. The Allied blockade of our ports is crippling our nation. If I execute this man, who is a peat farmer, what do you think could happen?"

Klein scratched his head. "Well, local fuel production will suffer."

"Exactly." Oberlott rubbed his clean-shaven jaw. "Where there is no fuel there is unrest. I will not have disorder in my region which is exactly what will happen if he dies."

He turned and grabbed a handful of letters which he tossed onto the table. "Furthermore, this Burkhard is quite popular for a farmer. Dozens of letters have come pouring in as news of his arrest spread. Neighbors describe him as a saint. Business leaders call him an asset. His execution could lead to riots, such as those in Berlin." Oberlott shook his head. "*Nein.* I refuse to take such a chance."

Now it was Klein who passed his hand over his grizzled chin. The first Berlin riots had begun over a year ago, sparked by women grousing over low food supplies and high prices. As civilian morale ebbed across the country, the riots had become more common place. Oberlott was right. Burkhard's execution could easily become the focal point for the people's anger, leading to a fresh wave of riots.

Doubtless the *kommandant* also intended to protect his own political career. If the Fatherland's generals did indeed take power, a man who could not control his own region would be viewed as ineffective. In preventing an uprising, Oberlott was, in effect, protecting his reputation.

The thought gave rise to another, one that made Klein's collar itch. Many would remember that it was he who had arrested Burkhard.

Klein cleared his throat. "I see. So, what will you do?"

"What is practical. I will find him to be innocent." Oberlott picked up his helmet and tucked it beneath his arm.

"Innocent?" His superior's words had punched the air from Klein's lungs. "How can he be innocent?"

Instead of answering, the *kommandant* marched toward the door, jerked it open, and entered the courtroom.

—◆●◆—

Katja pulled away from her mother as the commander stormed back into the room. His eyes, a merciless gray, raked over her as though she were the source of all Germany's troubles.

No. That would be the war. Not me.

She wiped her cheeks with her palms, steeling her nerves for the coming condemnation. This part of the trial was a charade. Papa had admitted his guilt, or rather, had taken the blame for her crime and there could be no doubt of the verdict.

But had she committed a crime? She had liberated the man she loved, sacrificing everything she had wanted so he could return to the woman who had first claims on his heart. Could that be considered a crime?

No. The crime would have been to keep him for herself, to lure him down a path they both would have regretted.

For her part, Katja knew she could never love again. She did not want to. She had tasted the heady sweetness of love's wine once and some part of her found a sort of contentment in that alone.

Her mind flipped through cherished memories, like a reader turning the pages of a book. Will, hanging from the post after being whipped for fighting on her behalf. Will, broken and lost in a tormented whirlpool of hate only to realize that Germans bled as red as he did.

The papers had carried the story of a prisoner exchange gone awry in Rotterdam. Despite the kaiser's claims to the contrary, the paper quoted military sources in both Germany and the Netherlands that claimed the British had humiliated both nations by forcing them to release a prisoner who had unexpectedly appeared on the docks.

A faint smile tugged at Katja's lips as she closed her eyes, seeing his handsome face again in her mind and savoring the knowledge that her sacrifice had not been in vain.

No other man could touch her life as he had. The memories of his gallantry and tenderness were enough to sustain her, if not fill her heart, until she died.

"Burkhard Meier." The *kommandant's* stentorian voice jerked her eyes open. "After due consideration, the court has reached a verdict."

Due consideration? Katja's jaw clenched even as her eyes flew open. There had been no jury, no trial by her father's peers. No defense to find some legal loophole, to—

"The court finds you innocent of treason."

Mama gasped. "Innocent?"

Katja's hand flew to her mouth. *Innocent?*

General Oberlott's steely gaze flickered over the two women then shifted back to her father. "However, the fact remains that a prisoner of the empire escaped while in your care. You are therefore found guilty of neglect of duty."

"M-my punishment?" Papa clutched his manacled fists against his chest.

"You will be placed under house arrest for the duration of the war. Aside from deliveries of peat to your regular clients, you will not leave your farm. You will also agree not to participate in any acts of protest against the ruling government. Fail to do so, and you will be tried again, this time with no leniency."

Papa gaped first at him then at his chains. "Y-you mean, I am free?"

"No, you are condemned to house arrest." Oberlott's eyes narrowed. "If you prefer to stay here, or if you find the penalty too lenient, I can adjust the sentence."

"No, no!" Papa dipped his head. "House arrest is harsh indeed."

"Release him." General Klein snapped his fingers as he stepped forward. The chains had no sooner fallen from Papa's wrists than Mama leapt from her seat and hurried toward him, losing herself in his embrace.

"I never thought . . . " Her words ended in a half-choked sob.

Papa reached an arm out and Katja, scarcely able to breathe, slid into his reach.

"You're free." She reached up and touched his weathered face. "Oh, Papa!"

He chuckled, a wheezing cough that soon matured into a full, belly laugh. "How I prayed to hold you both in my arms again!"

The three of them remained, clutching each other for several long moments, unable to give voice to the emotions that played about in their hearts.

"If you're ready, Burkhard, I will escort you all back to the farm." General Klein's voice cast a momentary shadow over the small group, but her father pulled away from them and stepped forward with arm extended.

"I understand, Uther." Burkhard clasped the general's arm. "It had to be done. For honor."

"I cannot tell you how happy I am with the court's decision."

"Neither can I." Papa stepped back. "Neither can I."

Then, with a smile on his pale face and a twinkle in his eye, he curled an arm around both his wife's and his daughter's waists. "Let's go home."

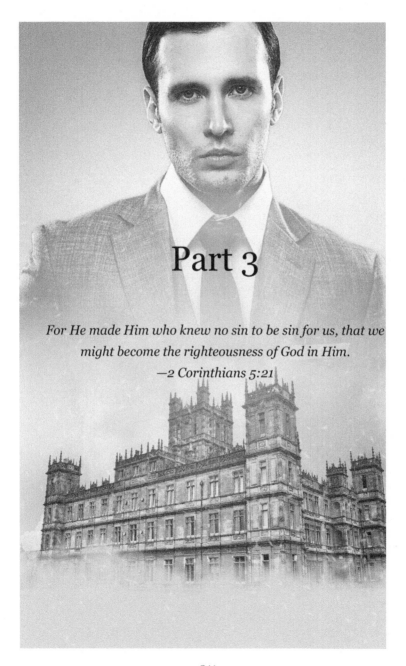

Part 3

For He made Him who knew no sin to be sin for us, that we might become the righteousness of God in Him.

—*2 Corinthians 5:21*

JP ROBINSON

Chapter 27

Château des Aigles, Switzerland, August 1917.

Jutting out over the clear, sapphire waters of Lake Thun, Thomas Steele's secluded castle was nothing short of an architectural masterpiece. Known as the *Château des Aigles* because of its lofty perch in the Swiss Alps —and the massive bronze eagle that glared down at the few guests bold enough to traverse the castle's main entrance— the *château* traced its origins to the 13ᵗʰ century.

It was a mélange of various architectural styles. Variegated Romanesque turrets gently sloped upward while patches of ivy curled around the white Turkish towers. It all combined to create a sort of magical aura that Isabella Steele had adored.

Thomas had acquired the castle over a decade earlier as a second property, hoping that the pristine Alpine climate would help his beloved wife recover her health or, at the least, ease the pain that consumed her.

But Isabella had passed away in his study which overlooked the water. Lake Thun had been her favorite view. She had gazed upon it until the angels carried her away to a castle more magnificent than human hands could ever fashion. The loss had altered the course of Thomas's life.

Now, as he gazed into the lake's depths, standing with arms folded across his starched, white shirt and his chin resting on the ball of his thumb, Thomas could not escape the feeling that his destiny would once more change course in this very room.

As a warm evening breeze rose off the lake and passed through the study's open bay windows, his mind rolled through the events that had made him a voluntary exile in neutral Switzerland. Greyson, his resourceful butler, had managed to telephone him after the failed attack on Northshire, warning him to stay out of Great Britain.

Despite the gravity of the moment, the corners of Thomas's lips curved upward. Greyson's report had included a detailed account of Malcolm's defense of the estate. A surge of pride made his shoulders rise a little higher. *You were right all along, Isabella. The prodigal has become a man of honor.*

The fact that Malcolm had returned to the Front lines instead of launching some foolhardy attempt to liberate his wife from the Tower only increased Thomas's confidence in his son. Malcolm clearly realized that he had a duty that was greater than his own desires, a concept he had been unable to grasp only two years before.

But then his smile faded.

Duty. He was a soldier. He understood the importance of responsibility. Duty was powerful, compelling blind obedience to a higher purpose. It was the force that had driven him to leave his family and wage war across continents in the name of an Empire. But now there was an even higher call, a stronger force.

With a grimace, he glanced around the spacious room. The walls were covered in a kaleidoscope of pastel oranges and greens, allowing the natural light from the large bay windows and the glass ceiling to create an inviting atmosphere. Despite the warmth of the summer evening, however, a chill spread through Thomas's chest as his mind wrestled with the decision that lay before him. He had to decide where his duty lay.

His brow furrowed. Robert Hughes, head of British foreign intelligence, believed that Thomas was complicit in a plot against the Empire and had imprisoned Leila in the tower. She would be granted a farce of a trial and then executed. Britain had no tolerance for foreign spies, not with millions of her sons lying cold on the battlefields of Europe and the Orient.

But Hughes had not stopped with Leila's arrest. The press, no doubt eager for a detailed account of the excitement at Northshire, had carried a story dubbed the "Steele Scandal." It was the latest proof of the German collaborators—the enemy that hid in plain sight. Hughes had played upon the people's need for security in order to increase the government's power while decreasing their rights to privacy.

According to Greyson, polls carried in the London Times indicated that the nation was divided on the issue with a little less than half the country believing that Thomas Steele was a traitor. To date, confidence in the Bank of England remained largely unshaken, but while this news was encouraging, Thomas knew that the support of the people was fickle.

It was only a matter of time before he would be officially removed from his role as head of the Bank of England—a move that many shareholders would support. No one would want to associate with a man tainted with the stench of treason, even if he was innocent. No, Thomas knew he had to strike, hard and fast, before Hughes's manipulation eroded whatever support remained to him.

At the core of the problem lay one person: Leila. She was his daughter-in-law, and while Hughes did not know this, she stood to inherit Northshire upon his death.

But it was not only Leila's life at stake. Thomas rubbed the grizzled stubble along his chin. Greyson had informed him of the possibility that Leila carried his unborn grandchild. The British government would not execute a pregnant woman but, in the Tower, Leila's health could easily be compromised, putting both herself and his grandchild at risk. Once the child was born, she would be shot.

Turning from the view of the tranquil lake, Thomas shoved his hands into the pockets of his navy-blue slacks and moved toward a painting on the opposite wall. It depicted a small vessel tossed about on a dark, wind-swept sea. The scene would indeed be depressing were it not for the solitary figure of Christ who strode across the white-capped waters, arm outstretched to His fearful disciples.

Thomas considered the painting for several long minutes then sunk into a dark brown leather armchair, slowly tapping his fingertips together.

"How, Father?" He slumped forward, covering his face with his hands. "How can I do it?" The question was not how to go about gaining Leila's freedom as much as it was how to pay the price that would be required.

The price. To save her, he would have to violate every principle by which he had lived up to this moment: honor, justice, and truth. His reputation would be destroyed. In fact, he would become the very traitor that Hughes already proclaimed him to be. But to let her die without lifting a finger . . .

Hughes would expect him to offer some sort of exchange; his life for Leila's. Thomas shook his head, scoffing. Not only was it against his nature to surrender without a fight but, if he agreed, Hughes would simply try them, then execute them both.

He tilted his head from side to side, as the burden of decision pressed down on his shoulders. On one hand, it seemed ludicrous to even consider waging political war against his own country. War was messy. It could only be justified by a cause that outweighed its brutality.

His eyes narrowed as he probed the causes for this war against the nation he loved. First, he needed to safeguard his family. Leila's words, spoken so long ago, passed through his mind like fog in the early morning.

I don't want to be your enemy, Thomas. I want to be what I was meant to be . . . your family. She carried his grandchild. In protecting her, he protected his descendants.

Second, despite Malcolm's reforms, it was clear that he would need Leila's shrewd mind to effectively manage the estate. By taking up the sword against Robert Hughes and his own government, Thomas would preserve the Steele heritage that he and his forefathers had labored to establish.

Beads of sweat broke out on his forehead. He was caught between two extremes. Patriotic love had driven him to fight for king and country for decades. Love for the empire had sustained him when he was wounded and bleeding on the battlefields of Asia and Africa. But now a higher love called out to him, twisting his mind in an agony of indecision.

"She's become my daughter." He pounded his fist on the arm of the chair. "I can't just let her die!"

When he had granted Leila leave to remain at Northshire and accepted her marriage to Malcolm, she had indeed become a part of his family. The transforming power of Christ, coupled with her passion for Northshire and its tenants, had bound her to him more closely than any natural ties of blood. Leila was a Steele. Equally important, it was possible that she now *carried* a Steele.

With a deep groan, he shoved himself upright, catching sight of his reflection in a mirror. The dying rays of sunlight glinted off the moisture that covered his face, giving the impression that it was blood, and not sweat, that dotted his furrowed brow.

"Father is there any other way?" He spoke through gritted teeth, barely noticing the dull ache in his jaw. "Surely there *must* be another way!"

But that was it. There was no other way.

Malcolm was fighting in Flanders. At the moment, it was the best place he could be. Few would question the loyalty of a man running *toward* the enemy. Not even Hughes would be able to impinge Malcolm's reputation as long as Thomas kept his distance.

His heart clenched. He was a father who would have to give the appearance of abandoning his own son in order to rescue the woman who had once been his enemy.

This was not a fight that Malcolm could win. Hughes was well entrenched, fortified behind the bulwarks of political power and an international network of formidable spies. To defeat him, the scale of his attack would have to be unprecedented.

"So it comes to this." He expelled his breath with a slow *whoosh*. "So be it."

Turning slowly, as though he had aged twenty years in as many minutes, Thomas limped toward the study's double doors. The moment of decision had come, and nothing would ever be the same.

Chapter 28

Tower of London, Great Britain, August 1917.

Leila shivered as she rebuttoned her stained, cream top then turned back to the physician. The man was like a spider, thin with long legs. It seemed fitting to compare a man who haunted the gloomy crevices of the Tower's dungeons to a spider.

The cell in which she had spent the past month was little more than an oblong hole in a rock wall, about seven feet across and eight feet long. The floor—if it could be called a floor—was an uneven mass of granite that made sitting difficult and sleep almost impossible.

Despite the summer temperatures, the days in the subterranean cell were cool. The nights were frigid. One rectangular window, cut into a teardrop-shaped hole in the wall, allowed a measure of light to enter, along with noxious fumes of prison sewage that was dumped into the moat that ringed the Tower walls. The entire picture was a garish nightmare that harked more of the Middle Ages than the modern world.

At times she forgot that, outside this archaic granite tomb, lay a bustling society filled with men and women who lived, dreamed, and loved . . . as she loved.

"Do you have the results of your test?" Coughing, Leila forced herself to look at the arachnid whose beady eyes darted about in all directions.

"Yes." The quiet tone of his voice did nothing to conceal its sinister edge. "Yes, I think the results are most conclusive."

She stepped forward, eyes drilling into his skull, her sense of loathing forgotten in an overpowering need to know the truth. "What are they?"

"When Sir Robert told me of your possible condition, I was delighted at the chance to test my latest theory." He sniggered, his silken voice making her brow crinkle with disgust. "Urine analysis is still a new field and one I don't often have the chance to explore on prisoners."

The gleam of gold in his crooked teeth glinted in the afternoon sunlight. "The results of my test, along with your missed menses, nausea, and fatigue means"—he steepled his thin fingertips together as his smile widened—"you are pregnant."

He continued speaking but Leila did not hear another word. A roaring sound filled her ears as though she were once again in the East End of London, witnessing the wholesale destruction caused by the bombs of the Zeppelins. But indeed, the physician's words were like those bombs, blowing craters in whatever semblance of peace she had managed to scrape together while locked away in this pit of stone.

She was arrested for treason, her husband was risking his life in the trenches of Flanders, her father-in-law was a fugitive and she—she was pregnant.

"Oh God." She groaned as she swayed and slumped to the ground, banging her knees on the rough stones. "No, this can't be!" Under normal circumstances, she would have been overjoyed. But these circumstances were *not* normal.

The doctor eyed her dispassionately. "I must report to Sir Hughes. He was most insistent that you be examined."

Rapping on the cell door twice, he waited as a guard unlocked it. "Look at the bright side."

"The bright side?" Leila's voice was dull.

"Well, they won't kill you while you're pregnant, now will they? They'll let you see the little one, rip it from your arms, then shoot you. Ha!" With the wild cackle of a madman, he scuttled through the gate, then slammed it shut behind him.

Sir Robert Hughes approached the cell with the distinct sensation that he was about to achieve a monumental victory. Leila Steele, the deceptive Delilah that had secreted information to the enemy while in his own employ, was at last a prisoner in a cage of stone.

A soft caw grated against his ear and Hughes smirked at the raven that sat on his shoulder. The thought struck him that, with his wooden leg, dark navy uniform and the bird, he was the quintessential image of a modern pirate.

I rather like that, actually. His grin widened, and he winced. He wasn't used to smiling.

The debacle at Northshire had become a national affair, one which divided London society from members of Parliament to beggars on the street. Despite the incontestable evidence—the transmitters, German code books, and more—retrieved from the estate of Northshire, a good portion of the public clung to the ridiculous speculation that the government was abusing its expanded wartime powers.

Pressure was mounting for Whitehall to rescind its charges against Thomas which intensified the pressure the Prime Minister placed upon Hughes. David Lloyd George had told him in no uncertain terms to, "finish this matter quickly or the people will forget everything you've done for them."

Hughes chuckled as he approached Leila's cell. The battle was all but over. He had Northshire Estate under constant military guard, Leila was locked away, and Thomas would be next.

Hughes peered at Leila through the iron bars. She was curled up in a ball in the corner of the room, blonde hair lying in a mess of tangles and dirt. He knew his treatment was harsh, but what else did the girl deserve? Spies, such as the beautiful menace before him, threatened the security of the Empire.

"You should be happy I've put you in this cell." She started at the sound of his voice and turned slowly toward him. "It's quite famous, you know. Thomas Moore was caged in here centuries ago." He paused, then said, "You probably don't know who he was though, you little savage."

Leila wiped a smudge of dirt from her cheek then pinned him with a glare. "Moore was a fifteenth century politician who was executed by King Henry VIII because he refused to support the king's wish to divorce his wife and start his own church."

Hughes arched an eyebrow. "Impressive. This is what they teach you in the *Kriegsnachrichtenstelle*?"

"That and other things."

"Ah." He thumped his walking stick against his palm. "One must know one's enemy, eh?"

Silence.

"You could count it an honor to be imprisoned in the cell of such a great man." He gestured expansively at the stone walls. "The best accommodations in the house I'd say. Then again, since Thomas was beheaded for treason . . . perhaps not."

Leila slowly pushed herself to a standing position. "I have no time for games."

"No time?" Hughes scratched the neck of the raven, earning a pleased *caw* in return. "I would think that time is all you have. Time to think. Time to grieve. Time to prepare to die."

She lifted her chin. "I am not afraid of death. Not anymore."

"Well I'm so glad to hear that. It makes ordering your execution *so* much less painful. I do hope your father-in-law shares your courage."

"Thomas?" Leila's pale face became ghostlike. "You know where he is?"

Hughes shifted his weight onto his left foot, easing the pressure on his stump. "Of course, I know where he is. Where else would the buffoon go but to his mansion in Switzerland? He's safe there because the Swiss are too busy flirting with every European nation to pick a side. Our government will never authorize direct military action against Thomas for fear of pushing the Swiss into bed with the Germans. My hands are tied." He leaned forward and grinned once more. "Or so Thomas thinks."

"You plan to use me as bait."

The smile froze on Hughes's face. The girl's cleverness was actually quite annoying. Not that it was totally unexpected; she had managed to pull the wool over his eyes when serving as his cleaner.

"It won't work." Leila folded her arms across her chest. "Thomas will never sacrifice himself for me."

Robert pursed his lips, tilting his head to one side. "Oh, I wouldn't be so sure of that. I think you underestimate him."

"What exactly are you saying?"

Instead of answering, Hughes motioned for the nearest of the eight guards surrounding the cell to open the door. Inside, he slammed the door shut then leaned against the far wall while ensuring that Leila could see the butt of a revolver that protruded from the holster on his hip.

"Thomas knew from the moment he gave you shelter that he was betraying his country. Harboring an enemy agent?" Hughes scoffed and shook his head. "Of all the stupid—"

"He wanted to win me over to your cause. He's done nothing wrong."

"Oh, spare me the pitiful platitudes. I've heard all I care to and more about Steele's supposed innocence." His voice hardened. "The fact remains that Thomas *will* trade himself for you, especially when he learns you are carrying his grandchild!"

Leila swayed, steadying herself by thrusting her hands out against the rough face of the granite wall. "And you call *me* a savage? You would use an innocent child to your own ends?"

"If the child is yours, it is not innocent, madam. *Nothing* about you is innocent. You manipulate men like a puppeteer pulling strings."

"But surely your conscience—"

"Conscience?" Hughes barked out a laugh. "I am a spy. Spies cannot afford the luxury of a conscience . . . as you well know." He lifted a finger as though suddenly recalling a forgotten detail. "Wasn't it you who used a young man's heart as a means of gaining access to classified information?"

Her head drooped.

"You corrupted one of Britain's best, a man who was my *friend,* and you *dare* speak to me of conscience?"

The raven's caws broke the silence that filled the cramped cell.

"I make no excuses for what I was." Slowly, Leila lifted her head. "But I am different now and whatever you plan will fail. I *will* not let Thomas die in my place."

Hughes leaned forward. "Do you know why these ravens are here?"

She did not answer.

"Almost a thousand years ago, William the Conqueror prophesied that 'if the ravens ever leave the tower, the kingdom will fall.'" He stroked the bird's maw again. "That's what you Germans want. To bring down the greatest empire ever to rise on European soil."

Heat crept along the back of his neck. "Well it won't happen! You lot will stop at nothing to destroy us. I have no choice but to retaliate using every weapon at my disposal! Like these birds, you will die here, a captive inside this mound of stone. Your fate is to die so that the kingdom is secure. Thomas *will* come and you will never see the light of day."

He rapped sharply on the door and a soldier unbolted the lock. Slipping outside, he turned back for one parting blow, but Leila spoke first.

"You will fail, Robert. God is on my side."

"Is He?" Hughes let the question hiss through the dank air. When he spoke again, his voice was a low growl. "How interesting. Thomas Moore thought the same thing."

With those words, he turned and shuffled off, leaving the sadistic echo of the raven's caw.

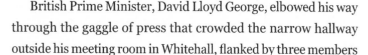

British Prime Minister, David Lloyd George, elbowed his way through the gaggle of press that crowded the narrow hallway outside his meeting room in Whitehall, flanked by three members of his security team.

"Any word on the Steele Scandal, sir?" A voice sang out the question from his right.

Another reporter leapt in front of David's twisted face, the flashbulb of his camera nearly blinding him in a pop of light. "Yeah, guv'nor, we've got a right to know!"

"There have been no developments." David resumed his rapid march toward his office as security shoved the meddlesome man aside. "I have no further comment."

Voices, hungry for a morsel of information that could be misconstrued into a hundred variations of truth, shouted from the crowd.

"Will Steele be extradited from Switzerland?"

"How will this impact the country's finances, sir? Will the Bank of England still back the war effort?"

"C'mon guv', give us somethin'!"

Lips pressed into a tight line, the Prime Minister barged into his office, slamming the door behind him with a slight sigh. But his relief was short-lived as he took in the grim faces of the members of his War Cabinet.

"Quite the commotion out there." Milner, assistant to the Council, loosened the black necktie around his throat. "I barely made it in alive."

"Journalists!" The heavy voice of the Exchequer filled the small room. "They're like harpies, just waiting for a chance to glut themselves on the wounded."

"Wounded?" David jerked off his black suit jacket, threw himself into a short, wooden chair, and propped his elbows on the round table that was situated in the center of the room. "Our government isn't just *wounded* gentlemen; we're at the point of death!"

Silence claimed them all.

Brows knitted together, David's stern gaze slid to Robert Hughes who, while not a member of the War Cabinet, had been instructed to join them for today's meeting. "Hughes, did you even stop to consider the impact of blabbing your mouth?"

"Of course, Prime Minister." Robert straightened in his seat. "There were too many witnesses at Northshire to conceal the affair. The public was bound to unearth the truth."

"That's not what I mean, and you know it." David slammed his fist against the table. "I'm talking about Thomas, man, Thomas! Was the public *bound* to unearth that as well?"

"I did my duty, Prime Minister."

Cynicism dripped like acid from David's voice. "Yes, well, you must be chuffed about it!"

Lord Curzon, President of the War Council, spoke next. He was an arrogant bigot, tall with a curved nose, whose ruthlessness mirrored his character.

"For once, I must agree with the Prime Minister. Informing the rabble that a man privy to government secrets has been in bed with the enemy is truly not in our best interests. How could you have been such an utter fool, Robert?"

"Gentlemen, gentlemen." The soft voice of the Prime Minister's assistant, Henderson, rose over Hughes's mangled protest. He removed the small oval glasses from his eyes as if, in so doing, he could better see the emotions that flickered across their faces. "Perhaps, now is not the best time to begin a war of words. As we all know, there is another war, one that is quite real, raging just across the Channel and we do have more important considerations at hand."

"Yes." David glared at the seemingly undaunted spymaster, "Foremost of which is how to continue to finance our military operations now that we've publicly accused the leader of the Bank of England—which happens to be our strongest domestic financial backer—of treason!"

He sucked in a deep breath, barely restraining himself from leaping out of his chair, wrapping his Welsh hands around the man's scrawny neck and squeezing with all his might. But murder, although definitely justifiable in this case, would not enhance either his political career or the well-being of his country.

"Thomas will retaliate, gentlemen." David exhaled slowly. We must be prepared."

"Retaliate?" Hughes scoffed. "How? We have him boxed in a corner. His daughter-in-law is expecting. She's locked up in the Tower. I've sent him an ultimatum and he'll be here within a fortnight."

"An ultimatum?" Milner raised a skeptical eyebrow. "I applaud your patriotism Hughes but—"

"I was Viceroy of India back in '99," Lord Curzon cut Milner off without a hint of apology. "Steele was a general I assigned to the eastern Bengal region. I showed up at his barracks for a surprise inspection and made the mistake of staying the night."

His eyes glazed over. "The locals must have gotten word that I was coming. That night a group of armed Hindu nationalists surrounded the barracks, ready to burn it and us to the ground. We were outnumbered you see, the Empire's resources were already stretched quite thin. To retreat would be to lose face and to attack would be suicidal. Reinforcements were at least three days away."

"What happened?" Milner leaned forward.

Curzon shrugged. "Steele happened. He ordered his men to hold their fire. He walked out—alone and unarmed—in front of those howling savages and demanded to talk to their leader. God knows I've never seen such pluck in all my days. Steele negotiated a deal with the Indian leader and within an hour they were gone. All of us owed him our lives."

He shook his head then continued. "If you think you've got him in a box, Robert, you're wrong."

At this, David pivoted to the Exchequer, Bonar Law, who sat on his right. "Has there been any word from the Bank of England?"

"Yes, actually. Joseph Mara, Steele's second-in-command at the Bank, rang me just this morning regarding our request for additional funding." Running his fingers over his short moustache, Law added, "I was told that some of the necessary paperwork is missing. There will be a processing delay of about a fortnight."

"Balderdash!" David leapt to his feet. "Joseph has always been Thomas's secret devotee. I'm willing to wager that Thomas has contacted him somehow and given him orders to delay. He knows we're desperate!"

The Exchequer nodded. "He knows better than most that war runs on money not just manpower. I have, of course, spoken to Parliament and the King, requesting that the Bank of England's governing structure be legally reexamined. After all, we can't have a traitor heading one of our most prestigious financial institutions. But such a procedure will take time."

"Time that we don't have." Milner drummed the dark surface of the table with his fingertips.

Hughes spoke up quickly, the hint of a smug smile on his face. "I've beaten you to the punch, gentlemen. Last week I sent a wire to Thomas, giving him thirty days to turn himself in if he wants his daughter-in-law to live." He leaned back in his chair, fingers laced behind his head. "I included a postscript telling him that he'll soon be a grandfather. Thomas will show up and we'll nab him quicker than you can say 'Bob's your uncle!'"

"Thirty days?" David threw back his head with a snort. "The man's no fool, Robert. He knows we can't legally execute a pregnant woman. Even if she is a Hun. And he knows jolly well that you won't let her go if he shows up. No, Thomas will take his time, plotting a blow that will cripple the nation."

"Well, I for one refuse to believe it." Henderson pushed back his chair from the table and stood up. "Thomas would never forsake his own. He loves this Empire. Sweat drops of blood for it, he has!"

A few voices around the table murmured their assent and Hughes, face flushed, pushed himself upright.

"Sweat drops of blood? Ha!" He leaned against the table for support. "Consider the following, gentlemen. First, Thomas amassed a private army on his estate, citing a need for security. Second, two of my men sent to infiltrate his property turned up dead. Third, information that only he, myself, and the Prime Minister had access to was transmitted to the enemy. Finally, I confiscated professionally assembled radio transmission equipment worth over three hundred quid. Again, on his property!" His voice dropped to a scathing hiss. "And you still insist that he is a loyal subject of the crown?"

Silence claimed the small group once more.

David clasped his hands together, as though praying, and pressed his forehead against the knuckles of his thumbs. "The die has been cast, gentlemen. I too find it hard to believe but, no matter what Thomas originally intended, when Hughes made this situation a public show, he forced Thomas's hand. We pushed him over to the enemy's side."

Slowly, he lifted his head, locking eyes with each member of his cabinet. "This bit with the bank is just the beginning. Something bigger is coming, you mark my words."

David pushed himself upright. They hadn't discussed anything on their agenda but at the moment, he doubted anyone was in a frame of mind to do so. "Right. Let's take a break and meet back here at half past three. Do try to dodge the press on your way out."

Then he slumped forward, lost in a world of private speculations, leaving the members of his cabinet to face the mob of howling reporters.

Chapter 29

Château des Aigles, Switzerland, August 1917.
Arthur Hoffman pulled his thin, five-foot three-inch frame to its maximum height while tugging sharply on the lapels of his plaid suit jacket. It was an effort to convince himself that he was not intimidated by the metallic glare of the domineering eagle that guarded the arched entrance to the *Château des Aigles.*

He pushed aside the niggling voice in his mind that insisted he *was* afraid—perhaps not of the statue itself, but of the family it represented. Or, more specifically, of the man who had become the stuff of legend: Sir Thomas Steele.

As a stakeholder in Switzerland's seven-member government called the Federal Council, Arthur was intimately acquainted with Thomas's strong involvement in Switzerland's economy. Thomas bled business and politics just as he had once bled military strategy. Now, as Arthur wiped moist palms on the legs of his maroon slacks, he mentally reviewed what he knew of the man.

Over the past three decades, Thomas had used his vast wealth to develop a string of manufacturing plants, specializing in the fields of metallurgy and precision engineering. He employed at least a thousand Swiss workers in various cantons across the country. Based on a recent economic report, his companies had indirectly produced almost ten percent of the nation's exports.

Hoffman sniffed as he stepped past the eagle and began the trek up the white polished limestone steps that graced the outside of the château. The view from this elevated perch was nothing short of breathtaking, making him feel almost like an eagle himself.

To his left, Lake Thun lay tranquil, the dewdrops of a thousand years collected into a bowl of quartz and limestone. A low mist swirled about the peaks of the lower hills to his right, while straight ahead rose the white foundations of the castle, bathed in colors painted by the light of the setting sun.

As he approached the door, which was pulled open by a bowing steward, Hoffman could not escape the feeling that he had left the world of mortals and now approached the home of an Olympian deity.

"Please wait in the study." The servant dipped his head as he took Hoffman's maroon top hat and cane. "His Lordship will join you shortly."

Arthur hurriedly pulled out his pocket watch and flipped it open. Aegis. The word scrawled across the back of the watch's face in bold print identified it as having been produced in one of Steele's factories. He had hoped that wearing the Aegis brand to this meeting would bring him a measure of luck, or at least, impress the man.

A good politician never misses an opportunity to make an impression.

Those had been his father's words. Now, as Arthur loosened his necktie which suddenly seemed too tight, he hoped that Steele's reasons for summoning him to his personal paradise, whatever they were, would provide an opportunity to make the impression of a political lifetime.

————————◆◆●◆◆————————

"*Gueten Abig* Arthur." Thomas let his powerful voice precede his entry into the large study, eyes fixed on his guest. As he passed through the door, his mind flitted through the mental profile of Arthur Hoffmann that he had formed after days of intense planning and research.

Arthur was a politician of German descent, born and raised in the canton of Saint Gallen. Affiliating himself with the Free Democratic Party, he held rather liberal views that could be shaped to Thomas's purpose. He had extensive political but also military connections, thanks to his position on the Federal Council. His father, Karl Hoffman, had successfully campaigned to be President of the Council thirty-six years prior but had declined the honor in the end, citing his family's need for his undivided attention.

It was this last kernel of information that had cemented Thomas's choice. Arthur Hoffman had witnessed his father make a hard decision, putting family above personal ambition. Some applauded his father's decision. But Arthur was not one of them. He had openly criticized his father's choice when he had entered the political arena. Arthur was the kind of man who would risk much in order to gain more. The kind of man that Thomas needed on his side.

"Ahem, *guten Abig, Härr* Steele." Hoffman leapt to his feet, arm thrust forward in greeting. Thomas noticed the slight quaver in the man's voice.

Thomas clasped his hand firmly, gestured to a suave armchair then continued the conversation in French, one of Switzerland's official languages. Although Hoffmann hailed from a German district, Switzerland's mixed demographics mandated that successful politicians speak French, the lingua franca. "*Veilleuz vous assoir,* Arthur. Please, sit."

Closing the door firmly, Thomas stepped to a nearby table and filled two small glasses with port. "I must thank you for making time to see me on such short notice."

"No, the honor is all mine. Truly." Arthur blinked rapidly behind his narrow, oval glasses as he accepted the small chalice from Thomas's outstretched hand.

He gulped down the amber liquid then spoke again. "I confess that I'm a little . . . " His voice trailed off as his eyes rolled around the room's lavish furnishings—"surprised at your invitation. We have never spoken until this moment."

Thomas sat with a soft sigh and sipped at the contents of his glass. "Nonetheless, we are connected, albeit indirectly. One of your cousins heads the production department of Aegis near Geneva, *n'est-ce pas?*"

Thomas's intent was straightforward. Before the battle for Arthur's mind began, the politician needed to be reminded that there were those in his family who depended upon Thomas's goodwill. From the sharp glance that he threw in Thomas's direction, it appeared the point had hit home.

"Yes, my cousin Hans." Arthur held up a gold watch for Thomas's inspection. "It is he who, gave this magnificent timepiece to me. I-it was made by your company."

"Ah." Thomas gave a noncommittal nod. The ground had been prepared. Now it was time for the first assault.

"Did your cousin accompany you on your recent trip to Russia?"

Hoffman froze, hand poised with the glass against his lips. Slowly he put it down on the table.

"No doubt you are wondering, how I knew that you, the head of the Swiss foreign ministry, went to Russia with the hopes of negotiating peace between the Germans and the Russians?" Thomas sucked in a deep breath. *This will not be easy.*

At this moment, he was struggling not to pound the reptile before him into the ground. Like all of Europe's politicians, Hoffmann knew that a separate peace treaty between the Russians and the Germans would ensure Germany's victory.

If Russia and Germany came to terms, the kaiser's generals would simply pull their barbaric horde from Russia's borders on the Eastern Front and redeploy them in an all-out assault on the British, French, and American troops.

The Russians needed to remain in the war until a lasting peace between all parties involved could be declared. Despite knowing this, Hoffmann had gone to Russia to bring about a peace that would destroy everything. And yet, it was precisely this deadly bargain that drew Thomas to him.

"I'm afraid I really don't know what you're talking about." Hoffmann leaned back in the chair, a smile on his thin lips. "Me? Negotiating a separate peace with the Germans? Absurd."

Thomas's face hardened. "Unlike politicians, we businessmen prefer not to waste time. I never divulge information that I have not verified." He leaned forward, setting his glass to one side. "Now, I'm going to *pretend* that you didn't just insult my intelligence."

Silence stretched between the two men, one that was short-lived but profound.

"How did you know?" Hoffmann spoke at last, folding his right leg over his left knee.

Thomas's lips twitched but humor was the last thing on his mind. "Simple, really. I rang last week to schedule this meeting.

Your man—Godfrey is it?—mentioned that you were away on business in Petrograd."

He reached again for his glass. "Now everything has a purpose. I asked myself, why would an experienced politician, a member of a neutral country's government no less, go to the capital of Russia? Keep in mind that Russia is a beleaguered ally of the British and one that everyone knows is crumbling from within."

He laid a finger on his pursed lips. "The only plausible reason is that you wanted to negotiate some sort of peace agreement between the Russians and the Germans. A peace that would not extend to the rest of Russia's allies."

Silence, broken only by the soft *tick, tick* of the pocket watch that was still in Hoffman's hand filled the room.

Sipping at his glass, Thomas leaned back in his chair. "Of course, since Switzerland is officially a neutral country, such activity would have to be done with utmost secrecy, or you, my good man, could find yourself answerable for charges of treason by your own government."

The thin man pulled his glasses from his face and wiped them on a handkerchief. "I ought to have Godfrey horsewhipped! He knew better than to let on where I was. The fool is getting old and careless."

Thomas said nothing. Silence often yielded the most fruitful conversations.

Hoffmann continued. "Perhaps I'd better explain."

"Please do."

"A-as you know, Switzerland is composed of many ethnic heritages. Those of French origin naturally want Switzerland to fight on the side of the Allies while those of German origin—such as myself—feel that an alliance with Germany is the right thing to do. Needless to say, this puts our government in an awful predicament."

"One that you hope to solve."

Hoffmann swallowed. "Well, yes. You see, I've learned that peace between the Russians and the Germans is indeed possible. The kaiser's generals are becoming more powerful." He lowered his voice to a confidential whisper. "I have it on good authority that they only want a trifle in return for peace with Russia."

His eyes gleamed with anticipation, and Thomas felt his gut clench. This was the moment. This was his point of no return. Until now, he had been innocent, but now he was about to plunge headlong into a dark world of clandestine manipulation.

Hoffmann expected him to rebuke his illegal attempt at brokering a treaty. Instead, Thomas was about to go against his every instinct and encourage Hoffmann to take his duplicity even further.

It will be worth it, Thomas. He imagined the expression on Malcolm's face when he saw his beloved wife again. *And when he learns she's carrying his child?* Anything, *everything*, was worth that.

"Some would argue"—Thomas cleared his throat, shifting in his seat—"s-some would argue that this is the path of a true leader. To see beyond the established convention and reach for unexplored possibilities."

Hoffmann leaned back in his chair and slanted him a speculative glance. "Forgive me, Sir Thomas, but are you saying that Switzerland should *break* its policy of neutrality and align itself with Germany?"

Don't do it. Turn back, it's not too late.

The persistent voice of his mind screamed its outrage at this charade, this defilement of his character. Decades of loyal service begged him not to cross the line. Memories of comrades who had died in his arms, men who had sacrificed everything for the British Empire stared at him with cold accusing eyes.

"Yes."

One word. One word by which Thomas fell from grace and became sin itself.

Again, silence claimed the small room. Again, it was Hoffmann who spoke first. "Then the rumors are true? You, Thomas Steele, have betrayed your country?"

Thomas lifted his eyes to Arthur's, hoping that the ugly pain he felt, the self-loathing that churned within his gut, did not reflect itself in them.

This is war. A war to save the ones I love more than life itself.

He understood war. War was a game he played only to win.

"What is the difference between a patriot and a traitor, Arthur?"

"I would think that is obvious." Hoffmann hiked his thin shoulders together. "Loyalty?"

"Loyalty to what is *best* for the country, wouldn't you agree?"

"Well, yes, I suppose."

"Then ask yourself this question." Thomas set his jaw and leaned forward once again, eyes drilling into the politician's skull. "Is it truly in Switzerland's best interests to remain neutral in this conflict?"

Hoffmann's response was immediate. "Absolutely not. An alliance with Germany would benefit all of us."

"Then your enquiry into a separate peace between Russia and Germany is not treason; it is patriotism at its best."

Arthur stared at him, mouth agape, and Thomas pressed harder. "It is not only your moral responsibility but your *duty*, as a patriot, to support this initiative."

340

"I . . . "

"The most adverse of times, produce the strongest heroes." Thomas lifted his chin. It was time for the deathblow to Hoffmann's doubts. "What would your father have done?"

Hoffmann crinkled his nose. "He wouldn't have come this far. He would've never gone to Russia in the first place."

"But you have." Thomas gentled his tone. "You've gone farther than he ever did. Will it all be for nothing?"

Rising, he closed the small distance between them and laid a compassionate hand upon the younger man's shoulder. "We old men leave the future to our children. They must pave roads where we feared to walk."

Arthur stared up at him, eyes glittering. It was obvious that his ambition was working relentlessly to overcome his fears. "Why you? You who have so much to lose?"

"Because, in the end, Arthur, we must all choose where our true loyalties lie."

"But—" Arthur stood, ready to ask another question, but Thomas forestalled his words.

"Now is your chance to make your mark on history. Let the world hear your voice. Tell the Council of your negotiations with Russia and urge them to abandon their neutral position. Urge them to side with Germany."

"And if I don't? What if I just walk away and pretend this conversation never happened?"

Thomas's eyes narrowed. He had just committed treason, raw and ugly. He wouldn't let Arthur's fears make light of his sacrifice. "I've been told by my financial advisors that the Geneva branch of Aegis has taken a downturn in profits thanks to the war. I may need to reevaluate the number of management personnel I currently employ." He let the thinly veiled threat hang in the air.

"My cousin, Hans?" Hoffmann retreated a step, eyes darting to the watch in his hand. "You're saying that if I don't do what you want, he'll lose his job?"

Thomas evaded his question. "Think about it, Arthur. You've been given the singular opportunity to rewrite Switzerland's history. Not only Switzerland's history but that of the world! Why do you hesitate?"

The younger man tugged at his mustache for several moments before looking up at Thomas. "I will speak to the Council on the condition that you agree to do so as well. Your companies are responsible for a large portion of our national fiscal gain. They will think twice before crossing you. Will you speak?"

"If necessary."

"Then we have an agreement. The Council meets tomorrow. I will speak to them then." Arthur cocked his head to one side. "I may lose my position for this, you know. I'm gambling with my political career."

"Every investment has its share of risk."

Arthur nodded, tapping the tips of his fingers together. "You are a hard man, Sir Thomas."

"I am a businessman."

Arthur rose slowly. "Somehow, I have the impression that you have gotten the better end of this deal."

Thomas did not smile as he too stood up, his lips pressed into a thin line. "Time alone will tell, *Härr* Hoffmann. Time alone will tell."

Chapter 30

London, Great Britain. August 1917.

L ord Curzon, Earl of Kedleston and President of the British War Council, flicked an invisible piece of lint from the ivory sleeve of his silk shirt then crinkled a brow as he took in the messy confines of the Prime Minister's office. Crumpled sheaves of paper crowded the top of a wastebasket that could barely fit beneath David Lloyd George's desk and littered the carpets that covered the scratched surface of the hardwood floor.

Maps, demarking various military positions, hung at odd angles on the white wainscoted walls, making it impossible to appreciate the crown molding that ran along the edges of the walls to the cathedral ceilings.

Chaos. Utter chaos.

Curzon shifted slightly in his uncomfortable chair to get a better view of the comedy that was unfolding before him. For as his beloved wife, the late Mary Victoria, would have undoubtedly agreed, the shouting match that was taking place between the irate Prime Minister George and the dour-faced cripple, Roger Hughes, was nothing short of comical.

343

"I tell you, Hughes, that this move by Switzerland's government is Thomas's retaliation for *your* stupidity." The Prime Minister thrust a newspaper whose bold headline screamed IS SWITZERLAND STILL NEUTRAL? in front of Hughes's pallid face. "I warned you a week ago that something terrible was coming. Well, here it is. You expected Thomas to hand you his head on a platter, but he's served you up a diplomatic catastrophe instead!"

Yes. Curzon nodded slowly. *This is all a desperate game, an act in a theatre with the devil's own spawn as the cast.*

A wistful smile tugged at his lips. Mary had loved the theatre, both in the literal sense and the political. It was her intoxication with the melodramatic that had led him to bring her with him to India during his time as Viceroy. She had almost died there.

His silver brows knitted together at the memory. Mary had been with him the night the Indian nationalists had swarmed outside, lusting for British blood. It was Thomas who had risked everything to singlehandedly challenge the horde. Were it not for him, Mary would have been murdered. He would not have had one more precious year with his wife before the illness claimed her.

I owe Thomas much, and now, businessman that he is, he has called on me to repay my debt.

Curzon's mind shifted to the short note he had received yesterday afternoon. Thomas, doubtless anticipating that Hughes's agents would open all London-bound mail from Switzerland, had somehow managed to have the letter posted from France. As an Earl and member of the Prime Minister's War Cabinet, Curzon was immune from the government's censorship policy and the letter had arrived at his desk unopened.

344

"Prime Minister." Hughes gestured toward the newspaper. "With all due respect, that accusation is nothing short of ludicrous. How could Thomas convince the Swiss government to negotiate a separate peace treaty between the Germans and the Russians? What political influence does he have? No, I insist that this debacle is totally unrelated to our problems!"

Curzon didn't bother to listen to David's sharp retort. Instead, he leaned over in his chair and nudged Bonar Law, the Exchequer. "I say, old boy, have you been able to break Thomas's hold on the Bank of England?"

Bonar snorted then, leaning closer, he raised his voice to be heard over the quarreling men. "It is like trying to pull a whale from the sea with naught but a string and hook. Parliament has said it will take at least another two weeks before legislation can be passed demanding the Bank reorganize its leadership. I expect another fortnight will pass before Thomas's puppet, Joseph Mara, will be forced to resign and a new head of the bank is found."

Bonar sighed. "If Switzerland does indeed negotiate a peace between the Huns and the Russians, we can't afford to wait that long. The Empire needs money. Now."

"I see." Curzon straightened, tapping his fingers lightly on the arm of his chair. His mind probed Thomas's battle plan. After a moment, he gave an approving nod. Evidently, the years in retirement had not dulled either the general's calculating nature or his flair for the dramatic.

Perhaps that's why I admire him. Thomas didn't just act, he did it in a way that was histrionic. Knowing that it would be several weeks before the government could take direct action against his bank or its shareholders, Thomas had struck first.

He had engineered a diplomatic crisis of epic proportions while simultaneously reaching out to Curzon, reminding him of the incident in India and asking for his help. He needed an ally and Curzon was prepared to be just that man.

Thomas had asked him to communicate with his son, Malcolm, and Malcolm's superior officer on Thomas's behalf. Malcolm was to request leave of absence and to be in Geneva within a week. Curzon was to use his influence to ensure that the leave was granted.

Curzon was about to resume his conversation when the Prime Minister's voice rose from a shout to an enraged howl.

"I warned you time and again, Hughes, but your wounded pride wouldn't let you leave sleeping dogs lie." David slammed his fist against the table. "You had to arrest the girl because you couldn't stand the shame of being put over by a German spy!"

Hughes? Deceived? How interesting. Curzon stroked his smooth chin and spoke into the abrupt silence. "It appears, Sir Hughes, that there is more to this tale than first meets the ear."

He glanced at the faces of the other five men around the table, all members of the Prime Minister's War Cabinet. All eyes were riveted on the spymaster, all faces were white with shock.

"Please." Curzon settled back into his chair. "Tell us the whole drama."

"There's really nothing—"

"You *will* tell them, Robert, or I swear that I will." The Prime Minister's voice was the low growl of a stalking bear.

Hughes pressed his lips into a tight line then pushed himself upright. "I have acted purely as a patriot. However"—he raised his voice over David's loud snort—"I admit that there are certain . . . aspects of this debacle that I would rather not disclose."

Curzon motioned for him to continue. "Such as?"

"I-I hired Leila Steele as a cleaner in my office."

Bonar made a choking sound as though Hughes' words had somehow jumped out of his ears and shoved their way into his throat. "You hired a German spy as your cleaner?"

Silence.

"Well, didn't you check her references?"

"Of course I did, you blithering idiot." Hughes ground the words out between clenched teeth. "A thorough investigation was conducted by my agents. E-everything appeared to be in order."

"Apparently, it was not." Curzon stroked his chin.

Bonar regained his breath. "So, you are covering up your failure by imprisoning the girl."

"No." Hughes jutted his chin. "I imprisoned her because she is an enemy of the Empire."

The shrill cry of a black telephone that sat in the center of the Prime Minister's desk drowned out Bonar's reply. David yanked the receiver and shoved it next to his ear. "What is it? You've been my secretary long enough to know that I'm not to be interrupted—"

His tirade died on his mustachioed lips. His face, red and flushed, became as pale as the cream suit that he wore. Curzon didn't need to guess who was on the other end of the line.

"Thomas."

A collective gasp sounded from the other men around the table. David spoke again, holding up a hand for silence from the men around him. "Yes, Thomas. Yes, it's all over the newspapers. Switzerland has been acting as negotiator between the Russians and Germans. You're saying this is your doing?" David's voice was choked. Apparently, this was one time the Prime Minister was not happy to be right.

"For goodness sakes, you're an *earl*, Thomas. If the Russians make peace with the Germans, we'll all be destroyed. What do you hope to gain by backing such a move?"

A pause filled the room as David listened to Thomas's reply and Curzon took advantage of that silence to observe Hughes. Lips clenched, eyes glaring, the man leaned forward like a wolf ready to rip into its prey. If Thomas were here...

"I see." The Prime Minister spoke again at length, shooting Hughes a recriminatory glare. "Yes, yes, I understand."

David closed his eyes for a moment, listening then said, "You're holding us hostage, Thomas. Freezing our assets in one hand and threatening us with diplomatic sanctions in the next. You're a traitor. Thomas?" He pulled the small round earpiece away from his ear then put it back. "Thomas?"

David turned back to his advisors, a stupefied look on his face. "The cheeky blighter hung up on me!" Returning the telephone to its base, he regained his seat, face set in a grimace.

"He wants his daughter-in-law and two of his servants brought to Geneva, Switzerland on the twentieth of September. They're to be accompanied by a member of this War Council. If the girl does not arrive, Thomas will personally again urge the Swiss government to abandon their neutral position and negotiate a treaty between the Russians and the Germans." He eyed each member of his War Cabinet. "You all know what's at stake. What do you propose?"

Bonar shook his head. "He's sacrificing his honor and turning his back on his own people, to save an enemy. The girl's a raw heathen—a German!"

"Incredible." Henderson, assistant to the Prime Minister, flopped back in his chair, arms spread wide. "A man we thought was incorruptible has chosen to become a sinner so he can save a life."

"You can't possibly be thinking to give into his demands." Hughes gripped the edge of the table with bloodless fingers.

At this, Curzon released a burst of mocking laughter. He let his chuckles hang in the air, then dabbed at his eyes with the corner of his silk sleeve. "Thanks to you, good fellow, we have no choice. Thomas has us right where he wants us."

"What do you mean?" Bonar Law shrugged.

Curzon rose and leaned over the table. It was time for him to play his part. "Think, man. Thomas has gone too far to turn back now. He's desperate to save his family from this fellow's clutches."

He jerked his chin toward Hughes. "He's found someone to go to the Council with the idea of negotiating a separate peace between our ally, the Russians, and our enemy, the Germans. If that happens, we *will* lose this war."

"But the Swiss have always maintained an armed neutrality. I-it's in their charter!" Henderson tapped his finger on the table. "How could Thomas convince them to do otherwise?"

It was David, the Prime Minister, who answered the question. "Over the past three decades, Thomas has built extensive financial investments in Switzerland, a country that depends on manufacturing to boost its economy. If we don't give the man what he wants, he'll tell the Swiss to either negotiate peace or he'll shut down his businesses in Switzerland. They can't afford to lose his business. Not now."

"B-but the cheek of it!" Henderson shook his head. "What about honor?"

David shrugged. "Governments run on economics, not principles. A large percentage of the Swiss population already supports the German cause. Besides, Switzerland loses nothing if the Germans and Russians make peace. They will, however, face a surge in unemployment and lose millions of francs each year if Thomas closes down his companies. Without a doubt, the Council will follow Thomas's lead."

Curzon spoke up, annoyed at David's interruption. "The Prime Minister is right. Now that this scandal has become public knowledge, the Swiss government will also need to fear riots from the pro-German populace if they do not acquiesce to Thomas's demands."

"So." Bonar Law loosened his collar. "The choice is, we either set a German spy free in neutral territory or risk losing the war?"

"Essentially, yes." Curzon tilted his head to one side. "If we release his daughter-in-law, I believe that Thomas will reverse his position. This is a calculated gamble, nothing more."

He did not mention, of course, that Thomas had sworn in his letter that he would do everything in his power to stop Switzerland from negotiating peace if Leila was released. At this moment, Curzon doubted that the other members would believe a word Thomas said—but *he* did. Trust, forged in the fires of war, was a hard bond to break.

"Why?" Hughes snapped out the word, his gray eyes glittering. "What's to prevent him from simply taking his daughter-in-law and leaving us all to burn?"

Curzon raised a cynical eyebrow then held up two fingers. "For two reasons. First, in his heart of hearts I still do not believe that Thomas wishes us ill. I believe this is an act of desperation." He pinned Hughes with a steady gaze. "Desperation brought on by your incompetence."

Hughes choked back a mangled cry, but Curzon ignored him and continued speaking. "Second, his son is at the Front and Thomas obviously wants him to remain alive. The odds of Malcolm's survival will plummet if the Germans double the number of soldiers already at the Front."

"He's a businessman used to taking risks." Hughes clenched a fist.

"Yes, but he's not a fool," Curzon said pointedly. "I assume you have been monitoring all mail sent to Malcolm Steele, Hughes, so I ask you, has Thomas written to his son?"

"No."

"It's quite odd, really. It almost seems as if he's trying to distance himself from his son." Bonar Law tapped the side of his nose. "As though he doesn't want to taint Malcolm with the stain of his treason."

"Forget that." Hughes's lip curled back in a snarl. "Malcolm Steele should be arrested upon suspicion of collaboration with the enemy."

"Have you taken leave of your senses?" David eyed him askance. "Arrest a man who is rising to prominence on the Front Lines? You know as well as I, that Thomas's son returned to the Front with the rank due the son of an Earl. He was reassigned to a new battalion as a Major and showed he was worthy of the promotion by his heroism at Passchendaele." He scoffed. "Arrest a hero when we need heroes now more than ever? Take my advice, Robert. Stick to spying and stay out of politics."

"Yes, I read the report in the Times." Bonar puffed out his cheeks, releasing a breath. "Though outnumbered, Steele's cohort wiped out a gang of German snipers that were slaughtering our lads who were pinned down in Passchendaele's mud. Quite impressive, really."

Curzon stifled a yawn. As entertaining as it was, this show had gone on long enough. "Yes, well, all things considered, I propose that we accede to Thomas's demands."

"I second the notion." Henderson's voice was closely followed by the rest. "And I."

"It's hard to believe that he'd go to such lengths, though." The corners of Bonar's lips turned downward. "To polarize an entire nation!"

"I suppose one must say that his love is greater than his hatred of evil." David stood, shoving his hands into the pockets of his white trousers. "He's taken the shame of it all upon himself. None but us know that Thomas is the driving force behind Switzerland's move."

His brown eyes lingered on Hughes. "And not a word of the truth to the press. The world must never know that Steele was behind this. There's no telling what he'll do. Is that clear?"

The voices around the table murmured their assent and David spoke once more.

"So, it is decided. Thomas's daughter-in-law will be immediately freed and taken to Geneva. Which one of you will accompany her?"

Curzon felt a flush of victory steal through him. He had played the role of neutral negotiator, bringing the War Cabinet to the point where they accepted Thomas's terms. After a decade of indebtment, his obligation to his friend had been repaid without tainting his own personal honor.

"If it is the wish of the Prime Minister and the members of the Cabinet,"Curzon said, dipping his head to hide the smile that played about the edges of his mouth, "I will undertake that mission."

It is all theatrics in the end, Mary, my love. I can only hope that, somewhere in Heaven, you are proud of the part I have played today.

Chapter 31

Geneva, Switzerland, September 1917.

The shrill cry of the train as it hurtled along the *Schweizerische Nationalbahn,* or Swiss National Railway, jerked Malcolm from a fitful sleep. He blinked several times, trying to clear his mind of a fragmented nightmare in which Leila was dragged before a merciless firing squad.

He rubbed his face, feeling the stubble on his chin, then turned to gaze out the small window to his left at the pristine view that scudded by. The afternoon sun glinted off grass, green and lush. Grass was a miracle in itself. The land near the trenches was utterly void of any sign of life for miles in any direction. He stared, mesmerized at the verdant scenery.

Switzerland, touching borders with both France and Germany, played a desperate game in adopting a policy of armed neutrality. So far—judging by the peaceful countryside and sparkling lakes—it seemed the Swiss were winning their gamble. But life, as well as war, was full of surprises. In a moment, everything could change.

With a slight frown, he reached into the breast pocket of his dark checkered suit jacket and withdrew a letter from a man he did not know but who evidently knew him—or at least, knew his father. His eyes roamed over the short note once more.

Major Steele, I trust this missive finds you well in both body, and as much as can be, in spirit. I have been requested by a man, who is loved by you and admired by me, to instruct you to join him in Geneva, Switzerland on 20 September. Your request for leave will be granted, I assure you. Acquire civilian clothing in France prior to boarding the train. Continue in your gallant service to the Empire. More depends upon it than you know.

May God keep you safe and may God preserve our empire.

Lord Nathaniel Curzon, Earl of Kedleston

Malcolm let his head fall back against the headrest of the leather seat as his mind probed the implications of Curzon's note. While he had never met the man, Malcolm knew that Curzon had held the prestigious position of viceroy in India for several years and that his father had served under his command.

As to why such a man would obey his father's wishes, Malcolm couldn't begin to speculate. Now more than ever, he regretted the rebellion that had pushed him to shut his father out of his life. There was so much he didn't know about his family's past.

Brow furrowed, Malcolm pushed his mind back to the issue at hand. Leila was in the Tower, condemned to die for crimes against the state. As he had promised, he wrote daily to Northshire but none of his letters had been answered, which could only mean that she was still imprisoned.

The absence of news nearly drove him mad. Every day he repeated her words more times than he could count. *You need to focus on staying alive, Malcolm.*

354

Alive. He expelled a ragged breath. A word that meant everything to the men in the trenches. But living, real living, was impossible without knowing that she was safe. It didn't surprise him that Thomas had not contacted him directly nor that his father was in Switzerland. Leila's arrest would undoubtedly implicate Thomas; the safest place for him would be their castle near Lake Thun.

What *did* surprise him was Curzon's statement that more depended upon Malcom's service to the Empire than he knew. Could Curzon be implying that, since Thomas had tarnished the Steele reputation by harboring a spy, it fell to Malcolm to restore the family honor?

Malcolm shifted in his seat. He felt uncomfortable traveling to foreign terrain out of uniform. But Curzon's note had been explicit. Despite the fact that the Swiss sheltered wounded soldiers from both Allied and Axis armies, he would be less conspicuous if he did not walk the streets in a British uniform.

The train's whistle sounded again, and this time, Malcolm could clearly see the flat, steel roof of the approaching depot. As the train slowed down, he felt his pulse spike. Somewhere in the crowd that lined both sides of the quay waited his father. He didn't know why Thomas had sent for him, but it could only mean that he had news of Leila. Together, they would formulate a plan to secure his wife's freedom. And free her they would—no matter the cost.

———◆◆●◆◆———

Leila, followed closely by Jenny and Greyson, sucked in a deep breath of fresh, evening air as she stepped off the black shrieking train and onto the wooden platform that bordered the tracks of Geneva railway station.

After a month in the dank confines of the Tower, each puff of wind that ruffled through her hair felt like a kiss from heaven. She kept her eyes on the tall, broad back of the man before her—a stranger who identified himself only as 'a friend'. Her mind still reeled with the rapid change in her situation.

Two days ago, Hughes had limped up to her cell and tersely ordered the guards to set her free. She had been handed over to the man before her while Hughes looked on, face tight and jaw clenched. Their nameless leader had escorted her to Northshire where she had found a pile of letters from Malcolm waiting bundled on her bed.

Tears stung the back of Leila's eyes as she remembered the moment he had promised to write each day until she was free. Over the past two days, she had spent every waking moment poring over the letters, reliving Malcolm's experiences at war.

The morning after arriving at Northshire, the small group had crossed the English Channel and boarded a train that followed a circuitous path through northern France, around hostile territory, then crossed into Switzerland. In all that time, Leila had been unable to obtain any information about the man who directed their small party, although she suspected that Greyson recognized him. She had chosen not to press the butler for information, trusting in his judgment.

In the end, what did it matter as long as she was free? *If only Malcolm could be here!* Her heart lurched at the thought. There was so much to share. But he was away, fighting by day and writing letters to her by night.

The group's leader paused, then gestured toward a sign that read "*Wartezimmer.*" Waiting room. "Let's go in here."

Greyson stepped in front and opened the door with a slight dip of his head.

"Thank you, Greyson." Leila slipped around him, trying to quench the nausea that rippled through her stomach. She paused, sagging against the doorframe.

"Are you all right, my Lady?" Jenny gave her arm a gentle squeeze.

Leila nodded, breathing in through her nose and out through her mouth. "It will pass." After a few seconds, she hiked up her gray skirt, squared her shoulders and stepped inside. Within the building, a long, narrow corridor opened up to a spacious lobby while, on both sides of the hallway, were small rooms in which couples or small groups could say their goodbyes.

The tall man before her walked purposefully forward, carrying himself like a man used to authority. He strode to the eighth room on the right then pushed down on the handle and opened the door. Leila noted that he did not knock despite the fact that there were no windows in the full-length wooden door. It was clear that he expected the room to be empty, which could only mean that this meeting was all part of a larger, pre-arranged plan.

Thomas? She knew that her father-in-law was in Switzerland, and now, the question that had haunted her since leaving Britain burned once more at the forefront of her thoughts. Hughes's words, spoken just as she left the Tower, echoed in her mind.

Tell your traitorous father-in-law that every businessman must settle his debts. His time will come.

At first, she had thought Hughes was referring to the fact that Thomas had offered her shelter but, as she saw the man before her motion for her to enter the room, Leila could not help but wonder if Thomas had somehow engineered her freedom.

"Wait here." His voice was firm but not unkind. Leila scanned the small room then stepped inside. She drew a measure of

JP ROBINSON

comfort from the small Luger she had strapped around her waist before leaving Northshire.

Jenny started to follow her, but the stranger barred her way then motioned to several benches that lined the corridor. "You may both wait outside."

Turning to Leila, "He will join you in a few moments." Then, without another word, he closed the door and left.

———————◆◆●◆◆———————

Thomas watched through the narrow space of the partially opened door of his cubby as Lord Curzon motioned for Leila to enter the eighth waiting room. He had closeted himself in a room diagonally from her in order to better observe without being seen. In reality, the clandestine nature of this reunion was as much to protect Lord Curzon as it was to safeguard his own interests.

As a neutral nation, Switzerland was a hotbed of spies from both the Allied and Axis powers. Thomas had demanded that a member of the Prime Minister's War Cabinet accompany Leila to ensure that Hughes would not sabotage his carefully laid plans.

Curzon had been the ideal candidate. But Switzerland boasted a large number of German loyalists and it was possible that Curzon would be recognized. He was therefore in danger as long as he remained.

The fact that Curzon had agreed to come, despite the obvious risk, showed how much he wanted Thomas to back down from his threat to influence the Swiss government. If he did not keep his promise to Curzon after the man had gone to such lengths, Thomas knew he was doomed.

Thomas glanced at his watch as Curzon made his way toward the waiting room in which he was closeted. Noon. Malcolm should

358

arrive at any moment. Curzon had barely stopped outside the waiting room when Thomas pushed the door open.

He grasped Curzon's outstretched hand then pulled the door shut behind him. "Well met, old friend."

"Indeed, Sir Thomas. Indeed." Curzon peered down at him, a slight smile on his face. "I must confess that I commend your diligence in regard to my security. Your instructions were precise, as always."

"Without you, none of this would have been possible."

"True," Curzon said in the blunt manner for which he was known. "But I feel that in complying with your plan I have not only repaid an old debt but acted in my country's best interests."

The smile faded. "You will keep your word?" It was more a statement than a question. "You will persuade the Swiss to abort this ludicrous notion of negotiating a separate peace between our ally and our enemy?"

Thomas did not hesitate. "I swear to you that I will do everything in my power to convince the government to maintain their current policy."

"Hmm . . ." Curzon's eyes drilled into his skull as though he wished to read the very thoughts that flitted through Thomas's mind. "I know you have considerable influence. In part, it is your financial enterprises that have kept Switzerland neutral throughout this war. See that the status quo is maintained."

Before Thomas could reply, Curzon spoke again. This time his voice had lost its sharp edge. "It can't end well, old chap. You do realize that." He tilted his head to one side. "I don't know how you concocted this debacle, but we both know that no man can manipulate both sides and win. Someone, either in Switzerland or in Britain, will retaliate and I fear that you will fall. Even if you convince the Swiss Council to remain neutral, Britain will still consider you a traitor."

He laid a gentle hand on Thomas's arm. "Either you remain an exile in Switzerland for the rest of your life or you face the charge of treason against you in England. Hughes the Cripple is ready to rip your head off if you ever touch British soil again."

Thomas met his gaze. "You know I don't fear death. My wife, like yours, waits for me just beyond the shadowed vale. All that matters is that I protect the welfare of those who will outlive me. My sacrifice must not be in vain."

"Yes, well, perhaps your son will somehow manage to clear up this whole affair." Curzon tugged at the lapel of his simple navy-blue suit. "It is possible you know, especially given that Hughes hasn't made your part in this Swiss charade public knowledge. The Prime Minister has expressly forbidden it."

Silence filled the small room, but it was short lived.

"In the event that we do not meet again in this life, it has been a privilege to call you a friend." Curzon held out his hand. "God speed, Thomas. God speed."

◆◆●◆▶

Malcolm stepped out of the small coach and onto the landing dock, eyes scanning the clumps of pedestrians who loitered about the quay. Only one train made the trip from France to Switzerland each day, so his father would have had no difficulty knowing his arrival time.

He pressed his way forward, again subtly remarking the difference between the Swiss and the residents of France. The cheerful look in the eyes of the people, the murmurs of genuine conversation. They were all small mercies that had dissipated like the smoke of an exploding canon from the lives of those who lived in the shadow of the Great War.

He could see definite evidence of the conflict around him. Medical contingencies bearing the red cross on their shoulders carried both French and German wounded soldiers away from the depot. Posters decrying the war hung on the walls of buildings and armed Swiss soldiers stood in small clumps around the station. But it was all from the perspective of a nation of observers.

Malcolm slowed his walk to a crawl as the cherubic sound of children's voices, raised in song, reached his ears. Following the sound, he caught sight of a small, impromptu choir singing hymns to the wounded veterans as they were carted off the train.

His heart churned. There was hope in Switzerland, hope that the rest of Europe seemed to have forgotten.

With a sigh, he turned away from the poignant scene, searching once more for evidence of his father. It was unlikely that Thomas would meet him openly, not with the possibility that they could be watched.

The lack of direct communication from Thomas could only mean that he wanted to keep Malcolm clear of any accusation of treason.

He'd send someone, a friend or—

He froze, catching sight of a familiar face. A bulky figure stepped out of the shadows, swathed in a long, gray coat. Malcolm pressed forward, wending his way around the crowd toward the butler.

"Greyson!"

Greyson, as composed as if it were teatime at Northshire, waited until Malcolm neared him then dipped his head. "Lord Malcolm. Welcome to Switzerland."

Malcolm gripped the man's hand. "So good to see you, Greyson." He stepped closer, lowering his voice. "Any word on my wife? My father?"

Greyson smiled then motioned for Malcolm to follow. "Please follow me."

His excitement degenerating into impatience, Malcolm followed him inside a narrow corridor lined with a series of waiting rooms. Greyson motioned toward a woman who rose to meet him then bobbed in a curtsy.

"Jenny?" Malcolm stared at them both, mind reeling. "Are you . . . ?" His gaze shifted from one to the other. "Where is Lady Steele?"

It was Greyson who spoke in low, measured tones. "I have just spoken with your father. He was here but felt it best not to risk being seen with you in public. He has returned to his castle and wishes for you to join him there."

Malcolm nodded briskly. His father's plan made sense. What did *not* make sense was why Greyson had chosen to answer his second question instead of his first.

"My wife, Greyson?" He edged closer, trying to curb his impatience. But it was not only impatience that clawed at his mind. It was fear, the terrible fear that something had gone wrong and both servants knew the truth of the matter while he was in ignorance.

"Please, Your Lordship." Jenny's tenor voice sounded in his ear as though from a distance. "There's something that must be said in private. Follow me."

Private? Malcolm felt his blood turn to ice. *She's dead. They don't want me to make a scene so Jenny's taking me into this waiting room.* Dumbly, he followed the maid, his mind struggling to cope with this crippling news. *God . . . she's dead? My wife is dead?*

He staggered against the door, dimly hearing the thud of his body against its wooden frame.

Jenny laid a cool hand on his arm. "Inside, sir."

Malcolm, unable to focus, fumbled with the handle. *Why won't it open?* He slammed the handle downward, grunting. Yielding to his strength, the door flew open and he crashed inside.

———◆◆●◆◆———

The moment her guide left, Leila withdrew her Luger from its holster in the small of her back. With detached precision, she slipped several bullets into the chamber, verified that the silencer was in place and cocked the gun, ignoring the sick feeling that swirled again in her gut.

She didn't know who the man was, but she would be a fool to trust anyone. Especially now.

Her mind ticked through the facts. First, he had refused to give his name. Second, he had spoken little in two days. The lack of conversation certainly did not increase her trust. Third, he had forbidden her servants to enter the room citing only that "he" would arrive soon. Who was this *he*?

She doubted that Thomas would meet her in a train station in Switzerland. At least a quarter of the people outside were possible agents for one of the belligerent nations. If Thomas was involved in this affair at all, he would wait for her at his home near Lake Thun.

Her eyes rolled around the room, seeking a way out. There was none but the door, which only increased her sense of malaise. A few months ago, she might have tried knocking a hole in the wood paneling with the butt of her gun then making her way through a crawl space.

But now, her hand dropped protectively over her stomach where the faintest of bulges curved, *I can't afford to chance things like I used to.*

So, she waited for just shy of ten minutes and it was then that she heard the crash of a body against the door.

Someone's attacked Greyson!

Instantly, Leila moved out of her seat, positioning herself against the back wall. She lifted the Luger coolly, despite the pulse that ticked in her jaw.

The door handle jerked downward. Whoever wanted to get in was obviously too hurried to focus which meant he was an amateur.

Good.

Her mind calculated the odds of survival. While the outside of the station had been decently crowded, the corridor lining the waiting rooms was virtually empty since no train was departing. This was a problem, because whoever wanted to kill her would have a clear shot once she got out of the room.

That is not good. Leila's brow creased in a frown. Jenny had not cried out. *Is she dead?*

She pushed the thought away, trying to focus.

Hughes's men? It was possible but unlikely. If Hughes had wanted to kill her, he wouldn't have released her in the first place.

Werner? No, he was dead. Hughes had told her as much. Her tongue flickered over her dry lips. She would have one, maybe two shots at best. She could only hope there was only one killer involved.

Father, help me now.

At that moment, the door flew open.

Leila dropped to one knee.

A dark-haired man stumbled into the room, eyes wide and face pale.

Her finger curled around the trigger and—

"Malcolm!"

Chapter 32

Château des Aigles, Switzerland, September 1917.

The sun had just begun its brilliant arc across the azure Swiss skies when Jenny, lugging a small basket of freshly-washed laundry, stepped into a small enclosed garden over which ran several wire clotheslines. Humming a slow but cheerful tune, the sprightly maid set the basket down on the bricks below, pulled several clothespins from her pocket, then, flicking back a strand of brown hair from her face, began to hang the laundry.

Sir Thomas did not keep many servants in his employ at his Swiss castle, probably because he was here so infrequently.

But that's all goin' to change, now won't it?

A frown puckered Jenny's face as she recalled the fragments of conversation she had overheard during last evening's dinner. It had been a festive affair, but the joy everyone felt at being reunited had been overshadowed by the reality that it had all come at a heavy price.

Jenny's frown deepened. If she had understood correctly, returning to England was out of the question, at least for the moment. Not that she minded. She had no ties to Britain beyond the family that she served. *As long as Lady Steele is safe, 'tis all the same to me.*

"Good morning, Jenny."

The maid let out a squeak at the unexpected voice, then whirled around to find Sir Thomas himself behind her. He removed his black Fedora and dipped his head even as she bobbed out a curtsey.

"Beggin' your pardon Your Lordship. I-I didn't know you were about or I wouldn't have come. So sorry to have disturbed you!"

"Not at all." Thomas slipped his hat back in place. "Isabella and I used to greet the dawn with prayer here in this garden whenever we were in Switzerland. I still maintain the practice."

Jenny laid a hand on her chest. "I didn't know your wife for long, but it was enough to see that she was a great woman. You must miss her very much."

"More than life." The crowfeet around Thomas's eyes were more noticeable now, as though the past few months had taken their toll upon him in years. His eyes misted, and he looked away at the shimmering blue lake whose translucent waves lapped gently against the brick patio's edge. Then, shifting the conversation, he glanced back at her. "Are Lord Malcolm and Lady Steele about?"

"Um, not yet." Jenny flushed and lowered her gaze to hide the twinkle in her eye. "I was about to bring somethin' up earlier, but Lord Malcolm met me at the door and said they'd prefer not to be disturbed this mornin'."

"I see."

She glanced up just in time to catch the faint outline of a smile on Thomas's face.

"Well, I have an appointment with the Swiss Council this morning." His smile faded. "But inform my son that I will be back around half-past two. I will speak with him then."

He turned to leave and Jenny, knowing she was out of place but unable to contain the curiosity that ate her up from within, called him.

"Your Lordship."

Thomas turned slowly.

"I-I didn't mean to eavesdrop durin' your private dinner last evenin' but I couldn't help but overhear certain things that were said."

"Such as?"

Hesitantly she met his austere gaze. "How you managed to set Lady Steele free. 'Tis a fine thing you've done, sir, and I just want to say how grateful I am. Workin' for Lady Steele is not just a job. Please don't think I'm puttin' on airs, but I love her as though she were my own sister. A kinder, more noble soul, I've never met."

She expelled a deep breath. "Now, I know that some are sayin' you're a traitor back home in England, but in my eyes, there's no greater man in all the world. 'Tis proud I am to serve this family, truly."

Thomas held her gaze without speaking for several long minutes then his brow crinkled as he smiled once more. "Jenny, I don't think I've ever heard you say so many words at once in all the years I've known you."

The maid flushed again. "Beggin' your pardon, sir, I—"

"Thank you. Your words were much needed." Then with a slight bow in her direction, he left the lofty garden's tranquility to descend into the chaotic world of mortals.

———————◆◆●◆◆———————

Leila awoke to the gentle caress of Malcolm's lips on her face and neck. For a moment she lay still, letting his mouth wander where it wished but then she slid closer to him, resting her head against his taut chest and listening to the steady beat of his heart.

"You amaze me." She breathed out the words then snuggled still closer, savoring the security he offered.

Malcolm ran his right hand lazily through her hair, letting the gold tresses curl around his fingers. "Hmm . . . the woman who almost blew my head off last evening finds me amazing today." His voice this early in the morning was a deep bass that made her spine tingle. "Sounds like quite a contradiction, don't you think?"

She gasped. "I did *not* almost blow your head off!"

"Oh, really?" He propped himself up on one elbow, eyes glinting with humor. "Did you or did you not have your Luger pointed at my head with your finger about to press the trigger?"

"That, that was different!"

He stared at her, one eyebrow raised.

"I mean . . . I didn't know it was you."

"Hmm . . . " Reaching over, Malcolm traced the outline of her chin with the ball of his thumb. "It's a good thing I'm mad about you. So, what about me is 'amazing'?"

"Well, I was in the Tower for forty-five days. When I went to Northshire there were forty-six letters waiting for me." She pulled his hand free then kissed it. "You didn't miss a single day."

"I wrote you twice on the day my platoon was pinned down in the mud at Passchendaele. I was sure I would die that morning." The light faded from Malcolm's eyes as he sat up, the pants of his black, silk pajamas contrasting sharply with the white sheets of their bed. "So many of us did die."

Gathering the sheets around her, Leila sat up as well. "There was nothing you could've done about it, Malcolm. We both know the cost of war."

"Yes, but there are times when I feel so helpless." He turned to her, jaw set and eyes hard. "I couldn't save my men in Passchendaele—at least not all of them. But what really hurts is that I couldn't save . . . you."

"Me?"

"Last night, Father told us how he forced Whitehall to give you up. We all know what that means for him."

She nodded, closing her eyes. The price Thomas had paid hung heavy on her own heart.

If I'd have known he'd have gone to such lengths . . .

But if he hadn't, she wouldn't have been the only one to die. Her child would have perished as well. She had wanted to tell Malcolm the news, but the atmosphere after last night's dinner had been too poignant to reveal that she was expecting. But she realized now that he needed to know.

Malcolm expelled a ragged breath. "He did all that for you, but you're *my* wife, Leila. This was *my* fight, not his. But Father had to manipulate the will of nations and now he has to bear the brunt of it all while I get off scot-free."

He ran a hand through his black hair. "Don't think I'm jealous, of course I'm not. It's just that I'm not a shirker. Not anymore. I won't have any man—not even my father—handle my responsibilities for me."

Her brow creased. "Would you rather he had done nothing?"

"Of course not." Twisting, Malcolm cupped her face in both his hands. "Don't ever think that. It's just that there are times I feel so useless!"

"Oh, Malcolm." Leila leaned over and draped her bare arms around his neck. "Nothing could be further from the truth. Think of what you've done instead of what you have not done."

"And what have I done? Nothing."

"That's not true, Malcolm. So many of your men are alive today because of your leadership. I've read your letters and I know you weren't boasting. Those men followed you in the worst of circumstances, not because you're the son of Thomas Steele, but because you've proven that you're a leader. A man worthy of their respect. And if it weren't for all the prayers you sent up, I probably wouldn't be here."

She kissed him, then after a long moment, pulled away. "Because of you, Malcolm, I believe in love again. Because of you, your father has hope that the Steele name will one day shine as brightly as it ever has."

She paused, sensing that the time was right. "Because of you, our child will live in a safer world."

He sighed, shaking his head. "Yes, perhaps someday. If we ever have a child. If this war ever ends. *If* we win. Sometimes I wonder—"

"Malcolm."

He shrugged, a helpless gesture. "I know you're right, Leila, I should have faith, and I do, really. But it's hard to keep positive when I'm out there watching my men being blown into bloody chunks all—"

"Malcolm."

Frowning, he broke off his flow of words. "Yes?"

The corners of Leila's mouth tipped upward as excitement mingled with nervousness swirled within her. This was the moment she had prayed would come for months. Now at last they were together. Now at last he could know.

"*Our child* will be safer because of you."

"Yes." He blinked several times then shrugged again. "You said that already."

Leila couldn't suppress a giggle. "But you're not listening."

"Of course, I'm listening. You said, 'our child will be safer because of me—'"

He choked on the end of his sentence then pulled away, his face going as white as the sheets on the bed. "Our child? You mean *our* child?"

She nodded, then laid his hand upon her stomach while chewing on the inside of her lip.

What will he think?

"Leila, are you . . . ?"

"Yes, darling." Sliding closer she placed her mouth inches from his ear. "In about six months, you are going to be a father."

He sat rigid, as though her words had transformed him into ice. Then shock melted into a wave of supreme happiness. His face, so melancholy only moments before, seemed to blaze with some inner joy. Malcolm jumped from the bed, tripped as the sheets entangled themselves around his legs, then shoved himself upright while pumping his fists in the air.

"Yes!" His whoop made her ears ring, but then, she supposed her peals of laughter were making his ring as well. "Yes, yes!"

"Shhh . . . Malcolm." Kneeling, she grabbed a pillow and threw it at his head. "You'll wake the servants."

In an instant he was at her side, cupping her head with his broad palm. "I don't know what words to say." His brown eyes glowed with a warmth that touched the core of her soul. "Nor, in truth, whether I'm more ecstatic or terrified at the thought of having a child."

He brushed her cheek with the backs of his knuckles. "But what I do know is that I love you."

Leila covered her mouth with her hands, choking back tears.

371

"What?" Malcolm pulled away, staring at her in horror. "Did I hurt you? Are you sick?"

He immediately fluffed the silk-encased down pillows then pushed her to lean back against them. "Here, lie down."

"No, no." Leila waved him off, laughing now. "It's not that at all." Sobering, she interlaced her fingers with his own. "I was afraid that you wouldn't want the child."

"Not *want* him? How could I not want our child?"

"Because your own childhood was difficult. And because the war is still raging."

"I understand." He fell silent for a moment then squeezed her hand. "Like I said, I'm petrified. I-I don't know the first step of parenting and I'll be even more reluctant to go back when my leave is up." He lifted his eyes toward the ceiling. "But perhaps this is where *our* Father's advice to trust Him becomes even more real."

He pressed her fingers against his lips. "Faith, Leila. We forget it sometimes but it's still there, waiting for us to wake up and realize how lost we are without it. We'll stick together, and everything will be fine."

Love and admiration congealed in an explosive ball within her chest. What a man he had become. A man she could follow. A man she could trust. "Do you know what I think?"

"No, what?"

"I think the Tower was a very lonely place."

A grin split his face as the meaning behind her words sunk into his mind. "What are you saying ?"

"I'm saying,"Leila said in a whisper as she crooked a finger and leaned back against the pillows, "that I am madly in love with the man I married. Right now, I want that man to show *me* how much he loves me."

"Is that an order, Commander?" A teasing note slipped into his voice as he moved closer, devouring her with his eyes.

"But of course, Major Steele." She looped an arm around his neck and pulled him downward. "Whenever do I give anything else?"

Chapter 33

Federal Palace, Bern, Switzerland, September 1917.

The sea-green dome of the Swiss Federal Palace held Thomas's gaze as he crossed the large concrete slabs of the plaza known as the *Bundesplatz* and stepped under the second of three arched doorways. The palatial structure was the meeting place of the Federal Council, Switzerland's chief governing body that was comprised of seven men—each overseeing a different aspect of social affairs as well as the legislative body known as the Federal Assembly.

Adorning the top of the dome was a glittering golden cross. Below it, three angels perched atop the granite roof, holding the nation's coat of arms. Thomas slowed his walk to a crawl as he read the Latin phrase that was etched in the rectangular building's white limestone façade.

Unus pro omnibus, omnes pro uno.

"One for all, and all for one." He vocalized the words as his mind flitted through the tumultuous events of the past month, his thoughts transforming the original meaning of the words into a message of sacrifice.

One for all.

To protect his family, Thomas had taken advantage of Arthur Hoffmann's political ambition. Now, his own government saw him as a traitor.

One for all. One lifetime of service sacrificed for the well-being of all the members of his family.

Now that the goal had been achieved, Thomas had to extinguish the fire that he himself had ignited. Arthur was counting on him to support his proposal to the Council for Switzerland to negotiate a separate treaty between Russia and Germany.

However, as part of his agreement with Lord Curzon, Thomas had sworn that he would convince the Council to reject Hoffmann's plan and maintain Switzerland's position of neutrality if Leila was released. London had kept its part of the bargain and he had to keep his. Thomas had already betrayed his country. Now he had to betray Arthur.

"One for all, and all for one." He repeated the words as he thumped his brass handled walking stick against his palm.

"Inspiring words are they not?" The voice at his side carried the distinct trace of a whine.

Thomas glanced down at the politician then returned his gaze to the mural. "Good morning Arthur."

Arthur Hoffmann cleared his throat and jerked his chin toward the building. "Some believe the saying alludes to Christ. You know, one man dying for all humanity."

Thomas tilted his head to one side, considering this interpretation. "And the 'all for one' part?"

"Well, Christ was willing to give up everything for each one of us. I suppose one could say that it was *all for one.*"

"I see. Are you a Christian, *Härr* Hoffmann?" Thomas resumed his walk toward the building's doors.

Hoffmann snorted. "No, not me. I've no time for myths of divine power—not when there's real power to be had on this earth. Politics offer us a world of opportunity, the ability to shape history."

He paused, brow furrowing and glanced up at Thomas. "I don't mean to offend. I know that you are a religious man and there's nothing wrong with that. But"—he pulled the door open and gestured for Thomas to enter first—"I prefer more tangible power. I have been a member of the council for six years now. I have garnered enough support among the other members and the Federal Assembly to rise to the Presidency next year."

He rubbed his hands together like a child about to open a long-awaited Christmas present. "When the Council members hear your endorsement of my plan, my victory will be assured. The value they place upon your support of my political agenda will pave the way for my success in the coming election."

Thomas came to an abrupt halt, grounded by the politician's words.

Arthur is using me!

Realization flooded his mind, bringing with it a sense of recrimination. He had been outmaneuvered by the cunning politician. In Arthur's mind, this whole affair wasn't just about a peace treaty; it was about achieving his lifelong ambition to become president of the Federal Council.

Arthur had led Thomas to believe that he had been reluctant to share his plans with the Council when, in reality, he had been planning all along to present Thomas's endorsement of his proposed treaty between Germany and Russia as support for his bid for the presidency.

The manipulative snake.

"And this is what you want?" Thomas chose his words carefully. "To become president?" He turned to better observe

377

Arthur's face. The man was more vindictive than he appeared which made him nothing short of dangerous.

"Y-yes!" Arthur stepped around him. Lowering his voice, he glanced around then continued. "I know what you're thinking. You're assuming that I wish to be greater than my father, that I'm a power-hungry despot."

"And are you not?"

"No!" Arthur thrust a finger against Thomas's chest, his eyes burning. "I want this country to rise to a glory unlike anything we've known. I want Switzerland to lead the world in the coming century. It can happen if the right man is at the helm of the ship."

"And you are that man, hm?" Thomas drilled him with a hard stare.

"Of course." Hoffman shrugged as though the question had been redundant. Turning, he placed his foot on the first step of a massive granite staircase. "Come, the Council is waiting."

Thomas let Hoffman move ahead of him, his mind weaving a picture of what the next few moments would bring. He was about to crush Hoffmann's dreams, but he felt no regret. Every war had its casualties; this one was no exception.

Pausing outside the open door of the meeting room in which the leaders of the nation waited, he thought through the words with which he would unleash the final stage of his battle plan. It had to be done. Here. Now.

"One for all," he murmured, "and all for one."

Then, squaring his shoulders and lifting his chin, Thomas strode inside.

Arthur Hoffmann did not bother to hide the flush of victory that crept across his thin face as Thomas Steele entered the spacious *salle*. Rubbing his mustache, he felt a thrill of anticipation as the renowned businessman seated himself in a leather-padded chair on the right side of the room.

Small, cream tables had been arranged in a series of short rows behind which the members of the council sat. Together, they formed a layered, concentric semi-circle that faced the desk behind which the President of the Federal Council, Edmund Schulthess, scratched his balding head like the monkey he was.

Soon. Soon I will be the man in the presidential chair.

As Schulthess droned out his welcoming remarks, Arthur's mind flitted through the intricate steps that had led up to this moment. After hearing rumors of Thomas Steele's alleged treason in Britain, he had reasoned that it was only a matter of time before the international business tycoon brought his political agenda to Switzerland.

Given that Thomas was not a politician, if he wished to accomplish anything in Switzerland's political circles, he would need an ally. Who better than Arthur himself, the head of Swiss Foreign Ministry?

As such, prior to leaving for Russia, Hoffman had instructed his secretary, Godfrey, to mention his whereabouts *if* Sir Thomas—and only Sir Thomas—happened to call during his absence. What Thomas had assumed to be a slip of the tongue had, in fact, been a morsel of information that had been intentionally released.

When Thomas had demanded that he share his proposal with the Swiss Council, it had been all Arthur could do to maintain the mask of reluctance. In reality, he had been exhilarated.

Thomas had played right into his hands when he had agreed to back his proposal to the Council.

After Arthur made a few deliberate remarks to guide their thinking, the councilmen would see that the man whose ideas Thomas Steele backed was the man to lead the assembly. Once President of the Council, Arthur would be in a unique position to rewrite Switzerland's role in this war.

Arthur scoffed as he shuffled the sheaf of papers containing his notes. Thomas, ancient and deluded, thought he was manipulating Arthur while the younger man had, in fact, neatly turned the situation to his own advantage.

It's time the old horse was put out to pasture.

Clearing his throat, he stepped around his desk to a roar of applause and made his way to the center stage.

"Thank you, fellow councilors, and thank you, President Schulthess, for this opportunity to address the Council on an important matter of national security." Arthur made a slight bow in the direction of his peers.

"As you no doubt will remember, a few weeks ago I approached this esteemed body with a proposition that, if approved, will alter Switzerland's role in this war."

His eyes scanned their faces. They were neutral, void of expression.

They're waiting to see which way Thomas will lean.

The corners of his mouth tipped upward. That was exactly where he wanted them.

"As a nation we are divided, with many of our residents aligning themselves with either the Axis or the Allied powers. Therefore, it falls to us, the heads of the nation, to make the hard choice and *lead*." He paused for a moment, letting the insinuation that, unless they followed his will they were *not* leading, sink into their minds.

Arthur made a conciliatory gesture with his hands. "None of you are surprised by this, however. The papers across Europe recently announced that a treaty between our German neighbors and our Russian friends is possible. I have made it so. But the real question here is not whether the warring nations find my proposal acceptable—it is whether *you*, the members of this council will support my vision."

President Schulthess interrupted his climatic moment. "We all know what is at stake, Councilor Hoffman. We knew this at our Council's last session. Get to the point and tell us something we *don't* know."

Arthur stiffened, but he drew in a deep breath and, forcing a smile, bowed to the ape. "Of course, President Schulthess."

To the audience, "I have invited a man known to all of you to share his thoughts. Recall, gentlemen, that this man's financial leadership has propelled Switzerland's economy before and during this devastating war. Sir Thomas?" Hoffmann stepped to one side, leading the thunderous applause that accompanied Thomas as he came forward.

───────◆◆●◆◆───────

"Gentlemen." Thomas bowed to both the councilors and the President. "I thank you for your time."

President Schulthess straightened in his chair. "It is an honor to have you with us. I rarely agree with Councilman Hoffman but one thing he says is true. Your wisdom and leadership have contributed to our economic stability in this time of chaos."

His eyes narrowed. "Which is why I find it difficult to believe that you, of all people, support Councilman Hoffman's plan.

As a British citizen, have you not often spoken *for* neutrality? Yet now you endorse this atrocity proposed by Hoffmann?"

Thomas's gaze shifted from the president to the politician on his right. Hoffman waited with bated breath, hands bunched into fists at his sides. Thomas realized now that he had misjudged the man, a mistake that could be costly. But that would be a fight for another day.

He snapped his head back to President Schulthess. "You are not mistaken. I stand here today, not to encourage Switzerland's participation in this barbarous act of duplicity but to ask that you *reject* Councilman Hoffmann's proposal. I ask you, the Council, to crush any proposal that could even remotely violate Switzerland's policy of neutrality."

A ripple of murmurs swelled among the ranks of the councilmen behind him, but it failed to cover Hoffmann's strangled cry.

Thomas ignored him.

"Switzerland must think of the consequences. Any attempt to negotiate a treaty between warring nations could cause Allied soldiers to invade this country. We all know that the Americans have joined the conflict. There is little doubt in my mind that, with their help, Britain will win this war. Think gentlemen: after having worked so hard to remain untouched by this global conflict, do you really want to risk everything now?"

He continued without pausing, knowing that Hoffmann would only be silent for so long. "Furthermore, the citizens of Switzerland, who are loyal to France, would resist anything they perceive to be favorable to the Germans. Unrest and riots that this great nation *cannot* afford will become commonplace."

He paused, letting the wave of murmurs die down before unleashing his last and most deadly weapon.

"Finally, if Switzerland violates its policy of armed neutrality, the possibility of Allied invasion places my financial investments at risk." Turning, Thomas pinned each councilman beneath his stern gaze. "I will have no choice but to liquidate all my assets in Switzerland, shut down my factories, and stop all lines of Swiss production if this body supports Councilman Hoffman's proposal."

The murmurs swelled into a roar of animated shouts. Hoffman, face as white as the walls around them, staggered forward.

"Liar!" He brandished a fist under Thomas's nose. "Traitor! We had an agreement!"

Thomas coolly took the measure of the impudent pup, then pushed Arthur's fist to one side with his walking stick. "I agreed to speak to the Council, Arthur. I have done so."

"But you knew what I wanted. You were my ally!"

Thomas lowered his voice, so only the politician could hear his next words. "Then I suggest you learn this rule well, boy. In business—as in war—today's ally may well be tomorrow's adversary."

"Oh, well said, Thomas." Arthur staggered backward, lip curled in a snarl. "Well said indeed. That is exactly what I will be—an enemy. An adversary who will crush your dreams just as you have destroyed mine!"

"Order. Order!" The president banged his gavel several times on his desk to still the commotion. When silence at length reclaimed the courtroom, his severe gaze flitted over each councilman then came to rest on Thomas.

"Sir Thomas Steele, as President of the Federal Council I must thank you for your pointed reminder about our commitment to neutrality."

He cleared his throat then glared at the livid Hoffman. "Without official endorsement, Councilman Hoffmann has abused his office of Foreign Minister to misrepresent himself as an agent authorized to speak on behalf of our government to foreign powers. In so doing, he has placed our reputation as a neutral nation at great risk."

He removed his oval glasses, wiped them, then tapped them against the desk. "With this Council's endorsement, I propose that Switzerland publicly reaffirm its commitment to neutrality. To show our unwavering support for all nations, we demand the immediate resignation of Arthur Hoffmann, banning him from ever again holding office in the Council. Those in support of this motion, signify the same by raising your right hand."

"No!" Hoffmann reeled, clutching the desk behind him. "You can't. I-I've given my life to this nation." He pointed a trembling finger at Thomas. "It's him. It's all his fault. He's the one behind this!"

Schulthess spoke again, his voice as unfeeling as the stone walls around them. "Arthur Hoffmann, your conduct is unbecoming of a minister of the Council. Unlike your father, who served this nation with dignity, you have failed. By virtue of this Council's resolution, you are hereby removed from our political body."

Thomas turned away from the sight of the defeated man, unwilling to witness his humiliation. Arthur had been a useful tool, a man whose ambition had driven him to play a dangerous game, but he had lost. And losing was never easy.

Making his way to the rear of the great hall, Thomas stepped outside, closed the door behind him, and released a deep, long breath. Remorse swirled within him but with it came a sense of accomplishment. He had won the war to save his family. Leila was secure, his grandchild was safe, and Malcolm had been kept clear of the entire affair.

His head slumped back against the cool granite walls.

I'm tired, Isabella. So very tired.

Arthur wasn't the only one who had paid a high price. Like the war that engulfed Europe, his own campaign had been costly, plundering his emotions and ravaging his conscience. If there had been any other way, he would have taken it. He had been ruthless in his manipulation of both his country and Arthur, becoming the very definition of sin itself in order to save a life. But the objectives had been noble.

"And that," Thomas murmured, straightening as he passed his right hand through his silver hair, "makes all the difference."

JP ROBINSON

Chapter 34

Château des Aigles, Switzerland, October 1917.

Light spilled into every corner of Thomas's majestic castle, cast by dozens of flaming torches that enhanced the celestial brilliance of a million stars above. Strolling violinists filled the air with music. Some songs were the poignant melodies of Switzerland while others characterized the robust spirit of Great Britain.

To Leila, who stood with about thirty other guests on an elongated wraparound patio that buttressed the shimmering waters of Lake Thun, the entire atmosphere was a fusion of reality and the surreal. It seemed impossible that she was here with her husband, instead of locked away in a cold, dark cell in London's Tower. But she was.

Closing her eyes, she laid a hand on her abdomen, feeling again the first flutters of movement. A smile slipped across her lips. How could she, who had never conceived in the years of her first marriage, be carrying a child?

But she was.

And the surge of faith that flooded her mind each time she thought about the baby brought with it the whisper of promise that this child would not be born under a curse. This child *would* know a happy home now that Christ had entered it.

It was hard to believe that this was her husband's final night in Switzerland before returning to face the evil of war.

But it is.

She pushed aside the knot of worry and loneliness that swelled in her stomach, choosing instead to focus on Malcolm's presence at this farewell gathering that Thomas had organized in honor of his son's departure. Nothing must mar this moment, for indeed, there was no guarantee it would ever come again.

Leila looked up as Malcolm's arm curled around her waist. He was resplendent in a solid white tuxedo, embossed with gold trim on the shoulders and the edges of the lapel. A silk, gold waistcoat peaked out beneath his jacket and the stars themselves seemed to dim beneath the brilliance of his smile.

"Each time I see you, I have to remind myself that this gorgeous woman is not a creature of my imagination."

She reached up, touching the neatly trimmed beard that curled about his chin. "I was just thinking the same about you."

"How is our little one?" Pulling her closer, Malcolm gently laid his hands on her stomach.

"Active." Leila leaned back against his chest. "He must know his father's around."

"He?"

She cocked her head to one side as she looked up at him. "Your side of the family has always had boys. Mine has always had girls."

He grinned at her and she felt her anxiety begin to melt. "So we have a fifty-fifty chance, I take it."

"Oh, Malcolm." Laughing, she pulled away. He had always been able to brighten her mood with just a few words.

God, keep him safe. I can't live without him.

Sobering, Malcolm reached for her hand, his gaze still on her womb. "I understand now why he did it."

"He?" She crinkled a brow.

Malcolm's mouth thinned into a firm line. "Will Thompson, the man I told you about. After his child was killed he went crazy. Now, I think I understand why."

He looked away. "That's one thing I'd give anything to make right. I wrecked his whole life with one lie."

"Malcolm." Leila squeezed his arm. "Don't look back. I understand how you feel, but some things we just have to leave in the past. You told me his wife, Eleanor, forgave you. Be content with that, at least. Even if you never see him again, you did what you could to make amends."

He was silent for several moments. "All the same, I'm glad you'll be here away from it all. Safe."

She could see the subdued worry that clouded his eyes despite his brave words. They had spent long hours discussing their future, but knowing they only had a few hours left brought a strain of its own.

"Malcolm, tonight is *your* night." She forced a smile then pointed to Thomas who was surrounded by a small cortege of businessmen and politicians. "Your father went through all this expense for you. Let's leave tomorrow's battles where they belong."

At that moment, Thomas caught her eye and motioned.

"He's calling you." She put her hand in the small of his back and gave him a gentle push.

"Hmm." The twinkle was back in his voice. "He's been introducing me to his business partners all evening. It's as though he's preparing them—or me—for something."

"I know." Leila tried to keep the note of anticipation out of her voice. Tonight was about much more than just a sendoff for Malcolm. "There's a reason for it."

Malcolm slanted her a curious glance. "What do you know that I don't?"

"Go to him." She gave him a mischievous smile. "I'll be your ears among the people and tonight we'll compare notes."

Malcolm chuckled. "All right, my little spy." Then, with a quick peck on her cheek, he strode off in his father's direction.

Leila let him move ahead before ambling toward a group of women—wives of Thomas's guests. Though a number of the women spoke English passably well, French had been her language of choice throughout tonight's dinner. To speak German would raise too many questions, questions she didn't want to answer.

"Ah, Madame Steele, won't you join us?" One of the women beckoned to her eagerly. "You look absolutely stunning in that shade of blue. No wonder you have such a charming man for your husband! You simply *must* tell us how you two met."

A chorus of agreement rose on all sides.

Warmth spread through Leila even as she realized that she would have to eliminate the most interesting parts of their story. "Well, we met in England one evening. It was just at the start of the war . . . "

───────◆◆●◆───────

"Son, let me introduce President Schulthess, leader of the Federal Council." Thomas stepped aside as Malcolm strode forward, arm outstretched.

"An honor, sir." Malcolm clasped the older man's hand in his own.

"The honor is mine, Lord Malcolm." Schulthess gave him a shrewd glance. "Your father is a wise man, one who only a few weeks ago showed us the benefit of his wisdom."

A flush of pride crept into Malcolm's heart. "If I could be half the man my father is, I would count myself fortunate indeed."

Thomas stood next to his son, placing his arm on Malcolm's shoulder. "President Schulthess, I do not exaggerate when I say that no father could be prouder of his son's accomplishments than I am of mine."

Malcolm did not hear Schulthess's reply. His mind was still trying to process the depth of his father's words. Never had Thomas spoken so openly of his feelings, of pride in fact. A bewildering surge of emotion, raw and powerful, swelled within him. But, before he could speak again, Thomas turned to the crowd that milled about.

"I would ask you all to join me in my study." He pointed to a room on their right whose ceiling-high windows and glass roof reflected the light of the torches that lined the courtyard. "I would like to conclude this most auspicious of occasions with a tribute to my son, Malcolm."

Applause rose from those around him, but Malcolm shook his head. "Father, you don't have to do anything." He placed a hand on Thomas's shoulder. "This"—he gestured to the crowds—"this is more than enough."

Thomas cupped his neck with his broad palm. "Nothing could ever be enough to show how much I love you, Son."

"W-why?" Malcolm could barely speak past the lump in his throat.

"You are a Steele." Thomas jutted his chin forward and looked deep into his son's eyes. Those words conveyed far more than a family name. His father was saying that he had what it took to lead their family forward. "It is time the world recognized you as such. Follow me."

Thomas turned away as Leila moved to stand next to Malcolm.

"Come." She pulled Malcolm forward. It was obvious that she was privy to whatever his father had planned. Her hair, carefully styled and topped by a diamond tiara, fell in a glorious cascade of gold over her vibrant blue dress and her emerald eyes were rich with the promise of life.

"What is it?" Malcolm glanced over his shoulder, seeing the rest of the guests following him.

"You'll see." Mischief tinged her voice.

Despite his sense of building anticipation, Malcolm's feet slowed as he neared the doors that led into the brightly-colored chamber.

Leila must have sensed his misgivings for she turned and echoed his question. "What is it?"

Malcolm stood to one side, letting some of the guests enter first. "I . . . " He leaned over and whispered in her ear, "Mother passed away in this room. I haven't entered it since she died."

"Then think of this." Leila slipped her small hand in his. "Tonight she'll be here, in this room, to celebrate with us." She smiled up at him then squeezed his hand.

Malcolm inhaled a deep breath through his nose, then expelled it through his mouth. "All right."

He waited until the last of the guests entered, then, with Leila at his side, Malcolm entered the room.

◆◆●◆◆

Thomas watched his son and daughter-in-law stroll into the spacious hall, arms around each other as though they were newlyweds just returned from their honeymoon. They were as he and Isabella had been forty years ago.

Time, disease, and death had altered Thomas's world, but as he gazed upon the happy couple before him, he knew beyond a shadow of doubt that the decision he had made was the right one.

They are the future. Everything is for them.

"My friends." Thomas stepped to the center of the room which was lined with smiling faces, among them Greyson and Jenny. The room held little furniture, just a small writing desk and a few seats. Its walls were covered in a kaleidoscope of pastel oranges and greens that bespoke happiness and life. "It is every father's dream that his descendants will carry on his legacy, perpetuating both his name and values to those that will come after him."

A few heads nodded among the men.

Thomas continued. "Unfortunately, because of the darkness that is swallowing the world, too many fathers are outliving their sons." Again, more nods, this time from both men and women.

"But God has blessed me above measure." His eyes shifted from the crowd to Malcolm who stood, shoulders set back, and chest thrust forward, as true a soldier of Britain as he himself had ever been. "I have been granted the privilege of seeing my son, Malcolm, become the man I always knew he could be."

A knot rose in his throat and Thomas blinked several times to clear his eyes.

It's taken so many years, Isabella, but he's arrived at last.

How many prayers had he launched for his prodigal? Like bullets, each prayer had been another shot, aimed at an unseen enemy that threatened to steal his child's soul. But, just as he had pulled the trigger time after time in battlefields across Asia and Africa, in service to his king, so Thomas had sent volleys of prayers in the defense of his son. And he had won.

"Now, Malcolm is everything any father could ask. A decorated war hero, a Major in the army of Great Britain, a defender of his ancestral home at Northshire, and a faithful husband who treasures the woman he has been given." Motion caught Thomas's eye and he glimpsed Leila wiping her cheeks. "Soon, he will be a father himself!"

Applause again filled the room and Thomas waited until it died down before coming to the heart of his speech.

"But there is one thing my son lacks."

Abrupt silence gripped them all.

"It is something that, according to our family tradition, only I can give him." Thomas motioned, and Greyson stepped from the side door to the rear of the room. The butler made his way toward a large, oddly-shaped object that lay covered in a simple cloth drape.

"May the memory of this expression of my esteem bring you comfort on the battlefield and honor in days to come, my son." Thomas nodded, and Greyson pulled the drape away to reveal a massive portrait of Malcolm set in a heavy frame of dark wood.

"Father?" Malcolm staggered forward, eyes wide. "Is this . . . ?"

Thomas turned from the portrait to his son. "You have shown that you are worthy. One day you will return to our estate and this portrait will hang next to mine and those of your predecessors in the great hall of Northshire." His voice softened. "Your mother would be proud."

"Father, I . . . " Malcolm's voice trailed off. "This means so much . . . "

Stepping toward him, Thomas pulled a ring from his right hand and held it high for all to see. "This ring once belonged to my great-grandfather, Louis-Charles, son of King Louis and Marie-Antoinette of France."

394

A collective gasp rose from the assembly. Thomas heard the whispers, some believing and others incredulous. But he had no time for the speculations of others. Tonight, for the first time he had publicly revealed the truth behind the Steele heritage. It mattered not if the world believed, only that his son knew the truth. Malcolm was of royal blood.

"The wearer of this ring is legally entitled to act on my behalf." Taking Malcolm's right hand, he slipped it onto his son's third finger. "I have already drawn up all the necessary paperwork, however, tonight I proclaim by ceremony that Lord Malcolm is the heir of this castle, the *Château des Aigles*."

His gaze fell upon the President of the Federal Council.

"President Schulthess, I have requested that you and every director of my various Swiss enterprises be present to witness that I hereby name my son, Malcolm Steele, the beneficiary of all my financial assets in Switzerland. He and his wife, the lovely Lady Steele, will be coheirs of Northshire Estate, my property in Great Britain. It shall belong to them and their descendants forever."

Thomas, chest tight with emotion, held the crowd beneath his stern gaze. "Are there any that dare contest my claim?"

Again, silence swept through the room, stilling the voices that murmured in wonder only seconds before. He waited for several moments, then his face softened as he turned and clasped his son in his arms.

Cheers filled the room as the spectators witnessed the conclusion of this powerful night.

"All that I have is yours, Malcolm." Thomas patted his son's back. "I know that you will rebuild what I have brought down. You will carve out the path back to our home in Northshire and will make our name greater than it has ever been before."

Malcolm gripped him, face buried in his father's shoulder. Thomas noted that they were equal height now, but whereas his own arms were growing thin and his shoulders stooping, Malcolm had the strength of a lion.

"Thank you, Father." His son's voice broke. "Thank you."

Thomas patted him once more, closing his eyes as he felt an echo of his wife's presence in the room. He turned his face heavenward, gazing through the glass ceiling at the stars that seemed to sing for joy. He could take no credit for the happiness of this night. After all, it was not his doing. It was the work of his Father who, against all odds, had brought his prodigal home.

"Thank *You,* Father," Thomas whispered. "Thank You."

Epilogue

December 1917. Kaiser Wilhelm Institute. Berlin.

Fritz Haber's laboratory was a physical depiction of the scientist himself. It was a paradoxical conglomeration of chaos and order, ingenuity and tradition. Now, as the chemist puttered about his workspace with his white lab coat thrown over the tuxedo he had worn to his wedding this afternoon, one thought held his mind prisoner like a block of wood in a vice:

Find the antidote.

Seven months earlier, Fritz had been commissioned by the kaiser to develop an antidote for German agents in the event that the Fatherland lost the war. Now, as the coils of Europe's blockade crippled Germany from within and the Americans brought increased military pressure upon the Triple Entente from without, the project Fritz had codenamed *Hubris* had become of vital interest to the few who knew of its existence.

Haber grimaced as he laced his fingers together behind his bald head and stared at the intricate notes on his chalkboard. Charlotte, his wife as of three o'clock this afternoon, had been the catalyst behind his recent irresponsible choices—choices he already regretted.

If I'd only kept walking the day she showed up at my wife's grave.

If only...

Those were the words that had haunted him when his first wife, Clara, lay cold and stiff on the ground before him—a victim of his fierce pride and infidelity. He had resolved to change that night. He thought he had succeeded. He even went to church. For a while.

But reform could only go so far. The allure of power had intertwined with Charlotte's siren call, wooing him with irresistible force back to the old life of achievement at all costs. This came at a price, however. Karl Schmidt, his friend and colleague, for two decades had disagreed with Fritz's dreams of using gas as a weapon. Now Karl was dead, executed by Fritz's own order.

A shiver ran down the scientist's spine. He had no faith in the afterlife but there were times he swore Karl's ghost haunted the corners of his mind. Karl's last words violated every principle of nature, every animal instinct to survive that lay embedded in the human psyche.

I forgive you, Fritz. May God forgive you too.

Those nine words drummed through Haber's mind without reprieve. He had given the order to fire, one word that had ended Karl's life. How many times had he wished he could turn back the clock?

If only...

But Charlotte had told him that Karl was working against him. The clever vixen had used his rabid hatred of competition as a tool to bend him to her will.

Strike to kill, Fritz.

Those had been her words and, like a dog on a leash, he had obeyed. He had killed. Murdered Karl and slaughtered his conscience. Now, his laboratory was his only escape—from the world, from Charlotte, from his past.

Haber picked up a glass vial filled with the experimental antidote that he had used in his last failed test. "Why didn't you work?" He turned the vial around in his hand, examining the clear liquid from different angles.

"It won't talk back to you, Fritz."

Haber jumped at the unexpected voice behind him, and the glass vial slipped from his fingers. It shattered on the white tiles. He whirled around to face his wife.

"You wretched fool. Now look what you've done!" Fritz knew he was overreacting, but this was about more than a broken vial. This was about his broken life.

Despite the late hour, Charlotte was still dressed in the same pink blouse and black slacks she had worn after they returned from their wedding ceremony. They had spent the afternoon apart, each lost in their dreams of the future.

Charlotte flung her head backward, a short-lived cynical laugh erupting from her throat. "What I've done? Don't blame me for your mess."

"Who else is to blame?"

"I'm the best thing that ever happened to you." She tapped a finger against her chest. "If it weren't for me, that wretched friend of yours, Karl—whatever-his-name-was—would've told the whole world what you're planning in this disgusting lab of yours."

Haber glared at her, jaw set. "If you hadn't turned me against him, this problem would have been solved by now. I need his mind!"

"Oh, so you're telling me I married the wrong man?" Charlotte arched an eyebrow. "Perhaps he's the one I should have seduced?"

"You devil!" Fritz stormed forward, tramping on shards of glass.

Charlotte didn't back down. Instead her lips pulled back in a cunning smile. "Call me what you like; it doesn't change the fact that I'm your wife."

Her words jerked him to a stop like a puppet on a string.

"Another loveless marriage, Fritz?" Clara slunk forward, her dark eyes intent on his own. "More years without a woman's touch? Is that what you want?"

A sickening feeling swirled around in his gut. He couldn't endure the same isolation that he had suffered in his first marriage. He had no choice but to give Charlotte what she wanted.

"Yes." He drew in a deep breath, held it, then released it. "You are my wife. I, um . . . " He swallowed. "I apologize."

Charlotte tossed her head, flicking his face with a few strands of her dark hair. "If you expect me to say that you're forgiven, think again. Forgiveness is *earned* in my book, not given. All the same, your temper is grating on my nerves."

Fritz had been about to spit out an angry retort but, as Charlotte's last words registered in his mind, his anger melted before a shockwave of inspiration. "What . . . what did you say?" He had heard her, but the microcosm of recognition demanded she say the words again in order to crystalize his understanding.

Charlotte's foot tapped a staccato rhythm on the floor. "I said 'your temper is grating on my nerves.'"

"The nerves!" Fritz spun back to his chalkboard and began scrawling out figures. "It's the nerves." He shouted as he continued writing. "Don't you see?"

Glass crunched behind him as Charlotte came closer. "No, I don't. All I see is your bald head bobbing up and down like an apple in a bucket of water."

Fritz was too carried away to respond. He turned back to Charlotte, gesticulating as he pointed to the board.

"What we need is an antidote that works on the *nerves,* not the lungs. Now, what drug has been used for thousands of years, of course in a rather primitive way?"

She wouldn't know the answer. This was a subtle way of reminding her that his *bald head* contained more knowledge in a single cell than her entire cranium could ever hope to obtain.

Charlotte glared at him in silence.

"Oh, you don't know, do you?" A smile tugged at the edges of his mouth. "Let me educate you. It's called atropine. First used by the Egyptians and also implemented by the Greeks. Over a decade ago, atropine was synthetically produced for the first time."

"So, you're using someone else's work?" She scoffed. "This is the best that you can come up with?"

Fritz felt the back of his neck begin to burn. "No, Charlotte. Atropine is the *cure,* but I have just created the disease." He pointed again to the board, sensing his frustration fade as he lost himself in the molecular miracles of chemistry.

"You made me realize that I needed to focus on the nerves. Well, it is obvious that atropine's formula will allow me to save German lives provided, of course, that a poison gas with a reciprocal chemical structure is engineered."

"And that's what you just did?" Her tone was a little more subdued, holding a slight trace of respect. "You diagrammed this gas?"

"Yes." Fritz stuck his chest out. There was a time, before their marriage, when she had praised his genius incessantly. Sadly, after their child had begun to grow in her womb and her position as his wife was secure, Charlotte's stream of compliments had evaporated.

Why? Why can I never make a woman happy?

"This gas will make *Hubris* a success?" Charlotte turned to him, eyes drilling into his skull.

"You mean, will the gas make *you* a success?" Haber was not fooled. He had no doubt that, if Charlotte wasn't persuaded of his ability to perform, she would leave him. In that respect she was much like him—driven by a relentless ambition that left no room for mediocrity.

Charlotte's smile did not reach her eyes. She minced forward, pulling him toward her by the edges of his lapel. "You know I only settle for the best."

Then she kissed him, a tantalizing reminder of what she offered. "Answer the question, Fritz." She whispered the words in his ear. "Will it work?"

Haber hesitated, knowing this woman would not settle for an indirect answer. He had sown to the wind. Now he held the whirlwind in his arms.

I only settle for the best. If he failed to be the best, he would not only lose his reputation but his second wife—this time to a cause more shameful than suicide.

"Will it?" A harsh edge crept into her tone.

Fritz knew that whatever he said now would alter the course of his life. To lie would be to dig the grave of his second marriage. He needed to perform tests, to verify the data but Charlotte, his draconian taskmaster, would not wait on tests. She wanted results.

He licked his lips, unable to put off the inevitable any longer. "Y-yes. Yes, it will work."

"You're sure?"

"I'm sure." The lie slipped smoothly off his tongue. Compared to the growing mountain of regrets that pressed down on his shoulders, this was but a trifle. But his marriage, if not his political future, was at stake.

Something within him rebelled at the thought of failing a second time. He was the greatest scientific mind in modern history. Surely, he could find a way to save his marriage.

The thought struck him that acknowledging her part in the discovery might be a step in the right direction. Clara had killed herself because of his neglect, after all. "This discovery is what I've been looking for all these months." He shrugged. "Without you I would still be lost."

"Hmm, is that so?" Leaning into his arms, Charlotte nuzzled his neck, nibbling on it the way she knew he liked. "Well, since you're sure this will work, you are forgiven. This time. When will the attack take place?"

"I don't know." Fritz closed his eyes, trying to shut out the guilt that her touch aroused. Clara had killed herself after finding him with this woman and the memory plagued him each time Charlotte's hands caressed him. Biology had its laws and he was a man after all. But, unlike his body, his mind was not subject to nature's dictates.

He pulled away. "I'll have to give the kaiser's generals a live demonstration. They won't act until a treaty is in place. My guess is at least a year. You'll have to be patient."

"Patience was never one of my virtues." Charlotte undid the knot of his tie then kissed him again. "The world is waiting, Fritz. Let's unleash chaos."

In the Dead of the Night Prologue

January 1918. Whitehall, London. Great Britain.

Sir Robert Hughes stood in his office before a wall-length, oval window and let his eyes roam over the crenelated spires and rectangular rooftops that made up the Whitehall complex.

Whitehall was the administrative center of British government. It was just a road, really. A simple road that trudged through a host of brick buildings filled with snub-nosed politicians and draconian bureaucrats, all of which obscured progress like an army of Goliaths.

Hughes shoved his hands in his pockets and continued to count the raindrops that spattered against this one window into his world of lies and secrets.

Politicians.

The thought turned the lingering taste of his afternoon tea sour in his mouth. He wanted to spit.

"Let it go, Robert." The voice of Prime Minister David Lloyd George threw him off count. "You've won your share of battles; leave Thomas Steele with his victory."

David snorted as he sank into a brown leather armchair. "Think of it, man. In the year since we released his daughter-in-law, you've helped put down a rebellion in Ireland and your men obtained vital information that helped us end the butchery of Passchendaele. You've redeemed yourself, Robert. Now let the past be."

Hughes turned around slowly. "Nine hundred seventy-six."

"I beg your pardon?"

"Nine hundred seventy-six raindrops dripped onto my window pane in the last three minutes."

David blinked twice then stared at him, jaw slack, for a full thirty seconds. "You know, Robert," he said at length, "there are moments when I truly question your sanity. Why on earth are you counting raindrops? Aren't there more important things to count, like the mounting number of dead in this ridiculous war?"

A momentary silence filled the space between the two men. Then Hughes broke it.

"Raindrops are like our soldiers." Hughes gave a tight smile then stumped to his desk. "Almost a thousand raindrops ended their miserable lives in three minutes. Across the globe, probably as many British soldiers have died fighting for law and order while you insist that a criminal like Thomas Steele remains free."

David tilted his head to one side, eying him like a hawk might eye a potential rival. But Hughes had no interest in political games. Not anymore. One desire only burned in his mind.

"What is it about Thomas that galls you, Robert? What is it, really?"

"Thomas is a transgressor." His jaw tightened into an inflexible line. "He broke the law. He must be punished."

"And unless he is punished by law, you will not be satisfied?"

"How can I?" Hughes laced his fingers together behind his back and began to pace, an awkward thumping rhythm. "Every transgression, every infraction of the law must receive just retribution."

"I suppose the idea of mercy is a foreign concept?"

"Mercy?" Hughes felt bile rise in the back of his throat. "There is no mercy. There is only the law. The law, Prime Minister!" He released a ragged breath. "Did you know that when my wife and I were married, I took her last name?"

"Really?" David arched a silver eyebrow. "How very . . . progressive of you."

"Hmm. It was part of our marriage contract. Her father wanted it to be that way so his name wouldn't be lost when his only daughter died. I wanted her inheritance. After the marriage I could have worked to change the situation, but you see, in my mind every word of the document had to be kept or else my entire marriage would become a tainted affair."

"But surely—"

"Every . . . word." He drilled the Prime Minister with his eyes. "That is why Thomas must be brought back to England. He must face our justice. Not our mercy. In violating one part of the law, he is guilty of breaking the whole."

"I see." David leaned back in his seat, resting his forearms over his slight paunch. "But you know that he is untouchable in Switzerland."

For the first time all day, the hint of a smile creased the corners of Hughes's lips. Yes, political figures stood in his way like an army of Goliaths. But the story didn't end with the giant's boasting. Every Goliath must have a conqueror.

"I have a guest who is scheduled to arrive"—he pulled out his bronze pocket watch, glanced briefly at the insignia of the British Navy on its polished surface, and flipped it open—"now."

A knock sounded on the door and Hughes turned to it, while thrusting the watch back into his pocket. "Enter!"

The Prime Minister stood up as a thin, pale man wearing a plaid jacket and maroon pants skulked into the room. He carried a small black briefcase in his left hand and smoothed out his short-cropped moustache with his right. Hughes narrowed his eyes. The man was small and unimpressive, like the giant-killer of Biblical times. But, more to the point, this man carried a weapon that, if used correctly, would wreak havoc.

"You are Sir Robert Hughes, head of British Foreign Intelligence?" His guest looked the spymaster up and down.

"Yes." Hughes leaned forward, peering at him through his monocle. At length he nodded. The man before him matched the description he had received from his agents abroad. Now, his guest leaned forward, extending his arm even as a merciless smile slid across his pointed, sallow face.

"I am Arthur Hoffman of Switzerland. And I have come to help you destroy . . . Thomas Steele."

Author's Note

Isn't it a wonderful feeling when a long-awaited prayer is answered? For Thomas, this moment defines the power of a faith that defies circumstances. Malcolm and Leila as well as Eleanor and Will have all experienced their own miracles. But so many battles remain to be fought. How will it all come together? Find out in the riveting conclusion to the Northshire Heritage trilogy, *In the Dead of the Night* (available Summer 2020).

For dramatic purposes, some alterations to the historical record were made in this novel. For example, the British camp of Étaples was attacked in 1918 not 1917. The German plot *Hubris* is purely a concept of my imagination, but it does reflect the nationalistic spirit of the times.

Eleanor's friend Veronica was inspired by the historical figure Vera Brittain whose monumental eye-witness account, *Testament of Youth,* provided a wealth of information for my research. Whereas Veronica dies (as did many nurses on the frontlines), Vera Brittain survived the war.

At the conclusion of the Great War, millions around the world were left with one question: *why?* The pointless loss of life robbed the world of hope. A century later, the world again hinges on the brink of global catastrophe. But there is a hope in the Person of Jesus Christ. If you're like Will or Malcolm who has wandered away from the love of the Father, take the first step home right now.

As the hour of Christ's return draws near, the window of opportunity is closing. Come home today.

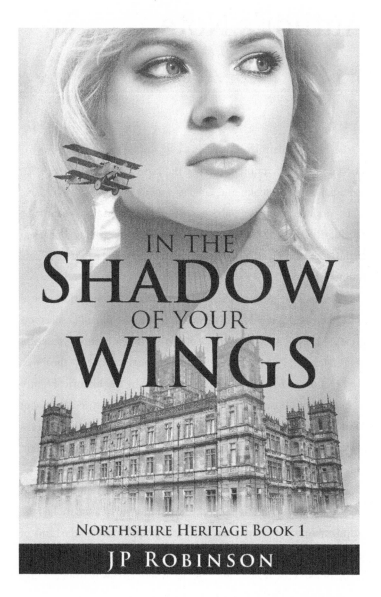

JP ROBINSON

IN THE
SHADOW
OF YOUR
WINGS

NORTHSHIRE HERITAGE BOOK 1

JP ROBINSON

In the Shadow of Your Wings
(Northshire Heritage I)

Leila Durand, an elite German spy charged with infiltrating the home of British icon Thomas Steele, sees the war as a chance to move beyond the pain of st. But everything changes when she falls in love with Thomas's son, Malcolm. Is there a way to reconcile her love for Germany and her love for the enemy?

Thomas Steele sees the war as an opportunity for his profligate son, Malcolm, to find a purpose greater than himself. But when Malcolm rebels, it falls to Thomas to make tough decisions.

The war's reach extends to the heart. Eleanor Thompson finds her faith is pushed to the breaking point when her husband disappears on the battle front and her daughter is killed in a German air raid. Where is God in the midst of her pain?

In the Shadow of Your Wings presents inescapable truth that resonates across the past century. Then as now, the struggle for faith is real. Then as now, there is a refuge for all who will come beneath the shadow of God's wings.

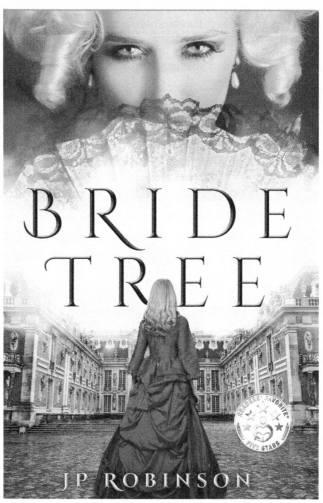

BRIDE TREE

JP ROBINSON

SECRETS OF VERSAILLES II

Bride Tree
(Secrets of Versailles II)

UNMASK THE TRUTH

Bride Tree, a sweeping allegory of the Church set in the tumultuous French Revolution era, fuses alternative history with romantic suspense.

The year is 1789. France is reeling under the impact of a civil war between its social classes. When a secret agent from Rome joins forces with a vindictive politician bent on revenge, the stage is set for an explosive outcome that will shake the country to its core.

Meanwhile, Queen Marie-Antoinette engages the help of her lady-in-waiting, Viviane de Lussan, in a desperate battle to keep her throne . . . and her head. But how can she win a struggle she seems fated to lose?

Amid the chaos of the revolution, Viviane's heart is torn between a nobleman who sacrifices everything for her and a peasant who promises true freedom.

Buy your copy today.
JPRobinsonBooks.com

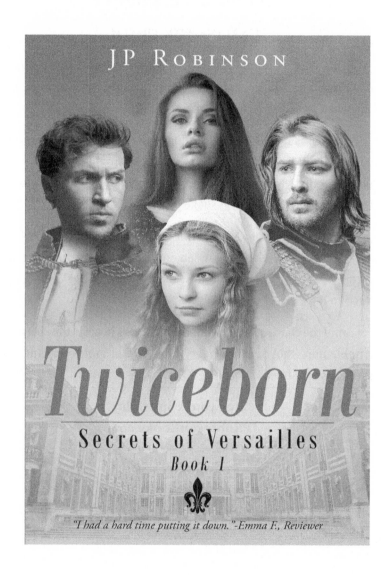

Twiceborn
(Secrets of Versailles I)

SOME SECRETS CAN KILL

Versailles is the center of European power, but the court of King Louis XIV is also a hotbed of intrigue and political manipulation.

Despite the rigid structure of Angélique's upbringing, temptation proves stronger than her principles. She gives birth to twins, Antoine and Hugo, who are ripped apart by their mother's shadowed past.

Twenty-five years later, Antoine is caught in a web of intrigue when his jealous brother, now a powerful member of the clergy, accuses him of treason and threatens to destroy the woman he loves.

But Hugo has bigger plans than just his brother's downfall. He ignites a plot that threatens to bring the Kingdom of France to its knees, little suspecting the cataclysmic forces his actions will unleash.

Tears will fall, blood will flow, and in the end, only one man will remain standing.

Buy your copy today.

JPRobinsonBooks.com

Are you a writer?

Workshop-in-your-Pocket

- **Write History:** Establish compelling settings, create authentic 3D historical characters, hook reader emotions and more.

- **Write Business:** Learn the fundamentals of setting up a writing system that pays.

- **Write 3D (2020):** Discover the secret of crafting unforgettable characters in a personalized, easy-to-follow book complete with activities.

- **Write Strategy (2020)** Backed by data and interviews with some of today's most successful authors, *Write Strategy* teaches cost-effective strategies to market, promote and sell your book.

Bookmark his exciting website: www.JPRobinsonBooks.com and connect with him on social media.

Facebook.com/JPRobinsonAuthor

@JPRobinsonBooks

Instagram.com/jprobinsonbooks

About the author

JP Robinson began writing as a teen and soon gained local recognition for his writing, has been a guest speaker on several radio networks and is known for leading dynamic author education workshops across the nation.

He holds degrees in English and French from SUNY Stonybrook and is a state-certified teacher.

Together with his wonderful wife, JP runs Fearless Marriage, a ministry dedicated to Christian couples.

Made in the USA
Monee, IL
16 August 2020